THE KEY OF H

By J. H. Brogden

Published by New Generation Publishing in 2013

First Edition

www.newgeneration-publishing.com

 New Generation Publishing

Music is the answer to the mystery of life. It is the most profound of all the arts. (Schopenhauer)

With grateful thanks to Trevor Ward for his astute proof-reading and advice on grammar and syntax, and also to Ian Browne for his suggestions on style and characterisation.

This book is dedicated to the memory of Jim Shanahan.

CHAPTER 1

Greg's meeting with Mr. Manktelow had been short and informal. His head of 'Ideal Listening' at Deci-Belle had stopped him in the corridor to ask him to compose some appropriate music for optimum domestic settings. Their impromptu venue had been between Greg's tiny office and the utility room. Greg often referred to his own space as the '*futility* room' as he never quite knew what his role at Deci-Belle was now that the company had withdrawn the practice of home visits for hi-fi checks and which he'd always performed more for the customer's benefit rather than creating additional revenue for his employers.

"I'd like you to go away for a short break", announced Mr. Manktelow brusquely. "Come back refreshed, and with a few marvellous tunes - songs, jingles, anthems, symphonies even - tailor-made for our domestic market in their living rooms, cars, or even their headphones if within the confines of their approved domestic settings. 'Buy one of our systems; get two personalised modern classics thrown in!'"

Greg thought that a time frame of two weeks to acquire the inspiration and expertise to create a repertoire of music of all types slightly over-ambitious. He also didn't particularly like the concept of linking any such output with a specified retailer of audio equipment, although he did accept the principles of copyright.

"We thought Lincolnshire for you, Greg. It's between Yorkshire and Norfolk, basically, so the

1

landscape should be a nice balance between - well....sharps and flats!"

He'd taken Greg's expression of mild incredulity as that of an artist in the act of formulating a great work, and so he shook his hand warmly, treated him to a plastic cup of tepid water from the adjacent vending machine, then gazed out of a window at a flat roof below.

"I love the way pigeons strut, those little heads nodding rhythmically", said his senior colleague. "Learn your craft from the fowls of the air where the Lincolnshire Poacher spent his Friday nights, then put pen to paper. It'll come!"

Greg nodded but was dubious. He looked out vacantly just as the pigeon was taking to the air, presumably in quest of some surplus crumbs that had been dispensed at ground level by Mrs. Anstruther, the kindly tea and biscuit lady.

"You could set off tomorrow, if you like", said Mr. Manktelow encouragingly, assuming that Greg had accepted the working holiday offer. "Would express coach suit you?"

"As long as the company's paying all my expenses, and you don't mind if I return with some blank pages!" said Greg.

"I'm sure you'll be able to tap into whatever it is that composers use to find the right themes. You're a good listener! Mahler found the Austrian Alps inspirational, but we don't want too many peaks. Our speakers perform best when handling a more compressed input. More than one octave and they begin to rattle."

With that he was off, leaving Greg alone in the corridor to muse on his mission, and dispose of his plastic cup. Apart from successfully processing an expenses claim form from accounts, but failing to retrieve any manuscript books from the store cupboard, Greg spent the rest of the afternoon perfecting treble clefs in his pocket diary. He'd polish his skills with the bass clef if and when the need arose.

Thus the following day Greg found himself - although he'd not actually *lost* himself - on a coach, heading south from his adoptive home town in the Scottish lowlands all the way down to some inspirational retreat in the English fenlands. He remembered that he'd got no manuscript paper in his rucksack, but he very much doubted that he'd fulfil his employers' expectations of his - as yet unexplored - composing skills. His own forte lay in musical appreciation, but this didn't include the trivialisation of great tunes, such as the fanfare from Carl Orff heralding yet another phone conversation for the passenger sitting next to him that someone called Mel wished to share with her. Fortunately, arrival in the city of Lincoln was imminent, and so he began to wriggle expectantly in his seat and check that he had all his personal belongings, thankful for travelling on Ash & Knowles' Express, and yes, they *would* see him again soon - in two weeks time for his journey home.

After alighting at Lincoln Bus Station he immediately headed in what he assumed to be the right direction for the nearest hotels. However, his instinct told him that he'd been spotted making a futile foray towards a flower bed which he then discovered to have no pedestrian access. He turned round, feeling slightly disorientated and headed the other way, but his observer, a rather short man in his twenties, wearing a tattered tartan jacket and a welcoming expression, was approaching him purposefully. Greg kept his head down, but knew he was about to be accosted.

"Are you lost?" asked the man. "You can't get out that way! They've blocked it in!"

Greg could see now that those who had arrived with him on the same bus were either walking confidently to, or already milling around, the timetable displays at the opposite corner of the bus station. He was concerned that being seen wandering aimlessly amidst a maze of municipal shrubs might suggest to the man that he was in need of care and protection. He grinned and shook his head at his own confusion, and tried to think of something noncommittal to say, but the man seized his chance. Greg gripped the holdall he was carrying that bit tighter in case it too might be seized, but already the encounter was becoming more intense.

"Are you looking for anywhere in particular?" asked the young man pleasantly. "I'm as good as a guide to the city!"

"Well, I'm really on my way to wherever the B&Bs are," said Greg, hardly stopping for the now stationary stranger. "Just point the way and I'll be fine!" he called out cheerily.

"Well....It's gone seven o'clock. There won't be many vacancies now. You should have booked!" said the man, running to catch up and confident he knew best. "Tell you what, why not ring round a few first, if you've got any numbers!"

"Well, I do have some numbers and addresses," said Greg, warily, "but...."

"Good man! That's a start!"

He was now striding alongside Greg, and a row of

public telephones was facing them. He seemed so keen to help that Greg felt he had no option other than to accept the man's advice, although his breezy manner was slightly threatening, especially the way in which he now held the door of the first of the telephone boxes wide open for the two of them to enter.

"The mobile signal's useless here; it's those mountains, but these 'phones are no problem, except for the end one - been jammed since last week!" said his impromptu guide, in full command of the situation, as he squeezed into the confined space.

"You give me the number you want and I'll ring them for you. Have you got some coins?"

"I don't really want to fork out money unnecessarily," said Greg, lamely, hoping he too wouldn't be jammed in for a whole week. "I'm sure I'll soon find a 'Vacancies' sign if I...."

"Tell you what," said the man, "you give me 60 pence and tell me what to dial. We might just be in time before someone beats you to it!"

Greg felt in his pocket for some change, although this was awkward with his elbow restricted by the man's chest. "It's very good of you," he said reluctantly as he passed the coins into an eager sweaty palm. "You could try ringing The Lindsey Lodge."

The man stared at him expectantly. Greg took the cue with an "Oh yes," and produced his diary, then leafed through it quickly until he found a list of numbers and dictated one. The man pressed the silver keys, repeating each number in what sounded like a south eastern accent. "It's ringing!" he announced, looking at Greg as though this were a miracle. "We'll soon get you fixed up. How many nights shall I say

5

you want?"

"Well, one to start with, I suppose," said Greg.

Was he an unofficial agent for the local tourist board? thought Greg, and were all visitors to the city accorded such assistance? He felt uncomfortable sharing a callbox with the pushy stranger, and he was also developing a dislike for the slightly malodorous tartan jacket. Was he going to be able to talk to the hotel himself, or were all his requirements to be handled through a very keen third party whose eyes darted around him like frenzied searchlights? If the offer of a double room came up he'd make a swift exit if he could extricate his holdall from under the telephone assembly.

"You're in luck! They've just got one room left, with a nice view and full English en suite TV!" said the man proudly, putting the receiver down after minimal interaction with whoever had answered.

It occurred to Greg, though, that perhaps there hadn't been any meaningful dialogue at all, especially when his eager guide grabbed 60p which had just been pumped out from the machine.

"Told you I'd get you fixed up, didn't I?" he continued, satisfied with his stewardship.

"I believe you did. Thank you," said Greg, reversing carefully to open the door wide and wondering whether a brief handshake might be appropriate so as to indicate the parting of the ways.

"Er, before you head off, and it's the second street on your right, by the way, I wonder if you could help me out," said the man, now wearing a more serious expression. "Only, I need to get the bus to Sleaford, but I've not got the fare, unless I get off less than halfway, and walk home in the dark. (He was toying with a rip in his sleeve at this point, whilst glancing furtively towards a limited stop bus discharging its complement of vague-looking arrivals.) "Any chance you could sort of help me out a bit with the er....fare?"

Greg put down his holdall and thought quickly. The person standing in front of him had either been very kind or very clever, but if his assistance had been no more than a scam to get the price of a bus fare, well, then his time was surely worth a small recompense. Greg smiled and reached again into his pocket, his fingers touching the milled edge of a coin. "How much is it to Sleaford?" he asked, looking around him to see if anyone nearby was aware of a scam possibly taking place.

"Well, £3 would help, but if you give me your name and address, I'll definitely send the money back to you!" replied the dodgy guide, now beaming with expectation. "Yes, sorry, the fares went up recently."

"Have you lived in Sleaford long?" asked Greg, his fingers now grabbing hold of several coins within his pocket. The clink alerted the man, whose smile broadened.

"Lived there all my life!" he replied in a distinctly southern accent, as he rummaged in his own pocket, presumably for some paper to write down his putative benefactor's name and address. Both men then stood for several seconds with their hands frozen in their pockets, neither wishing to be first to extract them. It was Lincoln Bus station's answer to High Noon, albeit an early evening version.

"I'll walk over with you to the bus," suggested Greg. "I can see the one you want loading up there on the stand!"

"No, no, no, there's really no need, mate!" countered the man urgently. "Here, let me write your address down on this."

He pulled out a scrap of paper, obviously intended for disposal. Greg produced a pen, and wrote down his address on it, but with a false name. He handed it back to the man who put it unread back into his pocket, and in return received another expectant stare.

"Tell you what!" said Greg moving quickly towards the bus, "I'll buy your ticket for you….then you just send me the whole amount when you can!"

The 'local' halted, expressionless. Greg thought he'd called his bluff - Sleafordians surely didn't pronounce chance as '*charnce*', and the full English en suite TV didn't sound quite right either. He walked the last few steps towards the bus, and boarded. Its engine was already running. He wondered what to do next, but then the sound of running footsteps behind him converted him from his scepticism. The driver looked at him querulously, but Greg felt awkward about his lack of trust in the natives of, or even *newcomers* to Lincolnshire, and avoided eye contact. "A single to Sleaford, please," he asked, and duly paid the fare demanded. He received little change from the note tendered but he took the ticket, then turned round to present it to his unofficial accommodation agent, only to see - instead of a short young man in tartan - a large middle-aged lady in a nurse's uniform. She offered the driver a return ticket, which he duly stamped, before summarily closing the doors and slowly moving off. The nurse took her seat near the front, but Greg remained standing, stunned. He realised that he *had* been conned - albeit in a voluntary and impulsive sort of way - after all. He'd talked himself into going somewhere he didn't want to go, whilst out of the window he watched a figure in a tartan jacket chatting cheerfully with a young lady, as she extracted coins from her purse. Greg stood open-mouthed, his hands gripping the handrail surrounding the luggage storage area.

"I see that Topsy boy's about again!" called a young lady from the front seat, grinning wryly, together with an older lady sitting next to her.

Greg's reactions were slowed down by his own disbelief, whereas the bus was gaining speed as it turned a corner. He kept his balance and asked the driver if he could get a refund and get off at the next stop.

"No, I can't do that, sorry," said the driver. "It's a valid ticket and it's gone through the system now. Where did you want to be then?"

"Well, here, really!"

"Here? Well, I can let you off at the Lindsey Lodge round the next corner, but I'm not allowed to reverse the revenue, you see."

Greg considered the option of getting off at the hotel which might or might not have vacancies, but felt the urge of natural justice. He'd paid for this journey, and so he'd see it through.

"Never mind, I'll stay on," he said, resignedly, as he went to sit down behind the two ladies.

"I see you've met that Turvey character!" said the older of the two. "He's been had up for cadging more than once. Did he ask you to help him out?"

"Well, sort of," replied Greg, as though it didn't

9

really matter now.

"You do see life here!" added her younger companion, shaking her head.

"Not much life in Mr. Scrimshaw now," said the nurse sitting across, hardly looking up from her Sudoku.

"No change then?" asked the older lady.

"He just lies there."

The ladies nodded knowingly. Greg noticed his own head nodding in unison, although this was just a polite reflex. He also noticed that the driver's left elbow was now resting on his cab door. Experience told him that the driver probably wanted to announce something. Sympathy for Mr. Scrimshaw, perhaps?

"You're sure you want to stay on, then?" called the driver, his face just visible in the mirror.

This question precisely coincided with the older lady asking: "Are you on holiday, dear?"

Greg was musing on his immediate plans and so the dual interrogation threw him slightly.

"Yes, I've got two weeks!" he shouted at the driver.

"That's what they're saying about Mr. Scrimshaw," said the nurse, resignedly, and abandoning her Sudoku.

Greg noticed the driver withdraw his elbow - presumably in response to his odd reply.

"I mean…." he said quietly to the ladies, but they were shaking their heads this time and expressing regret. He waved to the driver as though to say 'carry on', and tried to appear normal.

The younger one beamed at him and addressed him for the first time. He assumed them to be mother and daughter - they shared the same manner of tilting their necks.

"Have you been to Sleaford before, love?" she asked, as though it were an experience to be savoured.

All three ladies were watching him now, and the driver's elbow was back in attentive mode also.

"No, but I'm not too sure if I want to go there after all, really," he replied, wondering whether getting off at the next cheap hotel might be the best option. Now the nurse was shaking her head, whilst the other women were conferring in hushed tones.

"Is someone meeting you, dear?" asked the older lady, concerned, turning her head to study him in perfect synchronicity with that of her daughter. "Only we're getting off soon and, well, we don't want to read about you in the Boston Bugle tomorrow starving to death in a ditch somewhere, do we Monica?"

Monica shook her head and referred to feral dogs that allegedly roamed the highways after dusk.

"You're not diabetic are you?" asked the nurse, abruptly.

"No!" said Greg, defensively, but he thought it might be as well to quell some of the mystery that he'd somehow created.

"My employers have given me two weeks holiday to do some....composing."

The nurse turned her attention to her magazine's wordsearch, whilst mother and daughter smiled approvingly.

"Really! Meston, my husband used to say he wanted to write a symphony but he couldn't find the right key," said Monica.

"He won't get far without a key," added the nurse as she encircled a diagonal series of letters in green ink.

"How far are *you* going, dear?" asked Mother.

11

"There's a nice old inn near where we get off. Oak beams."

"Pine," corrected the nurse.

"Anyway, I'm sure they'll let you stay and compose something there if you ask!" continued the mother.

He hadn't meant to 'go public' about the purpose of his visit, but was glad it hadn't invited cross-examination about what skills he had with 'writing dots'. He'd try not to mention the subject again, unless asked specifically, but he feared that his fibre tip pens could well remain as pristine as when Mr. Langrish in 'Stationery' issued them to him that morning.

"Thank you, I might try booking in there if you can recommend it," he replied, reassured that he was getting good advice.

"You must have a word with Meston about composition. He's meeting us off the bus!" she added. "We'll be there soon!"

Greg smiled and hoped that being met off the bus this time wouldn't involve paying another 'booking fee' for accommodation.

"There aren't any mountains around here, are there?" he asked, changing the subject. and remembering the Turvey character referring to them.

"You won't find any mountains round here," replied the nurse peremptorily. "You should have done your homework!"

He exchanged a knowing glance with Monica, then bowed his head remorsefully. She giggled, and offered him a 'fun size' packet of cheese biscuits from the carrier bag at her feet. "I buy these for my husband. He's a bit underweight."

"What's his body mass index?" asked the nurse, as

her green fibre tip hunted for names of famous weather forecasters.

"I don't know. He's never mentioned it, has he, Mam?"

"He doesn't say a lot," agreed Mother.

"Perhaps there's a personal problem page for such cases in *Pravda*," said the nurse. "No offence, Mrs. Throstlethwaite."

Mother took a deep breath but said nothing with it.

Greg was relieved when the nurse looked as though she was about to leave, although she appeared to be assessing him briefly for his BMI whilst simultaneously taking the pulse of the bell push.

"Enjoy your stay, then!" she instructed him forcibly before ringing the bell, passing her magazine to Mother, and then marching to the front of the bus.

The driver duly stopped in the middle of nowhere where she alighted on a grassy verge, from which she peered in at them as the bus moved away.

"That was Nurse Newnes," advised Mother. "We're next!"

Greg was glad that he hadn't begun to eat the biscuits, especially now as he'd just noticed a warning against consuming food on the bus which implied that such behaviour was a serious offence. However, Nurse Newnes had definitely been chewing a peppermint.

A minute later the ladies rose, and made their way to the front, glancing behind as though to make sure their fellow traveller was still present. He picked up his bag, and noticed the driver observing him in the mirror.

"You're going to stay at 'The Fenman's Rest' then?" he asked.

'Mother' spoke proudly on his behalf. "He's got to

meet my son-in-law first - this young man's a composer!"

"That accounts for it," laughed the driver. "Songs about mountains, is it?"

"Well, er....I need to be inspired," replied Greg diffidently, wondering whether he could actually fulfil his employers' expectations of him.

The bus stopped diagonally opposite the brightly-lit whitewashed 'Fenman's Rest'. Greg saw a car parked in a lay-by and wondered what on earth he was going to say when introduced to Meston.

"I'd better see if they've got a room first," he said as he stepped off the bus.

"Wait, I'll come with you," said Monica as she took his arm to cross the road. "I want a bottle of Advocaat for tomorrow."

As they reached the inn he glanced at the illuminated glass case on the wall displaying menus typed in copperplate script - all in French. This was an expensive place to stay - more than his allowances would permit.

"You sit in the car, Mam!" called Monica to her mother across the road. "I want to get a surprise for Mesty."

She checked the contents of her purse, then opened the door for them to enter. "Mesty would like it here but he's not keen on crowds," she confided in him as they heard a party of diners toasting someone called Piers. "We've got a men's awareness group camping in the field at home, but he's a bit wary of them too," she added.

Greg nodded, wondering whether he might end up sleeping in a tent if the inn was full, then have his own awareness - of damp grass.

They walked along the thickly-carpeted hall and approached a mahogany reception desk, where he rang a brass bell with trepidation. Monica moved to one side and admired the prints on the wall of 17th century windmills with multiple sails and equanimity. The bell was immediately answered by the sound of footsteps on a tiled floor, and interest in the windmills was suspended.

"Good evening, sir!" said an efficient man in a waistcoat hurrying in though a doorway. "A double, is it? We've just got one left!"

"No, just a single, actually," said Greg as he heard the bus departing from the stop, making its way to Sleaford without him. Monica returned to stand resolutely at his side. She seemed as keen as he was to get him fixed up for the night.

"I'm afraid we don't have any single rooms left," said the receptionist, looking quizzically at Greg's companion.

Greg braced himself to ask how much they charged for a double, even though Monica only wanted to buy a bottle of Advocaat, but the answer preceded his question, and it was three times the amount that Mr. Manktelow could sanction.

"It's got a four poster bed!" added the hopeful receptionist, encouragingly. "With ruched curtains for madam!"

"No, I just wanted to buy a bottle of something!" blurted Monica, realising the misapprehension. "My husband likes us to indulge occasionally!"

"I can have a bottle sent up to your room!" said the eager man, not giving up. "The house white?"

"Is the...well, the rendering at the front is a bit patchy but it's basically white," she replied, pleasantly surprised. "How did you know? Have you called there to buy King Edwards from us?"

Greg had forgotten his concern about sleeping arrangements and was giggling to himself, but the man behind the counter now appeared to be trembling slightly.

"Actually I think we *might* be full tonight after all, but the 'Blue Moon', three miles up the road, will probably have vacancies," said the receptionist nervously as he deftly withdrew the register that had lain open on the desk.

"I know it, it's in all the guide books! We can drop you off there in the car," said Monica, taking Greg's arm once more. "You'd better sit in the back, though. Dawn's in the front seat. She's on heat."

She tilted her head at a brick-built windmill, advised the bemused receptionist: "Nice clapboards!", and accompanied Greg back outside.

He peered anxiously at the car in the distance and hoped that Dawn was a dog. However, he could only make out Mother in the back, and a male figure in the driver's seat. Monica escorted Greg across the road, but on reaching the kerb she broke into a trot. He assumed there was a time factor involved and so he began to run behind her, but then slowed down. It might have alarmed Meston to see a strange man running after his wife, and Dawn, whoever she was, might scream - or bark. He overcompensated and slowly ambled along for the last few yards, but then realised that his pace might now be too nonchalant if they were being kind enough to give him a lift to the

16

Blue Moon.   He therefore compromised by adopting the brisk gait of the receptionist as Monica stood holding the nearside rear door open for him invitingly. The car was dark grey, and seemed to blend in with the road surface.

"This is….Oh! I don't know your name, do I?"

A hitherto silent collie on the floor in front began barking loudly.   The driver, a slight man, attired in a chunky pullover, tried nervously calming the animal down with a succession of "No, no, no, no, no."

"Hello, I'm Greg!" said Greg as he climbed in, but the barks and the 'no's drowned out anything he uttered.   "It's very kind of you!" he called out, adding to the din.   "I understand you've been working on a symphony!"

Meston either couldn't hear him, or didn't wish to discuss his attempts at composition, and merely carried on repeating "no".

Greg sat down with Mother on his right, but she was wincing at the noise.   She added to it by shouting: "Dawn, Dawn, Dawn!" to complement the "no"s.   It reminded him of some of the more dramatic passages from Shostakovich.   Mother then leaned towards him.

"You can call me Thelma!" she invited him, smiling as though allowing the name to sink in.

"Thelma, right," said Greg, innocently, but this seemed to amuse her slightly.

"My Bill used to call me that," she said wistfully. "Gone now, though."

Monica squeezed in on his left and slammed the door.   "He's a composer!" she announced.   "Can we take him to The Blue Moon?"

Meston turned to face the visitor with a faint smile

and held out his right hand, but when Greg reached across to shake it with his own he was instead kissed by the dog's wet tongue.

"Cloth, cloth, cloth!" demanded Monica, but then she saw a dirty towel on the front seat and handed it to Greg. "Found it!"

He wiped his hand methodically on the only clean bit of the towel and then fastened his seat belt. The dog had now become less excited, as had the humans who began to talk in sentences.

"Nice to meet you," said Meston, dispensing with handshakes. "You probably already know my name."

"Yes, no doubt it's local," said Greg, diplomatically. "I've not been to these parts before, but my line manager sent me here. He thought the flat landscapes would be inspirational!"

Meston nodded, patted the dog's head, and started the engine, whilst Monica and her mother talked across Greg about having enough bread for the morning. Apparently the men in the tent ate huge quantities of toast but were quite cavalier with their crumbs. Greg proffered the back of his hand to the now docile Dawn but she kept knocking it upwards with her strong and slender nose.

"Sorry, I can't go fast due to the exhaust being loose," explained Meston as they drove along ultra-cautiously, but then Thelma gestured to him that he shouldn't ride the clutch either as it too required attention.

"How long are you staying here?" asked Meston, but the car began juddering.

"Meston, the revs!" shouted Thelma, prompting acceleration with apologies.

"Mind the exhaust!" reminded Monica. "There's a pothole somewhere along here!"

"Yes, I know," replied Meston, again apologetically. "I think there's another seven after the next bend."

"Two weeks," said Greg, as he removed his hand from Dawn's sphere of influence. "I want to go for some long walks, it might help me to…."

"Meston, the revs!"

"We live down a very rutted farm track," explained Monica, breezily. "We hold our breaths every time we drive along it, but Nurse Newnes said we shouldn't. It could starve the brain of oxygen! A bit faster here, Mesty, I think."

Thus they drove for several miles along the deserted road with alternating advice from the two ladies, and corresponding acceleration or braking, according to the immediate perceived risk. Greg eventually saw the shape of a large building looming up in the distance, together with a sign at the side of the road indicating it being '*The Blue Moon*', and serving evening meals.' This looked to be even more grand than the previous place. He imagined gold-braided commissionaires meeting guests at the door with formal courtesy as they stepped out of plush gas-guzzlers, but his own imminent arrival from a limping banger with canine guard and driver-support might attract less of a welcome. Meston duly turned in through the gates and allowed the car to judder along up the tree-lined driveway.

"Meston, the revs!" reminded his mother-in-law.

"Careful, Mesty, there are loose chippings!" advised the second navigator.

"It's very good of you, but I can easily walk from

here," suggested Greg, but it was then obvious that the place was in darkness, apart from three well-lit downstairs windows.

"We want to see you settled in, love, don't we?" asked Monica, to which a chorus of 'yes!' and another bout of barking ensued.

As they approached the door to what appeared to be an annexe, they noticed a young man sitting on the steps watching them. He had the typical young smoker's manner of scrutinising someone intently whilst pausing on the next inhalation, lips gripping the cigarette as though it were about to fly out. This was definitely no gold-braided commissionaire establishment - the man's visage implied "Keep Out!" Meston stalled the car a respectable distance away from the unwelcoming committee of one.

"I'll wait here," he said as the ladies opened their doors to get out.

Monica put Dawn on her lead and held her on a tight rein. Greg pondered on whether getting out via the left or right passenger door was better, but he chose the right so as not to appear churlish to Meston. "Once again, many thanks," he said as he hauled out his bag, but Meston was anxious about the proximity of a redundant rusty lager can near Greg's foot.

"Don't trip over that, but it's probably nice inside!" he said encouragingly.

"They're usually lined with tin, I think," said Greg, wondering why a used can was being recommended to him. He followed the ladies and barking dog towards the steps, hoping that the hotel's unlit upper floor windows indicated that there were rooms to spare, and possibly negotiable. The smoker tensed, and removed his cigarette, but then grinned and stretched out his arms to cuddle the approaching dog.

"Hello!" he said, before looking up and asking: "What's his name?"

"Her," corrected Thelma, peering in through one of the windows. "What a state!"

"Hi Herb!" said the young man as he stroked the dog's neck. "What brings *you* here?"

Greg took his cue and got down to business, literally, by bending slightly to address his seated, although occupied, prospective host.

"Hello, do you have a single room for perhaps two weeks…." but the man was already shaking his head.

"We haven't even got a *double* room for perhaps two hours. We're closed pending major repairs."

Another, slightly older person wearing overalls appeared in the doorway. "Can I help?" he asked. "We're in a bit of a muddle!"

The younger man stood up and Dawn ran off to sniff a bag of cement. "I'll get Herb a bowl of water," he said, cheerily. "Do you think he'd like sparkling?"

Greg could see that Dawn's requirements were being prioritised, whereas his own were of minor importance to the staff. He approached the older man in order to tell him he didn't mind muddle, but Monica was asking him the name of the shrub near the door. Whilst the man tried to remember, Greg tried again to secure a room. "It said you were open on the sign outside!"

"It's a berberis, I think!" came the reply, followed by: "No I'm sorry but the kitchen's out of action - the ceiling collapsed. It's in a right mess!"

"Goodness. What a shock that must have been!"

said Thelma, as she joined Monica in fondling the prickly leaves of the berberis. "You have to be so careful these days."

"We came here because it said 'open'!" pleaded Greg, although he realised that any forthcoming apology wouldn't necessarily provide him with a bed. "It doesn't need to be a four-poster!"

Both ladies were now engrossed in the shrub, whilst Meston remained in the car, filling in a crossword.

Greg was beginning to feel rather incidental, but then the man took pity on him. "You're welcome to come and see the damage for yourself. There's still rubble on the hobs!"

The younger man had just served Dawn with mineral water on the steps, before resuming his place next to a cast iron foot-scraper. He tried unsuccessfully to light another cigarette, but his plastic lighter merely clicked impotently. "You haven't got a light, have you?" he asked, but Greg merely shook his head, and made his way past him to view the kitchen. At least he was being allowed in.

He paused in the entrance, as the two ladies having heard the invitation, decided to accompany him. Meston watched them from the comfort of the car with a puzzled expression. Was he stuck on an anagram?

"Mesty, there's rubble on the hobs!" shouted Monica.

He put down his paper down and wound down the window. "Sorry", he called out.

The visitors were ushered into the large kitchen where they stared at the festoons of plasterwork draped like mosquito nets above the metal sinks. Thelma gasped, and whispered something about 'Auntie

Edith's' to Monica. Greg stood respectfully next to a tall fridge, and wondered what the point of this inspection might be.

The man stood to one side as though allowing them to drink in the scene, but then he coughed slightly and apologised, presumably from having broken the reverential silence. "See that superior quality piece of carpet through the hole up there?" he asked quietly, pointing up. "That's room number 3. Empty at the time, fortunately. The occupant was enjoying our reconditioned billiard room when it happened, but of course we had to tell him that his room was temporarily no longer of the highest standard."

Greg remembered newsreels of royalty visiting bomb damage and selected an appropriate comment. "Something must be done!" he said.

Dawn scampered in and examined the oven door. Greg hoped that the oven, like room number 3, was also empty.

"Is she all right in here?" asked Monica, concerned about the dog being in a hotel kitchen.

"There's no danger now," assured the man. "the joists are quite safe. The chef became hysterical, though, when it happened."

"Well, thank you very much," said Thelma, after giving due respect, turning to make her way out. "It's been very…."

Dawn led the way by rushing outside and barking, and the man looked at Greg and forced a bittersweet smile as though to say "Well, there you are!" The two ladies filed out, pausing briefly on their way to inspect a dust-filled lemon squeezer.

"You can't beat glass for a good squeeze, Monica,"

advised her mother.

It occurred to Greg that if he hadn't been so keen to buy a bus ticket for a dodgy stranger he wouldn't now be standing in a condemned kitchen with no prospect of accommodation. He almost wanted to laugh, but it was probably the alkalinity of the suspended ceiling that was actually making him want to sneeze instead.

"So as you can see, there's no way we can function as a hotel for some time yet!" said the man. "There's no milk either!"

Greg nodded, but tried not to appear too positive about it. "I'll try somewhere else then," he said patiently, then sneezed violently and dispersed a film of plaster from a tray of eggs. "Somewhere that really *is* open!"

"Do come again when we re-open!" said the man, accompanying Greg to the outer door. "That's why we've kept the 'open' sign, so people won't think we've closed for good. I'm thinking August!"

Greg was thinking 'walkies' as Dawn had returned to 'collect' him, but she then placed her wet nose and tongue in the palm of his hand, and there was nothing in the kitchen to wipe it on. He picked up his bag with the clean hand and glanced through a doorway to a utility room in which the younger man was cutting a length of pipe with a hacksaw. He waited until he got outside and knelt on a small patch of lawn to wipe his contaminated hand vigorously on some grass. He then turned round to see both men staring at him. "Nature's towel!" he called out, before standing up and walking towards the car. Meston had locked himself in, and was now releasing the doors to allow the others in. Greg was relieved that Dawn's invitation for him to return to them was being echoed by her owners who were all beckoning him to rejoin them and weren't going to see him stranded.

"You sit in the middle, Greg," said Monica, allowing him to enter first. Thelma got in next and smiled, encouragingly.

"Sorry, wasn't it all that good?" asked Meston. "It seemed nice and quiet, I thought."

"Not really, Mesty," sighed Monica as she squeezed herself in. "One of the rooms was broken. Then the chef had run out of milk and became hysterical. We thought Greg could stay in the caravan."

"He should be safe in there," said Meston as he switched on the engine. "anyway, there's too much of a crowd in the tent tonight."

CHAPTER 2

Greg hadn't slept in a caravan for many years, but he remembered that almost everything inside such vehicles was usually within easy reach. It also sounded preferable to the overcrowded tent, although he had a slight fear of caravans losing their balance during the night. During the day, however, they were probably as safe as....garden sheds."That's *very* kind of you!" he said, again feeling rather beholden to the family. "I'll look for somewhere nearer the coast tomorrow, although I've always wanted to visit Quadring Fen!"

The others glanced at him sympathetically. He responded by diverting his eyes to his holdall on the front seat, loyally guarded by Dawn. "Well, not *always*, of course," he added. "That would suggest I was fixated with....fens."

Meston was manoeuvring the car round on the loud crunchy gravel, and heading towards the main gate. As the indicators were ticking, apparently showing left - the way they'd come - Greg realised that they'd made a minor detour to bring him to the hotel. Thus, after a pause at the entrance, the car duly moved sedately to the left.

"Meston, the revs!" instructed Thelma in a friendly cajoling manner, before turning to Greg as though about to kiss him. "You'll be very comfortable in the van. There's a little table where you can sit and compose!"

"Mesty, don't forget that rough bit round the next bend," advised Monica, before she too confided in

Greg. "It's got a captain's bed!"

Meston thanked his team, and continued along the road in an effort to please both them and the car. Greg wasn't sure what to say about his composing aspirations, although he would like to have known more about Meston's ambitions for a symphony. He thanked his companions again, collectively, and wondered why a captain had loaned the family a bed. "Is it a big campsite that you have?" he asked.

"Just you in the van and the boys in the tent!" replied Monica. "You'll probably meet them in the morning - Norman, their leader, is quite....Watch out, Mesty! I think the exhaust's rattling again!"

Greg felt himself lurch forward, meeting Dawn's eyes as she lay protecting his bag. He smiled briefly at her, before another injunction from Thelma made him recline as the car sped on again. Had Monica said that the leader of the campers was *quite*, or quiet?

"Hold on!" announced Meston, a few moments later. "I'm just about to turn into the lane. Sorry for any bumps!"

Greg braced himself for both the anticipated rough ride and the onslaught of further backseat vehicle verbiage. They were such an amiable group, however, that as soon as the car lurched on to the rutted track laughter immediately accompanied the violent movements of both passengers and exhaust assembly. The commands "Meston, don't stall!" and "It's working loose, Mesty!" formed a unity of good-humoured instruction, as did the simultaneous reply of "Almost there!" from the ultra-patient driver. Even Dawn exhibited glee at her imminent arrival home, whereas Greg remained blissfully silent as he peered through the high hedges past which they crept / lurched / sped.

Looking ahead he saw a farmhouse looming up in the near distance, dark in the dusk. A gap through the hawthorn hedge on the right revealed a small group of Jersey cows watching the car from the vantage point of a metallic gate. They appeared to be only mildly interested as the party by turns trundled and careered past.

"Are they yours?" asked Greg, realising he'd said nothing for several minutes.

"My dad kept a herd of Friesians once," replied Meston. "Those you can see on the right belong to the...."

"Mesty, mind that chair!" interrupted Monica.

"Ooh, thanks, love!" said Meston as he swerved to avoid a basket chair projecting on to the track.

Greg then noticed a white triangle standing on a patch of grass on the left. A washing line bearing numerous vests connected it to a curved box painted lime green with a window. The curved box was, of course, the caravan - his bijou residence for the night. The white triangle, he realised, was the tent, proportionately even smaller - perhaps *too* small - judging by the number of vests that appeared to be edging their way along the line to the slightly more commodious caravan.

The car lurched to a decisive stop a few yards short of the front door to the old house. The two ladies baled out, along with Dawn, who skipped and sniffed her way to the open porch.

"I'll be making coffee!" called Monica, cordially. "Or you can have something weaker if you'd rather!"

"Whatever you're making!" called Greg as he leaned towards the door on his left, but he noticed that Meston remained steadfastly in his seat. He wondered whether the man ever left the car. Was his foot somehow trapped by the problematic clutch pedal? Taking his leave once more from the offside passenger door, Greg paused. "Well, thank you for the ride, and for the use of the caravan!" he said, although there were probably more interesting conversational gambits he could have used, like: "So, have you written any other music lately?" or "Are the caravan's tyres correctly inflated?"

"We'll show you round," said Meston, as he handed him a key. "While it's calm!"

Greg thanked him once more, then stood expectantly, waiting for Meston to try and get out, but he still didn't move. Greg wondered whether he needed assistance, and offered his hand to help him out.

"I'll just park it round the side first," said Meston, smiling at the outstretched arm, then gesturing backwards towards the mini-camp-site. "Far from the madding crowd!"

Greg modified his redundant arm into one employed in waving off his host as Meston drove the car at walking pace riding the clutch for the final few yards to the other side of the house. He lifted his bag, and wondered whether to go to the front door to await a cup of whatever Monica was making; go and unlock the caravan door to let himself in; or follow Meston to extricate him from the ambivalent car. One of the cows mooed loudly. A corresponding moo seemed to emanate from the tent, but it sounded more human than bovine. This all seemed a world away from the accommodation he might have had in the centre of Lincoln.

Dawn then came dashing out of the house, stopping first to examine some brickwork as though choosing a perfume, before bounding towards Greg and sitting on his feet. He had little option now but to await developments; trying to move might invoke friskiness, or barking that could well incite further mooing from the adjacent field, and another response from the tent.

Thelma appeared at the door and waved. "I'm off to bed now, dear. Meston and Monica will sort you out!"

"See you in the morning, then!" called Greg, cheerily. "Meston's given me the key!"

"Well, that's good," she laughed. "Now you can get started on your music!"

Meston then appeared round the corner as Thelma went inside. He was walking quickly, but Dawn moved even quicker as she raced to greet him. Perhaps she too had never seen him walk before.

"I'll show you what's what," he called to Greg as he paused to usher the dog back in to the house. "Then you can have a Welsh rabbit with us in the kitchen!"

"Well, if you're sure it's all right," said Greg, hesitantly, as he lifted his bag.

"It'll be fine. We've not been poisoned yet!" said Meston, unoffended by Greg's politeness. Then he pointed towards the tent. "We'd better lower our voices. I think the leader's in there, although the others are probably in the woods trying to find their inner warrior."

"I see," said Greg, quietly, giving the tent a wide berth. "Is their leader the one who moos?"

"Sorry, I don't know. I want to avoid them - like

these nettles. They can even sting you through cotton."

"I'll take extra long strides," said Greg, wondering whether the vests on the line symbolised the inner warrior's liberation. "Anyway, I wasn't suggesting the rabbit was past its best. I just hoped it wasn't any trouble for you!"

"No problem, but it's not a real rabbit," whispered Meston. "It's cheese on toast - Caerphilly!"

"Oh," said Greg as he trod softly through the nettles. "That sounds even better!"

As they approached the door of the caravan, Greg surreptitiously checked out the supports. A few bricks underneath might have provided more security for him, but at least the little legs looked to be intact, and the caravan itself seemed to be level. He inserted the key in the lock and pushed slowly on the handle. As the door was virtually in the centre, he hoped the chassis wouldn't tip up yet.

"Shhhhh!" said Meston as the squeaky door yielded to Greg's gentle pressure. "You'd better let me go first!"

Greg stood aside and hoped that with two men inside it would still maintain equilibrium.

"I'll light the gas mantle for you," whispered Meston. "Watch what I do, though. It's delicate."

Once inside, Greg felt more confident about the safety of his night's abode. He watched the lighted match ignite the gas with a soft pop, then surveyed his living space as the mellow light illuminated what appeared to be a well-kept study in compactness, but then he noticed Monica standing in the doorway, beaming, and holding a large enamel water jug.

31

"Mother spruced it up this morning in case. Just as well, as it's turned out!" she said as she entered and placed the jug on a small shelf next to the sink. She remained standing there, admiring the cosy interior. "There's no plumbing in here, but you can use the bathroom in the house. You don't mind sharing it with the men's group, do you?"

"Er....is it a very large bathroom?" asked Greg, slightly dubious.

"No, but only one of them is tall," Monica assured him. "Anyway, show him the folding table, Mesty!"

"Sorry, this is the table," said Meston proudly. "It folds up!"

Greg observed how close the table was to the narrow bed, assuming that the cupboard with cushions on top was indeed the bed. "It looks very neat," he said, coming to terms with his limited space. "I can even lie in bed at the table and try song writing!"

Meston turned to face him, grinning. "You can tell me more over the Welsh rabbit!" he replied, enthusiastically. "Perhaps you can show me...." but he was stopped in his tracks by the sound of low throaty chanting from somewhere outside.

"Mother said they told her they might want to invoke the *animus,* apparently," advised Monica, as she walked over to hold Meston's hand.

Greg hoped the pulsating rhythms wouldn't provoke the animals, and give him a disturbed night. However, he was more concerned about the shift in weight distribution, and so he moved over to the sink and hoisted himself on to the draining board. "It's probably just a ritual before settling down for the night," he said, but as the couple were both staring at him leaning back

32

with his head against the wall-mounted plate rack he felt he had to qualify his statement. "Out there, I mean. The men singing!"

"Sorry, is *that* the sort of music you write?" asked Meston, clutching his wife's hand.

"No, actually I've not written a note yet," Greg confessed as he slid down self-consciously from the draining board. "By the way, this caravan *will* bear the weight of three adults randomly positioned, I trust?"

Monica averted her stare, and instead smiled nervously at the enamel jug. Meston dropped the support of the table which crashed to the floor. The caravan wobbled, and a cow mooed. The man in the tent then responded with another moo of his own.

"Sorry, it's been a long day," said Meston as he fiddled with the table. "I think we're all a bit anxious."

Greg drew the curtain above the sink and tried to instil a peaceful mood. "Of course. Thanks for the water, Monica. It looks....so still!"

The chanting was now ominously increasing in volume. Meston peered out of the window above the bed, then quickly drew the thin curtains. "Shall we all be getting back to the house?" he suggested, trying to appear calm. "Dawn will be wondering where we've got to."

"She will. She's eight now!" said Monica, breezily, as she moved towards the door. "See you two in a minute, then!"

Meston stood up and peered out again, warily. "Sorry about the table," he said before turning out the light. "Shall we go and eat?"

Greg agreed, then waited for him outside whilst he gently closed the door. The chanting was getting

33

closer. "It's a lovely even...."

"Shhh!" whispered Meston as he parted the thermal vests suspended before them. "Anyway, have you been writing music long?"

Greg followed his lead and loped through clumps of nettles towards the house. "Well, actually I've never written a note in my life!"

"Wow, it's that avant garde stuff, then!" said Meston as he raced ahead. "To be honest, I didn't really have the skills to write a symphony. I wouldn't even know a treble clef from a…..the other sort!"

"I see," said Greg, seeing little point in advising him on the bass or alto clefs.

By now they'd reached the sanctuary of the back door where Meston conscientiously wiped his feet on the metal scraper. As Greg waited his turn he looked across at the rather cute little caravan. "It's quite oval in shape, isn't it?"

"The treble clef, you mean?" said Meston, puzzled. "Like an egg?"

"Would I....on my cheese on toast?" asked Greg. "Well, I wouldn't mind, or even a tomato, thank you!"

Meanwhile the higher registers of male chanting were steadily advancing, although Greg thought there was a distinct reediness in their voices. Meston opened the door and beckoned him inside. "Sorry about the mess, although when my dad ran the place we had hens strutting about the floor! They always kept it free of crumbs."

Greg wiped his feet for what he presumed to be the statutory period, then entered and stood to one side as Meston closed the door behind him. The crescendo outside stopped suddenly, and was followed by a unison of coughing.

"I think they're a bit hoarse," said Greg as he chose a chair at the long table. "Shall I sit here?"

"Sorry, yes, of course, make yourself at home," said Meston as he sat on a well-worn sofa to remove his shoes. "Monica's upstairs reading to her mother. She reads with such feeling. She'll be down soon."

The room was comfortably disorganised, but crumbs weren't in evidence, and it reminded Greg of a typical farmhouse kitchen. He studied the Aga opposite where he sat, then took his cue from his host and removed his own shoes. He was about to ask about the Aga's running costs, but Meston had donned a pair of slippers and was gesturing him towards a half-open door. "Would you like to see round the place? That's if you don't mind looking at rooms!"

Greg didn't particularly need to inspect the house, especially as he wasn't going to stay in it, but it was obvious that Meston was keen to show off his domain.

"I've just taken off my shoes," said Greg. "Is it carpeted throughout?"

His host reassured him of the foot-friendly floors, and invited him into a small hall, where the dulcet tones of Monica reading to her mother drifted down the stairs. Greg gazed appreciatively at a Chinese ceramic umbrella stand and pretended to ignore the intrusive vocal instructions from above to "Drain the vegetables before covering with oatmeal and grated cheese."

"I suppose it rains a fair bit in China," said Greg, quietly, keen to avoid interrupting the denouement of Monica's Woolton Pie.

"It's a big country!" advised Meston. "Sorry, would you like to borrow a brolly in case it's raining in the morning?"

"Then serve with gravy from the stock you saved earlier," intoned the soothing bedside voice from above. "Hmm, lovely!" came Thelma's response.

"Hmm, if you think I might need one," came Greg's.

"The forecast wasn't good, sorry. I still listen avidly to the weather reports for farmers every morning," explained Meston as he opened another door. "Anyway, this is our sitting room. You're welcome to look inside the piano stool!"

Greg didn't have any urge to see what the furniture contained, but again, he followed up the invitation, and proceeded to enter the cosy, and yet rather cramped room. He hesitantly raised the upholstered lid of the stool that stood half under the protective canopy of an antique piano. "Oh, manuscript paper!" he announced pleasantly as he discovered a pile of ageing but unmarked sheets, plus some tutorials on harmony. He assumed that these were being offered to him, and so he selected a small manuscript book, and feigned gratitude. "I'll try and compose something tomorrow!" he said, as he looked round the happily cluttered room, but he wanted to change the subject from that of his working holiday. "I like the old radiogram!" he enthused as he spotted the large item standing in one of the alcoves. "I shouldn't be saying that, though, in my line of work!"

"It's all right," assured Meston. "The room isn't bugged!"

A door closed gently upstairs, and an equally gentle footfall followed as Monica crept down the stairs. "I think she's off!" she whispered to Meston, now standing in the hall. "She really loves those wartime recipes!"

Greg joined them, clutching his manuscript book, and politely smiled. "And so few eggs around!" he said.

"Quite right!" said Monica, thoughtfully, before opening the door to the kitchen. "So, who's for those Welsh rabbits?"

"I think we all are!" said Meston, cheerfully, as he ushered Greg back to his chair at the table, but then he became serious as he stood to one side by the window and peered out. "It's all quiet out there now," he said eventually, somewhat relieved.

"Mother says they might drum tomorrow," said Monica casually, as she collected large plates from a cupboard. "You won't mind that, will you Greg?"

"Well er, I'll probably be moving on after breakfast," replied Greg, assuming that the men's forthcoming drumbeats were more likely to form an evening ritual.

"You're welcome to stay as long as you like!" said Monica, an invitation seconded by Meston as he sank into the low sofa and removed a rubber bone that had somehow intruded into his trouser pocket.

"Sorry," he said as it squeaked plaintively.

"Thank you, that's very kind of you both. I'll see how I feel," said Greg impassively, keeping open his options, and aware that any extramural rhythms might impair his first attempt at composition.

"I can show you round the rest of the house tomorrow!" said Meston. "It was always a great place for playing hide and seek!" He excused himself to go and attend to Dawn, now presumably bedded down in

37

her own room.

Would the dog be benefiting too from a lullaby of food-related prose? And might games that required counting to a hundred be on the agenda for tomorrow? Monica had, after all, wanted to surprise her husband with a bottle of Advocaat the next day. Greg watched as she laid slices of bread on the grill pan, adding a basinful of grated cheese. He wondered about correcting her pronunciation of 'rabbit' to 'rarebit' but the word could sound pretentious and he was merely an unexpected guest. Anyway, she was concentrating on the task in hand, and so he refrained from mentioning anything. Thus he sat thoughtfully at the table, anticipating the snack, and hoping that the caravan would remain level through the night.

"You're very quiet!" she said as she provided him with cutlery. "You've probably got a tune running through your head!"

The responsibility of being paid to come up with at least one creditable musical composition to be marketed specifically for clients' own homes was preying on his mind. He knew of the concept of 'House' music, but there were so many other genres and perhaps 'Caravan' or 'Tent' were styles that he should also consider. "I'm a bit new to all this!" he admitted after a four beat pause.

"Don't worry, you'll soon get used to us!" she laughed, before checking the grill and slicing a tomato.

"No, not you!" he exclaimed, but immediately regretted how the phrase could have been misconstrued. "I mean...." but she suddenly left the room to stand in the hall and whisper loudly: "Mesty! It's nearly ready!"

Meston returned and took his place opposite Greg. "Sorry, I was just checking …." but his words tailed off as a cistern flushed outside and footsteps were heard hurriedly passing by the window. "Was that one of them?" he asked nervously, turning round towards Monica.

"What did he look like?" she asked, apparently not too concerned.

"I don't know," replied Meston. "Sorry, I didn't actually see him."

She glanced at Greg who responded by shaking his head whilst trying to look suitably disappointed.

"It probably was, then," she said, casually. "Mother didn't see anything of them either, apart from a man in a beret who called in to pay in advance. Said he wasn't very chatty - a bit short."

"Probably a bit miffed about the size of the tent, then," said Meston, wryly. "Greg understands!"

This time Greg nodded, indicating his support for the overcrowding theory. "I'm sure they'll survive if they move about slowly!" He thought about genres again. A cow mooed, but this time there was no response. Mood music, perhaps?

"Have they lit a campfire?" asked Meston, springing to his feet after a short lull. "I can smell something burning!"

"It's the rabbits!" shrieked Monica as she rushed to turn down the grill. "Thanks. Just caught them in time!"

Heavy footsteps crunching on gravel drew the men's attention back to the window. Again they saw no-one, but the raising of the latch on an external door was heard.

"Sorry about that," said Meston. "It's probably nerves."

"Probably," said Greg, unsure as to whether it was the low profile campers', or Meston's own repentant nerves that were on edge.

"Mesty, did we run out of Worcestershire?" asked Monica as she began serving up.

Greg wondered if it was nerves again that had been responsible for such an epic escape, but the recalling of the memory prompted Meston to hit his head in mock remorse. "Sorry, that's my fault, it went straight out of my head."

"Never mind," she laughed as she presented Greg with his plate. "We've got H.P. if you want any."

Further plumbing and gravel-crunching sounds sidetracked the men's attention, but Greg declined any H.P. commitments and waited politely for Meston to be served. Finally, Monica took her place at the head of the table, facing the window and leading the supper.

"I once lived near the Forest of Dean!" declared Greg, wondering what had driven them out of Worcestershire.

They studied him with expressions of kind concern, but then the cistern flushed again, followed by rapid footsteps. Could he create something *alla marcia*, perhaps? With an intro of pan pipes? He suppressed the urge to giggle, but his hosts were now too engaged in eating to have noticed if he had.

A generally staccato sequence of unconnected phrases ensued between savoury mouthfuls. "So, what are your plans for....", "Some pepper?", "Hmm, no, I'm fine", "There's another one", "Going to the...?", "Is it going to be choral?", "Sorry, can I just reach for....", "Yes, there might be a soprano...." but conversation abated suddenly when the now cooling grill banged loudly as its metal parts contracted. Then an owl hooted in the woods beyond, but the mood of slight unease was relieved by Monica as she cleared away the plates and touched Meston's shoulder.

"Mesty, do you want to get the....?" she asked, quietly.

"Oh, yes, of course!" he replied willingly. He stood up, and stepped on to the old sofa, his feet sinking into the amorphous cushions. He then opened the two panelled doors of the fitted cupboard set into the wall above, and peered into the vast repository of jars, cans and bottles. Greg's interest in architecture included all sorts of domestic features, and so he peered in and tried to assess how far the capacious cupboard might project into the next room. Meston concentrated on assessing a wide shelf, before casting three very large packets of broad bean and basil flavoured crisps onto the table.

"Sorry!" said Meston as he stepped down from the sofa. "I hope I didn't break any. I thought I heard a crack."

Greg helped himself to the mug of tea that had been placed by his elbow, then looked discreetly at his watch.

"I think one of the men trod on a twig," said Monica. "I hope they've got torches."

This conjured up for Greg an image of burning sticks held aloft by the small army of outdoorsmen. They probably ran barefoot on hot coals too. However, the prospect of his bare fingers wading through quantities of unsavoury crisps, broken or otherwise, in the company of his garrulous hosts didn't really appeal.

The inevitable loud munching would make listening to speech exhausting, unless, of course, it was customary in this house to suck the contents instead.

"Is that the time?" he announced, after downing his tea and with his ears already assaulted by Meston and Monica's synchronised bag-opening. "I'd better go and get ready for bed!"

The couple had only that minute sat down again at the table, but they shot up in unison, as though intent on preventing his departure.

"Oh, nearly forgot these!" he said as he took his seat once more, and ducked under the table to retrieve his shoes - invaluable if he were to be waylaid on his way back to the caravan, and invited to partake in fire-walking, he thought.

"Feel free to let yourself in for breakfast any time," said Monica. "There'll be someone around all morning."

"Thanks, I'll probably make an early start," he said, picking up his manuscript book. "I'd like to spend the day amongst nature!" Wasn't there a genre of music called *Rock Steady*, he wondered? He could perhaps focus on a well-bedded rock and adapt it for clientele with stone fireplaces.

Meston was putting on his own shoes, but his method of doing so was to lie on his back on the floor and force them on with his legs doubled-up above his chest. Greg stared for a moment, but he assumed that the shoes might be tight, or that their owner had been influenced by the family farrier.

"I can see you back to the van," said Meston, his voice affected by his unusual posture. "I don't want to hang about, though, sorry!"

Greg had no worries about losing his way, but it would be churlish to decline the offer now that the man was shod. "That's very kind," he said politely, as he tied his laces in the more conventional position.

Monica had opened the door and was taking a deep breath. "So many stars!" she sighed. "Do you see the same constellations from where you live?"

"More than likely. I believe Orion especially has quite a few fans," said Greg, joining her at the door, but already disorientated.

"That's the one with a belt, isn't it?" she asked.

"Ready when you are!" said Meston, now standing behind them. "Sorry it's so dark out there."

Monica gave her husband a farewell kiss, then waved the two men off.

"Yes, there are three stars that form the...." called Greg, but Meston had already closed the door.

They sprinted towards the caravan, now but a silhouette in what moonlight there was, ducking under the washing line, then pausing at the door for Greg to place the key in Meston's waiting hand.

"I believe they're known as giants!" said Greg as he gazed up in wonder at Orion's belt.

Meston unlocked the door, then slowly withdrew the key and handed it cautiously to Greg, gazing in apprehension at the small tent. "Giants?" he asked, cautiously.

"Super giants, I understand," said Greg, casually.

"Is that what my mother-in-law told you?" he asked, his voice betraying some alarm.

"I read about them. Apparently one day our own sun will become a red giant!"

"Your son?" gasped Meston, looking round anxiously. He glanced at the medium size vests and scratched his head, then jumped when he heard a rasping cough. "Perhaps you wouldn't mind seeing me back to the house," he said after a short pause. "Just in case I er....catch my foot in a rabbit hole or something. Sorry about this."

Greg was surprised at this request to escort his escort back to the house, but he readily agreed, and together they loped off again, dodging the vests and the nettles.

"I'll see you some time during the day, no doubt," said Meston, relieved to have been returned safely to the back door. "I leave early for work, but they'll look after you - food etc. You could use the piano too, if you want, but one of the pedals is broken, like in the car. Sorry."

With that he dashed inside and locked the door, before calling back to Greg through the window. "There's a key to let yourself in on top of the cistern!"

Dawn barked, a cow mooed, and an owl hooted. Greg mouthed his thanks, waved, then went to make use of the facility. He felt on top of the old vitreous china cistern and his fingers found the key. He wondered what the policy was on flushing at this late hour, but he pulled the sturdy chain anyway, wincing at the resultant noisy cascade. He let himself out, and crunched as quietly as possible along the gravel path, then loped once more through the nettles. He entered his retreat and lit the gas light, happy to hear its soft hiss as it illuminated his small space. He rinsed his hands in the cold water from Monica's jug, half-undressed in the rather cool, and yet cosy glow from the flame, then deftly squeezed into the narrow bed. He reached up to turn off the gas, and all became quiet and dark. He'd forgotten his fears about the caravan tipping up during the night, and yet he felt slightly uneasy when he realised that on his final return, the vests on the line had all disappeared.

CHAPTER 3

Greg woke early and, after shedding the fleeting amnesia that resulted from waking up in a strange oval caravan, he pieced together the events that had brought him here. Paid leave to compose made-to-measure music for the domestic market had somehow led to him catching a bus against his will. Then, after meeting an intimidating nurse, he'd been invited by the family of a nervous ex-farmer to view the damaged kitchen of a country hotel, having previously unnerved a receptionist at an inn by requesting a single room. Finally, an erratically driven lift to a farmhouse where he was served a Welsh 'rabbit' and then endowed with manuscript paper had led to him spending the night on their mini-campsite, currently shared by a group of wild men. He lifted the corner of the thin curtain to peep out. The sun was shining, and he could hear what sounded like someone nearby brushing shoes vigorously, with occasional coughs as an accompaniment. He then lay back and surveyed his small metallic domain, and wondered what his neighbours were like - formidable, but with shiny shoes? Then he thought about work. Did his employers really believe that his finely-tuned listening skills would progress to him composing fine tunes? Could he, as Schubert had done, write energetic songs before even getting out of bed? In such a compact environment he could perform almost any task in the comfort of his bed, but he'd been invited to eat breakfast in the house, and an inspirational walk was on his agenda too.

He no longer cared about the floor being pivoted on a single axle, although any space underneath had probably now succumbed to rampant load-bearing nettles. He arose from the cupboard / sofa / bed and got dressed. Then he drew all the curtains, saving those at the larger end window until last. Its aspect was towards the field where the cows lived, and as he drew the final curtain he saw Meston driving off tentatively down the uneven lane. He also caught sight of a black beret passing almost as slowly under the window. This dual sighting reinforced his opinion that he was destined to look out of windows at their busiest moments. He picked up a towel from a towel rail-cum-bookshelf and prepared to visit the shower that he'd noticed last night in the bathroom. Getting dressed to go outside, only to get undressed again to undergo saturation seemed a waste of time and effort, but he had an abundance of time today, rather like that famous work for piano written with no notes - just a challenging four and a half minute rest. He opened the door and stepped down onto the dewy grass, avoiding eye contact with the tent in case its occupants were sitting outside purposefully engaged in being resolute and empowered. He wended his way through the vegetation, then trod carefully along the short gravel path to the door with the heavy latch. He entered the room, surprised to find a red sock on the back of the door, then proceeded to undress before standing under the half-hearted shower.

Glad to have survived the lukewarm downpour he dried and dressed, then felt for the key on top of the cistern, momentarily pondering on home security. Finally he went to the kitchen door with his towel around his neck and let himself in. It wasn't locked, and so he assumed Monica or her mother were around. He took his place once more at the table and awaited developments, placing the wet towel behind him on the back of the chair. He considered attending to a rather hot kettle that whistled slightly on the stove, but then he heard Thelma whistling from within the house. He assumed it must be her signature tune; his own grandpa had been wont to whistle whenever he'd been summoned for his mid-day meal, although no-one in the family had ever been able to identify the tune. This one was just as unrecognisable - perhaps she could teach him composition.

Entering the room she was initially startled to find him sitting there expectantly at the table, but then she laughed and greeted him. "And did you sleep all right in that captain's bed?" she enquired, shaking her head slightly as though to prompt him to say that he hadn't.

"Like a log, thanks!" he replied, nodding as though to prove that indeed he had. "A *captain's* log!"

"That's good," she said wistfully as she looked out of the window towards a vegetable plot. "My husband bought that caravan the year Britain went decimal."

She continued gazing out. Greg had a look too and thought the brassicas were impressive, but he knew she must be reminiscing about the old coinage.

"Yes, all those chunky half-crowns," he said fondly. "It's a pity we can't bring them back, isn't it?"

She turned her gaze on him, although she seemed slightly distracted by the white twill that was draped on his chair. "They told you about what happened, did they?" she asked before lifting the simpering kettle to somewhere less intense in a sort of underarm action.

"The demonetisation process, you mean?" suggested Greg.

She turned her back and set about preparing breakfast whilst imparting a sad story. "I mean my husband. He went missing during a conjuring trick at a theatre in Mablethorpe."

"Sorry, no, I didn't know," said Greg, wondering whether he should assist her in her culinary activities.

"He volunteered to go and stand behind a black screen. Then he was supposed to be released from a locked trunk."

She paused to peer inside the grill pan. "What happened here?" she asked quietly as she examined fragments of carbonised cheese.

Greg pretended to be absorbed in a red cabbage, avoiding giving anything away about the late supper. "Was the key to the trunk missing?" he asked, wondering if it too might be kept on top of the cistern.

"The trunk was empty, dear, apart from some young man who'd wandered on to the stage. A double blow for the magician - his assistant was never seen again either."

Greg thought that the double disappearance might have been more than coincidence, but refrained from saying so. "How terrible," he said, but wishing he could have said something more positive.

"That's why Meston went and got us a puppy from a rescue centre to make up for it. He's thoughtful like that - I suppose that comes from being brought up with Friesians!" she said, slightly more upbeat, whilst turning round to face him. "We still miss him though, well sometimes."

"I see," said Greg, hoping that Dawn's continued

49

silence wasn't a bad sign.

She walked over to the sofa and stepped on to it, sinking into its billowing cushions. Opening the cupboard doors she teetered slightly, but nimbly grasped a huge packet of muesli from within. She then turned precariously to show it to him, but it was upside-down. "Bill loved this stuff. You're not allergic to pine nuts, are you, dear?"

He leapt up from his chair to grab it from her, concerned that she might fall, and accidentally dropped it on to the table.

"Goodness, you are keen!" she said, as she closed the doors and stepped down. "Would you like hot milk with it?"

He considered the suggestion but her attention was diverted by barking from within the house. Dawn was either stirring from her slumbers, or wished to summon Thelma away from the guest in the kitchen.

"Oh dear. Do you mind if I see to our precious one first?" she asked as she trotted towards the door. "Feel free to help yourself!"

He refrained from barking himself at being deserted, but gestured: a 'be my guest!' kind of wave and set about heating some milk. He reached up for a small pan from a large shelf and examined it for foreign bodies. It was bright and clean, and so he half-filled it with semi-skimmed and put it on the stove. Soon, though, as he stood watching it begin to swell and hiss in the pan, a sixth sense told him that he too was being watched. He swivelled his head in a stealthy scanning movement until he spotted a man of pensionable age standing at the back door, peering through and exuding an air of solemnity. Greg moved the hot pan to join the kettle and assumed that the visitor had come for some payment. "Can I help you?" he asked as he opened the door. (He often used that phrase when responding to customers at work but here he added a more defensive tone.)

"I want to see Mrs. Throstlethwaite," said the man, slightly out of breath. "She should remember me."

Greg studied the visitor for a few seconds. He stood to attention on the doormat, wore outsize shorts, and held a black beret in his hand. He also wore one red sock and seemed quite intense. Had Thelma's recollection of her missing husband actually manifested his return? "Er, are you....er...?" he asked, willing the man to reveal his identity. "Have you, er..." but this line of enquiry only made the man's lips quiver.

"I'll just see if I can find her," said Greg, trying to put the visitor at ease, but then another man of similar age, accompanied by a huge knobbly stick arrived at the door and took his place next to the intense man. However, visitor number two was much taller, and he whistled something that sounded vaguely Mongolian. Could this be the magician's ex-assistant, returning Mr. Throstlethwaite to his wife, wondered Greg? Ought he to advise the estranged husband that he'd been replaced by a rescue dog? It was hardly his place to prevent a reunion and so he invited them in. "Would you like some hot milk?" he asked, warmly, but then a cow mooed loudly, prompting the two men to enter in haste.

Greg went to the foot of the stairs and called up. "Mrs. Throstlethwaite, I think there's someone to see you!", but he didn't hear her reply due to a repeated cacophony of barking. He returned to the kitchen and stood facing the two men in a communion of silence,

51

apart from the faint and possibly pentatonic whistling. Had they said yes or no to the offer of milk? He wouldn't press it - Thelma might need to lace some of it with brandy when she came down and saw who had returned, but next time she needed to visit the great cupboard he'd assist her to step on to the sofa safely.

"What d'you think it's going to do?" asked the tall man suddenly, leaning on his gnarled stick. "Have you heard?"

"Ted said he felt a spot of rain when he was brushing his shoe," said his friend, despondently. "We might have to stay in the tent today and drum quietly."

"I think we must be neighbours!" said Greg as it dawned on him who the visitors really were. He gazed at them for a moment and tried to reassess his expectations of the band of brothers, whilst they muttered privately about the hazards of residual dew.

"I suppose we are," said the first one before craning his neck slightly to peer at a dark package on the worktop. "The lady's got a loaf of rye bread for us to collect. I can't take wheat. Joe'll tell you that."

"He can't take wheat," confirmed his tall companion. "Some of it has germs."

"Wheat doesn't suit me," added the first, quietly.

"We're seeking our inner lion!" announced Joe, proudly.

"Aye, that's the one," said his friend, obviously the leader. "We roar, and we're raw!" he proclaimed.

Greg nodded and excused himself to recall Thelma. The barking had ceased at that last statement, but Joe's whistling had resumed - this time possibly more Balkan in style.

A third member of their clique then arrived, wearing

a tracksuit and a knitted balaclava in bright yellow. He entered silently and stood behind the other two men. "That spider under my camp bed seems to have gone!" he said in a relieved but plaintive voice.

"Coming!" called Thelma as she made her way downstairs.

Greg remained near the stove, waiting for a suitable moment to pour the hot milk, and yet mindful of the skin forming. The thought of the milky membrane made him shudder, although he suspected that visitor number three would have fainted, had he seen it too. All three of them appeared to be slightly fearful of the senior lady of the house as they heard her descending the stairs. The leader glanced nervously at the rye bread as though considering grabbing hold of it and running back to the safety of the tiny camp, but she was now standing framed in the doorway that led from the hall, and obviously surprised at the assembled company in the kitchen.

"Ooh, a deputation!" she laughed, as their leader shuffled nervously and forced a smile. "I suppose you'd like your loaf, you boys."

She picked up the package and pressed it into the leader's hands, but he averted his eyes from her friendly gaze. They thanked her in unison, each stumbling over his own variation on the name 'Throstlethwaite', and then made a swift exit back to the sanctuary of their spider-free tent.

"See you again tomorrow!" called Joe jovially as he closed the door behind them. "We won't go far today, might do a press-up, though."

"They're a grand bunch, aren't they?" said Thelma as she watched them march down the path.

53

"Yes, they're….quite unusual," said Greg as he inundated a bowl of muesli with hot milk.

"Meston would probably get on well with them but I think he's slightly intimidated by such tough individuals," said Thelma as she stood writing items on her shopping list. "He works as a security guard at an umbrella museum in Louth but he won't patrol."

"I see," said Greg as he began to digest both the cereal and the news of Meston's sedentary security operations. He wondered where Monica had got to this morning, but to enquire might seem insensitive, especially after the disappearance in Mablethorpe. Even his bath towel had performed a vanishing act, although it had merely slipped off his chair on to the less than pristine floor. He picked it up slowly and tried flicking the crumbs off it inconspicuously, but then stopped when she glanced at him pityingly.

"Oh by the way, I do like your deep cupboard!" he said as she flung its doors wide open to check the weight of a tea caddy.

"You're not the only one! Meston used to come and hide in there when he was young, apparently," she explained. "Doesn't do it so much now, though."

"I see," said Greg once more, but then he heard Joe outside whistling in - perhaps - Paraguayan, and remembered his calling to compose. "I think I'll just wander about the locality today. I'm sure there are some commanding views."

She only half-heard him, being preoccupied with stock-taking, and so he ate in silence, allowing random notes to play in his mind. What *was* the secret of being able to pluck any of only twelve notes out of the air and form a tune? Perhaps air itself was the medium, and a walk in the country would aerate his lungs with music. After all, J.S. Bach had written a notable air on a G string, so perhaps a single note if arranged well, and in an inspiring rhythm, might become his opus one. Thelma had left the room and was out of earshot by now, and so he cleaned up after himself, and returned to his caravan.

He was aware of activity taking place within the tent, but he was glad that he wouldn't be subject to the rather delicate trio's possible attempts at roaring like lions inside their triangular enclosure. What were his intentions for meals, though? He hadn't thought to ask about shops nearby, although he'd probably find a café at some point, and he might even graze from hedgerows, just like the gang next door would - if only they dared to brave the threat of unsettled weather. He filled a flask with water from the jug, but then worried that it might have attracted pathogens overnight. He poured it away again, and decided to fill it up instead from the kitchen tap. Thus with an adequate reserve of emergency rations in his rucksack, he returned once more to the house and crept in. Thelma was still absent, and so he laboriously replenished his flask from the barely running tap, not wishing to alert her with tell-tale plumbing noises that he was stealing a pint of water. Now, however, he felt ashamed at his own reservoir of guilt - until he decided to dispense with that too, but to retain the water. Emboldened, he resolved to spend the day striding purposefully along highways and by-ways, filling his body with endorphins, and his lungs with music - he would empower himself with nature!

Beyond the back of the house a short lane led

towards a gate, next to which a faded sign announced a public right of way. A narrower path then ascended gradually towards a wooded area, but hopefully not so densely packed with trees that a map would be required. Greg felt that the path was urging him to follow it and as the only alternatives for a leisurely walk would be either back the way he'd come in the car, or through thick hummocky vegetation past his neighbours' tent, he opted for the enticing route towards the woods. Thus he set off, conscientiously waving as he passed the windows of the house in case either of his hostesses should have noticed him begin his trek. The ground beyond the gate was fairly even, and soon he found himself moving to a rhythm that might have inspired some musical theme to enter his mind, but his concentration was focused upon his employers' misplaced faith in his creative talents. He knew that solitary walking sometimes allowed the mind to obsess on personal matters, but whatever might fail to transpire, either today, tomorrow, or the next, he'd definitely not be returning home shamefully, nor bearing a shamelessly plagiarised manuscript. However, Mr. Scantlebury, head of 'Creative Planning', and formerly a student of 'Creative Accountancy', already knew that Greg's forte lay in channelling existing music, rather than producing 'made-to-measure'. If he were to return from Lincolnshire without even a duo for dining room, or a quartet for extended kitchen, then he'd obviously been dispatched to the wrong county. Nevertheless, he was aware of the wealth of specialist music around. The Garage Music scene in London was almost writing itself, due, no doubt, to an abundance of inspirational lock-ups. Plus there was an extensive Underground - the Piccadilly Line in particular - and quite a few houses belonging to customers with quality audio had basements that could benefit from that style of musical ambience. He trod on a lump of erratic granite and wondered whether Hard Rock also had a place within domestic dwellings, but if it did, encountering it today hadn't had any effect upon his muse as yet. He recalled recently having heard of Acid House - how might that sound? Rather fizzy, probably, and he knew enough about chemistry to know that it could compromise the alkalinity of Meston and Monica's lime mortar. Perhaps a theme derived from a visit to the chalky uplands of Kent would be a safer bet for most houses. Soft Rock was probably much more versatile too. He trusted that if any of these strange genres was worthy of listening to, then with enough receptivity and by exposing himself to the right stimulus the inspiration to add to the canon of tailor-made domestic music might well occur.

He pressed on up the gentle incline, but as he stopped and turned round to survey his progress, he heard the kind of chanting typical of American GIs when they jog collectively, although this was even less tuneful. He then noticed three familiar, disparately-sized men toiling breathlessly in the distance behind him. It was the campers, and they'd obviously decided to brave the elements of what was a fairly mild and dry day. He assumed that as long as they continued struggling and chanting while he continued pacing and pondering, there was little imminent danger of them catching him up.

They hadn't spotted him, but as he had no wish to

intrude upon their adventures, he turned again and continued towards the enfolding trees ahead. Very soon he was trekking through an arcade of brown and green, where, for the moment, his immediate surroundings seemed to be for his exclusive benefit. He hummed aloud notes at random, hoping they might form themselves into some original theme, but then he felt self-conscious when his attempts briefly attracted the attention of a passing rabbit. He wondered if it was a Welsh one, but knew it would have ignored such a flippant question, even though its gait did incorporate the Hip Hop form of locomotion. Could such creatures have also influenced that staccato dance style which apparently taught gangsters how to wrap? His left boot squeaked slightly upon the hardened mud as he strode on. Was this the sound of Sole Music to which young Lennie Leadbetter, the catering manager at work, covertly listened during his frequent coffee breaks?

The men were gaining on him - he could almost hear the combined wheezing of cardiovascular systems in overdrive. He decided to pause until they actually hove into view before moving on himself, but he didn't want his departure to look too obvious - the protocols and etiquette of the great outdoors were probably as keenly observed as were the niceties of listening - until the bitter end - to an orchestra tuning up.

He looked back to see the three heads once more, this time just above a horizon of hawthorn, gasping, grimacing, and gurning. He waved, partly in greeting, partly in valediction, but only the tallest of the trio responded, painfully flourishing his walking branch in repeated arcs of amiability. His comrades, however, were too involved in their tortuous progress to waste any energy in waving; besides, they all appeared to be encumbered with foldable chairs and tea trays. Greg quite liked the spot by the tree that he'd now chosen for himself, but he moved round to the opposite side; there he could remain undisturbed by the party as they trudged by. He repositioned himself within a hollow, and looked down at his blank manuscript paper, as though having it opened on his knees would provide the awaited inspiration. He carefully drew a treble clef at the beginning of the first stave - anything more creative than that was beyond him. The voices and occasional coughing from the gang of three formed a crescendo, but he was well out of sight as they approached. What he hadn't anticipated was that they too might wish to install themselves in his arboreal domain. He put down his fibre tip pen - at least he'd made a start.

After due deliberation on whether the ground was sufficiently even to situate their chairs safely, they thus sat down with maximum fuss where just a few minutes previously he'd been sitting safely on a thick knot of tree root. He assumed this was to be just a breather for them, but the constant resiting and scraping of the tubular chairs suggested that they intended to make themselves quite comfortable, although Norman was complaining about his nylon seat. "I might be in danger of sliding off! We should have insisted on canvas at the outdoor shop," he complained.

"Do you think he's their new cowman - that man in the caravan?" asked one.

"Possibly. They weren't in the field this morning, so perhaps he's taken them for a nice walk."

"He might be a cattle drover, like John Wayne was!"

Norman's foot was making him wince, and he complained that his bunion was worse than his next-door neighbour's.

"You share your side gate with her, don't you?" said one.

"Indeed. I usually put her wheelie bin out on Tuesdays if she's not up."

"Friday's our day!" said another. "You know where you are with Fridays!"

"Shall we do some shouting now?"

"Soon."

Greg tried to suppress the trivia emanating from behind the tree by focussing on the song of a nearby chaffinch. Would the men be staying there long? If he were to move off now he might cause panic and be rumbled. What would John Wayne have done in a case like this? Single-handedly face them and tell them to head on out of town? Threaten them with a spell in a wheelie bin?

"Is he good, your podiatrist?"

"Well, yes and no, if you know what I mean."

"Always know what you mean, Norman!"

"His hands can be cold at times. I dread going."

"Nothing worse than cold hands. They can lead to frostbite!"

Greg pondered on the pentatonic scale consisting of fewer notes than most western ears were accustomed to, and yet it seemed quite adequate for some oriental nations. Perhaps the severe cold in the

Far East made playing only five notes more amenable. He looked again at his manuscript and considered whether the chaffinch held the copyright to its tune, but now he was aware of something thundering towards him.

Against the sunlight his visitor appeared to be a wolf, and his mind recalled the warnings from Thelma on the bus yesterday about strange dogs roaming the highways. He braced himself, and held his incomplete opus high above his shoulder, but the being almost knocked him over when it reached him. However, it was neither wolf nor hob hound, but a German Shepherd dog, and it seemed delighted to meet him. Presumably the delicate warriors behind the tree were aware of its presence in their midst; although they were probably right now fleeing for their lives, gently and carefully. Moments later a man approached hurriedly, his face also obscured by the rays of the sun.

"Spike! Come back here!" he shouted. "It's all right. He won't hurt you!"

Greg assumed that it was Spike, not himself, that was being declared harmless. However the dog was quite keen to give him an intimate examination first before sitting down and leaning firmly against his shoulder, almost pushing him over sideways. He obviously had no interest in sniffing out whoever might still be behind the tree, although his owner stared with great interest at both his now pacified dog and the dog's new friend. Greg in turn shielded his eyes from the sun with his manuscript as he tried to gauge the expression on the man's face. "I'm sure he just wants to say hello!" he said as the cranial eclipse

61

of the sun continued.

"Can I ask you something?" barked the man suddenly.

Greg didn't get a chance to answer either way before the second question was inevitably fired at him.

"What would you do if your neighbours smashed all the glass in your garage windows?" His tone was menacing, accusatory even, as he continued standing there facing him, while the dog nuzzled Greg's neck affectionately. Greg didn't have a garage, and so any answer would be hypothetical, but he did have neighbours - Mr. and Mrs. Cathcart, although they were very quiet people and kept to themselves. Clear up the broken glass and mention the inconvenience next time they gave him a jar of home-made gooseberry jam, he mused?

"Leave the doors open so they don't get locked in again?" he suggested, emboldened by his supportive canine companion.

The man fidgeted slightly and crumpled a cigarette packet in his hand. "It's like Bei-whatsit where I live, believe me," he said, as he awkwardly lowered himself on to the ground on Greg's other side.

"Bayreuth?" suggested Greg, wondering if the man lived in some Wagnerian fantasy-world. He looked at his visitor's care-worn face, but didn't wish to linger on it long. He decided to lower the book that he still held aloft, but discreetly, so as not to draw attention to its embarrassing incompletion.

"Looks like a dull book you've got there," stated the man, attempting chit-chat. "What's it about?"

"It's just my....tabula rasa," replied Greg, not

62

wishing to qualify the statement.

"Are you doing community service?" asked his inquisitor as he studied Greg's attire. "I've tried to stay clean myself, but that lot next door….!"

Greg shook his head, and wondered why anyone should have sought him out in the woods to discuss their problems. Had Beethoven been interrupted when he was sketching the 'Pastoral'? The man removed a crumpled object from his jacket pocket. Did he assuage his anger by crumpling everything? Greg glanced at it - it was an ex-tennis ball, which was then thrown aimlessly into the middle distance. This was immediately followed by the impatient command: "Go on then!"

Greg nudged the dog, assuming the command was for him to retrieve the squashed ball. He licked Greg's ear, then rose reluctantly and remembered his obligation to play the part of servant to his irritated master.

With him briefly gone, the man leaned towards Greg. "We're in dispute over the rights of access to my driveway."

"Oh dear," said Greg, adopting an appropriate expression of resignation. "You mean - you and Spike?"

"The Jacksons!" barked the man, before receiving the old tennis ball from his dog. "I found a pair of trainers slung over my TV aerial yesterday!"

"The Jacksons again?" enquired Greg, wondering if he'd get any time to himself today.

"No, Spike's!" came the impatient reply. "He loved chewing those old things. Now he's just got his tennis ball."

A catalogue of further revelations about arguments at the local express check-out, plus details of his siblings' counter-claims regarding an intestate cuckoo clock were shared with his hapless acquaintance, but Greg's attention was waning, and he watched idly at the successive throws and catches of the flattened ball. He wondered if the old men had found somewhere more peaceful for their delayed war cries, but then he put away his manuscript and decided to add a bass clef some other time.

"What a trauma!" he said as he made a discreet move to leave. "Although perhaps your tin-opener wasn't really compatible with the tub of potato salad?" he suggested after hearing the man's latest bone of contention.

"I hate that sort," came another embittered reply.

The ball-throwing had ceased, and Spike's eyes were looking soulfully into Greg's. "See what I have to live with?" he seemed to be saying. Greg nodded and heard some quavery shouting permeating the woods. The dog whimpered and the man threw a stone and muttered about yobs scaring birds.

He was still droning on when Greg stood up, but he probably stood up a bit too quickly. It was the familiar sensation of low blood pressure that he'd sometimes experienced when standing up after kneeling in bookshops to peruse a low shelf. His vision was temporarily absent and he could almost feel the blood rushing too quickly from his brain to his feet. This time, however, when his body finally adjusted, he found himself standing neither in a bookshop, nor in a wood, but instead he was now upright inside a vertical trunk with views through

64

peepholes of an audience watching his container expectantly. This was obviously going to be one of those days.

CHAPTER 4

Greg tried to rationalise what might have happened. Had he dozed off under the tree, dreamt some composition, and then been brought here to hear his opus one being given its première? He heard chains rattling as though his viewing chamber was about to be opened. Would he receive a round of applause prior to conducting his new work, whatever it was? He surveyed the audience apprehensively through a convenient knothole. There weren't all that many present, which reassured him slightly, but the two ladies in the third row bore a strong resemblance to Thelma Throstlethwaite and Monica, and their eyes were fixed upon the box in which he stood with first night nerves. Had *they* towed him and the crate here behind their delicate car? As he tried to make sense of things, he recalled Thelma mentioning that her husband had vanished during a conjuring trick in pre-millennial Mablethorpe. At this point he felt a cold sweat run down his back as he reflected on his part in usurping Mr. Throstlethwaite.

Stepping back in time could adversely affect his pension scheme contributions too, as well as making it difficult to access his thick pullover, futuristically left in the caravan. He acknowledged that his present predicament was all due to having been diverted by a conman in a tartan jacket at Lincoln bus station, although these perceptions could merely be due to low blood sugar. Perhaps this was all a rather lucid dream, and yet the loosening of the chains around his tiny storeroom sounded so real, as did the accompanying loud percussion. Surely he hadn't written that - the cymbal clash was pure Tchaikovsky!

At last the door was ceremonially opened by a man in a dark suit who bowed to a stunned audience. Greg stepped out hesitantly and faced his public. A bow was probably the correct form of etiquette for him too, but the audience didn't seem too pleased at his entrance. A few giggled, some clapped politely, but the rest remained silent. The two ladies, however, gasped and then looked round desperately at the others in the small auditorium. The magician turned round as though to present his exhibit proudly to them, but as he looked at the stranger's bemused face he took a sharp intake of breath before collapsing on to the stage. Would *he* now be replacing Greg under the tree? Perhaps it was the man's magical powers that had brought Greg retrospectively to this venue, so as to repeat the illusion.

"Who the 'eck's that?" someone heckled. "He's not ours!" shouted Thelma, but Monica smiled at her reassuringly and whispered something about claiming compensation.

"Sorry," said Greg, avoiding too much eye contact with those facing him. "I....I think I might have taken a wrong turning." He glanced at the two ladies and wondered how it was that even though he recognised them, they apparently didn't know him. Should he introduce - *re-introduce* himself? People were now staring at the crumpled magician. Greg felt an obligation to assist and so he knelt down and rolled the man into the recovery position, which elicited a brief burst of solitary handclapping from a lady in the back row. Then he stood up very, very slowly - he didn't want to find himself relocated again so soon.

"Rubbish!" called out a disgruntled patron as he filed out behind several others for whom the show was now over.

Greg wondered where the traditional glamorous assistant might be, but then he remembered that she and Mr. Throstlethwaite had allegedly disappeared together. "Excuse me, have you got the date?" he asked one of the more sympathetic looking theatre-goers approaching the exit, but she smiled thinly and hurried on out. He took a bow, then decided to jump off the stage and follow the mother and daughter - presumably about to seek redress from the theatre manager for their missing spouse/father. It was possible, of course, that Meston was sitting outside in the car park. It might show greater sensitivity if he were to go and have a quiet word with him about the mishap and then ask him if there was any chance of a lift with them all to a caravan site somewhere…

It wasn't his place to break the news of a missing person to Meston, who would probably have no recollection of having previously met Greg anyway. It was also quite likely that they were all staying here in the town, rather than going home straight after the show. He entered the foyer, still undecided as to what to do, but then he spotted Meston sitting on one of the well-upholstered seats, anxiously watching the stragglers as they made their way out into the street. Greg probably stared at him slightly too long, as eye contact being made, Meston rose to approach him.

"Excuse me, but have you seen an older couple with their daughter in there?" asked Meston, his politeness masking his concern. "Sorry but she's my fiancée. I think she's wearing red, or it might be blue. Oh, and sort of softish hair."

The temptation for Greg to respond with far more detailed information was overwhelming, but he masked his concern with the same degree of restraint as Meston. "Yes, I think I did see them. Might the younger lady have been wearing green trousers?"

"That's the colour!" said Meston, noticeably relieved. "Are they still in there, would you know?"

"I think they're having a chat with someone about lost property," replied Greg nonchalantly, but eager to ask something himself that wouldn't keep any longer. "Excuse me, but are we in Mablethorpe in the nineties?" he blurted out.

"Well, it has been hot this week, but....sorry, do you mean lost property as in....chocolate eclairs?"

"Actually I think they're waiting for Mr. Thr..., I mean....yes, perhaps it's eclairs," said Greg, cautiously. "This is *Mablethorpe*, though, isn't it?"

"Er, yes, this is Mablethorpe. Are you a bit lost?"

"Misplaced, really," said Greg, resigning himself to some complex adjustments to his life. "Actually I think I might have heard them mention waiting for your future father-in-law."

"Oh, I see," said Meston as though it all made sense. "He's been having waterworks problems. Nuisance for him."

Greg knew nothing about any ongoing dispute with the waterworks, but nodded sagely as though it was a common occurrence. He wondered if it was worry over the last quarter's bill that had led to Mr. Throstlethwaite's disappearance.

"I'm sure they'll be out soon," he said, wondering what else to say. "Er, hasn't it been warm for…." he added, hoping that Meston might supply the name of the month, but then he noticed the dates on an adjacent poster for a forthcoming performance of 'Hamlet On Ice'. "July 1998!" he exclaimed, before sitting down and staring vacantly at a vending machine with very reasonable prices.

"Only another week, then!" said Meston. "Sorry, are you meeting someone here too?"

"To be honest, I've no idea what I'm doing here," said Greg as he fumbled in his pocket for coins for the vending machine. "I seem to keep getting diverted, and I sort of feel responsible for the magician. He passed out."

"Really? He might just be resting between engagements," suggested Meston. "I'm sure it wasn't your fault. The heat probably. I've been sitting in the car with the window open."

Greg still couldn't reconcile the two Mestons, or the duplicated family, temporally split due to a decade which he'd carelessly mislaid that morning. He thought about the man recumbent on the stage and hoped that he hadn't come to and rolled into the front stalls. "I think I'll just have a peep through the door and see if the magician's stirring."

"It's all right, you stay here and relax. I'll have a look," said Meston, as though bracing himself for something daunting. "Bill's probably ready now, no doubt waiting for Monica and…."

"Thelma," interjected Greg, but he noticed Meston look at him oddly. "Er….fill ma, I need to *fill ma* stomach! What do you recommend from the snacks cabinet?" He smiled and pointed to the illustrated selection of items, which seemed to dispel the quizzical look on Meston's face.

"I always go for crisps, myself!" said Meston, before walking over to the door to the small auditorium. He pushed it open gingerly and went in.

Greg meanwhile tried to operate the machine, but it was rejecting his coins. He adopted a fixed grin at each successive failure to buy anything, conscious of attention from a young lady in a top hat and very short dress staring at him from beside a door marked 'Stage'. Her manner was as furtive as his as he stood pressing buttons earnestly, whilst pretending to be perfectly calm. He looked across to her as though to share some pleasantry about the show, but then he noticed an older man emerge from the stage door with a suitcase. He took her arm, relieving her of a wand still clutched in her hand, and together they ran towards the main door which opened on to the street. They paused before leaving, at which point he grabbed hold of her hat, which he tossed aimlessly back into the foyer. "Thelma will understand," he said hopefully as he ushered the young lady outside.

Greg was still at a loss to understand anything himself, but then he noticed Meston reappear, apparently with an air of confusion too. Perhaps he'd tried out the box in which Greg had 'arrived', and lost twelve years himself.

"How's Mr...have they found whatever they...." asked Greg, leaning awkwardly against the unyielding cabinet.

"The magician's fine, but his assistant's missing, and so is Bill!" said Meston, as he returned to the seat.

71

"Oh dear," said Greg, realising he was watching history unfold. He remembered Thelma telling him that her errant husband had subsequently been replaced by Dawn, the rescue dog, but right now might not be the best time to assure Meston of such a feel-good outcome. "I can't seem to get this thing to work," he complained, his hunger pangs intensifying.

Meston stood up and took hold of Greg's coins. "Can I see if I can get it to…?" but he tailed off and looked closely at the small change in his hand. "Sorry, someone's passed you some duds here. Look at the size of this one, and the *date*!"

Greg felt his heart-rate quicken. "It must be from that magic act!" he exclaimed, with a laugh as false as the money. He pretended to delve into his other pockets to find some 'proper' legal tender, but in the process his manuscript book fell out. Meston picked it up off the floor and shook his head in amazement.

"Are you a musician, then?" he asked. "My dad used to love the 1812 Overture. Played it over and over again on a mouth organ to the cows - said it helped the yield. They loved it when he pretended to light the cannons!"

"Actually I've been trying to compose, but I just don't know where all the notes come from," admitted Greg.

Meston stared hard at him, and handed back the unfamiliar money in slow motion. Had Greg let slip something else that he shouldn't have known about yet?

"When I was young I wanted to write music," said Meston as he stared vacantly at the picture of a *Marathon* that Greg had been unable to win from the

72

machine. "My dad often mentioned that Mozart had already written his first symphony when he was eight years old. I think he was trying to tell me something."

Greg remembered this piece of information too, and willed him to carry on. "He was quite a prodigy, was Mozart!" he enthused.

"I thought about this only yesterday and looked for the manuscript book my dad bought me once when our chief milker caught mastitis," continued Meston. "I thought to myself - 'where do all the notes come from?'"

Greg's jaw dropped, and now it was his turn to sit down to collect his thoughts. He'd arrived at the precise point in time at which young Meston was attempting to create music, although in his case, not at the behest of an impatient employer. He presumably didn't have the problem of having the wrong type of change, or a debit card that wouldn't be creditworthy, either. How Greg envied him, and anyone else who was able to buy chocolate bars for cash, or work with easy-going cows. The two men began to bond by chatting about treble clefs.

The door to the auditorium suddenly opened to reveal Monica and her mother being reassured by a man in a suit. He shook hands with each of them in turn, expressing his regrets, and hopes for the future. "These misadventures happen occasionally," he sighed. "But at least you've both got complementary season tickets for this theatre for the rest of the season."

They thanked him, and did what they could to reassure him too with stoical nods and smiles. Then they noticed Meston, standing facing them across the foyer - now almost deserted - except for Meston himself and the man standing beside him: the man who had taken Mr. Throstlethwaite's place in the wooden trunk. They smiled, and hurried over. Greg was obviously not going to be blamed for Mr. T's disappearance, but he wondered whether there was any precedent for this kind of situation. He sat down again, giving the family a modicum of privacy in which to commiserate and exchange news of recent events and their ramifications, but this discussion passed by quickly. An employee of the theatre also passed by quickly, picking up a top hat and a wand on her way through. "Never trusted that one," she muttered.

"What a to-do!" said Thelma, placing her hand on Greg's shoulder. "We're not blaming you for what happened, dear. It's a bit like that film about the scientist getting mixed up with the fly!"

Greg smiled, and offered his condolences, although he felt the similarities between himself and a fictional teleported fly were rather unflattering. It would certainly solve his immediate quandary of being unable to purchase food, though, if he could buzz round the foyer and feast on the contents of a nearby sugar pourer. "I must have thought I was in a kiosk," he said, unconvincingly, but with thoughts of eating uppermost in his mind. "I don't really know how I got in there."

"He's going to teach me how to compose!" said Meston. "It'll help to take our minds off...."

"Oh, Mesty," said Monica, wiping away a tear, before gazing at the stranger in their midst. "Today might have a happy ending after all." She whispered

74

something to her mother, who scrutinised Greg briefly, before nodding, and initiating introductions.

"Young man," said Thelma. "You're welcome to come back with us for the evening. You look hungry!"

Greg wondered why he should be feeling so hungry when he'd only recently eaten at her table, even though that particular meal wouldn't be happening until twelve years in the future. However, it was now late afternoon, so perhaps time travel was far slower than the recommended speed of light. He thanked her profusely, and stood eagerly to accompany them to wherever they were staying. He tried to think of something incidental to say as they moved towards the exit, but in the circumstances it was hard to think of anything appropriate.

"Where are you staying?" asked Monica, tilting her head to one side in synch with her mother.

"Er, I was staying in a caravan last night, but I'm not sure where I'll be tonight," said Greg, selecting his words carefully. He noticed Thelma's eyebrows raise at this revelation, and her jaw drop correspondingly. "I made the bed before I left," he added.

"We're all staying with my sister," she interjected. "She's a bit of a fusspot, but she won't mind another mouth to feed!"

"That's very kind of her too, then!" said Greg, hoping that the sister would provide him with his own cutlery to feed himself.

Thus the four of them made their way to a car park at the back of the theatre, and thence towards a line of cars in the shade of a high wall. Greg recognised the car - although it looked in better condition than it did yesterday - but he made a point of pretending not to know it.

"Sorry, can I have a look at that manuscript book again?" asked Meston after being deep in thought for several moments. "It looked identical to one...." but Thelma pulled Greg to one side as they reached the car. He thought she was about to frisk him for illegal substances, but he didn't even have any legal ones. She waited until Meston and Monica had got into the front, then looked squarely at him.

"Don't mention caravans!" she whispered to him at point blank range. "We're giving them our old one as a wedding present!"

"It'll look perfect next to the hou....next to....wrapped in giftwrap!" stuttered Greg.

"I only hope my husband's back in time for the wedding," she continued. "It needs towing from Market Harborough!"

Greg was conscious of Meston waiting to see the manuscript book. He edged away from her to present it to him at the driver's window. "It's just one that I was given recently," he said, slightly apprehensive of Meston's expression of amazement as he took it from him. He sat holding it in his right hand and examined a minute inkblot on the cover. Then he reached with his left into the glove compartment in front of Monica and slowly pulled out a book that appeared to be identical - including an inkblot. He looked up at Greg wide-eyed, as though about to perform something never attempted before, and then placed the two books together in order to make a more thorough comparison. It was at this point that something even stranger happened - the books, when they made contact, appeared to fuse together, as though their individual existence was no longer viable. Mother and daughter, who had been discussing modified sleeping arrangements, fell silent. Were they asleep, or had they amalgamated too?

CHAPTER 5

Greg continued standing, and Meston remained sitting, but instead of being inside and outside a car, they found themselves in an extremely elaborate high-ceilinged room, Meston relaxing on a sumptuous gilt-embossed chair, Greg leaning against its high back. He wondered if his hunger had unduly affected him, and that he'd blanked out on the ride to Thelma's sister, but Meston was still holding the book, and was obviously not familiar with his surroundings either. They surveyed their elegant location with a mixture of admiration and unease.

"Are we still in Mablethorpe?" asked Greg, leaning across to Meston, but his companion appeared to be unnerved at seeing a man resembling an eighteenth century courtier wearing a wig approaching them with haste.

Meston sprang to his feet politely. "It doesn't look familiar but I've not been driving long," he replied softly. "We could be anywhere. This man probably knows."

The man lowered his head respectfully, studied the visitors for a moment, and then addressed Greg in a German accent. "Sir, the distinguished gentlemen are ready to meet you both in the morning room. Please!" He held out his arm as though to usher the way, and the two visitors duly looked at each other, lost for words, and followed the deferential messenger out of the large room.

"Sorry," whispered Greg as Meston looked all

about him while they followed the man along a corridor. "I seem to have landed you in another of my diversions. I think we could *both* have cash problems here - we might need marks."

"You think they're Marxist guerrillas?" asked Meston. "Do you think they're holding Bill?"

Greg shook his head and anticipated a rather awkward audience. They reached a double door, which the servant opened for them before standing to one side and bowing his head. Greg thanked him, etiquette overriding bewilderment, and so they entered a room of even grander size than the one from which they'd just been summoned. They noticed at the far end an elderly man, also in a wig, who rose from his chair and encouraged them to meet him, together with a younger man of mixed lineage who wore a moustache and who was sitting on a harpsichord, swinging his feet. Greg gulped as he recognised the two men, and advised Meston discreetly whose exalted presence they were now in. "I believe it's Josef Haydn and Jimi Hendrix!" he whispered loudly.

"Hi, I'm Joe's interpreter!" said Jimi, jumping off the harpsichord and making an arpeggio with his fingers on the exposed strings. "You two have come for some kind of workshop on chords and stuff, yeah?"

Haydn nodded amiably and waved from his chair. "Did you have a good journey from Great Britain?" he asked, pleasantly.

"Very swift, thank you!" said Greg as he shook the grand old man's hand respectfully, but trembling slightly. "It was all spur of the moment, actually!"

"Spur of the moment?" queried Haydn. "Did you hear that, Herr Hendrix? It was the spur of the moment!"

Jimi leafed quickly through a well-thumbed German / English dictionary but decided it was an idiomatic phrase. "Man, they mean they suddenly had to come and see us!"

"Yes, we really had to!" said Greg, endorsed by nods and smiles from Meston. "It was written in the... inkblots!"

Haydn laughed heartily, shaking his head in mock modesty. "I shall dedicate my next string quartet to you both! With a scherzo but no smudges. The Esterhazys find my chamber music quite pleasant to the ear when they er....gamble at cards. Is gamble correct?" He glanced at Jimi who quickly checked the dictionary again.

"Luftspringen," he announced, shaking his head at the dictionary in his hand in disbelief. "Yes, to leap about like lambs. Wowww."

"Indeed!" laughed Haydn. "While they leap about - with playing cards!" He then installed himself at the harpsichord and played a few bars of pianissimo improvisation. Greg was intrigued, but Jimi looked keen to have a go himself. Haydn then stood up and bowed, chuckling with both pride and modesty. Jimi took his place and raised the theme an octave, but this time fortissimo, until the F above middle C flew off the keyboard due to ebony fatigue resulting from such energetic treatment. It landed in Haydn's lap, which prompted some more amusement. He in turn handed it to Greg, which prompted gasps of gratitude from the visiting composer-in-waiting. "There's your key, young sir. Don't worry, the Esterhazys will replace the instrument when I ask them. I might claim for a pianoforte! They provide me with what I require and I provide them with what they deserve! You see, it's all a joke, really."

"I sure miss my geedar," said Jimi regretfully.

"Sorry," said Meston. "I really should be getting back quite soon. I was just about to drive off when we ended up here. I might already have flooded the carburettor."

"Flooded the carbur....." enquired Haydn.

"Yeah, we usually call it a carb," explained Jimi.

"A carp? Then you must return at once or it will drown! Don't forget those spurs."

Meston looked even more confused now, but he glanced at each of the group in turn, as though to elicit information of the next carriage to Mablethorpe. Greg wished he could help, and yet he felt as though the answer to his quest to understand where music originated might possibly be revealed if he were to stay and listen to the two accomplished men. However, Jimi wasn't about to arrange transport, but instead proceeded to play a crashing discord in the bass register. Haydn then resolved it, and Meston, patiently expectant, spontaneously vanished from view, like a diminishing fourth. Only Greg was surprised at his sudden disappearance, but he was confident that his companion would return home safely - there was a futuristic inevitability about it.

"Your friend had more pressing matters to attend to," said Haydn, already nodding acceptingly.

"He wasn't quite as motivated as we are, man," said Jimi. "Hey Joe! I think the goulash has arrived!"

Two servants entered the room carrying a foldable card table and a large tureen. They immediately began to chat to Haydn in a respectful, and yet familiar manner, as they set about erecting the table and placing the dining chairs. Greg assumed that the composer's status here was that of staff, but with privileges. As for Jimi, who had now picked up Greg's 'F' and was currently engaged in using it to pluck the open strings of the harpsichord, Greg assumed that he had been 'called' to assist in some joint venture. Was that venture to teach, or advise Greg in his quest to understand the arcane nature of creating music out of thin air? Both men were from different eras, and yet it was apparent that it was only Jimi and Greg who had actually travelled back in time. Meston had visited also, of course, but had elected to return to his loved ones, after rescuing his carburettor from potential flood damage.

Another member of staff had now arrived with plates and cutlery, and was speaking to one of his colleagues in a language other than German. Could this really be the Esterhazy Palace in the Austro-Hungarian Empire - Haydn's symphony factory? Where next on the itinerary - was he destined to make a whistle-stop tour of all the great composers? He decided to confer with Jimi. After all, they were almost contemporaries, but a casual approach would probably work best. He sidled up to him and spoke quietly.

"You can really smell the paprika!" he said, perhaps rather excitedly, but the young man stared at him, as though uninterested in any small talk. "Oh, I think we're about to eat," added Greg, pointing to the table, but then he expanded the subject matter. "I don't really know any of your music, but I was sorry to hear about the fire."

"Fire?" asked Jimi, handing him back the F. He put his hand on Greg's shoulder. "I'm sure it wasn't your fault, man."

"I mean your guitar - didn't it get destroyed?" asked Greg. "I read it was spontaneous combustion!"

The stare was repeated. Greg's commiseration had drawn a blank. "You've had a long journey, buddy. Let's eat!"

Had Greg made a gaffe, or had such an incident yet to happen? Was it possible that everyone whom he'd met in this room was living in an alternative reality?What if there were a multiplicity of Gregs each pursuing the 'highest of all the arts' all over the world, and spanning the centuries? Which one of him would be returning to work in two weeks with a canon of 'house music'? The Hungarian-sounding man was ladling out the goulash, and Greg was keen to eat before being whisked away to his next surprise appointment. He therefore took his place at the table, replete with wine, and a quantity of bread. The goulash looked and smelled delicious, but although he was by now ravenous, protocol kept him waiting whilst the others were seated. He held his spoon ready, awaiting the subtle signal that declared 'let's begin', but then waited some more as Jimi collected the dictionary. He wondered if there was to be a toast, but he took advantage of this pause to attempt to clarify something. "Herr Haydn," he began, as respectfully as he could. "Can you tell me how many symphonies you've written?"

The old man smiled at him and leaned forward. "One hundred and eight at the last count!"

By now Greg had grabbed a chunk of bread and was keen to start, but he choked slightly before he even had the chance to nibble. He knew that Haydn's total symphonic output had been only one hundred and four. This version of Josef Haydn sitting serenely to his left must have lived longer, and this version of Jimi Hendrix sitting agitatedly to his right still owned a working guitar. "What a lot!" he exclaimed, slightly anxiously.

"Yes, do help yourself. We knew you'd be starving!" said Haydn, winking. "The cooks are used to your appetite!"

The old man chuckled, whereas Greg just pretended to. It was apparent that the servants had remained in the room, and were sitting nearby listening intently to the conversation, and so he assumed that it was at such meals that the musical theory lessons took place. He took it upon himself to raise his glass and propose a toast. Was it 'Prost' in German, or was it 'Proust'? Or was Proust the author who, having run out of ideas, dipped a cake in his tea and was inspired to write three more volumes? If he were to dip his bread now in the goulash would he find the inspiration to write vast amounts of music? Haydn was leaning towards him again. Greg lowered the wineglass and proffered his head to meet him. The wig smelled musty.

"It just comes to me, my young friend. A tune will suddenly skip into my mind! One must be decept... recept... empfänglich..." He looked at Jimi for assistance. The young man leafed quickly through the

84

dictionary, then called out: "To take one's leave," before resuming his interrupted meal.

"Indeed, one must take one's leave to be inspired!" concluded Haydn. "My 'Farewell' Symphony is full of departures!"

Greg paused and wondered whether this was his cue to go, but then he thought that Jimi must have supplied the wrong translation. Greg regretted that so far he hadn't obtained much in the way of wisdom. The Hungarians seemed slightly disappointed too, but now it was Jimi's turn to impart some wisdom to him. Heads met, while the young man finished chewing another spoonful. Greg smiled patiently and waited.

"You need someone to base yourself on," said Jimi at last. "I was heavily influenced by Muddy Waters."

"Really," replied Greg, as he took this advice on board. "I know Beethoven was once inspired by a babbling brook, but you think somewhere more *stagnant* might help?"

Jimi stared at him again. Greg thought he was getting nowhere, but then both his companions proceeded to give spontaneous advice. He tried to take it all in, but it was a virtual onslaught of tips and hints on how to create. "Exposition, development"; "Get your mojo working, man"; "Some light recapitul...."; "Yeah, recap too"; "Think of Bach's '48'"; "Keep the bass very light"; "Thrash the bass"; "Use repetition, then you'll earn more and satisfy them"; "Be different each time and electrify them."

Greg tried to synthesise the disparate advice assailing his ears, but then he excused himself to collect his manuscript book from the chair where Meston had been sitting until he disappeared. It seemed churlish to pick it up when its real owner had had to return home suddenly. He hoped Thelma and Monica wouldn't mind him staying on in central Europe, although it was perhaps possible that another Greg was already back with them all - a sort of transpersonal time share, but more fragmented. He decided to pick up the book and turned to return to the table, but now the table had gone. He thought that the servants had been ultra-efficient and respectfully quiet, but then he realised that Haydn and Hendrix had been removed too.

CHAPTER 6

The smell of damp laundry suggested to Greg that once again he'd been subject to the whims of the little book. Had he landed in the parlour of a much more impoverished composer, or was it someone's twenty first century utility room? A newspaper lay open upon a cluttered draining board. He moved towards it tentatively and covered the date at the top with his hand before gradually removing it so as to delay the shock of revealing which year it actually was. However, there was no shock; just relief, as he discovered that he was indeed back in the present day - the actual date on which he'd been dispatched to the Austro-Hungarian Empire via Mablethorpe.

He hoped that his body clock had now settled down and that he could continue normally, and yet the fact that he was in the 'now' didn't necessarily mean that he was in the 'here.' Surely he should have been returned safely to the tree under which he'd sat that morning before the man with the dog had bored him with his catalogue of foes. He looked out of the old sash window into a small overgrown garden, but he'd need to venture further than the garden to get his bearings. He turned the handle of a door, but then he heard voices - a group of people had apparently just entered the house. They'd probably be taken aback to find a stranger lurking in their utility room, and he had no idea how to explain his presence. He carefully closed the door again, then sat down on a set of steps and wondered what to do.

He noticed a basketful of folded clothes under the sink, and so he reasoned that he might look less suspicious if he were to hang them up on the nearby clothes horse - they were rather damp, after all. He grabbed hold of a pillowcase to give himself some credibility should the householders suddenly enter, then listened intently at the door. Whoever they were they sounded to be in good spirits, but then he gasped audibly as he recognised not only the familiar voices of Meston, Thelma, and Monica, but that of a fourth person conversing with them. It was a man's voice, and it definitely wasn't the missing Bill who had returned to the fold, if indeed this was his fold. The person now expressing his appreciation of the collection of begonias in the conservatory was Greg *himself.*

His grip on the pillowcase tightened, as he wondered if such crises of identity had occurred to other musical antecedents, but then he relaxed slightly as he assumed Meston must have been impersonating him. His main concerns now were whether to open the door and announce his presence to the others; his as yet unresolved quest to find the inspiration he sought; or why his old stripy green shirt should be at the top of the clothes basket. Footsteps approached the door. He trusted it wasn't going to be his younger self - the inevitable staring would be awkward. He watched the handle go down and the door begin to open. This was his cue to turn round and hang the pillowcase on the top of the clothes horse, as though this was his function.

"You don't need to worry about that now!" said an older lady wearing a floral apron as she bustled in carrying a bowl full of assorted clothes pegs.

Greg hadn't included the airing of the pillowcase in his list of worries, but he was relieved that she hadn't screamed.

"Why don't you go on up and join the others?" she suggested

"Go…on up?" he asked, as he duly placed the damp item back in the basket.

"You're meant to be the Duchess of Hamilton, go on, off you go!" she insisted, ushering him out of the door.

Was this some kind of fancy dress party he'd gate-crashed, its venue being upstairs? He looked at her for a few seconds, hoping that she might elucidate, but she merely raised her eyebrows, shook her head, and emulated the sound of a mechanical whistle. Greg considered this to be preferable to screaming, although he neither knew who she was, nor what she meant, but he trusted that the answer lay upstairs, whatever this building was. He'd no doubt meet familiar faces too up there. "I'm on my way!" he assured her as he left the room and hovered in the passageway until he found the stairs.

This was certainly an unusual day, but he was already resigned to the fact that he'd relinquished full control of his life for a while, and that the lady's attempt at soprano indicated that singing was involved. Surely he wasn't playing the part of a duchess in some badly cast opera? He climbed the stairs to the landing, but voices were coming from the floor above. Another flight of stairs beckoned him higher, where the sound of whirring and appreciative comments about 'dinky hand painted figures' drew him towards the doorway of a darkened room. He knocked delicately on the open door, as his eyes adjusted to the sight of people standing around a billiard table watching the action. They were too engrossed in it to notice him, and so he mimicked a cough, as it began to make sense. There was enough light from the various tiny lamps on the surface of the table for him to recognise Monica, Thelma, and Meston, and the activity in which they were keenly participating was the running of a railway. Meston spotted him first but didn't seem at all surprised to see him again.

"Sorry, I'm the saddle tank, so I hope you don't mind being the big engine!"

"I painted the scenery," said Thelma, proudly. "It's my nephew Tom's really but he became a bank manager and lost interest."

"He kept up his guitar, though, didn't he, Ma?" added Monica.

"Wrote a march for it, he did," said Thelma as she wiped some dust off the roof of a signal box. "He'll be coming round later."

Meston then invited Greg to operate the controls. "Don't worry about the signals. Monica's goods train will give priority to the Express."

"Thanks for giving me the franchise," said Greg guardedly. "By the way, what's the engine's name?"

"The Duchess of Hamilton," replied Meston.

"Of course," said Greg as he sent her on her way past some unusually oblivious sheep.

Footsteps were trudging up the stairs. "That's probably Tom," said Monica as she lined up some Highland cattle to watch Meston's saddle tank go roaring by.

"He's very early, then," said Thelma, surprised. "Perhaps there was a run on sterling."

Greg was nearest the door, and so he turned round to get a good look at the 'visitor', but then he lost control of his express train. The person who entered the room had made him visibly wilt, and his presence caused a major derailment of both trains too.

"Sorry for the delay!" said the man as his eyes adjusted to the darkness of the room. "I had to wash some sap off my fingers. Those three old gentlemen I met this morning got me hugging so many trees that I..." He stared back at Greg - or rather at himself. "Oh!"

Mother and daughter had also spotted the likeness and had now suspended their relocation of the more inappropriately placed telegraph poles. Meston was manually recovering his capsized rolling stock. A smell of fused electricity hung in the air.

"Well," said Greg, breaking the silence. "I think there might have been a bit of a.... mix-up."

"Do introduce your brother to us, Greg!" urged Monica as she nodded in harmony with her mother.

"This is...." said Greg, barely audible.

"He's very convincing!" said the double. "It must be your subdued lighting." He proffered his hand to shake Greg's, but the latter flinched as though anxious to avoid any contact with the perplexing visitor.

"Were you sitting under a tree this morning in the company of a large dog?" asked Greg, allowing himself to consider the possibility of being cloned.

"Well yes, but then I carried on walking, and caught up with three men who asked me to assist in

91

some sort of initiation ceremony." He thought about it for a moment. "Actually, they *said* that after drinking the tea I might feel different later."

"Tea's ready!" called a lady's voice from the ground floor. "It's nothing posh!"

"We're coming, Edith," replied Thelma, nudging Monica to stop staring. "By the way, we've got an extra!"

"What, another one?" shouted the voice.

"Are you an extra?" asked Monica, addressing the stranger, but he gestured towards Greg and said: "No, I think *he* is!"

Meston was aware of there being some confusion by now, but it was only when he looked up that he realised there were *two* Gregs. "Sorry, I....I'd better switch off if we're going down," he said as he pressed a red button and looked at Monica for support.

She held his hand and together they dutifully left the room in silence, before proceeding down the two flights of stairs, with Thelma, Greg and his double close behind.

"I'm afraid there's not enough chairs for all of you," said Edith as she met them at the foot if the stairs. "The two extras had better sit and eat in the kitchen. You won't mind, you two, will you?" She moved towards the extra guests and demonstrated her kind side. "It's like the Everly Brothers, all over again. Welcome to Grantham! Thanks for taking the washing in!"

The two bemused men were shown into the small kitchen, and invited to sit on chairs which she'd placed in front of an old treadle-operated sewing machine and a gas stove. Both men asked each other

92

if they had a preference as to where to sit, but it wasn't all that important to either of them, although Greg sat down first, taking his place at the sewing machine to await developments. His new friend sat next to him facing the grill with its flap down, and was equally patient.

"There we are," said Edith as she brought them both plates of salad. "We'll be next door, but I'm sure you've got family matters to talk about!"

She left the room and closed the door.

"So, what do you think of the caravan, then?" asked Greg as he placed his feet on the treadle and rocked it gently.

"I was a bit worried about it tipping over last night," came the reply. "At least Monica's bucket of water helped to stabilise the wheelbase. That's if a single axle can constitute a wheelbase."

"Yes, you're definitely me," said Greg as he abruptly stopped the treadle. "I suppose the split must have happened in the woods this morning. I found myself in a trunk in Mablethorpe after I stood up, but then I went off to meet Haydn and Jimi Hendrix!"

"Incredible! What a busy morning! What did you learn?"

"They both speak English quite well, but I still didn't grasp where the notes come from."

"Hmm. I think you were probably dreaming. Anyway, we've got to get something down on manuscript by the time we get back to work. By the way, the old men invited me to join their initiation ceremony in the woods. They conferred upon me the name Hawthorn, anointing me with sap, and followed by tea and bourbon biscuits."

"That should make things easier while there are two of us - or two of *me*," said Greg. "How long are you er....staying here, Hawthorn?"

He shook his head in reply and stared vacantly at a pressure cooker on the back burner. "I think the plan is that we're going back to the farmhouse about nine o'clock. I can have another go at composition before I go to bed."

"I really did meet them," insisted Greg. "I asked Haydn how he composed and he said it was all a joke - just let it happen."

"The old men told me *not* to let anything happen in case it's a joke," said Hawthorn. "Apparently Norman was once bombarded by a snowball in a ball-games exclusion zone. Said it was icy cold."

Greg nodded sympathetically, and operated the treadle once more as though pumping air for a harmonium. He felt the urge to pedal faster, and the whirring rhythm was satisfying to both men's ears. Hawthorn then followed suit, and beat his fork on the pressure cooker as percussion, and for a while a rudimentary form of innovative musicianship occupied their minds.

They didn't hear the back door open, but gradually they came to realise that a young man in a suit was staring at them incredulously from the doorway. He held a briefcase in front of him defensively.

"Ah, you must be....er, I mean....are you Tom?" asked Greg as he brought the sewing machine to a standstill and the assault on the pressure cooker abated.

"Pleased to meet you," said Hawthorn during the man's ensuing silence. "We've just been to see your

94

layout!"

"I don't need this," grunted the young man as he stormed through the kitchen to declaim his presence to those in the next room.

"Does he mean his briefcase?" whispered Hawthorn, abandoning the rest of his tea and sliding it out of sight under the grill.

"I think he might be upset about meeting strangers," replied Greg. "Don't forget, he works in a bank."

Raised voices, notably Tom's and Edith's, were escaping from the other room. "Well who exactly are they, then?" was one question that carried well, to which the reply that "They help with the washing, dear!" seemed to be the stock answer. Greg pulled out the manuscript book from his jacket pocket as though to reassure himself of his *raison d'être,* but then he realised that not only was it he alone who possessed it at this moment, but that when he was whisked away from the car to the Austro-Hungarian Empire, another split must have taken place.

For the past twelve years, or at least since that morning, there would have been yet *another* version of Greg - one who had been abandoned in a car park in Mablethorpe. Would the other version be able to catch up, or would the contemporary Gregs need to stage some kind of rescue mission? The 'real' Greg tried doodling on the back of the book as he attempted to evaluate the quandary. However, his small circles and lines of events began to resemble a harmonic cadence. Hawthorn stared admiringly and hummed a few notes, whilst in the other room the heated discussion continued.

"They could be evangelicals, or even opportunist roofing contractors for all you know, Mother!" complained Tom. "And *you* should understand about home security, Meston!"

Both Greg and Hawthorn were too conscious of their presence causing concern to their host's protective son to be able to think creatively. They wondered what to do, but a quieter, more reflective mood seemed to take hold in the room beyond, and a consensus for greater vigilance produced acquiescence. Greg thought about locking the outer door to prevent further intrusion into the household, but Hawthorn was already there and about to turn the lock. However, he didn't actually succeed and the door suddenly burst open. Had the other Greg just arrived, hotfoot from the past with a mind full of melodic inspiration?

A young lady with arms balanced by bulging carrier bags entered the kitchen and deposited a mass of shopping on an already full table. She turned and smiled at the two strangers who were staring back at her.

"Hello!" she said, in a mixture of friendliness and amazement. "Do you know where all this stuff has to go?"

The duo rose as one and set about finding homes for the tins, packets and jars that seemed to issue continuously from the bags. She thanked them and folded the empty bags neatly. "Tom says his mother always forgets the folding," she confided in them before knocking at the door that led to the hall, and then again at the room in which the family sat talking. This prompted Tom to return to the kitchen, as hurriedly as he'd left, and his mood was still one of irritation as he watched Hawthorn lining up tins of tomato soup in a cupboard with their labels facing varying directions.

"I thought it best if the dents weren't showing," said Hawthorn, amiably. "Aesthetics always beats uniformity!"

Tom swore under his breath, before switching his attention to scrutiny of Greg's replenishment of a vegetable rack.

"Leave that!" he ordered, keen to prevent the erratic misplacement of a parsnip. "Stock rotation and accessibility. That's how we operate here." He reshuffled various salad items as though playing chess, then looked at the two men now back on their chairs. "This place is a tip," he informed them. "I call in here to see Mother every Friday after work and it's always the same."

They nodded, just enough to be polite, but not enough to agree. Greg re-examined his manuscript book and his doodle. Hawthorn leaned across and studied it too, but as he pointed to a squiggle and asked whether it was meant to be a crotchet, Tom interrupted.

"So what exactly is your business here?" he barked. "And what's that book you're both so engrossed in? A manual for lethargic salesmen?"

Getting no immediate response, he began tapping the lid of a jar of gherkins impatiently, then marched over to them and stretched out his hand. Hawthorn took the man's hand to shake, but his conciliatory gesture was rebuffed.

"I'm not playing games," said Tom, pointing to the

book. "And if you're doing market research, then we're divulging nothing about age, income, or thermostat settings."

CHAPTER 7

Greg had forgotten what happened last time, but as he proffered the book on Tom's insistence it seemed to glow on contact with the impatient hand that snatched it. Greg's sense of being in the kitchen immediately began to fade, merging into a hazy impression of sitting in a rowing boat on a choppy sea. Tom was still with him, his face looking as thundery as the stormy clouds above. There was no sign of Hawthorn, but Greg trusted that he would be able to explain his other half's sudden disappearance from the kitchen, although with Tom missing as well, Meston might be regretting not having locked the back door.

"Do you feel any better yet?" asked a young man in Victorian dress, jotting down dots in a small notebook. His comments were addressed to Tom, but he looked slightly off-colour himself. "The basalt is monumental, you must agree, no?"

"Well give me some of that, then!" snapped Tom. "Anyway, what's that island and what are we doing on this boat?"

"Iona!" shouted the man rowing the boat.

"Well if you own her, get us to the mainland - now!"

Greg watched the passenger as he made notes. He then noticed that he was humming, and that the note-taking was on staves of manuscript. He felt an adrenalin-rush and, looking more closely at the man's youthfully receding hair, he realised he was in the presence of Felix Mendelssohn and that he'd arrived at the very inception of the 'Hebrides Overture'. Either they were on their way to, or back from the isle of Staffa, but the composer didn't seem to be enjoying the journey. Right now, however, their progress was more in the manner of violent bobbing actions on the turbulent waves than in any apparent linear direction, but Greg already knew that the result of this trip would be a success for the composer, and that perhaps in this instance one of them was here to assist the other. He looked up at the brooding sky and grabbed his own manuscript book. He had little control over his pen in present conditions, but it seemed as though the lurching motion of the craft in which they sat was dictating the craft which he had sought - the combination of sea and weather were composing the music, whereas Mendelssohn himself was uncomposed and seasick.

Tom had also been subdued by the waves and was now looking ill himself. The boatman glanced at him, then winked at Greg. "Aye, it's a grand day, sir!" he roared from the now elevated prow of the boat.

Greg smiled back, whilst his pen continued jabbing the theme neatly in his book. This went on for some time, until he noticed that they were approaching land, and that the isle of Staffa was now in the distance.

"I think we're almost there!" he shouted at Tom comfortingly, but his now meek companion from the kitchen merely nodded. Mendelssohn rallied himself from his torpor and observed what the rough sea had etched in Greg's book. He enthused rapidly in German, then shook Greg's hand and switched to English. "Truly you are an amanuensis for the elements!" he declared. "Let me see what you have there."

Greg quickly withdrew the book - he didn't want to propel the esteemed composer to who-knows-where or when, and yet for the sake of art and posterity he had to share it with him. Felix's book had only a smattering of illegible notation, whereas Greg's markings were definitely substantial.

"Sorry, about earlier on," said Tom as the sea became less rough. "Well, even later on too. I'm under pressure at the bank."

"I understand," said Greg as he wondered what he should do about the gestating overture. "Er, are you still nauseous?"

"I'm sick of my job. I really wanted to have a career in musical journalism, but there was more money in the bank."

"Excuse me, but could I see?" asked Mendelssohn, his hand gently extending towards Greg's writings.

Tom was watching closely and had become suddenly protective of the mysterious book. Greg was now preoccupied with their imminent landing on shore, and hadn't noticed how keen Mendelssohn was to take hold of it, but then Tom leapt on top of him as the three men wrestled for control.

Whether or not the boat capsized during the course of the struggle was impossible to tell, but Greg, Tom, and Felix suddenly found themselves on dry land. It was actually extremely dry land and the proximity of what Greg summised to be the Great Pyramid of Cheops in the near distance was somewhat disconcerting, but he knew that he had to stay calm and take on the responsibility of tour guide to his two

101

companions. He trusted that the boatman would reach the shore safely, but then the question of his fee began to play on Greg's mind. Perhaps Mendelssohn had already negotiated with him for the hire of the boat by agreeing to pay him a percentage of any performing rights?

Tom was staring at the pyramid with an expression more of resignation than incredulity. "I knew a guy who said he made thousands out of selling those things," he said resentfully. "Didn't expect to see one here, though. Hey! Where's that boat gone?"

Greg didn't wish to alarm the young, and apparently historically naïve, bank manager by telling him that he'd probably just been transported to Egypt. "Well, the sun seems to have come out all of a sudden!" he replied merrily, dismissing the sea of parched sand spread out in front of them. He was now maintaining a tight control of the manuscript book that apparently doubled as an instant passport, but he noticed that Mendelssohn was paying more attention to a small group of men chatting in Arabic who were strolling nearby. "There's a lot of Gaelic spoken in these parts!" assured Greg. "Anyway, if I hold my book open for you, would you like to copy out the theme? We can say you wrote it…. if you don't mind teaching me some of your skills!"

A delighted grin from the young man indicated that a bargain had been struck. Greg smiled back, and wondered about the date. At least the stones of the pyramid looked ancient, which reassured him that he was probably within the right epoch.

"Those Picts certainly left a lot of monuments!" called Greg with mock bluster as Tom moved towards

102

the colossus.

"The who?" asked Tom. "I've only been to Tenerife."

He turned round as though he'd remembered something and walked back to rejoin the other two. "Did I get stoned in Mother's kitchen or bang my head on her old Ascot? I don't have a window for any ill health stuff - besides, I'm 110 over 75! I always get the young nurse at the gym to check me out after a workout."

Mendelssohn looked puzzled. "Allegro *and* moderato?" he asked, before resuming his transcription. "The work definitely needs to ripple, like this er....sand."

Greg was relieved that although he was responsible for taking these two men out of their comfort zone, at least there was some kind of memory loss that eased their passage. However, they were probably all copies, himself included, of the original Felix, Tom, and Greg. Might it be possible that every day, people wake up in one reality that is familiar, while another aspect of the same person fulfils adventures and pursues various quests? His companions didn't seem to be fulfilling much of an adventure here. They both looked discomfited by the blazing sun, and Mendelssohn couldn't get a signal on the strange mobile 'phone that Tom had given him in exasperation.

"Yes, it's very pretty but I really would like to be underway soon to have an audience with the Queen!" he said, handing the object back to Tom. "Is that her schloss?" he asked, pointing to the pyramid.

"Whose?" asked Greg, unsure as to whether

103

Mendelssohn recognised the building for what it was, and was perhaps expecting to meet Queen Nefertiti.

"Queen Victoria, of course!" he replied, with bemusement. "She also is German!"

Tom was checking his expensive watch ostentatiously. "I think I was supposed to be taking Jessica to watch me play squash tonight, but I can't quite remember the moves," he said distractedly before sitting down on a handy stone. "Anyway, not bad round here, is it? Our cashier's from this area; he's Scotch, or is he Dutch? One of the two."

Mendelssohn sighed contentedly as he completed his rough transcription, before addressing Greg. "Just be aware of the rhythms all around you. Hark; those men coming towards us are singing as they march!"

Greg had hoped for more than just a tip on composition, but he hadn't gleaned all that much from Haydn and Hendrix either. He seemed to be on an odyssey of only the briefest snippets of musical encouragement. He nodded his thanks, but thought that he might have done better to keep the theme to himself, although to do so might have violated the past and led to chaos. He looked across towards where the men were approaching, but this proved to be rather a shock. He wondered at first if the two figures might actually be a mirage, for which desert areas had a reputation, but Tom was staring also, and bracing himself to engage with them, as though keen to sell them investment bonds. The rhythmic chanting was in an American mode, but Greg had no idea how or why the two Englishmen had ventured so far. He wondered whether they would recognise him, and how to address them if they didn't.

"Lovely day, lovely day!" said the tall one in a prestissimo tempo. "We're looking for the temple of Thoth."

"Thauth? Are they saying sauce?" asked Tom, glancing at Greg for clarification. "Sorry, we can't help you with any sauce!" he shouted in a slow, barely patient manner.

"You want the source of the Nile?" asked a local, running towards them. "I'm afraid the blue one starts its journey in Ethiopia, but I can take you there, if sir wishes...." He tailed off when Tom shook his head at him as though his account was overdrawn. "Or there's a very nice white one I can show you! No?" he called out before running off after a group of wandering sightseers.

"I do need to be getting on now," said Mendelssohn as he rose to his feet. "And thank you for your assistance. Your semi-quavers are magnificent!"

Greg had failed to anticipate the composer's impending departure, too fixated was he with the two frail, but intrepid men from Thelma Throstlethwaite's tiny campsite. Had their quest for the 'inner man' propelled them here, and was Thoth to be their mentor? At least, thought Greg, there was no need to pretend to *them* that they were in the Inner Hebrides.

Mendelssohn was gazing at the pyramid in wonder. "This must be Prince Albert's finest architectural masterpiece - and yet it looks as though it's not quite complete! And there are no windows!"

The leader of the two men was more concerned about sand in his shoe. "It'll play havoc with my corn," he complained as he sat down next to Tom.

"How d'you do. Did I hear you say your friends have got sores too?"

"What?" snapped Tom. "No, no worries. I've probably got jet lag. By the way, have you got your ISAs yet for the current financial year?"

"Isis?" asked the bemused group leader. "No, she's the fertility goddess. We don't need her, but we *are* seeking the spirit of Thoth. He's the record keeper."

"Record keeper," repeated the tall man. "You should see his shelves!"

"Well, we also keep records of all our customers' investments!" advised Tom, but there was an element of doubt in his voice. Nevertheless, when he saw Mendelssohn searching for the way into the pyramid, he instinctively went after him in a half-hearted attempt at salesmanship in 'latest investment products' mode. Greg was keen to try and prevent people wandering too far, but the local guide was trying his best to separate them with gleeful recommendations of the Sphinx and of refreshments. Norman, at least, wasn't in wandering mode, and so he prepared to make himself comfortable.

"I take a size 9 shoe, but a size 10 will do if I wear thick socks," said Norman as he placed his folding chair next to Greg and checked that the ground was safe. "Don't want to risk sitting on quicksands," he explained.

Greg was considering the rhythms of life, but the pointless statement about shoes at least deserved a polite response.

"Russian soldiers apparently don't wear socks but wrap enough linen around their feet to fit the allocated boot."

"Alligator boot, eh?" said their tall companion. "It just goes to show!"

"Linen, you say?" said Norman as he removed a tea stain from the arm of his chair. "So they mummify in Russia too!"

Back at the pyramid Mendelssohn was selectively tapping ancient stones as though seeking to gain admission. Tom stood watching him in a disengaged manner, as though dreaming of lost commission.

"Excuse me, honey," drawled a female voice from Greg's side. "Maybe you can help us. We've just escaped from our party."

The speaker wore a tee shirt claiming allegiance to Detroit and looked up at him pleadingly. Norman stared at her disdainfully. An older lady hobbled up to them, her manner of walking resonating with Norman who showed solidarity with her by wincing.

"We wanted to see the geyser erupting but the others are round the other side of that triangle thing," she complained.

"We see *that* thing every day on our dollar bills," drawled lady number one, "although the big eye's not here!"

"It's probably closed", Greg advised her, although by now he was becoming concerned about how extensive his duty of care ought to be. Did he really have to protect Mendelssohn from the realities of Queen Victoria no longer residing in the Great Pyramid? And should he avoid shattering the delusions of the dames from Detroit who had assumed that Giza was a hot spring?

"So! You're both on hol....vacation, then!" he said

positively.

"We sure are!" said the younger one. "Now, do any of you men know what time we get to see the water display?"

"I think it's probably been turned off at the mains. Maintenance probably," suggested Greg, crossing his fingers.

"Told you so, Aldebaran!" said the old lady. "I guess we'll just have to go and gawp at that darned skinks thing again."

"Darned Sing Sing again! Well, well!" said Joe as he set up his own foldable chair next to Norman.

"Not too close," warned Norman. "The aluminium might expand in the sun and push mine over."

Tom had abandoned his networking by the pyramid and was heading back to the growing party. "I think I'd better get going," he called out as he approached. "Anyone remember where I'm parked?"

Greg was aware that car owners tended to refer to their vehicles in the first person. Only last week Mr. Langrish had complained of being 'hit' in the car park, when it was actually the inanimate number plate of his otherwise pristine Ford Escort that had been microscopically dented.

"No, I don't think you actually brought your car with…." called Greg, but Tom was already wandering off. He looked at the two men in their chairs, who in turn looked suspiciously at the two ladies as they conferred on what to do next. Hadn't there been a third man? Had he too wandered off, or had he not made it through the spatial and temporal doorway? Mendelssohn, meanwhile, had given up on seeking the doorway to the pyramid, and was making his way back to the small group. The younger lady took a picture of him with her digital camera. "A real Egyptian, Mommy!" she exclaimed proudly.

"What!" said Norman, as he stood up quickly causing his chair to capsize. However, the unbandaged composer seemed more impressed by Norman's apparent courtesy than annoyed by the ladies with their strange and intrusive camera.

"This gentleman has been my Hebridean amanuensis!" said Mendelssohn proudly, pointing to Greg now sitting down in the sand. "Pity about the young bank manager. He told me he expects to be replaced by a customer care team who live in the Far East, but he suggested to me that to Balmoral I should repair - right away!"

"Did you follow all that, Aldebaran?" asked the older lady of her open-mouthed daughter.

"I did some temping as his secretary on a boat," Greg interjected modestly. "Now he's off to a castle, but meanwhile, your money is safe and your call *is* important to them," he explained mischievously.

He winked at Norman, but the man already had a twitch of his own. The ladies moved away, muttering their goodbyes, and appeared to be chasing after Mendelssohn as he strode off purposefully. Greg knew that the prospect of a carriage bound for Balmoral from Cairo was highly unlikely. He was about to join in pursuit of Mendelssohn too, but when he observed that he'd now caught up with Tom, he knew that the composer would be in safe, if rather cynical, hands.

The third member of the outdoor team then approached Greg and his two companions, bearing

109

two ice creams as well as his trademark yellow balaclava. "I didn't get one for you Norman on account of your problem with cones," he announced as he slowly got down to sit at the feet of his sensitive parabola-phobic leader. This seemed to provide some reassurance to his leader, happy to have his loyal band around him, even if the elusive Thoth hadn't materialised yet.

"The best day's work I ever did was when I took early retirement from the print room," said Norman, apropos of nothing.

Greg nodded sagely and hoped the man had enjoyed a final burst of activity with Times New Roman - a much more elegant font than Helvetica, he thought.

"That was the day I decided I needed to find my wild side," added Norman as he deftly folded a used teabag for later use.

"We like to stroll on the wild side, don't we Norman?" suggested Joe. "Those gusts of wind at Skegness last year were quite bracing!"

Their leader nodded while his comrades slurped loudly at their rapidly melting mint and choc ices to a wind accompaniment of Cairo's motor horns as background. Greg meanwhile felt flattered by Felix's praise, and was buoyed at the thought of having unwittingly tapped into the creative process. He was keen, however, to know how, and what had brought the three gentle macho men here, as well as himself and his own small party, now dispersing.

"Excuse me, but this *is* the present day, isn't it?" he asked, before realising the inanity of the question. "What I meant was…."

110

"*Every* day's a present!" replied Norman with an air of authority. "Carpe diem!"

"Compendium!" echoed his second in command. "That's right, Norman. Lots of games!"

Greg felt a sense of inertia whilst the men in their tubular chairs felt the intensity of the sun beating down upon them as they passed around a small tube of sun-cream.

"Thirty factors in this, Norman!" said Joe as he checked the label.

"Quite possibly, but there's a lot more factors involved in seeking the inner warrior." said Norman, glancing at Greg as though he too was on the same errand. "And yet *thirty* of them just so we can sit here in a giant sandpit isn't quite what I had in mind for today."

"Well said, Norman," replied his more talkative comrade. "We need to seize and....and....and *touch* those trees!"

Norman nodded and distributed handy moisturised wipes to his friends as ice cream dripped down their arms.

"That ice cream man looked at me a bit odd when I paid him," said the small comrade, suddenly recalling the transaction.

"I suppose they don't usually take Grimsby money in these parts," said Joe.

Greg knew the feeling of having strange money when he tried to get a snack in Mablethorpe twelve years too early, but then he wondered about his alter ego left behind in the kitchen. Might other clones of himself have been forming since he left?

"I suppose I'd best be getting back too," said Greg,

standing up, fairly certain that this adventure wasn't doing much for any of them. "Can I ask you how you got here from....wherever you were before?"

"We willed ourselves here, I suppose," said Norman, as though the thought hadn't previously occurred to any of them. "I pressed a custard cream into a fissure in the trunk of a pedunculate oak and made an incantation, and suddenly we all arrived here! By the way, aren't you the man from the caravan?"

Greg sat down again, his look of amazement at that last question being its own answer. He nodded as a plethora of questions of his own welled up within his head. "That's the power of custard creams!" he stuttered. Then, with a greater degree of thought: "Did you really come straight here, or did you call in at other places *en route*?"

"Sat round a campfire with some Hopi tribesmen, didn't we, Norman!" said Joe, proudly. "Lovely fire, it was!"

"We didn't know what they were saying, but they sounded like they meant it, didn't they?" said the more mournful-sounding member of the trio.

"It was all experience," declared Norman, "but I don't think we're going to find out much more here."

Greg wondered what their means of transport might be. In his own case it was the manuscript book that acted as both visa and vehicle. Could a packet of custard creams really have the same powers for the three men? He stood up once more, and with sighs of resignation his companions conceded that there was no point in them hanging around either. They had all had enough of the outskirts of Cairo, and the ice

112

creams had given way to what were now merely dry stems. What had been the purpose of the visit? Greg gazed at the pyramid. Were its arcane mathematical dimensions a lesson in classical composition? Should he write a score for triangles? "How do you think it was built?" he asked with a tone of wonder, realising that someone ought to make the comment.

"Who knows!" said Norman. "Perhaps it wasn't built at all! Might have been carved out in situ - could be a mountain in disguise!"

"In the skies, in the skies, there's a thought!" said Joe. "Oh, mind you don't trap your fingers when you fold that chair, Norman."

"Yes, be careful," said the lugubrious one. "Remember those cake-forks we had to use in the café on Monday?…Or was it those fish-knives we had to use in the pub on Tuesday?"

"Don't remind me," said Norman as he scraped sand off the legs of his chair with a toothpick. "The handle was really digging into the palm of my hand." He turned to Greg and outlined the disadvantages of using cutlery with angular handles. "And some of the cheaper soup spoons can be hard-going, too - I blame the Scandinavians for all that contemporary tableware nonsense."

Greg changed the subject, slightly, for the sake of international relations. "I understand that the Finns are quite keen on the Tango, as are the Argentinians!"

There was no response to this snippet of information, but Greg himself pondered for a moment on intercontinental, and even interplanetary musical genres. Gustav Holst had presumably never set foot on Neptune, and yet he'd instinctively known that its inhabitants could sing in the soprano register. Was there any limit to the mysterious powers of man's creativity? The three men had now begun their ungainly jog towards the city. Greg thought he might as well accompany them, although he didn't wish to contribute to their quavery chanting.

"We storm our way across the sands, we're martyrs to our feet and hands," but the combination of singing and shuffling was proving a bit too much for them. Greg felt an obligation to compose a gentle march for the delicate adventurers, but he still hadn't been able to tap into the source. Neither had he checked on whether this latest exotic visit was within his comfort zone of it being the same day as the one on which he'd strolled in to the woods. Having become even a day younger or older could prove inconvenient for his diary, although not intrinsically for himself, perhaps. He assumed, optimistically, that it was still 'today', and that by now there were sufficient numbers of Gregs in other times and spaces all seeking the 'source', and that perhaps they could liaise. Possibly they too were all at this very moment considering where and when they were, but with no identity crises as to *who* they were. They were all aspects of his own ambitions, and one of them was bound to realise it. And somewhere, and at some time, an identical trio of delicate adventurers were consulting Thoth with important matters of their own, or had Thoth also been replicated to wander?

The party ground to a halt. Greg suspected they might be exhausted, but Norman wanted to find his sunglasses. "I've had them six years, and check the lenses over every spring for abrasions!" he declared

114

proudly. "Then I oil the hinges with three in one."

"That's right!" said Joe. "Three in one, one in three - the trinity!"

Greg wondered if he could assist the trinity by carrying the bag containing the thermos flasks but his outstretched hand seemed to alarm Ted who flinched and shook his head nervously.

"Sorry I couldn't let you pick any flowers in the woods this morning, Ted," said Norman, now protected by his annually serviced shades as the men continued to plod across the sand. "It contravenes the Wildflower and Countryside Act 1981."

"I see," said Ted, exuding pathos. "I can collect some twigs next time, perhaps, instead."

Greg wondered whether making daisy chains would be permissible, but they might chafe as the inner man sought freedom.

"He doesn't want to go to prison, does he, Norman!" said Joe, cheerily. "He'd have to tunnel his way out again!"

"Man was born to be free!" declared Norman, glancing at Greg for his approval. "But no. The creepy crawlies would deter him from digging."

"It's those woodlice I don't like," confessed Ted, pausing in his tracks briefly to transfer his load to his other hand. "I found one on my back door step the other day. I had to go out the front door instead."

"That's the spirit of adventure!" said Norman, proud of his team-mate's initiative. He glanced at Greg again for tacit approval. Greg nodded, and wondered whether their tent had an emergency exit. "Funny how we met up again. I never expected to find myself in Cairo when I set out this morning.

Anyway, now that we've sort of finished here, how will you be getting back?"

The thought had probably never occurred to the men. They shook their heads as one as they progressed doggedly towards the city. "Same way as we came, I suppose," said Norman. "We arrived under a palm tree!"

Greg appreciated the fact that certain trees had formed a network of travel centres. He nodded and smiled, then turned round to get another look at the pyramid. He thought he should at least see if it was possible to take advantage of his visit here by joining one of the guided tours into its interior. He paused. "I wonder if you need to book," he said to himself quietly.

Norman halted the others and looked hard at Greg, who suspected exhaustion - a condition with which he could empathise. "I'd offer to carry that book for you, only I almost burned my middle finger on a boiled egg yesterday. The trouble with egg cups is that they don't anchor the egg in place when you want to set to work on tapping the shell. It's ridiculous."

Greg had often thought the same, although not with the degree of angst that Norman was now feeling. He held on to the book tightly. "Perhaps wearing thimbles on your fingers might help?" he suggested, his mind now set upon returning to the pyramid.

"What a good idea!" said Norman, his face lighting up.

"You *have* some thimbles?" asked Greg.

"No, I mean the pyramid! It must be cooler in there. I can't really stand too much heat. Or cold for that matter," he admitted.

"You want to come too?" asked Greg. "What about your comrades?"

"They'd love it! They don't get out much. We're not as young as we were."

"How old were you before?" asked Greg, curious as to the effects of temporal shifts upon the aging process.

Norman laughed, but then without any key modulation his laughter evolved into a short bout of coughing before his voice returned. "Well, we were all aged twelve at one stage, but that was some years ago now. How about yourself?"

"I used to be twelve too," said Greg. He pondered on the words he'd just uttered. Might there be twelve Gregs in existence by now, assuming that the various choices of action that fate had presented today had resulted in further exponential cloning?

"I can see the other two sitting in front of that café," droned Ted as they surveyed a busy street.

Greg looked, alarmed. Was he already populating the streets of Cairo with his image? No, it was Tom and Mendelssohn who were sitting on plastic chairs under an umbrella, nursing small coffee cups. They looked fed up, and yet querulous as a Dromedary camel walked sedately past them, its expression apparently mocking their lack of purpose. Greg waved, but they hadn't seen him and he felt responsible for their welfare. After all, they presumably had neither visas nor the appropriate vaccinations, and probably no means of getting back home, wherever it was they wanted dropping off. Could he cope with taking a group of five rather vulnerable men on a diversion to the Great Pyramid of Cheops before getting them all safely home?

Ted was dispatched to invite the other two men to join them. "Don't run!" cautioned Norman. "You might fall over! Joe you'd better go with him. His balaclava might cause panic." He smiled patiently at Greg. "He knitted that himself when he was thinking of joining the SAS but somehow it didn't quite work out."

Greg nodded and began to move back towards the pyramid in a sort of 'Shall we go?' manner.

"Yes, lead on, Brother Hawthorn," said Norman, picking up his various items. "They can catch us up."

"Hawth….?" said Greg, wondering why a bell was ringing in his mind. Wasn't that the name of his double whom he'd met and chatted to in front of a gas stove in a strange kitchen?

"I always wanted to be a gang leader since Miss Moston appointed me ink monitor at school!" Norman confided in him. "I kept thirty two inkwells in Form 3A topped up with blue-black for our fountain pens."

"The pen is mightier than the sword," said Greg, now beginning to wonder whether he might have been substituted by Hawthorn.

"Well, it did give me a sense of power, and ball points were banned," said Norman. "Anyway it must have gone to my head because I decided to lead a boycott against the school milk being served at less than room temperature. Three of us refused to drink it!"

"The other two being…."

"Yes, Joe and Ted! Even though Ted was the drinking straw monitor."

118

"The ink wasn't too cold, though, I hope," said Greg, his attention somewhat dissipated.

"No complaints about that. I once drew a picture in ink on the inside of my desk lid. It was a clenched fist grasping a primrose. It was the decade of flower power!"

"And protest songs too, perhaps?" added Greg, deciding not to bother protesting that he wasn't actually Hawthorn.

"Indeed. The three of us tried to write a song about cold milk but we just couldn't seem to find the right tune. We even borrowed Danny Dent's harmonica but nothing came."

This time there wasn't a bell ringing in Greg's mind, but instead the clanging realisation of what he had in common with the three men. The thought stopped him in his tracks, not that they'd been doing more than shuffling along anyway.

"You tried....song writing, then," said Greg, trying to sound indifferent to what he now knew had united them all.

Norman merely responded with a weary 'yes', but then he turned to face the small group who were now catching them up. Greg turned too, and watched them, wondering how much sense any of them had made of all their recent shifts of location. Whereas he himself had full cognisance of his various transfers to different times and places, the others whom he met were all rather hazy about their previous setting. And yet might he also have forgotten bits of his own history whilst other Gregs had gained new memories? The young bank manager still retained his innate bank ego, and yet he didn't seem unduly concerned about his relocations.   Perhaps that was part of the job. Mendelssohn also appeared to be coping well with being whisked straight from a choppy boat trip in the Inner Hebrides to experiencing a dry sojourn in North Africa. Possibly that too was to aid inspiration. But they all seemed to be so resigned to where and when they were!   However, perhaps yet other aspects of themselves were panicking and desperate to return home, whilst here Greg and his companions apparently shared an equanimity and acceptance of their purpose.

CHAPTER 8

Greg gazed at the mighty pyramid. Was he going to treat them all to the entrance fee? He had only British money. Could Tom negotiate currency exchange, or could they all declare themselves to be friends of Thoth? He wondered where Norman had gone. Had he been whisked away to another....but that was absurd. At any split one would remain and another would venture elsewhere, or 'else-when'.

"Never stand when you can sit!" said a voice next to him. Norman was sitting down on his foldable chair, awaiting the others. "That's what I tell them. We follow a more relaxed version of seeking the Inner Warrior. Man can learn a lot from the sloth!"

Greg agreed. It seemed the polite thing to do, and besides, both men and sloths shared a love of trees. He looked at the approaching party. Ted and Joe seemed to have adopted the gait of cantering horses as they hurried back earnestly in a bobbing motion, but Felix and Tom were walking *alla marcia* as they avidly discussed overdraft facilities and woodwind, respectively. They gave the impression of being primary school teachers who had sent their excitable, and yet exhausted, children a few paces ahead. Greg wondered if they'd all appreciate the pyramid, or whether it would be too far removed from their lifestyles to hold any appeal for them. There might well be steps inside too, although pharaonic escalators might be available for those in need. The tour guide would accommodate their needs, but Greg resolved to try and stick closely with the great composer. If the others looked bored he'd perhaps encourage Tom to discuss share investments in Egyptian ice creams with them - although Grimsby currency might not be an option.

"We're nearly there!" said Greg, instantly regretting such an obvious statement, but it sounded appropriate and his tone of voice suggested fun for them all. "I once heard a recording of the late Tutankhamun's royal trumpets! It sent shivers down my spine!" he called out, glancing back to his small party, but Norman was about to demonstrate his leadership skills to Ted and Joe.

"There might be women inside so remember - they multitask. They might peer sensitively at bas reliefs, but at the same time they're planning shopping expeditions to buy pashmina tea towels or.... lavender-coated candles."

"Having to cope with scandals? They need to ignore them and move on!" laughed Joe as he paused for a rest.

"Indeed, but we *all* need to move on!" instructed Norman. "You and Ted can follow me."

"We always follow you Norman!" declared Joe, loyally. "Isn't that right, Ted?"

"In single file, for many a mile," intoned Ted in his most lamentable voice yet.

Tom glanced at Greg as though desperate for it all to stop.

"Nice to see the older ones enjoying themselves, isn't it?" said Greg, quietly. "I think they might be from Grimsby. Have you ever been there?"

Tom shook his head and sighed. "I gave a lift to a

girl from Goole once. I think Grimsby might have cropped up as we chatted."

"I wonder what it'll do tomorrow," said Joe, swivelling his head in various directions in quest of a sign.

"I believe the pound was level-pegging against the dollar this morning," said Tom. "Or was it the Euro? Can't really remember."

"I'll check my seaweed when I get home," whined Ted.

"Seaweed?" exclaimed Tom, suddenly vivified. "Yeah, it's quoted on the Japanese markets, but to be honest, I don't really know much about it. I think there's an index called the Nike or Nicky or something."

Greg knew he had to inspire a sense of eager anticipation. However, Felix appeared to have his eyes trained on the pyramid, but his lips were definitely engaged in some sub-audible whistling. The giant structure loomed ever closer, and a group of people stood close to it, whilst being harangued in French by a female guide holding aloft an unfurled umbrella. Men in white suits dashed here and there, approaching visitors and enthusing in various stilted versions of several European languages. Those plying their wares and services took little notice of Greg and his party, but the French guide noticed them and beckoned to them wildly, as her party moved towards what was presumably the entrance. "Quick! Is closing!" she called out, emphasising the fact by opening and closing her umbrella.

Norman conceded the need to run, or even scamper, and urged his men to make their way quickly towards the now vanishing group of visitors. Greg assumed the role of deputy team leader and encouraged Tom and Felix to move quickly also, which they accomplished with slightly more finesse, not being encumbered with any tubular chairs or picnic impedimenta.

"Tell you what," said Tom as he jogged alongside Greg. "Looks a really great place to hold corporate events. It'll be impressive to have on my CV too! I'm glad I came now!"

"Good!" said Greg, wondering what Tom was hoping to 'take back' from whatever intensive role play or sales techniques he was expecting. He looked at Felix and trusted he wasn't still hoping to meet Queen Victoria, holding court in some windowless chamber in semi-state. "Almost there now," he said, rather obviously as they tagged on to the end of the queue shuffling through a nondescript entrance. "I'm paying!"

"Hard hats? I've got them in blue, yellow, and red," called out a vendor in a white suit as Greg, Tom and Felix paused to await the three senior men still loping along and endeavouring to catch up.

"Do we need to wear them inside?" asked Greg. "The sun won't penetrate the stones, will it?"

"The sun won't get in but the stones are old and very heavy," advised the vendor seriously. "You should wear protective hats in case masonry should fall and injure you!"

Tom gazed at the man, almost menacingly, then gave him a low denomination British banknote. The man smiled nervously, and silently handed him six assorted hard hats, before moving off quickly. The three older men eventually arrived, and breathlessly accepted their hats from Tom, who had patiently waited. He also issued Greg and Felix with theirs, advising Felix that he might wish to wear his back-to-front, in order to be cool. Greg assumed that such attention to dress might be a daily ritual at Tom's bank.

They all stood for a moment outside the unassuming entrance, as though unsure about who should lead the party inside, but it was Norman who took it upon himself to volunteer someone.

"Joe, you've got a stick - you can go first. There might be cobwebs."

Ted shuddered at the thought, but Tom nudged him reassuringly, which made him tense up.

"The French ladies haven't screamed!" said Greg. "I'm sure we'll be safe in there!"

They duly ducked in unison as Joe bent almost double to lead them into the gloomy opening.

"It's smaller on the inside than it is on the outside!" he observed cheerily. "Who'd be an architect, eh! Measure this, draw that!"

"The walls are probably insulated," assured Greg. "To prevent heat loss!"

A lady in a booth inside the entrance asked for everyone's tickets, but then she waved them through. "You with French party, yes?"

"Actually, we're not...." said Greg, unsure what to say next.

"Sorry, this my first day!" said the lady in broken English. "I wasn't told you come do repairs." She looked at Ted and Joe, who had hoisted their tea trays in the manner of hod carriers, presumably anxious not to damage them on the walls.

"We need to give the impression of being builders," whispered Greg. "Perhaps if we all look up and point at the ceiling and confer."

"But our faces would be exposed to any falling masonry," warned Norman.

"We could adjust our headgear to cover our faces," suggested Felix.

"Hmm, needs a lot doing," said Greg, getting into the part and pointing up vaguely in the semi-darkness. "Probably needs a....an Irish jay?"

"RSJ" Norman corrected him. "Reinforced..."

"Yeah, whatever. Anyway, the way I see it, we're wandering round this badly-maintained pyramid thing, and yet I still can't remember how I got here!" said Tom, losing patience.

"I think we met on a boat," advised Felix. "The man with the manuscript book modestly wrote the sketch of an overture for me during a storm, and see - now he brings us all to this enormous summer house for a tour of inspection! *And* he found the entrance! Wunderbar!"

Greg sidestepped any adulation that might have ensued by suggesting that introductions be made. Thus a whole minute was then occupied by the complete cycle of handshakes and greetings. Greg asked Felix for his autograph, which he kindly wrote on the manuscript book - avoiding any manual contact with it, and Tom hunted in his pockets for his card, but gave up and emphasised: "Tom!" to each of the others. Old schoolboys Norman, Ted, and Joe mostly concentrated on reacquainting themselves with each other, but their attempts at high fives were hampered by the difficulty of holding on to their chairs and other paraphernalia.

"Why can't they just leave those things somewhere?" asked Tom, shaking his head, as he stood with knees bent in the low dark passage. "No-one's going to run off with them!"

"Wouldn't you like to leave those things somewhere?" called Greg, slightly more gently than Tom's impatient delivery.

The men conferred, until Norman decided that they should find a convenient recess somewhere to shed their baggage. The lady from the entrance desk had by this stage stepped outside and was chatting to someone, but her voice was now almost inaudible. Greg suggested that they concentrate on finding an alcove to act as left luggage area. They continued in the gloom, which was punctuated by low wattage electric lights, until they noticed another slightly wider passage. Even though the older men appeared to be growing weary from carrying their burden, they still had enough energy to break into their chant as they shuffled along to an inviting-looking recess. They seemed to have lost their inhibitions too, as even though they were inside what was actually a public building, the three of them found themselves responding to the acoustic qualities of the stone passages by, on the count of three, uniting to produce a quavery bellow. It sounded to Greg like "Ho!", or even "No!" Whatever it was, their timing had been perfect, even if their pitch was dissonant, but the stone walls happily resonated for several seconds. Greg hoped that the lady outside hadn't been alarmed, but her own voice was by now well out of earshot. The echo had created harmonics, but then an ominous rumbling formed a bass accompaniment. Could it be the advance of the cleaning team exercising mops and buckets, wondered Greg? Or might there be a thunderstorm developing? A rush of stale air then caressed them as they stood motionless, until the roar was accompanied by the sight of a massive piece of stone scraping and sliding its way out of a space on their left, and blocking their route ahead with a violent thud.

"Great!" snarled Tom. "I hate it when staff start closing off access just before closing time. They could at least be a bit less heavy-handed about it."

Greg thought it would have needed a very heavy hand to move the gigantic stone into such a tight fit. He suspected it might not have been intentional. "Settlement, probably!" he said cheerfully, hoping that the now accessible passage to the left would be a safe option for exploring the place before it closed.

"Listen!" said Felix, smiling beatifically with his eyes closed. "Isn't it wonderful?"

Greg knew what he meant as his own ears were also picking up something that he found captivating. The two men exchanged knowing glances as they listened intently to a sustained chord that overwhelmed them with its purity and mystery.

"This beats everything!" exclaimed Tom as he cocked his head attentively. "What is it, and what's the instrument?"

"We never thought to get the guidebook," said Norman, apologetically. "Perhaps Hawthorn might know."

Greg peered into the gloom whence the sound

came, but as his eyes adjusted he could make out a flight of steps bathed in a dim light. Felix was now standing alongside him, attempting to hum in tune, but he was unable to do so. "I can't find the right pitch to hum!" he said, baffled.

Greg rummaged in his pockets for his tuning fork - a gift from his Uncle Henry, and which he always kept with him - just in case. "It's A, when I can find it," he said as he checked his pockets. "Has anyone here got perfect pitch?"

Heads shook, and the older men attempted whistling to the sound, but Norman thought it might be disrespectful to whistle and instead issued a "Shhhhh".

"You don't think it's Thoth, do you?" asked Ted, but Tom gave the distinct impression of finding speculation and delay rather tedious.

"What are we waiting for?" he said brusquely. "Let's go on and find out."

Greg gave up on the search for the tuning fork, but he was in introspective mood as they progressed, and yet acutely aware of the ancient surroundings of both himself and his disparate companions. It was all so far removed from the daily routine at work where he would usually be allocating advisable compositions to the clientele, and even his previous night's sleep in a delicately-balanced caravan was out of the norm. Was he actually meant to be here in his quest for the source of musical inspiration? He had often felt that his place was wherever a logical sequence of events had led him, and even today he was quietly accepting his allocated location. The chord could indeed be fulfilling his quest. One of the ancient *Books of the*

Dead impelled those who are near death to 'go towards the light', and yet here were the living, albeit in a mausoleum, going towards the sound - drawn by a chord.

"That Ted in the balaclava - his breath smells of peppermint," complained Tom suddenly, in his ear. "Can't you say something?"

"He's probably been eating one," suggested Greg. "And yet some of the more wayward senior citizens go in for aniseed."

"I've sometimes detected the whiff of aniseed in our strong room at the branch," said Tom with a sigh. "I've got my suspicions who it is....and yet I can't remember the guy's name!"

"Hawthorn?" said Greg, only just realising that Norman had referred to him as his alternative self again.

"Don't think it was that," said Tom. "It all seems ages ago. Wouldn't mind a huge stone door like the one we just saw back there though. That would keep out the aniseed-munchers!"

"You might develop cravings for aniseed yourself when you get older," said Greg.

"That's possible, I suppose," said Tom, reflectively. "Wow, I'll be thirty next year. Do you get a telegram from Prince William when you reach that age?"

"I didn't," said Greg. "It was just like any other day for me."

"Not like this one, then."

Greg nodded again, but felt his hard hat wobble. He wondered if the memories retained by his companions were merely extracts from their lives, rather than coherent histories. Perhaps his own memories were merely extracts too. Perhaps he actually *was* Hawthorn, or any other composite or amalgam of his assumed identity.

"All those stairs to climb!" moaned Ted as he saw the long flight of stone steps in front of them. "And no handrail!"

"You'll cope," said Tom. "You might even meet that Goth character you were on about!"

Norman decided to take a head count as they reached the foot of what looked to be the longest flight of steps any of them had ever seen. "There should be six of us," he said, before pointing at each of the assembled company to make sure. "Yes, we haven't lost anyone, but I've got plasters and iodine in case of personal injury!"

Ted was looking up apprehensively at the ascent before him. Joe exchanged knowing nods with Norman, whilst Felix was bonding with Tom - apparently they both liked apricots. "I can live with them," admitted Tom.

"Shakespeare mentioned them too, I believe," said Felix as he temporarily removed his headgear. "Sorry, it was causing my head to sweat," he explained.

"Tell me about it," said Tom.

"Well, it's the pores on my scalp," said Felix. "Perspiration is another word, I think."

"Er, sorry about the delay," said Norman solicitously. "Ted's got a bit of a dilemma. He can't manage the stairs."

"Ted's lost some bitter lemon," explained Joe. "He can't manage the spares."

"What can't he do?" asked Felix.

"I don't know," said Tom, his patience apparently now in steep decline. "Something about not managing shares. He wants to try managing a bank with head office on his back to push high yield accounts with even higher penalties for unauthorised withdrawals!"

"He wants to do all that?" said Felix, surprised. "I hadn't realised before how keen the British people are on economics!"

Tom stared at him for a second, and shook his head. "Give me strength," he muttered.

"Here, take my arm!" suggested Felix helpfully, but it was Ted who grasped the extended arm for support as he stared in disbelief at the flight of stone steps before them.

Greg could see that the combination of steps, a potential nervous breakdown, and linguistic obtuseness were causing friction. He tried to find a distraction. "I wonder if we'll find any hieroglyphics up there!" he said cheerfully. "Apparently the Ancient Egyptians were great record keepers!"

"It's my knees," said Ted, despondently. "They lock up."

"They're locking up?" exclaimed Felix. "Surely not yet! That wonderful music is still playing!"

Norman had formed a huddle with Greg and Tom so as to discuss a strategy for assisting Ted. He spoke softly. "His next-door neighbours but seven invited him to have a go on their trampoline but he found the jumping rather stressful and he hadn't done any warming-up exercises. He really wants to go up there but his knees could seize up. Could we all carry him, do you think?"

Various alternative tactics were mooted, including pulling him up backwards, and even placing him on one of the tea trays and lifting it one step at a time. However, the consensus reached was that supporting him manually was the most feasible method.

The brims of their hard hats were knocking each other as they conferred until Tom suddenly removed his and flung it to the ground, then kicked it against the wall. "Stupid hat," he said impatiently. "Yes, go on then. Don't suppose he weighs much."

"Goodness, is that rugby they're playing?" asked Felix as a hard hat bounced off the wall. "Prince Albert tried to explain the rules but Her Majesty thought it sounded unbecoming."

His comments hung in the air, augmented by the increasingly sonorous sounds emanating from above.

"If we each take one limb," suggested Greg, positively. "No, that won't work - someone would have nothing to carry."

Norman was now conferring with Ted and Joe in another huddle, with lots of nodding going on and clattering of hard hats.

"Next door neighbours but seven," said Tom, disparagingly. "There's no such thing! Who's ever heard of such people?"

"I've never heard anything like *this*," said Felix, his sense of delight increasing. "Even J. S. Bach never produced such a chord!"

"Hmmm, it is funky, isn't it?" agreed Tom. "Let's get hold of that Ted, then, and frog-march him to where that band's playing."

Greg stood on the first step as though to assure the

others that it was safe. "If we take it slowly and take turns to support his shoulders it shouldn't be too difficult. I read that we can thank the Ancient Egyptians for inventing stairs. Before that there were just slopes!" He hadn't read any such thing, nor did he know how many steps there might be, but at least the practical suggestions were honest. "And we might see some of their hieroglyphics soon. Apparently they were very keen on chronicling corn inventories."

"Chronic corn injuries." responded Joe. "I blame tight sandals."

"Of course, we'd really need that Rosetta stone to make sense of them!" added Greg as he took another tentative step.

"Well, *that's* not going to happen!" said Tom, slightly more upbeat. "You should have brought a phrase book! Anyway, who cares about corn - let's get to this concert!"

The whole group had by now assembled at the foot of the stairs. Ted winced as he bent his leg to mount the first step, then shook his head in defeat. Norman praised him for his "courage in adversity", whilst Joe commended his "college university", then positioned themselves either side of him and took hold of his arms. Tom nodded at Greg and the two of them grabbed hold of Ted's feet and counted to three before hoisting him unevenly, prompting his two loyal comrades to jerk his shoulders upwards so that he cleared the first step. At this point the chord ceased. Felix, who had adopted a more passive role in the procession and was merely holding his hands outstretched as though to catch the hapless little man if he should fall backwards, gasped disappointedly at the music's demise. He tried to sing what they had just heard, but he still couldn't imitate the sublime sound. Dejectedly, they continued the awkward ascent, swaying and stumbling as they carried their little friend up the relentless and irregular steps. The silence was broken only by their laborious and clumsy footwork, with an accompaniment of grunts and gasps. Progress was slow, and morale was low, but Greg remembered the trio's penchant for inspirational chanting, which he tried to restore.

"Climb the steps right to the top, Ted's the man we must not drop." He saw Tom stare at him, pityingly, but the rhythm of his lone voice had briefly improved their co-ordination. However, he felt too self-conscious to provide any more lyrics, although Felix was scribbling something down enthusiastically into a ragged notebook.

"Ted's....the....man....we....must....not....did you say *shop*?" he asked.

Greg didn't answer, as suddenly a new chord had begun to emanate from above with greater resonance and mellifluousness.

"It's a perfect fifth above the previous sound!" exclaimed Felix, excitedly. He tried humming it this time, but its pitch still eluded him. The others tried also, and yet it was impossible to hum, sing, or whistle. Norman peered up into the lofty half-light ahead of them, then suddenly urged them all to stand still. His warning hung in the air, as did Ted.

"I can just make out someone's head up there!" whispered Norman. "We might need to present our tickets."

The prospect of showing tickets to someone's head

135

whilst climbing through an ancient structure in quest of an unidentified chord seemed to hold little trepidation for the group. Greg thought that whoever was up there wasn't likely to be that concerned about entrance tickets, but the possibility of discovering a unique musical experience was of far greater relevance to them all.

"We might even find the source!" he exclaimed excitedly, causing Ted to knock his feet upon a slightly more awkward step.

"What is this obsession with sauce?" said Tom, bemused. "Let's just concentrate on getting to the arena."

Greg's mind was more intent upon the possibility of each of their lifelong quests being finally met in some esoteric academy of musical theory, rather than engaging with Tom. He turned round to speak to Felix, causing Ted's feet to scrape another step like a badly strung puppet.

"Sorry, I think I scuffed your toecap," said Greg as he compensated by raising the man's left foot into a contorted semi-kneeling posture.

"It's all right," came the plaintive response. "I suppose they'll fit this place with an escalator one day."

Tom muttered something about the sauce fanatics disappearing under the grating and discovering ketchup, whilst Greg nodded amiably and turned round to face Felix once again.

"Mr. Mendelssohn, what sort of chord is that? It's as though it contains all the twelve notes and yet...."

"Reminds me of when I used to go to Glasto," said Tom. "The sounds carried for miles there, I can tell you. So did the mud, come to that."

Greg hoped they wouldn't be carrying Ted for miles, but he really wanted to hear Felix's appraisal of the chord.

"Well, it's rather like all the notes forming absolute concord, but it doesn't happen on any instrument that I know!"

"I hated the mud, but the atmosphere was brilliant!" continued Tom. "And then I went to the bank...."

"You took the air on a mud bank?" enquired Felix. "What extraordinary traditions you have in your country."

Greg wanted to laugh, but Ted's two senior puppeteers were wheezing and moving ever slower.

"We could stop for a break soon," suggested Greg, but as a figure was standing awaiting them on what appeared to be the top of the stairs it seemed inevitable that a rest stop was due. "I think she's waving at us!" he added.

They paused to stare at their apparent hostess, while they caught their breath, although Felix actually waved back to her. Norman acted more discreetly, glancing furtively, then whispering to his two team-mates. "Yes, there's a lady up there watching us. Remember, you don't have to give her any information when we meet. It's women's role to ask questions, and man's to keep reticent."

"A masterly president," said Joe, content with whatever Norman might have said. "Right, got that, Norman."

"It's probably Rosetta whatsaname," said Tom. "Wants to translate some Cairo glyphics for us all!"

Greg smiled patiently. He wondered whether Tom might suggest finding a 'Cairo practor' for Ted, but instead he asked the unfortunate man if they had any gyms in Grimsby. "You could try and get yourself fit on a treadmill!" he added, causing Ted to turn pale.

The music died away again, and after a respectful silence a voice called from above. "Wonderful to see you all! Would you all like iced tea?"

A general exchange of looks between the men ensued as though seeking a united response.

"You don't have to swallow the ice cube," advised Norman, but Ted seemed nervous about such a hazardous cocktail.

"Yes, we're on our way up!" called Tom, jerking Ted and nudging his comrades in front to get moving.

"Very kind of you! We'll be there soon!" added Greg, assuming the role of assistant spokesman.

Norman murmured quietly to Ted once more. "Try not to walk like an ancient Egyptian once we reach the top. And if she offers to embalm you with natron, then just say 'no thank you'.

"No matron for us men," said Joe. "We hear you, Norman!"

They continued to trudge up the steps in expectant silence, when suddenly the music resumed - a chord of unimaginable sonority, causing even Tom to exclaim a loud appreciative "Wow!" before instantly apologising for the interruption.

Felix shook his head in a display of complete bafflement. "Truly, there are notes there that don't exist!"

CHAPTER 9

As they approached the top of the stairs it was apparent that the lady was young, probably British, and that she was now sitting behind a large desk. There was no sign of any antiquities within the chamber, but it had the appearance of a reception area, with potted palms and easy chairs arranged in a semi-circle in front of her desk. She beamed at them as they emerged from the stairs, grabbing hold of a rope that formed a balustrade as they stood tentatively surveying the large room.

"Do come in!" she said welcomingly as she pulled a large lever at the side of her desk, but this coincided with a far less sonorous sound, making her wince. It was the noise of something enormous slamming against rock, and it came from below.

"The authorities don't know we're up here so we have to be discreet," she explained. "We're actually squatters!"

"You must be Rosetta....Stow?" said Tom as he stood smiling at her.

She beamed at her guests collectively, but with an air of puzzlement as she observed Ted dangling between his two comrades.

"Well no, I'm Tamara Trotman, actually," she declared. "Please make yourselves at home. Refreshments are on the way, but if any of you wish to....make yourself comfortable first, it's over on the right!"

Norman and Joe made themselves comfortable by

lowering Ted on to the floor, then flexing their shoulders. Tamara giggled slightly as the three men looked about them, lost. "It's over there," she said softly, pointing towards one of two panelled doors.

Norman thanked her, and led his men off towards the door, but then he halted and turned round. "It says 'Gentlemen' on the door, but we're not *gentle* men, we're *wild* men!" he complained.

"We roar, and we're raw," added Ted, rather meekly, as he began running very gently on the spot.

"We're like lions, or wolves, or something," added Joe. "Oh, no sugar in mine, please, dear."

She suppressed a giggle, but then released an expression of surprise when she noticed that Tom had now perched himself upon one side of her large desk. He had also picked up and was ostensibly examining an alabaster bust of Boccherini.

"Hmm, Tamara. Nice name," he said, as he stroked the composer's pale face. "I suppose it translates as.... tomorrow?"

Greg winced at the man's clumsy flirting skills, but Tamara was more intent on assisting the wild men maintain their integrity.

"You'll have to excuse me," she said. "Those gentle....those *wild* men need some assistance. Take a seat - on one of the chairs!"

After Boccherini had been randomly placed on the desk, its slightly dejected handler walked casually towards one of the chairs and sat down. Meanwhile, Tamara had taken a clipboard and was listening with sympathetic nodding to the men's concerns.

"You see, we took oaths about not accepting being defined by women as 'gentlemen'", said Norman.

"We feel the gender classifications should be *gentlewomen* and *wildmen*!"

Although the indefinable chord from above was entertaining Tom as he sat alone on his chair, he heard enough of the conversation to turn towards Greg and Felix and raise his eyes, then shake his head in a gesture of gentle mockery. Greg, however, was listening to Felix explaining diminished sevenths, but he noticed that the wild men had now been tamed into entering the forbidden room.

"The refreshments should be here soon," said Tamara as she returned to her desk and repositioned Boccherini to his correct place. "We have a dumb waiter."

"Agency staff, is he?" asked Tom. "You have to take what you can find, I suppose."

Tamara looked confused this time, but as the music tailed off once more, a clattering, rumbling sound emanated from the wall behind her desk. "I'm so glad we found this place, and no rent to pay either!" she said jovially, before walking towards a small door at waist height.

"I wonder if I could ask one of you gentle...sorry, *men* to help me with...." but Tom was already by her side and clearly eager to volunteer. "The ropes," she continued. "Sometimes they get caught on the old stonework and we have to haul it up."

"No probs. I'm your man," said Tom. "Just show me the ropes!"

Her expression remained serene, but whatever she was asking him to do was now blanked out by the resumption of the music - in another remote key. This time there were two alternating chords, so powerful in

141

their harmony and lyricism that very soon Tom had lost interest in assisting Tamara, and had excused himself to return to his seat for some attentive listening. Felix was listening intently too, but he was also mouthing and gesturing to Greg that unfortunately he couldn't define the harmonics to which they surrendered their ears in awe.

"There's a diminished fourth in there somewhere," he shouted incredulously. "This is totally beyond me!"

Greg, on a whim, finally decided to proffer his confidential manuscript book to the composer for whatever useful information might be imparted; his thirst for understanding now overwhelming his judgment. He handed it to him willingly, but then his attention was distracted by a plate smashing to the floor just after a consignment of food and drink had been collected from the cupboard in the wall. He assumed Tom would be rushing to assist in its retrieval, but he was instead held in thrall to the pervading music. He turned to see whatever Felix might be writing down in the book, but it was lying open on a seat and the man had vanished. He assumed that the great man had rushed to the gents to wash his hands first, but the three older men were only just emerging from the door. He reluctantly concluded that, yet again, the book had posted whoever had held it to some unknown region or time.

"Sorry about the noise!" said Tamara as she returned to her desk with a tray of tea and snacks. She smiled at Greg, who was now sitting down, but then she noticed the open book that he carefully picked up from the chair. Their eyes met, and the music ceased. Tom asked her if he could help her in some way, and she duly gestured towards the broken plate. "If you wouldn't mind," she said softly, but she was still focussed upon Greg, who was now putting the book away in his pocket.

"Hmm, that smells like tabouleh!" said Greg as he sniffed the air, but he also had something sad to announce. "I think we might be one missing."

She came and sat next to him. Tom watched them from behind the desk and cleared his throat exaggeratedly.

"I presume that book is what brought you all here?" she whispered to Greg.

"Well, some of us," he replied, slightly relieved that it made sense to her. "But I understand that the three older men made it out here by means of a biscuit. A custard cream, apparently."

She nodded, and smiled, vacantly looking across to Tom's head peeping over the top of her desk. "It was the right time for you all to come here," she said after a pause. "We get round to everyone who's on the quest eventually."

"We?" said Greg, just as another chord began to play and permeate the place with inexplicable and yet sublime tonality.

"I'm the liaison officer for the Hidden Harbingers of H", she announced. "I'll explain things after we've eaten. Ah, here come your other three friends. Do you think they could eat falafels?"

"They might," he replied, wondering what 'H' might mean. Hydrogen? Was there a covert group of gas importers within the pyramid disguising their activities with surround sound? He looked across at

Tom, still on his knees and peeping above the desk. He too appeared to be baffled by what he'd heard.

"She's going to tell us all about it soon," said Greg, straining his voice to the level of a tactful whisper.

Tamara was now ladling out food on a table within an ante-chamber. Meanwhile the three men were fussing over which chairs to sit on and grumbling about the hot tap having been painfully stiff to turn.

"The paper towels were rough too," added Ted dolefully. "Someone must have starched them."

"They're probably made of papyrus!" said Norman, confidently.

"A virus?" said Joe, surprised. "Well, well. Just as well we washed our hands first!"

They took their seats in the same row as Greg, nodding politely to him as they sat down. "That thing about coming to meet Thoth," said Norman, leaning over towards him across Ted, who dutifully leaned in the same direction to make adequate room for his leader. "I think it was the effects of the hallucinatory tea we drank. "We were....*smashed* - I think that's what they call it."

Greg did some polite nodding, too, and hoped that the smashed plate hadn't been high on enhanced tea. "Sorry but I think we might all have been brought here to learn about exporting hydrogen," he explained. "But Felix has had to leave early. At least they've laid food on - we're having falafels!"

"Having a raffle?" enquired Joe, enthusiastically.

"Hydrogen! Lighter than air, that stuff!" said Norman, authoritatively.

"Perhaps Felix was worried about drinking that

iced tea," observed Ted, dismally.

"Yes," said Greg to all three men. Accuracy wasn't important at this stage, but anticipation was probably a suitable starter.

Tom had finished his sweeping up and was taking his seat next to Greg. "That statue's staring at me," he said. "It's probably jealous. I know I'd be!" He nudged Greg, and grinned knowingly.

Greg adopted an expression halfway between Tom's grin and Boccherini's inscrutability, and threw in a nod. "Unfortunately I seem to have caused Felix to...."

"So what did she mean about hidden hot pictures of H?" Tom interrupted. "It all sounds a bit...."

This time it was Tom who was interrupted as a mighty but mellifluous melody began to waft down from above, instantly quelling its listeners into rapt attention. Tamara appeared too, with a trolley. Did she control these fanfares, wondered Greg? She certainly seemed to be in control as she stood distributing large plates of falafels and cous cous to her quintet of guests. Greg would have preferred to eat from a bowl, reasoning that as food requires volume, then it should be served in three dimensional containers. However, plates had long since won hearts and minds, and forks now held sway over spoons. As for liquid refreshments; tall glasses with handles containing iced tea stood clustered around Boccherini. These at least were preferable to the paper cups served at work - blisteringly hot to hold when full of tea, and with no protective handles. Although last Thursday he'd waited forty minutes during a focus meeting on audio-ambience before risking a tentative sip from some new insulated polystyrene mugs. Perhaps Mrs. Anstruther might be persuaded to serve *tepid* tea on request?

"Black or green?" said a soothing voice in his ear, as he sat holding his plate. Tamara was hovering in front of him holding a long narrow dish of mixed olives. "Freddie Mercury always went for the pimentos when he visited, but Jim Morrison's weakness was anchovies. We hadn't moved into the pyramid then, of course."

"Of course!" agreed Tom, eager to acquiesce in all her pronouncements.

Greg helped himself to both varieties of olive, before she served the others equally attentively, and Tom fleetingly.

"We had a music room near the top of the Eiffel Tower for several years but the locals objected to the drone," she added.

"He should have told them to stop whingeing," said Tom, supportively.

"What did she say happened?" whispered Ted to Norman as the latter acted as chief taster before nodding to pronounce the food safe.

"They complained to the drone," replied Norman equally discreetly, before casting his eyes around the large chamber. "Look at the workmanship in that lintel," he added, pointing to a doorway half-hidden behind a potted palm. "And no subsidence, either!"

"No subsidies?" queried Joe. "Perhaps they've got a collection box for contributions."

"It's very kind of that lady to entertain us like this," said Ted, dolefully. "Is it because of our uniform?"

Norman made a cursory inspection of the motley garb that he and his allies wore, then at Greg and Tom in casual conventional clothes, and shook his head. "It's the hospitality of someone well brought up. Like the waitress in that café in King's Lynn."

"Aye," said Joe, his fork busily attacking an olive. "She might have been the Princess of Lynn on Work Experience."

Norman hardly noticed Joe's latest misunderstanding, but the man was consistently happy within his own dodgy interpretations. Greg cast his eyes around the room too. The lintel did indeed look built to last, but he was puzzled at how light the place was with neither window nor artificial light. Could daylight be emanating, as well as the bursts of music, from the open doorway beyond which a flight of more steps was just about visible?

"Shall I wash up?" asked Tom, eyeing the men's almost empty plates as though keen to snatch them if Tamara were to answer 'yes'.

"That's not why you're here," she replied, benignly surveying her small audience. "You've come here to achieve your ambitions!"

A sudden tremendous chord on an unidentifiable instrument permeated the room, causing Ted's fingers to tremble in sympathy.

"Well, well!" she said, clapping her hands once in honour of the deep sound. "It's really coming through loud and clear today. Would you all like to go on up soon?"

A general consensus of nodding and conferring ensued, whilst she assumed a more formal position of sitting *at*, rather than on her desk. She appeared to be

147

making a cursory headcount, followed by placing her arms on the desk in front of her in a kind of 'Well, let's get started' mode. Greg wondered if she was ready to field questions from her small audience and Norman thought that this would be an opportunity to ask her about care of pot plants - judging by the way he raised one hand, and with the other pointed to the large palm adjacent to her desk. However, it was Tom who asked the first question.

"When did you first become interested in chilling-out music?" he asked, clasping and raising the calf of his left leg.

Greg had often observed that people attending meetings etc. were more curious about the presenter, than in the subject itself, but Tamara was aware of Tom's fascination with her and so she merely smiled at her fan graciously and wrote something down on a pad.

"One doesn't become *interested* in any particular musical genre!" she declared forcefully after a moment's reflection on what was obviously a crass suggestion. "One is *subsumed*!"

A deep throaty and pulsating chord had now replaced the previous higher and more ethereal notes, prompting her to proceed with the preliminaries. "So, everyone," she continued confidently, "would you all like to tell me your names first, and something about your latent musical urges?"

Norman conferred with his men and then cleared his throat. "I'm Norman Nacton. Do you mean when we were young?" he asked, diffidently.

"Young, old, you've obviously still got a gestating opus in you, or you wouldn't be here!" she assured him. "Art such as this *drives* you, and can sometimes ignore temporal and spatial laws to bring you to the source when you need it!"

After a stunned silence Tom clutched his other leg for a quick lift. "My name's Tom and I've got a….. chest dating opus in me," he said, hesitantly. "Can you tell us about this source, and how we got here? I can only remember feeling seasick."

"Ah yes," said Tamara, putting down her pen. "I take it you all had varying journeys; perhaps some minor detours?"

"We had some very strong tea, then arrived on what we thought was a beach at first, near a palm tree!" said Norman. "This young man then brought us to the pyramid. We'd already met him at a farmhouse, so we knew we were in safe hands!"

She looked at Greg, her expression anticipating his contribution.

"I'm Greg. I got side-tracked too, via Mablethorpe, and then I met...."

He wondered if he should mention meeting Haydn and Jimi Hendrix, but realised he'd feel awkward about name-dropping, and even more so about mentioning the time paradox. However, Ted had raised his hand, and caught her eye. (Greg winced, but he knew this accident was usually just a figure of speech.)

"My name's Ted, but I was christened Teddington. I'm wild as a....wild as a....cherry," he said nervously.

"Wolf!" corrected Norman.

"A wolf, yes, and I came with these two. We're a band of brothers. We....howl."

She surveyed the group in front of her, nodding all

149

the while, before concentrating once more on Greg.

"Mablethorpe, you say? Hmmm. That rings a bell," she said, before gazing across the room, deep in thought.

She didn't elaborate, but Greg noticed a thick rope gently swaying not far from the dumb waiter. Was she inviting him to pull it and summon a more vociferous waiter, one who might ask him if he'd enjoyed his falafels?

She clasped her hands and addressed her listeners. "We have lots of cases of people diversifying on the way here," she added. "You've probably all got clones of yourselves by now too, but don't worry: your other selves will merge with you again after you've been upstairs and met the Hidden Harbingers. It'll all make sense to you soon!"

Ted was trembling slightly. Tom looked lost. Norman patted Ted on the back with a 'well done'.

"We've all got cones?" said Joe. "Well, well!"

Greg would have preferred to know more about the issue of exponential cloning at key decision-making moments. So far he'd only met one other Greg, and that was in Tom's mother's house. He went by the name Hawthorn, and the two of them had got on quite well. As for the potentially awkward problems that could arise from cloning, Greg wondered whether talking to Tamara privately before going upstairs might be useful, or was there a Human Resources department within the pyramid where he could chat to an advisor? Meanwhile, Ted and Norman were speculating about the means of getting to the next floor, but the height of the room in which they now sat suggested that another long flight of stone steps was likely, and this was making Ted anxious. Joe was currently sharing his absurdist and carefree observations with Tom, who agreed with him about the statuette on Tamara's desk looking pale. "That's how I looked when I agreed to forgo my summer holiday last year due to staff shortages," said Tom, wryly.

"That's no good," said Joe. "You should have come with us to Cleethorpes. We paddled, made a fire on the beach from driftwood, and Ted got a splinter in his finger!"

"Sounds like fun," said Tom, wistfully. "Although I'm more into golf myself - when I get invited to play, that is - but I'm usually whacked after nine holes."

"Oh dear, oh dear," said Joe, supportively. "So much violence in the game these days. At least that shrunken head on the desk seemed to be keeping his cool!"

Tamara appeared to be slightly puzzled at this minor discourse, but then she seemed to have remembered something, and pursed her lips whilst looking around the room. "We're still one short, aren't we?" she said, resting her eyes on Greg as though he would be sure to know. "That young man with the German accent - he looked like a natural! Is he still missing?"

The latest musical offering tailed off, and was replaced by the sound of footsteps clattering on stone steps.

"I think he had to leave early," said Greg, making sure his manuscript book was well out of sight and regretting having let the great man touch it. "Actually I believe his name was Felix……"

"Ah!" said Tamara as the first of several rather spaced-out looking people of varying ages and nationalities entered the room from the upper staircase. "Sounds like it was coming through nicely! I suppose that means Dubai's on the blink again."

"We can't get anything in New Zealand either," said a lady who sounded as though she would know. "The southern hemisphere's always badly served, but this location is marvellous, isn't it! I wish I'd known about your organisation before!"

"I'm going shtraight home to tell my fellow shtudents about this place," enthused one young man in a tee shirt depicting Beethoven in manic creating mode. "No more shtruggling at complicated chord progressions for me now!"

Others were too overwhelmed with recent events up above to say anything, and merely beamed and whispered: "Good luck!" as they hurried towards the exit that would take them downstairs and presumably back home to apply whatever they had learned.

Greg often wondered why an initial letter S was slurred in some people's speech, although this mutation usually only occurred when followed by a T. Ironically, he'd heard colleagues praising the superb clarity of the treble in their shtereos! Were all these extra - or eckshtra - aitches being added by those who had already been upstairs and grasped the meaning and phonetic usage of H?

"Thank you and keep in touch!" called Tamara as she pulled the lever that opened the exit for the departing group. She then ushered Greg, Tom, and the band of brothers towards the sun-dappled flight of steps leading upwards. "Right. It's your turn!"

Tom seemed most keen to go on up, although it was obvious that he'd have liked Tamara to accompany him. However, he began to confide in Joe about his teenage attempts at writing theme music for his Double O gauge railway as they quickly walked towards the doorway to the stairs. "Not in a nerdy way," he assured him. "Just a fanfare for my express when I sent it round the track. It was in the attic and I wouldn't let anyone in there, so the family probably thought I was growing marijuana."

"Going to marry Lana?" said Joe as he joined him in climbing the stairs. "Well, well! You'd have to call it off with Tamara then!"

Tom stared at him briefly, then laughed in an ironic tone.

Ted was also staring, but apprehensively, up what appeared to be an infinity of steps. Norman stood by his side and muttered: "Three hundred at least, I'd say. What do you say, Teddington?"

Ted didn't actually say anything, but pointed to his knees and shook his head.

"Wear and tear, little Tedders," said Norman. "You'll have to rest them when we get back home. Focus on your elbows instead."

Tamara walked over to them to lend some slightly more practical advice. Conscious of the height disparity between Ted and herself, she knelt down in front of him and looked firmly into his eyes. His own eyes glanced at Norman for reassurance, but Norman trembled when an ascending perfect fifth from above began to permeate the walls with sound and, curiously, light.

"Don't be afraid," she urged them. "All you have

153

to do when you're up there is listen. It'll all make sense!"

Norman crouched down to the level of the heads, too. "It's not nerves," he insisted. "It's his knees. They're lockable."

Ted nodded. "It's true. I'm best on flat surfaces really," he confirmed despondently.

Greg then entered the community of lowered heads, and addressed Tamara. "They're right, but I'm sure we can support Ted up the steps, unless you have some form of disabled access?"

"Well, there's that thing over there," she said, pointing to the dumb waiter. "But it's very efficient!"

They all stared at the vacant fitted cupboard, waiting for its next load like some miniature taxi hoping for a fare. Tom and Joe had charged ahead up the steps and were gazing down at the huddled group, one frowning quizzically, the other grinning encouragingly.

"You're nearly there!" they called out in unison, although in contrasting tones on the patience scale.

The rising tones on the scale of A major failed to motivate any advance, but Norman agreed it was a feasible means of transport, and so he began to lead a reluctant Ted towards the hole in the wall.

"Have you conveyed people this way before?" asked Greg as he walked over to examine the thickness of the ropes. "One of our more wayward junior staff hitched a lift with a consignment of music for dulcimers in one of these, but the strain on the gantry produced a horrible screech!"

"You can brave any horrible screeches, can't you?" said Norman as he clasped his hands to make a

154

foothold for his hapless comrade to climb into the cupboard. "You might want to hold on to the rope. He *can* hold on to the rope, can't he?"

"Of course," said Tamara. "We encourage visitors to feel at home."

Ted bravely forsook the proffered handhold and instead clambered awkwardly in to the cupboard. He said nothing, but gasped a lot as he manoeuvred himself into a foetal position, before glancing painfully at the assembled company watching him as he settled himself next to an empty tureen.

"It won't take him long to get there, will it?" asked Norman.

"Not if I turn the wheel fast enough," said Tamara, pointing to what resembled a steering wheel on the wall nearby. She shook Ted's hand, or attempted to, even though he had his fingers splayed firmly down on the base of his conveyance to support himself. "Just sit there and enjoy the ride, then wait for your friends when you get to the top," she advised him.

"He won't plunge down the shaft, will he?" asked Greg, concerned. "He probably doesn't have any holiday insurance."

She laughed and shook her head. "Don't worry. It's music that has drawn you here - not gravity!"

"Is there a problem down there?" called Tom, his voice reverberating down the stone staircase and providing a dissonance to the angelic sonority now emanating from above.

Greg acted as messenger and hurried towards the foot of the steps to reassure him, attempting to do so by making a thumbs up sign, and a series of gestures designed to indicate a hunched figure holding on to a rope. Both Tom and Joe looked puzzled, to say the least. He then returned to the 'lift' where Tamara was busy turning the wheel just as Ted disappeared from view.

The feebly enunciated words: "Do I have to pay when I get out?" could just about be heard as he rose, at which point Norman nudged Greg and pointed to the stairs.

"We'd best go up now. He'll cope," said Norman. "He's got the constitution of a fox!"

"Wolf!" Greg corrected him.

Tamara wished them well, pausing momentarily for a rest, then waved them off as they went towards the stairs. "Don't be surprised who you meet up there!" she called out.

CHAPTER 10

The two men thanked her, waved goodbye, and began the climb. Greg was now prepared to meet anyone - students, teachers, transient composers - and whoever had been practising on unidentified instruments was obviously getting very good training. He was also was aware that Norman was counting the steps under his breath as they began their ascent. This ruled out the possibility of any conversation between them, but as the theme from above became a soaring sequence of augmented sevenths - one of Greg's favourite intervals - he relaxed into a state of eager anticipation. Neither of them was finding the climb tough-going, and the fact that Norman's voice was audible proved that he was taking the steps with ease. Greg still couldn't get his head round the series of seemingly haphazard events that had brought them all here, but he felt a personal responsibility for mislaying Mendelssohn. At least he'd acquitted himself on the boat by accidentally writing the overture for him, and he'd somehow brought Norman and his little platoon to an interesting ancient monument.

Tom also was having a break from his onerous job at the bank, and it seemed very likely that the entire group's long-standing and, in most cases dormant, musical ambitions were about to be fulfilled. Greg paused to survey the view ahead of them just as Norman noted the hundredth step with that classic higher intonation reserved for significant numbers. He peered into the cavernous chamber at the top, and at the stone lintel of what was possibly an archway beyond, but then he realised that what he'd previously taken to be sunlight was actually a diffusion of shimmering colours emanating from the mysterious musical workshop. The two men were now approaching an aurora of synaesthesic splendour. Greg tapped Norman's arm and pointed to the display, hoping his companion wouldn't mind the distraction from his inventory of the steps.

"You don't see that every day," said Norman, somewhere between egregiousness and curiosity. "Prisms, that's what's doing it."

Greg hoped that Joe at least had found wonder and enjoyment at the phenomenon and that Tom would find it cool. Ted would probably have arrived at the top by now too, depending on the stamina of Tamara's wheel-turning arm, and would, hopefully, not be too distressed at being released from his dark cupboard into the *son et lumière.*

They plodded on upwards, both sets of eyes almost permanently trained on the top. Norman's vocalised step-tally had tailed off at about 170, but as he was now striding up two at a time, and a rhythm in 3 / 4 time was permeating the space through which the men progressed, together with swathes of mauve and green in the air around them, the steps had become progressively easier. Greg expected to see familiar faces peering back at them, but then it occurred to him that the dumb waiter shaft would be some distance back from where the steps finished. Presumably, Joe and Ted would be waiting there for them in patient acceptance, whilst Tom searched for empty plates to send down to Tamara to show her he cared.

There was a subtle change in the echo of their footsteps as they finally reached the top, which was devoid of either pot plants or people, but the hugely impressive double doors that towered in front of them across the floor commanded Greg's attention. The music was at its most powerful in this spot too. A long passageway ran in the direction of the presumed access point for Ted's special delivery, but the temptation to open the doors was proving too much for Greg. "He might already be through there, with the others!" he said, justifying his intentions.

"They can catch us up," said Norman, the relaxed patrol leader. "Let's see what all this is about!"

Greg looked at him to gauge his consent. It was an expression of curiosity and excitement this time. Together they walked across to the imposing doors. There was no point in knocking - the currently-playing arpeggios and glissandos would prevent him from being heard, and he might miss the beat. He decided to grab the large brass, or perhaps they were gold, doorknobs and pull. The doors were stiff, but they yielded before flying open to reveal a square windowless room, bathed in light that flooded in from a hole at the apex of the pyramidal roof. Situated alongside each sloping wall were rows of tables with people sitting either side, animatedly talking and full of humour. It was like Simon Spottiswoode's description of his recent visit to a speed dating event in Dundee, except that none of the participants here looked earnest. Curiously, Greg and Norman were less aware of the music now, but they were aware of a young man walking purposefully towards them as they stood deferentially in the great doorway.

"Do you think he wants to see our tickets?" said Norman in the same hushed tones he used to count steps.

"I don't think so," replied Greg, eyes wide-open with amazement. Tamara had told him not to be surprised, but she'd said nothing about being amazed. "Norman, this is Meston - from the farm!!"

As Meston approached them it was obvious from his animated expression that he recognised at least one of the two visitors. Greg was delighted at this imminent reunion, and relieved to think that time was still on their side, with no awkward disparity of their respective calendars.

"Greg!" said Meston, reassuringly, stretching out his hand to shake that of his peripatetic pal. "Sorry, I must have missed you outside the Old Bailey. You didn't hurt yourself when you came down, did you?"

"Er, no, thankfully," replied Greg, glad that even though events were still unpredictable, he'd apparently not been injured. "I must have landed on my good side! Perhaps the streets of London really are paved with...."

"He bungee jumped all the way down from the roof!" explained Meston proudly, addressing Norman. "That's dedication!"

"He's made of strong stuff," said Norman, proffering his hand. "Like me and my little band. I'm Norman, by the way. You've not seen my two rugged companions, have you? A short serious one in a yellow balaclava and a tall jolly one without?"

Greg had almost forgotten about his other travelling companions and was now busily taking in the scene around him. Dozens of men and women,

160

mostly in pairs, were seated at the tables and were engaging with their tablemates in intense conversation. Music was still very much in evidence, and yet it was as though its audibility was being experienced within, rather than heard externally. The swirling colours were also unobtrusive, and Greg felt that at last his ambition to be 'in the music' rather than passively observing it was being achieved. Unfortunately, there was no sign as yet of either Norman's comrades nor of Tom, but what had brought Meston here, and what had been going on at the Old Bailey? Had Hawthorn or another of the Greg entities been staging a roof-top protest in the company of the Statue of Justice?

"Sorry, I don't think I've seen them," replied Meston after a brief appraisal of the occupants of the room. "And they say that lady on the roof wears a blindfold, so she can't have seen them either, although she must know her scales by now!"

Norman excused himself to conduct his own search, but conscious of being in a room full of such positive and enraptured people he tried to avoid betraying his concerns. He thus adopted a stiff upper lip, whilst only the lower one quivered slightly. Greg had no worries about the absent friends, and trusted that in such a benign setting all would be well. He concentrated on Meston with an expression of receptive innocence, eager to learn all he could.

"So, fancy seeing you here!" he began, casually. "Have you taken a holiday job? It seems quite a lively...."

"Sorry to interrupt, but you see that man in the far corner drawing those crotchets on the blackboard?"

said Meston, pointing towards a professorial figure surrounded by a group of adoring fans. "He's been a conduit for H since he was 37! The scales have truly been lifted from *his* eyes!"

"Would you like to come and take a seat?" asked a jolly middle-aged lady, rising from hers behind a table, and smiling at Greg. "I can see you've been waiting years for this!"

"We must talk later on," said Greg, before moving towards the welcoming lady. "Oh, and about the Old Bailey! Sorry you had to miss out on the goulash!"

"I'll watch out for you," replied Meston, looking slightly bemused. "Sorry, I'm just going to have a word with Ev and Sylv over by the bookstall. They get chords every morning from Coleridge Taylor!"

Greg didn't quite know how to respond to that last statement, but the lady about to greet him was already nodding sagely.

"That's quite true!" she said as she gestured to him to sit down. "This is where it all floods in - and the feedback! A devotee of Albert Einstein has been writing some quite good solo parts for violin recently, apparently, although it's all too profound for me."

A chorus of excitement erupted across the room as a blast of jazz-infused counterpoint swept in almost tangibly from a vent in the roof. This was followed by 'wows!' a 'yes!', and other appreciative mutterings from the 'staff' seated at the tables.

"It's all based on H, but you probably know that, don't you?" said Greg's advisor as she leaned across the table to gain his attention from the current commotion. Then she laughed. "We call this place our HQ!"

"I thought it might be," said Greg in a tone of questing humility. As the general excitement subsided he noticed an enamel badge clipped to her blouse bearing the name Barbara. Had Tamara worn a badge? Was it a safeguard against being cloned?

"Would a baton help?" she asked, as though misreading his thoughts.

"Er, well, I suppose it might...."

"There's a new branch opening in Milton Keynes this summer!" advised a man in dispatch rider boots, leaning across from the next table while Barbara hunted for the baton. "You could go there for refresher courses when you've got the hang of it."

"Er well, I suppose I might," said Greg, wondering what he was meant to do with the baton when it materialised. Was he being given permission to conduct further bursts of music that might enter the room? The late Otto Klemperer had guided his players merely by the charisma emanating from his hands but where did Greg himself stand on the fingertip / baton debate? And where might his other companions be standing right now? Would there be good transport links to Milton Keynes other than the service provided by his over-zealous manuscript book?

"There you are!" said Barbara, as she proudly presented him with an ultra-slim baton. "Now, let me explain what we're all doing here."

He received the baton gracefully and tried it out with a few inexperienced waves. She smiled, then drummed a rhythm on the table which Greg recognised as Ravel's Bolero. He thus conducted her knuckles until tedium set in, hoping that she too would soon tire, and that she would then impart some knowledge. However, she appeared to be quite willing to continue for the full unremitting fifteen minutes of the work's duration.

"Yes, it works well!" he said eventually, before bowing slightly. "So, what it is that you do here?"

She gazed up at the ceiling and pointed to the hatch through which blue sky could be seen.

"That's our collection point," she said, proudly. "We call it our serving hatch!"

Greg concentrated on the aperture and wondered if meals were served aerially, this floor being beyond the scope of the dumb waiter. Did H stand for hatch? "What do you collect?" he asked.

She laughed and shook her head as though it was a silly question. "Raw music, of course! Currently at a rate of eighty gigavibes a second!"

Greg slumped back in his seat. This was neither music workshop nor convention. This was where composers came to tap into the source. This was wonderful, but could it really be true?

A man in his thirties with a ponytail, and wearing a tee shirt depicting an elm tree was working his way round the room with a triangle. He stood and hovered behind each visitor in turn, serenading them; not to encourage romance, but to chivvy them into moving on to the next table. Several times this activity evoked light-hearted banter between him and the visitors, whilst the advisors would relax with a valedictory smile and enter details in a ledger. Greg wondered where the person at the last of the series of tables would go. He turned round to take a brief glance, and saw that a tall figure full of gratitude had taken his leave of a panel of

164

three, all beaming at him, and was joining a queue facing a diminutive lady wearing a peaked cap. Presumably these were bound for some kind of guided tour, although a study of the history or fabric of the pyramid itself was probably not on the agenda: this tour party would no doubt be initiated into the essence of H! Greg's advisor reclined in her chair and beamed encouragingly as the minstrel then took his place and played his instrument at Greg's right ear.

"You play well!" said Greg, trying not to sound facetious, but the man merely grinned and shuffled round, invading Greg's personal space.

Barbara then leaned across to him, giving him even less space. "I really feel I belong here," she whispered intensely. "My partner works in a shoe shop in Johannesburg, but life is what you make it, I suppose." She leaned back as though declaring the interview over, and with her arms folded, focused her attention on the ceiling. Greg agreed that life certainly could be what you made it. He knew of at least one person whose life had improved since going in for wide fittings.

He thanked her and stood up, prompting the strolling player to go and weave his magic on the man at the neighbouring table so that he might move also. This took a few seconds, but Greg promptly moved across to the now vacated chair, where his next host, a bearded figure in a tweed jacket, was already holding out his arm as he gazed penetratingly into the newcomer's eyes. Greg grabbed hold of the man's hand before he'd even sat down, but this was not to be a welcoming handshake - this was a meeting of radial artery and perceptive fingers as the examiner stared into space. Greg slid deftly into his seat, anxious to

165

avoid affecting the reading, or even accelerating his pulse. Thus they sat for half a minute of silence.

A man with a loud voice at another interview was responding to questions about the imitation patterns of curlews. "They evoke a world of marshes and estuaries for me," he proclaimed.

Greg nodded slightly in agreement, but then checked himself as he continued to surrender his wrist. "You're allegretto, my friend," said the examiner at last in a tone that betrayed neither alarm nor satisfaction.

"Show me your tongue and say C," he instructed as he ticked a box with a flourish.

Greg tried hard to accommodate both requests, and wondered if everyone else had passed this test.

"Don't worry, it's not important if you can't," the man assured him. "What matters is that you're in sound health, and I mean sound." He stared at Greg as though awaiting a reply. Greg looked up at the ceiling as though it might materialise up there. A man further along was imitating a cuckoo. Greg looked down and across at his interrogator's stare. He nodded, almost apologetically.

"Poor Beethoven had problems in that area," said the man as he shone a torch into Greg's left ear.

Two people sitting together for a joint interview repeated the name Beethoven and promptly knelt down, bowing their heads. Greg offered his right ear for inspection but apparently 'nurse' would examine that one later.

"Do you suffer from tremors, tinnitus, tunnel vision, tachycardia, or Towb's Syndrome?" asked his interrogator, gazing into his eyes.

"Towb's Syndrome?" queried Greg.

166

"Really!" replied the man, as he made a brief note. "You're the first one this year, then!"

"No, I…."

"Thank you. I can spell syndrome! Tell me - what do we find as the dominant of G#, the note of notes, the key of keys, the progenitor of the other seven?"

He moved to one side to reveal a Snellen chart hanging on the wall behind him. He covered Greg's left eye with his hand and asked him to read the massive top letter with his right.

"H!" said Greg.

"And now?" he asked, covering the right eye.

"Well, it's just your hand."

"Excellent again. You are receptive, healthy, and honest. Well done!"

Illustrated cards were then dealt and placed on the table between them. They were almost all of various musical instruments. Greg sat patiently and studied the dealer's concentrated expression.

"Now, which is the odd one out?" asked the man, satisfied the array was complete.

Greg leaned forwards to examine them carefully, although he'd already spotted that two of the cards were of an anvil and an empty milk bottle. He took his time choosing, in deference to the time taken to place them all before him so elegantly, but then he became aware of a minor disturbance taking place near the grand entrance. He turned round to get a better view, trusting that diverting his attention from the task in hand wasn't proof of Towb's Syndrome, but the scene he observed was of little Ted being helped up from the floor by Norman and Joe. Tom stood close by, looking rather passive, and yet keen for the incident to be over.

167

"He'll be fine," declared Norman to several anxious onlookers as Ted was pulled to his feet and adjusted his balaclava. "He does this sort of thing!"

Greg gave them a cursory wave, but only Tom noticed, before coming over to speak to him.

"How's it going, then?" he asked. "I only just got here. The others went a bit hyper and insisted on break-dancing all the way here from that dumb waiter thing! Are you having a tarot reading or something?"

The man adopted a stern gaze which he directed at the intruder. "He's being examined," he snapped. "Your time will come."

Greg smiled and pointed to the first table that was still free. Barbara gestured to him to sit down.

"So, have we found the odd one out yet?" asked the man, glancing briefly at Tom as he noisily shuffled his chair into its optimal place.

Greg looked again at the cards. He couldn't decide between the anvil or the bottle, although he'd had slightly more experience with the latter.

"Interesting that you saw them *all* as relevant," said his advisor. "A theme, a rhythm, or a note might emanate from anything, or anywhere!" he stated forcefully. "Imagine you're in captivity with just a radiator pipe on which to tap out a hymn of freedom."

"I think I might make arpeggios on any bars in my cell," suggested Greg.

"Quite. Remember that notes are all around us. Bars, jugs, motors, wolves, pipes, springs, kettles, saws, etc., etc. The list is endless!"

Two men nearby repeated the word 'list' and sank to their knees. Greg suspected they'd found a Z on their Snellen chart, and had recognised the progenitor of

168

keyboard mastery.

"Excellent yet again. You are sensitive, healthy, and a good communicator," said his examiner. "Who are you, though? Just for the record?"

"I'm Greg Ives," said Greg as though it was of no consequence.

"Indeed!" replied the man, thoughtfully, before entering a squiggle on a separate form. "Ives, you say. You didn't have an *unanswered question*, did you?"

"No, but I have!" said a young man passing by, carrying a jug of water. "Was that the work written by *Charles* Ives, 1874 to 1954?"

Greg answered the man with a nod, but he still had some unanswered questions of his own. He was delighted at his apparent progress, but curious about the assembly line method of imparting musical theory. Two interviews had now passed, and yet even though he was still in the dark about H, he was intrigued at the notion of it being the musical equivalent of light and its constituent primary colours.

"Isn't H what the Germans call B?" he asked cautiously.

The interviewer looked surprised for a moment and then smiled. "Indeed they do." He appeared willing to say more, but the triangularist had returned and was aurally nudging Greg with whatever single note it was that he played with such dedication and gusto.

"Well, goodbye then, Greg Ives," said the examiner with a brief handshake before gazing up at the ceiling. "Be open at all times!"

Greg glanced at Tom, now listening patiently to Barbara as she recounted a brief period in her life when she had specialised in retailing espadrilles. "The opening hours were too long," she complained. "I even longed for muzak!"

"Next please!" piped up a boy of about twelve years old from the Indian sub-continent who was seated behind the adjacent table with his hands clasped on a mouse mat.

Greg brushed carefully past the triangle player and took his place opposite the boy and clasped his hands in a similar manner. They both smiled politely and then in unison looked up at the ceiling. Greg accepted that this was the customary thing to do.

"Hello. I would like to introduce you to quarter tones," said the boy enthusiastically, after a few seconds. "And did you know that in traditional Indian culture we have ragas for the different times of day?"

"So I've heard," said Greg, relaxing in his chair. "Are the quarter tones intended for the quarter hours?"

The boy looked at him blank, then burst out laughing, before looking up at the ceiling again. Greg smiled, and looked around him. Good humour and rapt attention seemed to be a major part of events within this open-plan relaxed consulting room, but he did notice that the staff's fascination with the ceiling was becoming rather intense. Were there structural problems? Should he and his friends have retained their hard hats?

"You have come here on one of our very powerful days!" said the boy as he doodled on a sheet of paper. "That indicates that you probably understand time very well, and so you already know that time is merely the interval between two beats."

"Perhaps. But what is space?" asked Greg. "I travelled through some of that today."

"Space is merely a notional series of notational rests upon a sheet of manuscript paper," the young sage replied reflectively. "But we have to transcend all that, and some of us will even diversify until we attain it!"

"I think I've probably been diversified myself, only today, but what is it that I or we attain?"

The boy laughed. "Beyond H is the ultimate key of I, but even I am not precocious enough to explain that to you. However, soon you will be imbued with H, but right now you must put on these headphones to enjoy quartertonality. It is most gratifying!"

Greg took the headphones and hoped the marshal with the triangle wouldn't be wishing to move him on yet. However, the man was both out of sight and out of earshot. Greg put on the headphones whilst the boy attempted to stand a pencil on its end. This diversion was soon achieved, and Greg observed that the pencil was graded as H. The boy then flipped it over, and for several seconds it stood balancing on its sharp point. Its owner grinned at Greg with satisfaction and said something, but the languid twangs of a sitar had begun, and Greg's mind was now wandering gently into the realms of an early evening raga.

In this relaxed state he heard a soothing voice. "Sorry, one of those men in battledress is waving to you." This was followed by a gentle tap on his shoulder, at which point he realised that the voice had probably not emanated from the dreamy idyll after all. He turned round slowly to see Meston standing obsequiously at his side.

"Their leader said to tell you that he's got postcards of Skegness if you want to send one home. It'll save buying any local ones."

Greg thanked him, and waved to all three men who were standing looking rather out of place near to a Death Metal stand. Meston then carefully raised one of the headphones away from Greg's ear and whispered into it.

"Sorry, but I thought I'd better let you know that there's been a warning issued. I've been asked to assist on account of my security job and my history of herding cows."

By the time Greg had taken in what had been said Meston had already hurried off somewhere else. Was there a severe sandstorm expected? The boy looked oblivious to the polite intrusion and was now balancing the tip of one pencil on the tip of another. He was also oblivious to any impending sandstorm. Greg trusted that there was no immediate danger, but he felt he should at least act responsibly.

"Thank you for that!" he said, handing the headphones back to the boy. "You'll probably want to pack them away in their box now in case of....unsettled weather!"

The boy stared at him, then laughed out loud, but his breath control was so expert that both pencils remained perfectly poised.

Greg's own poise was now slightly off balance due to the general sense of impending drama within the room. He wondered who, if anyone, was actually in charge. So far, the only person who appeared to wield any authority was the man with the triangle whose ringing in visitors' ears announced it was time for them to move on, as though he were some musical chairs marshal, but he had presumably moved on himself. There was a degree of scurrying going on, but Tom remained at the previous table, unaffected by events, although he did appear to be nodding in time to some inwardly-heard theme. Joe was still waiting to begin his tour of the mini-interviews, passing the time with a contented expression as he darned a hole in his left sleeve with some emergency cotton. Ted stood stiffly to attention next to him, biting his lip, whilst Norman completed the line-up, exhaling loudly upon his sunglasses and wiping vigorously with a soft cloth. The Indian boy, meanwhile, was contemplating his deft pencil alignment. Therefore, this end of the room was relatively calm, whilst in the vicinity of the hatch a crisis was developing.

"It's 1996 all over again!" shouted one of a group of assorted monks and punks staring up at the hatch, some of whom were brandishing long poles in an attempt to close the shutters.

Surely the whole of the room, and presumably the pyramid itself, hadn't suddenly undergone a temporal regression - pondered Greg. After all, Tamara had previously eased his mind somewhat by advising him that any lapses and leaps of time were merely a means of bringing people here. A mass lurch backwards would make no sense. It would also make it impossible for Norman and his cohorts to collect their foldable chairs and tea trays on their way out.

"1996 was sixteen years ago," said a tall man as he attempted lassoing the shutter's handle. "We hadn't learned how to control it then!"

Greg felt slightly relieved. The reference to the year had merely meant that a *particular aspect of history* was now repeating itself. Would warnings soon be issued about the approaching sandstorm? Meston was

173

suddenly back at his side accompanied by a rotund man wearing a white suit and a serious but kindly expression.

"Sorry, I've been asked by Sir Lammington Lyons himself to take you to his room immediately," said the man, breathlessly.

"Who? What sort of room?" asked Greg, slightly wary of the summons.

"You. It's about three metres square with a large bed, and one wall slopes, naturally. That goes without saying," said the man.

"Sorry, that's about ten foot by ten," added Meston. "I've not been in there myself, though."

Was Greg also expected to go without saying? The command sounded a bit odd, and especially in view of the present situation. Perhaps Meston could accompany him too - if Sir Lammington was bedridden then the two of them could perhaps gently frogmarch him to safety, or better still, wheel him somewhere.

"Er....I've had experience of pushing moderately-laden wheelchairs," said Greg. "I could propel him to safety with Meston as guide."

"Actually he just wants a private audience with you," insisted the man. "However, I should warn you that he's rather bland."

"I see," said Greg as he considered his options. "Will I be required to sit on his bed?"

"There are scatter cushions, but sadly his time is drawing to a close," said the white-suited one. "Some say he's 176 years old, although no-one has ever asked him his age. I think it's just his leathery skin. He was knighted in London by King Edward VII!"

"I could take you to his door, I suppose," said

Meston. "Sorry, but we need to knock very quietly if he's resting."

Greg looked about him at the others within the room who all seemed slightly lost and awaiting instructions. However, his friends all appeared to be calm, and the group of men endeavouring to close the hatch were now humming softly. He wondered whether he might be able to assist in a more positive way than having a chat with a bland man with leathery skin. Perhaps wielding his baton at the choir under the non-yielding vent might bring results?

"You will be helping mankind if you come now," pleaded the man. "Your friend can wait for you outside the room."

Greg thought that the possibility of assisting mankind by sitting on a scatter cushion chatting to an elderly knight sounded far-fetched, even for this place, but he nodded his agreement and submitted himself to this next stage in what he supposed to be part of his quest.

"They showed me where he resides when I got here," said Meston as he quickly escorted Greg along a passageway. "Sorry about having to leave so abruptly before when we went to visit Haydn, by the way. That *was* you who I gave a lift to, wasn't it?"

"Yes, that was me. Don't worry, we caught up later....well *earlier*, if you understand", said Greg, now aware of a small door facing them at the end of the passage.

"You mean at the Old Bailey? I knew *that* was you - although it was an amazing act of bravery to rescue that pigeon!"

Greg had no recollection of any pigeon rescue,

although he knew there were several of him about, and guessed that the bird must have been carrying an important message relevant to his purpose.

They stopped in front of the small door through which Greg was presumably required to crawl. He looked at Meston who produced a white glove from his pocket.

"It's for knocking with," explained Meston. "It reduces the noise."

CHAPTER 11

Meston knelt down and gently tapped on the woodwork. Greg knelt next to him and listened for a response, but what they heard was a loud bang from the room they had just left, followed by a rousing cheer. The hatch had presumably been battened down safely. Immediately after the extraneous and reassuring sounds a soft voice issued from behind the door. "Do come in!" it said.

"I'll wait for you here," said Meston, as he pushed open the door to reveal a darkened room. "You're very privileged!"

Greg accepted the assessment, and duly burrowed his way into the room as his eyes adjusted to the low wattage light bulbs that cast a warm glow on the colourfully adorned bed before him. Its inhabitant, a tiny wizened and yet serene figure, sat facing him propped up by a pillow. "Please, come in," he whispered. "Would you like some mineral water? I have a blend of still and sparkling!"

Greg was already in, but he shuffled further forward to accede to the invitation, and wondered whether standing, sitting, or generally shuffling was the right etiquette. He heard the slight click of the door as Meston closed it after him, and realised that the private audience had begun.

"Thank you, that would be lovely!" he said, as he adopted a cross-legged position on the previously recommended scatter cushion. The old man stretched his hand slowly towards a jug on a bedside table and poured some of its contents into a tiny cup for his guest. Greg was loath to break the silence, and so he accepted the cup with a nod and a look of exaggerated pleasure. Was he meant to sip it slowly, or savour the very presence of the still / sparkling combo and formulate some interesting observation for later on?

"Have you eaten?" enquired the man, at an almost inaudible volume. "There will be bread soon!"

"Thank you. That would be nice," replied Greg equally softly as though desperate not to alarm his soporific host. He waited for the next trickle of activity or words, but there was nothing. He imagined Meston's ears pressed sneakily against the tiny door to catch some snippet, but he felt more guilty himself for providing such lacklustre interaction. Perhaps the arrival of the bread would produce some conversational stimulus. The man gave a deep sigh and then closed his eyes. Was he bored? Was it his bedtime? Was this even the right room?

"So," said the man at last. "Here we are."

Greg nodded sagely, and accepted that he *had* been brought to the right place, and then a silly thought flashed through his mind - what would the 'outdoorsmen' do in a situation like this? Would they invite the bedridden old gentleman to join them in their adventures with foldable chairs and tea trays? And how would little Ted cope? Would he stir his cocktail of plain and fancy water with a smoothly contoured plastic teaspoon and watch nervously for any scorpions emerging from under the bed? He controlled an emerging giggle and concentrated on the elaborately knitted quilt with its many squares, but then his eyes rested on the large bulbous feet that supported the sturdy bed. The whole thing looked as solid as the stone blocks that formed the walls and yet, curiously, the headboard's dimensions appeared to be substantially greater than the aperture of the room's only door. It was the equivalent of a ship in a bottle.

"Your removal men must have been quite skilful when you arrived here!" said Greg boldly, after a minute's silence. "I trust you didn't sustain any scuffs to your veneer."

The old man suddenly became enlivened, his eyes now opening wide and beaming at his guest. "You have just confirmed to me why I asked for you," he said, in a slightly stronger voice than before. "You are to be my successor!" His announcement was followed by laughter, or rather a succession of pedestrian chuckles interspersed with the words: 'scuffs to my veneer!' in a falsetto range.

"I see," said Greg, celebrating this news by gulping down his water all in one go. "Er, in what would you like me to succeed?"

"In what would I like you to succeed?" responded the magnanimous master before succumbing to convulsions of happy hysteria, and a voice too elevated to continue coherently.

Greg hoped that room service might soon bring the expected modest feast, and that his host would remain still enough to enjoy it, but for the moment he thought it best to allow Sir Lammington - if indeed this was he, for no introductions had taken place - free rein for his mirth.

"I want you to succeed me as Harbinger-in-Chief!" said Sir Lammington at last, having regained some calm. "I have no hesitation in passing you the baton before I float away blissfully on a perfectly resolved final chord."

"That's very....kind of you," said Greg, unsure about how to decline such an honour tactfully, or alternatively, how to fulfil it. "Sorry, I've already been given a baton, but I'm sure yours works really well!"

The man shook his head gently, smiling and chuckling. "The world is in such a parlous state. Did you know I was once shot at for refusing to sanction partition in a small Berkshire village during a conflict between New Wave and Power Metal?"

"No, I had no idea," said Greg, shocked at such a scenario. "My nephew Raymond sings in the church choir in Abingdon, and apparently the deployment of guitars at Evensong led to only the briefest of boycotts. Anyway, were you unscathed?"

"My hair bore the brunt of the attack, but....ah, the food has arrived," said Sir Lammington leaning slightly forward and peering at the small door.

Greg turned round and stared at the door also, but it was almost another minute before a gentle tapping indicated that they had a visitor. The senior of the two issued a reedy invitation to enter, which Greg repeated at a more workable volume, and the door duly opened to allow a maternal lady in a long apron to crawl in bearing a plastic lunchbox. She smiled briefly, then continued on her knees to the bedside table where she carefully placed the item next to the water jug. "It's getting serious out there!" she said, before turning round and shuffling out again.

"Sunspots, Mrs. Rosenbaum!" said Sir Lammington, as though their statements made sense to each other. "And thank you so much for the wonderful meal!"

180

Greg courteously closed the door behind her, perhaps a bit too speedily, judging from the slight whimper from the other side. However, her apron had appeared to be shock-proof, and was probably resistant to sunspots and gunfire too.

"Perhaps you would like to eat *my* share?" asked the elderly man as he carefully opened the box. "I ate a nice walnut yesterday. I don't think I've got room for anything else!"

"If you're sure," said Greg, as he received the small plate being proffered to him, on which lay a small slice of pitta bread adorned with a sliver of cucumber. "It's very kind of you."

Sir Lammington was chuckling again, but then he stopped and looked serious. "We are here for good! You understand, don't you?"

Greg gulped and hoped the tea lady hadn't locked them in. "You mean...."

"The Harbingers of H seek to bring good to the world through the auditory arts. You were chosen to take over from me. We have special dispensations with time and space, but it all balances out. What do you say?"

Greg wondered if anyone else who had climbed the many stairs had at some point been summoned to this unassuming bedroom to be asked by its equally unassuming, and yet charming, occupant to take control of operations. However, to more cynical minds than Greg's, it could appear that the administrators' pretext of being desperate for someone to take on the chief role disguised a kind of mystery adventure holiday scheme, paid for in some way by one of the unsuspecting customers' multiple identities. He tried to appear cool by taking his time in eating the treat, but his natural inclination was to get the food out of the way and learn all he could about the set-up. This was obviously more than an academy for teaching composition, and an introductory video film would have been useful at this point, but he'd just been asked to decide on a big career move. What exactly was the job description? "Have I been head-hunted?" he asked, smiling broadly as though to indicate he was flattered and yet not unduly ambitious.

"We have been waiting for you for many years, but we couldn't take action until you actually began your search," said Sir Lammington, closing his eyes and embodying contentment. "We must apologise for the temporal inconveniences you had to undergo - Miss Trotman downstairs will reimburse you for the bus fares incurred, as well as any sundry expenses by your various stand-ins, including the birdseed for that wood pigeon at the Old Bailey."

Greg regretted having doubts, and decided to listen uncritically to all that the grand old man had to say. "That's very generous. I've so far only had to fork out for a single bus ticket from Lincoln to Sleaford, but that was all due to the influence of a man in a tartan waistcoat who asked me to….."

"Did you know he once sang 'Old Man River' in a boy soprano range in court so as to get a reduced fine?" asked the man.

"No," gasped Greg, taking advantage of a reduced sentence. "Please tell me all you know!"

"All I know?" said Sir L. laughing again. "That will take some time. I hope I have enough of it left!"

Greg noticed a mini-mattress under the bed. He

discreetly pulled it towards him and lay down on it, with his allocated scatter cushion as a pillow. He closed his eyes and listened in rapt attention, anticipating the story that was about to unfold.

He waited, but the prolonged pause made him uneasy. Had the storyteller expired? Or just drifted off to sleep? He lifted his head to see if there were signs of breathing from the recumbent figure on the bed, but it was difficult to tell without actually invading the man's personal space. However, there was certainly an energy within the room, and especially around the bed, as the aurora he had first spotted when climbing the stairs was now manifesting the room with a growing prismatic intensity. Greg marvelled at the merry miasma that seemed to be emitting a melodic murmur, and so he instinctively knew that all was well. He lay down again and relaxed, happily watching the colour-shower, and listening to the concomitant notes, until they too settled down.

"So much prejudice and hostility in the world," said Sir Lammington at last when all was still. "People are afraid to express what their ears crave to hear and their hands crave to write. Dear Ludwig began his first symphony on an unexpected note and people almost fainted from the shock. Young Bob played a single chord on an electric guitar and a voice shouted out: 'Judas'. Young people are ridiculed by their peers if they're enamoured of Ambient when they're pressured to attune to Anti-Folk, etc. What is needed is less fission and more fusion! All notes are gifts and should be welcomed and honed."

Greg found himself nodding in agreement, but as he was supine, it was of little use. He knew better than to interrupt, and so he lay perfectly still, giving silent support for the wisdom being imparted from the bed.

"For many centuries we of the Order have been quietly acting as conduits for blessèd strains and sublime refrains that are captured in high places for men and women to craft into the highest of the arts. Did you know that the notes for three of Mozart's quartets and half of Glen Miller's works were collected via The Leaning Tower of Pisa? Sadly, it's leaning so far out now that any new themes are in danger of inspiring only extremely political views. Thankfully we've negotiated a five year contract with Blackpool Tower. Some of the music feeds directly into the Wurlitzer Organ in the ballroom below, but most of it is processed by ourselves and despatched to various Lancastrian composers. We have a branch at Glastonbury Tor as well, although I believe much of the music ends up in some field."

Greg almost interceded at this point with some additional information, but thought it best to keep listening respectfully.

There was a knock at the door. Greg sought tacit permission to open it, but it opened without any invitation and Mrs. Rosenbaum, replete with calf-length apron, duly shuffled in again, her mission this time to collect the empty lunchbox. She smiled first at Greg, and then at the lunchbox which she picked up with a satisfied sigh before backing out again. "So, you liked it, Sir?" she enquired as she raised her head to glimpse the venerable occupant of the bed.

"Thank you, Mrs. Rosenbaum," replied the voice from the pillow. "Compliments to the chef!"

"Such a wonderful man. Daily I tell him such kind

eyes he has!" she said before closing the door behind her.

"She's a kindly soul," said Sir L. reflecting on the departed visitor. "She says she'd love to write a sonata for cream horn if she could, but her main strengths lie in her omelette making - she can really make a skillet sing! Anyway, we wouldn't expect you to stay on here, of course. The dry heat wouldn't suit you, and I think you can do such invaluable work in the Fens."

"My employers only sent me there to get inspiration," said Greg. "I wasn't sure why."

Sir L. chuckled as though he, at least, knew the reason for Greg's sojourn there. "The Fens might well be the new Vienna one day or even another Nashville! What better environment could you have for your base! I see you as a rotating garden sprinkler - spraying the region, possibly the entire Northern Hemisphere, with copious quantities of notation from the comfort of your hub!"

Greg felt flattered to be allocated a hub, but the old man appeared to be getting over-excited and was coughing slightly. Notions of rotating garden sprinklers could well be exhausting him, thought Greg. A change of subject might be timely.

"I wonder," began Greg, tentatively, "how a small manuscript book allowed me to travel first from an oak tree to a locked trunk; then from a theatre car park to a soirée with Haydn and Hendrix; to a laundry room containing a familiar shirt; then as an amanuensis to Mendelssohn in a rowing boat from the Outer Hebrides to The Great Pyramid. Is there a precedent for such a mystery tour? There were several calendrical changes too!"

There was complete silence from the bed as though its occupant was slowly considering a cogent reply - or had Greg's questions sent him into shock? Perhaps Greg too had dreamt it all, and yet he'd had witnesses, some of whom had actually arrived here with him! A sigh emanated from the bed, or was it a final breath? Then a reassuring but faint chuckle. Relieved, Greg almost regretted having broached the subject of his convoluted journey, but the man then took a deep breath as though ready to impart more wisdom.

"Do you understand electronic mail?" asked Sir L. now gazing benignly at his guest.

"E mails?" said Greg. "Not all of them. Some recently bereaved people in Africa asked me to store huge sums of money for them, but they spelled 'dear' with two 'e's, so the message might have been intended for a safari park instead. Others keep offering me medicine at a reduced price - it's all a bit odd."

"Indeed, but anyway, when you send a message through the wide world net it's split into tiny fragments that travel through hundreds of different wires, then like you and all the other bits of you, they reassemble, as you have done, restored and ready to provide good news."

"I see," said Greg, on behalf of all his other co-creations, for want of anything more erudite to say. "But the calendrical anomaly?"

"Time travel is probably a fantastical speculation but of all the arts, music is the most connected with time - we slow it down with rubato, and speed it up with accelerando, and so in our great quest we have the power to override temporal considerations, but we use it sparingly, except in such circumstances as finding my

186

successor - such as yourself! However, the Pre-Raphaelite Brotherhood of painters, on the other hand, were very keen to return to a time *prior* to Raphael, but the appreciation of painting is static - not transient like music, drama, or driving - and so the muse refused their application."

"Is driving an art?" asked Greg. "Any creativity in propulsion seems to be so reliant on fuel."

"It certainly can be an art form. Your friend Meston handled his temperamental car with the grace and control of an aesthete. He might even be able to drive *without* fuel one day. There is no energy crisis - H is power, like hydrogen!"

Greg said nothing as he tried to take in the latest revelation. He envisaged all road vehicles being powered by their own stereo systems one day.

"Anyway, my friend," continued the sage. "Meston and the others will be ready soon. They're all going back with you."

"That's good, we'll appreciate that," said Greg. "Are we going by virtual express again? There doesn't seem to have been any vehicle at all involved in our recent journeys."

"Surely you know that music has the power to transport one?" said the old man. "Mrs. Rosenbaum has only to hear the opening bars of 'Oklahoma', and she's instantly back in a corn-filled meadow, even though she came to us from Golders Green!"

Greg nodded, and anticipated his responsibilities of getting his friends safely back to Lincolnshire, perhaps with the aid of the song of its famous poacher. He envisaged being part of a latter-day *Les Six,* and yet it was he alone who was being invited to become a virtual aerial for imbuing Lincolnshire and beyond with original music.

"What is your nephew's own musical predilection?" asked Sir L. "The one in Abingdon."

"He's firmly in the Soft Machine camp, I understand," said Greg.

"Then you must make sure that his family are exposed to soft machines too," Sir L. replied gently.

"But all genres are of equal merit, aren't they?" asked Greg.

"Indeed. But we must share our passions, and without any force!"

He propped himself up languidly on his pillow and beckoned Greg to come close, but the latter's left foot had lain so long compressed by his right calf on the lumpy scatter cushion that when he stood and attempted a tentative step towards the man he lost his balance. Both feet had the sensations of being pogo sticks, and his short journey to the bedhead resulted in him thrusting out his hand for support, accidentally hitting his mentor's nose in the process.

"So sorry!" exclaimed Greg as he fell against the headboard, grabbing a suspended egg-shaped light pull for support. Unfortunately, the cord was jerked from its coupling just below the ceiling, and whiplashed itself across the hapless man's chin.

"Oh dear," said Greg as he removed the serpentine light cord from his master's chin and gently patted the bruised nose. "I do apologise. I've got pins and needles in my feet. It's probably a fault in the cushion, although I believe a lack of iodine in the thyroid gland can also be a cause!"

Sir L. stared at Greg for a while, which prompted

another short burst of self-justifying hypochondria. "Perhaps I need to eat some seaweed. I hope your nose doesn't bleed, but did you want to tell me something, confidentially?"

The man felt his nose carefully. Greg tried standing on alternate feet in case he needed enough blood circulating in his lower limbs to go and summon a towel, but then his victim began convulsing. Was it inevitable that the transfer of power should involve such a cruel demise for the person relinquishing it?

"It's been lovely meeting you, but I think I should get someone to have a look at you," said Greg, hopping from one foot to the other. He then realised that the convulsing was actually due to an intense fit of giggling. This was probably contagious as Greg too began heaving with laughter - born of relief. Now, hopefully, all should be well and thus he would willingly agree to whatever the wise man had planned for him. He put his ear near to the master's mouth in order to listen carefully for the secret knowledge, whilst the bed rocked vigorously due to its occupant's fit of mirth. The message, when it came, was little more than a whisper in the falsetto range as its speaker attempted to transmit the teachings.

"H will need to be reduced to its constituent notes," he said, slightly hysterically, before pausing for excess giggles.

Greg nodded seriously, watching out for signs of delirium.

"Could you find an elevated spot from which to carry out the work?" asked Sir L, after drawing breath again.

"An elevated spot," repeated Greg, thoughtfully.

"About what height were you thinking?"

"Halfway up a horse chestnut would be about right. Mature, of course," he advised, although another onset of giggles detracted somewhat from his own sense of maturity.

Greg nodded, and tried to envisage himself in a commanding position swaying on a branch, but the thought unnerved him.

"Or an oak," added Sir L. "I believe you were led to a significant oak tree only this morning. Something similar, perhaps?"

"Well, I suppose I could ask around when I return," said Greg, in non-committal tones, amazed at the omniscience of the sage.

"There's no actual physical work involved," assured Sir L., his voice now down to a normal working pitch. "It's just your close proximity to an input that matters. When H transforms down, then your mind, and the minds of others in your immediate circle, should be able to receive both the inspiration and the notes to enable spontaneous composition. Pyramids aren't ideally suited, as you'll appreciate - we went critical this afternoon! Ah, nurse has arrived!"

Greg glanced at the door and felt his heart rate quicken. There was no-one there - yet, but he participated in another vigil, slightly anxious that tugging on the light pull cord had activated an alarm to summon help. He then glanced at the gentleman's nose, aware that any sign of bleeding would put himself in a very awkward position. Thus he made sure that his baton was safely in his pocket and out of sight, should it be construed as an offensive weapon. He smiled thinly at Sir L. and trusted that the incident would not give rise to any suspicion of a pillow fight that had got out of hand. "Sorry, it's just one of those things!" he said in mitigation. "They say most accidents happen in the home!"

Both men then stared at the little door, anticipating the visitor. Greg took the opportunity to rub both his feet to stimulate normal circulation, but the tingling had almost gone. "I'll just wait outside during the examination," he suggested respectfully, whilst putting aside his concerns. His 'victim' was, after all, still in good humour.

"No, please stay. Your assistance could be invaluable," said Sir L. "Don't worry: nurse has seen it all before!"

"Well, if you're sure," said Greg, not quite sure what it was that she would be seeing again.

A heavy pounding on the door made Greg jump and almost lose his balance again, but the patient remained calm and invited the visitor to enter with a gentle "Come in", which Greg echoed, although more audibly. He braced himself for someone with the attitude and bulk of Nurse Newnes, recently encountered on the bus, and wondered if forceps might be required to assist her entry into the room. However, when the door suddenly flew open it revealed a youngish man of slight build who stared for a moment at Greg before producing a clinical thermometer from his top pocket. "Under the tongue for half a minute," he instructed in an Irish lilt from his sphinx-like position halfway through the doorway.

Greg bent down to receive the instrument, which he accepted diffidently before taking it over towards the elderly figure on the bed.

"No! Not the sir!" cried the young man, refusing to let his lowly position compromise his authority. "His tongue is too frail. Put it under *your* tongue. This is stage two of your medical!"

Greg breathed a sigh of relief and dutifully did as he was asked and wondered whether Celsius or Fahrenheit was preferred in Cairo, although the nurse looked as though he was equally proficient in either scale. During the half minute's silence he reflected on his medical, psychological, and musical evaluation, although it seemed to be taken as read that he was being primed for the top job whatever the results. Meanwhile, Sir L. mused quietly on the subject of the flat Lincolnshire landscape being perfect as the new chief distribution centre for the super-tone. Obviously, Greg himself was going to be subservient to the topography, rather than being a conduit; similar to the way that ink is dependent upon manuscript paper.

"Thank you," said the nurse eventually, impatiently extending his right hand to receive the thermometer whilst propping himself up with his left. "Now I want a water sample." He reached round behind his left shoulder to drag a galvanised iron bucket noisily past him through the narrow doorway, drowning out whatever Sir L. was advising as a safe technique for tree-climbing. Greg looked at the bucket before him and thought briefly about garden sprinklers, but it had no effect, and circumstances were rather public within the room. He compensated by carrying the receptacle over to the bedside table where he poured in a glassful of water from the jug. He looked at Sir L. and half-nodded as though to gain his consent but the man's eyes were closed as he lay on his pillow continuing his monologue - now eulogising on the nature of E flat. "A beautiful sound!" he added.

Greg flicked his finger on the side of the bucket to produce another pleasing tone, then carried it back to Nurse and placed it in front of him. "Will this do?" he asked.

"If that's all you can provide," replied Nurse as he dragged the bucket past his shoulder and through the doorway. "Now we just need to weigh you and that's it."

"What was my temperature?" asked Greg as he watched Nurse drag in a set of bathroom scales.

"Average. Nothing to worry about."

Greg suspected that the thermometer hadn't even been read. They were merely going through the various formalities that paved the way for him to adopt a tree and channel music from the ether. He stood on the scales and watched the small window reveal his weight, and the weight of his outdoor clothing too....as well as his baton....plus the manuscript book. "It's....average. Nothing to worry about!" he said, proudly.

"Fine," said Nurse. "No need to bother with checking your blood pressure. You don't get nosebleeds, do you?"

Greg felt his blood pressure rise. "Er....no. And I always try to avoid internalising a sneeze." He glanced at Sir L. who was now shaking slightly and repeating the words 'internalising a sneeze' in a slightly high voice, possibly in E flat above middle C.

"You'll do," said Nurse as he lifted the scales sideways to drag past him, hitting the awaiting bucket with a satisfying clang.

"Sorry to have disturbed you, Sir Lammington," he called out as he retreated through the small doorway. "I'll let you get some rest."

Greg turned and looked at the figure on the bed, but his eyes were closed once more and he had now transcended both speech and laughter and bore an expression of complete contentment. "I'll see myself out," whispered Greg softly, but there was no reply. He watched him for a moment, then got down on his knees and quietly opened the little door, and shuffled out backwards. "I'll get you some more water!" he whispered, this time slightly louder, although he knew that his mentor wasn't listening. He also knew that he should seek advice from another quarter. Hopefully there would be an electrician somewhere who could repair the broken light pull. He closed the door quietly, and stood upright in the passageway, reflecting on the fact that he had reluctantly attained a very high ranking position, and without any mention of remuneration. He wondered whether he was up to it, but then a vision of dancing light seemed to come from nowhere and proceeded to enfold him, accompanied by the most sublime choral descants. He took this as a resounding 'Yes!' and submitted to the experience for an unspecifiable piece of eternity. Then it vanished, leaving him with a sense of peace, and the aroma of roast onions in his nostrils.

CHAPTER 12

Greg could hear footsteps approaching briskly along the now dimly lit passage but it wasn't Meston coming to collect him; this was the walk of someone less diffident. He hoped it might be one of the staff coming to replenish the water jug and so, being slightly disorientated after his 'important meeting', he thought he'd better ask for directions back to the main hall, as well as advising them about the faulty light. However, it was Tom who was patrolling the passageway.

"What kept you?" said Tom, as he stopped abruptly, clutching a bread roll that exuded a dark tangle of onion. "We'd almost given you up! Come and get some food and drink, although the atmosphere there's a bit naff."

"Yes, thank you," replied Greg after contemplating the invitation briefly. He was keen to eat, but felt that advising Tom that there might soon be vacancies 'in various branches' should take precedence. He began to outline his meeting as they walked. "I've just been visiting the main man. Meston brought me here to see him - in that little room!"

"I know. That's tough, but at least he had a good innings," said Tom as he led Greg towards a door.

Greg stared at him for a moment. Unless the sage had recently been successful at playing indoor cricket, the term 'a good innings' might have a much more serious connotation, and as they entered what seemed to be a refectory, he was aware of a number of people standing and staring compassionately at him. Some whispered, others smiled, whilst several clapped their hands gently as Tom led him towards a buffet. Word had obviously got round, but what was the word? Were they expecting him to say something memorable, or did they expect him to compliment them on the catering? Would his posting to the Fenlands be a poisoned chalice, and might Sir L.'s water jug also have been tainted?

Greg smiled back thinly towards his onlookers, then tried to concentrate on the food on offer, reluctant to ask anyone what might have transpired. He stared at a dish of black eyed beans and recalled Sir Lammington's gentle laughter and facial injuries. Tom stood next to him and suggested, conspiratorially, 'a bit of everything', before handing him a pair of serving tongs from the salad bowl whilst whispering in his ear: "I've decided on a career change. I want to devote myself to the musical field."

Greg smiled to himself after recovering from his initial shock of actually seeing Sir Lammington's plans begin to unfold. But did Tom realise that the musical field to which he aspired might involve some gentle tree-hugging within its boundaries, or assistance in gathering the aural harvest? And was that harvest indeed H; its objective being to permeate the kernels of oblate chestnuts, or even acorns, with the music of the spheres?

"I'm sure you'll find your new vocation fulfilling!" said Greg, as he garnished his plate with a sprinkling of chopped walnuts. "Did something, or someone this afternoon prompt you to move from commerce to creativity?"

"It was really the guy with the triangle. He looked

196

so spaced out playing his one note. I thought *I* want some of that!"

"I'm sure it'll happen," said Greg. "Triangles....tripods....trying things.... Have you ever tried....tree-climbing?"

"No. I tried climbing the corporate ladder until I got hacked off with it, but I did climb all those stairs to this place! Anyway, why do you ask about trees?"

Greg pretended not to hear, and distracted himself by trying to hum the triangle tune. He had no idea how Tom, let alone the others, would be persuaded or cajoled on to the project that Greg was destined to head. However, it could well be that events were already set in motion towards this end. Tom laughed when a small beetroot he was ladling out of a dish fell into his glass of iced tea. Gone was the restrained anger - in was the sense of fun. "That's a heavy beat!" he said as he tried to extricate it.

Greg winced and wondered whether trite lyrics might also ensue from the joint operation of processing music from its collecting point.

Meston then entered the room from a side door bearing a basket of dates. He also attracted a certain amount of kindly attention from those in the room. He placed the basket on the table next to a bowl of fruit salad and then noticed Greg and Tom standing on the opposite side. He reached across carefully and shook hands with both men warmly. "Sorry to hear about what happened, but life has to carry on," he said, directing his words at Greg. "Anyway, I'm sure we'll all get the hang of it!"

Several people clapped gently, murmuring pleasantries at him, whilst one man took a photograph of the three men shaking hands across the table, which they kindly repeated for the camera.

"Apparently we'll be going back home quite soon," said Meston, his arm accidentally nudging a bottle of vinaigrette dressing. "Sorry, I didn't know if you'd been told. The other three are seeing Nurse at the moment. They're discussing chiropody and allergies."

"They should get down to discussing opera and elegies!" said Tom, guffawing.

Greg pointed out the crisps to Meston, remembering his penchant for them; especially the broad bean and basil flavoured variety which formed part of the stock in the farm's Great Cupboard. He reached over to steady the wobbling vinaigrette bottle and quietly asked him if he'd known about the 'grand plan'.

"I sort of got swept up by it," said Meston modestly. "Sorry, I hope you don't mind becoming heir to the Chief Harbinger, but I did hear the Head of Modes say there was a legend that the successor would emerge unsuspecting from an oval caravan. Monica will be thrilled to think that her well-waxed captain's bed would give *berth* to a chief, so to speak!"

"Well, I only…." said Greg, keen to avoid even the slightest degree of exaltation, but then one of the group of appreciative onlookers clapped her hands gently and beamed at everyone in sight as a hush fell. The vinaigrette bottle also fell and the photographer captured the moment for posterity, before clasping his hands in front of him as though in prayer.

"I'd like to sing a refrain inspired by our late Harbinger-in-Chief, and dedicated to his memory," said the hush-inducing spokeswoman in what sounded like a Dutch accent. "Then we'll have a one minute silence."

198

Some conferring took place with amicable nodding and whispering, before an amendment was issued. "We've decided on a *two* minute silence - it gives us greater scope for reflection. I hope we can all benefit from it, as well as from the preceding choral expression of a life dedicated to the distribution of the muse."

Greg remained standing next to Tom in front of the table, with Meston standing opposite, all conscious of the group facing them, as though this was to be their own little benefit concert. Attention to accumulating food was put on hold, as the three men waited respectfully for the song to begin. The little triangle player scuttled into the room, appearing slightly lost, until he was directed to, and took his place in front of the Dutch lady, where he hovered, triangle at the ready, peering at her for the cue to begin his accompaniment.

She raised her arms in a gesture of spiritual connection. Then she threw back her head, and brought her arms down again, stretching them outwards in a gesture of worldly inclusion. The player ducked, in a gesture of avoidance. Then she parted her lips and imparted the hymn's first syllable. It was an exhalation that reminded Greg of some of the older men who browsed the aisles of supermarkets whilst emitting subdued but tuneless whistling sounds. His own grandpa had this gift, but he had not witnessed the phenomenon in women before. Perhaps this lady's minimalist recitation was influenced by shopping with other members of the fraternity who had retired from full-time whistling.

Her accompanist seemed to be responding to her understated performance, however, and his tinny instrument complemented her tiny voice, until they were augmented by the rest of the choir in a unity of exhalation. Could their raw emotions be sapping them all of the ability to vocalise? Greg was aware of the grand old man's demise, and he realised his resolution to float away blissfully on a final chord - also resolved - had been achieved perfectly; notwithstanding Greg's fist and the impact of the bakelite light fitting. Meston joined him and Tom in their respectful review of the choir, though rather than walk *round* the table to stand in fellowship beside them, he took a less conspicuous short cut so as to emerge from *under* it. A minor jolt caused the hapless vinaigrette bottle to lose its balance once more, this time resulting in it rolling off the table and smashing on to the stone floor at the precise moment of the choir finding their collective voice.

"MAY-Y-Y-Y-Y!!" they sang with gusto, before a long pause. The young triangle-player also performed with gusto, and at such a frenzied tempo that at one point he sank to his knees so as to continue the refrain without the danger of keeling over.

"Sorry I wasn't able to wait for you in the passageway," whispered Meston in Greg's ear. "I had to water the potted palms."

"Shhh," said Tom, standing rigidly in expectation of more sounds. "This is awesome!"

"WE-E-E-E-E-E!!" continued the choir, a perfect fifth above, followed by another spirited solo from the one-man percussion.

Tom was now in his element, raising his hands in an ecstatic swaying action. Greg and Meston felt that they should express their appreciation just as avidly, and so the three of them adopted the universal manner of open-air fans in communion with their heroes.

200

"SI-I-I-I-I-N-G-G-G!!" was the next word, completing the octave, and culminating in a sustained *tour de force* on the triangle until the man collapsed exhausted on the floor. Was that it? Were the songsters asking permission to sing, or were the lyrics rhetorical, and did their warm smiles indicate that applause was appropriate, or that a more sombre mood was called for? Greg lowered his arms and gestured to Tom and Meston to do likewise, which after a while they did. They then awaited further instruction. Clearing up the broken glass and its contents crossed Greg's mind, but a mood of introspection and lowered heads now enveloped the choir, and thus the three men joined in the silence. Greg closed his eyes, and trusted that someone would softly announce when the two minutes was up. He recalled having attended a Quaker meeting where anyone might interrupt the communal silence with words on which to ponder, but a strident voice declaring: "Nice spread, that'll do very nicely!" suddenly cut through the still air of the room.

"Ah, there's the rest of our little party!" said another in a breezy manner, unaware of current events. "Those people watching them look rather perturbed, though," he added, slightly more discreetly. "I think it might be a stand-off."

Greg had instantly recognised the loud hearty tones of the irrepressible Joe, and the more egregious, and yet cautious Norman. He half-turned to try and subdue the gatecrashers by means of subtle gesturing, but they just stood there between the doorway and the table looking puzzled.

"I wouldn't say no to a nice cup of tea," said Ted, the third, and rather gloomy, member of the trio, as he hesitantly entered the room and saw the buffet. "If it's loose leaf, I'll need a strainer, though. My doctor told me it might it be best if I don't choke on anything."

Greg felt a growing sense of embarrassment, and hoped that the old soldiers might have realised that a quiet time had been convened, and that any excessively loose tea would have been scrutinised in the kitchen before serving. He tried to lead by example and so he resumed his original position; head lowered in respectful silence opposite the dormant choir. However, Norman's brief observation of the quietness within the room led him to issue a warning to his food-foraging comrades.

"Pay attention! Our man Greg seems to have been spared, but I think that broken bottle on the floor has released some sort of nerve gas. They're all stunned! Quick, one of you, get that nurse!"

Joe took on the role of the one to summon assistance. He loped out through the doorway, shouting as he went: "Quick, Man-nurse, emergency! Some sort of gas is getting on people's nerves!"

Norman steered Ted away from the comparative safety of the tea cup array, and pointed out the broken glass on the floor with its seeping slick of yellowish vinaigrette dressing. Greg sneaked a glance at the two men. Norman bravely sniffed the air, whilst Ted covered his nose and mouth with his hankie as he cowered from the deadly dressing. Tom looked at the mess disdainfully and Meston apologised. A collective throat-clearing and shuffling of feet from the choir indicated that the silence was over. Closed-lip smiles beamed generally to anyone who might catch them, whilst Tom was approached by several people who shook his hand warmly.

"You'll make a wonderful Harbinger," said one man, emotionally. "You all will!"

"I don't know if I'll make much money from it," said Tom nonchalantly. "No-one explained the salary structure, but I can't wait to be chilling out amongst nature, setting up barbecues with dead twigs, whilst getting raw music to play at live gigs! It'll be amazing!"

The man patted him on the back and glanced at Greg with an expression that implied: "Keep him straight, won't you."

Norman stared in open-mouthed disbelief at the increasingly enlivened choir, whilst Ted kept his mouth tightly closed and his nose shielded by his hankie. Joe then hurried back into the room like a breathless messenger and loyally returned to stand side by side with Norman. "Nurse is coming, he's brought a thermometer," he whispered. "Is it safe to inhale now? My breathable fabric needs air too!"

Norman nodded and wondered if he might have over-reacted. "There's a health and safety issue over the broken glass, of course," he said. "You probably know the ancients were accident-prone and heavily bandaged."

Greg noticed Norman had his fingers crossed, but then he began to recognise people within the choir as being some of his mentors in the great hall. The man who had given him the eye test came over to him whilst Meston excused himself to assist Ted in pouring himself a cup of tea, maintaining a sharp lookout for stray tea leaves.

"So!" said the man, gazing at Greg as though he

were in the presence of greatness. "He chose you!"

"Well, there should be six of us altogether," said Greg, modestly. "Although I'm not exactly sure what we do about receiving…."

"Don't worry. Some of you will start writing spontaneously, and any surplus will find others with pens poised over blank manuscript paper so that harmony may ensue across the Wolds and beyond. Think of yourselves as photovoltaic cells feeding into the national grid!"

"Someone sent for me?" called the male nurse as he entered the room, surveying the gathering of apparently healthy and rather talkative occupants. "I was told there was an outbreak of gas. Who wants bicarbonate of soda?"

The answer he received was kindly but bemused stares from those who actually heard him above the general hubbub of polite and encouraging conversations, but no-one admitted to there being any problems.

"No, but I'll have a *cream* soda if there's some on the table, thank you!" said a lady with a Texan twang. "Easy on the cream, honey!"

The nurse affected a degree of mild annoyance, and muttered something incoherent before slamming a large drum of sodium bicarbonate on the table, together with a packet of charcoal biscuits. He looked at Greg with an expression of comradeship in adversity. "High spirits, that's all, I suppose. Anyway, that's the way Sir Lammington wanted it. Good luck!"

"Yes, my congratulations too," said the tutor as he gripped Greg's hand, rather like he had done when taking his pulse. "We'll arrange transport, although budgetary restrictions won't allow for any more temporal diversions. From now on, any rubato would have to come from your etheric downloads!"

"You won't be meeting any more 'aspects of yourself' as we usually refer to them," assured one lady who had sidled up to him with a small tub of apricot yogurt in her hand. "I had *four* existential sisters on the go at one time until I gave up market research and followed my heart and began to listen out for the wind in the wires."

"I see," said Greg, thoughtfully. "I did encounter a double but we didn't shake hands. I've seen similar encounters in films where the two people concerned have to avoid physical contact due to the limitations of the cameras."

"He's probably completed his task now you've found your calling," she said, emphasising the point by tapping the lid of her yogurt with a plastic spoon. "After I joined the Harbingers my sister aspects all spontaneously vaporised during a moving recital of wind chimes."

Greg's mentor concurred with her reassurances about his single identity, before drawing him to one side. "It's only since we moved into this pyramid that we got involved in the transmigration of souls business, but we can see where they're coming from."

Greg nodded, and wondered where the draught was coming from, but then he observed a section of wall slowly opening up on his right to reveal what looked to be a narrow unlit passage. Was Mrs. Rosenbaum about to make an appearance in her mission to remove the broken bottle and its greasy rivulet of salad garnish? No-one emerged from the passage, but then he noticed that people were staring benignly at him again. He averted his eyes from their admiring faces and looked at his five companions, all tucking into the buffet on the table.

"See, he's already Sir Lammington, mark two!" said a male voice, louder than had been intended. "No interest in eating - he gets all his nourishment from the source!"

"For the journey," whispered the lady with the yogurt as she discreetly dropped the tub, together with its percussive spoon, into his jacket pocket. "The chief would have done the same. Well, not a flavoured one, naturally."

"Er, if you're all ready I'll show you the way out!" said a rotund man in a white suit whom Greg recognised as being he who had summoned him to visit Sir Lammington.

"And, if we're not quite ready yet?" said Tom, winking at a young lady wearing a tee shirt emblazoned with the legend $E = D\#2$.

"Well, then I can show you the way to the scullery and a pile of dirty dishes instead!" said the man, smugly.

"I think we're all ready to leave now, actually," said Norman, marshalling and ushering his two comrades towards the presumed exit.

The guide smiled, beckoned the rest of the men and then shook his head. "I'll miss this place when we transfer operations over to you as you scale your tree. Anyway, I know you'll achieve great things at that latitude. This place was only meant to be a stop-gap, but it's too close to the Tropic of Cancer and the very shape of the pyramid was attracting too much musical energy. We couldn't filter it fast enough! That's why people wander around with iPods strapped to their ears, trying to absorb the excess."

"They can only absorb bits of it. The rest escapes," said Greg. "Last week I stood behind someone at a delicatessen counter leaking treble."

"Delegates out looking for trouble? Dear oh dear," said Joe. "You had a lucky escape!"

"Joe has perfect pitch, isn't that right, Joe?" said Norman proudly, but his friend didn't hear him. "By the way, Ted, you've got some turmeric on your dentures. You don't want to tarnish your image before you've even begun your rock star career, do you!"

This was received with a plaintive apology and the application of some remedial lemon juice. Greg wondered if he should have a quiet word with both Tom and Norman about the more introspective aspects of collecting crude art.

"This way, gentlemen," said the guide. "I'll take you to the departure chamber."

Greg turned and waved goodbye to the group of choral advisors as they stood dabbing their tearful eyes with hankies.

"Mustard gas," whispered Norman to Greg as they moved towards the exit. "That canister on the floor. Probably left behind by the conspirators of the late Queen Hatshepsut. Tchhh."

Greg nodded impartially and checked that he had what he needed for the journey - small manuscript book in one pocket, tub of apricot yogurt in the other.

Meanwhile, an emotional exchange of waving was taking place between the new Harbingers of H and the old. Kisses were also being blown, some of them between Tom and the lady with the T-shirt proclaiming her own favourite notational formula. Meston then waved farewell and called out a final 'sorry', before joining the other new Harbingers as they grouped themselves at the top of a flight of steps to await orders.

"It's this way down!" the guide advised them, helpfully. "There's absolutely nothing to fear, and once you get back to England and you're settled into your new routine, you'll see that everything will fall into place."

They watched as a lump of masonry fell from its place on the ceiling and shattered onto the middle of a step some way below them. The guide ignored it and handed each of them a form to fill in at their leisure, with various questions on whether they'd found the course location: 1. Well-appointed; 2. Professionally staffed; and 3. Adequately signposted. Greg noticed that the largest box for preferential ticking related to the standards of catering and seating accommodation. The subject of musical channelling seemed to be absent.

"Sorry, we've run out of questionnaires that deal specifically with hard hat size and colour," said the guide. "Anyway, can I ask if you all found the headgear at the start of your visit: A. Extremely useful; B. Useful; C. Reassuring; or D. Would rather not say?"

No-one answered at first, but Greg thought that the provision of hard hats themselves, rather than questionnaires about them, might be useful at the end of their visit too. "Isn't there perhaps another dumb waiter we could use to go down?" he asked, endorsed by his friends' nodding heads.

"Well, that would mean having to go back through the room we just left," said the guide. "But then you'd have to go through all those emotional farewells again, not to mention the reunions."

"I wouldn't mind going back through there, not to mention reunions!" said Tom.

"I'm sure if we all move quickly and quietly and pull our collars up we can brave any minor masonry spills," said Norman as he peered up at the colossal stone lintels above. "You have to expect a bit of settlement in old buildings!"

The guide agreed and went first, followed by Greg and Norman. Meston and Tom held Ted's hands, and Joe happily acted as rear lookout.

"When I was small my parents sometimes left items on the first step of our staircase at home that needed taking upstairs," said Norman to Greg. "Then as I grew taller they'd place anything to go up on the second, then the *third* step, which kept pace with my advancing height, of course."

"Of course," said Greg, in non-judgmental acceptance of this revelation from Norman's past. "And did they ever leave anything on the *top* step that needed bringing *down*?"

"Well, now you mention it, I did sometimes see an empty mug or a hot water bottle tucked in next to the newel post on the landing but I just assumed....oh well, it's too late now," he sighed.

"I'm sure they ended up in the right place," assured Greg.

"They retired to sheltered accommodation in Sheringham. Single storey, and protection from the weather for their wheelie bins," said Norman.

Greg nodded, and wondered how significant the subject of wheelie bins had been in Norman's life. So far the man had said very little about any passion for music. Meanwhile, Ted was getting tired, and had asked if they could rest for a few moments. Greg looked up at the ceiling and thought that it looked in good shape from this point onwards. He then looked down, and noticed that the foot of the stairs wasn't far off. "If the rest of you want to carry on, I'll wait here with Ted," said Greg. "We'll join you when he's ready!"

His motive was to sound Ted out on the subject of his willingness and ability to gather unrefined music by means of a certain amount of climbing. He even sat with him on the step until the others had continued downwards, with promises from the guide of a nice sit down once they arrived in the 'Departure Lounge'.

"Do you have a stairlift at home?" asked Greg, wondering how to broach the subject of tree climbing.

"No, but I live in a ground floor flat so I don't qualify for one," replied Ted, resignedly. I lift *weights* though. I've got two heavy bottles of thick bleach with added lemon at home. Every Saturday I exercise by lifting them both six times up to waist level, although I still can't release the screwcaps."

"Have you pinched them?" asked Greg, but Ted's reaction to this question was to become flustered and for his face to turn red.

"Shall we press on, now?" he replied, scrambling to his feet. "Tell me about this musical tree we're going to look after. I once wrote a song about a tree. I called it 'The Tree!'

Greg smiled at the sudden willingness to ask about their mission, although he suspected that the bottles of bleach might have been lifted illicitly. "If you're ready," he said as he assisted the little man to his feet, now surprisingly more agile. "But tell me about your song."

"Well, it's in 2/4 time and it's rather sad because the tree dies of Dutch Elm disease," said Ted. "I sent it to some publishers, but a Mr. Van Der Goot returned it and said it was too controversial, so I gave up and concentrated on collecting matchbox labels. You don't think there'll be any diseases in *our* tree, do you? I've heard of infectious music."

"The notes should be pure, and your song might get the harmonies it deserves," said Greg as he proffered Ted his arm for support. "You could even modify your lyrics and refer to a healthy wych elm instead! What I think we'll actually be doing there is sit quietly in the branches and await inspiration in a sort of hands-on way."

Ted seemed to accept this, and even began to hum what was presumably his long-neglected opus. Thus they wended their way down the steps until they reached an uneven floor strewn with debris due to centuries of 'settlement' from masonry fatigue. Familiar voices from within an ante-chamber invited them in, where they found the rest of their little group assembled around a small boat.

"This is where I bid you all farewell," said their guide, although the dry floor suggested that any voyage would be metaphysical. Norman gave Greg a knowing glance, as though pharaonic journeys of the soul had been reintroduced, but Greg in turn glanced nervously around the room. Fortunately there were no Canopic jars visible, and so evisceration prior to journeying to the Netherworld looked highly unlikely.

211

"The boat looks very similar to the one that brought us here!" said Greg, keen to relieve any tension.

"It was actually built for transporting the souls of the dead," said the guide, "but you're all alive and well, of course, so I suppose we could call it a *lifeboat* in your case, although it won't actually move itself. It's the property of the Director of Antiquities, and he has no idea of our illegal occupation of this place!"

"You're not going to leave us here in this vault, are you?" said Tom, nervously hiding his apprehension with a grin.

"Well, I'm going to see you off, of course, but I'll play you out with some Elgar to help transport...."

"Look!" shouted Norman, alarming Ted by his delivery. "In the boat - our rucksacks and tea trays, and the folding chairs!"

"All aboard the Bismarck!" said Joe enthusiastically.

Meston apologised and moved to one side to allow access to the reunion between the older men and their impedimenta.

"Thank you for all you've done," said Greg to the white-suited one. "I hope we can be worthy successors to Sir Lammington."

"We'll be in touch, and you don't have to worry about the process at all," said the guide. "Just relax and let things happen. Like Mahler in the mountains, except you'll be up a tree. Now, if you'd all like to stand inside the boat...."

Edward Elgar's Theme and Variations began to permeate the chamber whilst the men considered the request to board their *lifeboat*. The guide watched them as they ponderously took their places, quietly assisting each other to huddle together in the confined space.

"It's a rite of passage," said Norman to his companions, proudly. "For men who know where they're going!"

The guide had now positioned himself in the doorway and bore an expression of satisfaction that the men on the landlocked vessel were ready. He began waving to them, and although only half the crew were actually facing him, they all began to respond with waves themselves.

"We'd better humour him," whispered Tom. "Although if I feel sick again, I'm getting out."

Ted was now humming the music that surrounded them, prompting the others to join in. Greg instinctively knew that he had something in his pocket that might be appropriate for this moment, but the tub of yogurt would do for later on. Now was the time to take out his manuscript book and hold it for a moment....

CHAPTER 13

During a soaring crescendo in the strings, Greg realised that they had made the transition from the stationary boat, and were now standing somewhere much more cube-shaped. He put the book back in his pocket and stood impassively as though waiting for the doors of a lift to open. However, their present location was a large cupboard, furnished with tins, packets, and bottles. Standing room was restricted, and so Ted and Joe were sitting on the top shelf either side of some economy size jars of chutney. There was stunned silence at first, then a mood of resignation as though a holiday had ended abruptly. Then voices were heard from beyond their well-stocked enclosure, and there was no doubt as to where they were. Mrs. Throstlethwaite and her daughter Monica were sitting just feet away discussing Meston's birthday cake.

"Well, we've lit the candles. How long do you think he's going to be?" asked Mrs. T. "Let's hope he's not disappeared like your father."

There was no latch on the doors of the Great Cupboard, and so they were permanently slightly ajar. Thus enough light from the kitchen penetrated the gap to allow Greg to see Meston's expression of concern about his absenteeism. However, Tom's immediate niggle was that a small tin of gooseberries on the shelf opposite was perched on top of an A1 size tin of tomato soup. "Their flanges don't mesh, either," he complained. "What was Auntie Thelma thinking?"

"Sorry, I'm going to have to join the party very

214

soon," said Meston, peering out. "They're still missing Monica's father, and the candles are in danger of burning down to the fondant."

"It might traumatise them if you were to appear suddenly from the cupboard, though," advised Greg as he conscientiously repositioned the ill-harmonised tins. "Might be best to knock gently on the doors first before making an entrance?"

"If I could just suggest something," said Norman, as he parted Joe's feet dangling in front of his face. "we could wait until the two ladies turn the lights out for the candle-blowing, then move in swiftly."

"And then what," said Tom, contemptuously. "tie up my relations with string and interrogate them by candlelight? We're just about to become musical emissaries, right? We'll enter the room with dignity and a tin of gooseberries in natural liquors."

"Actual figures?" said Joe, just loud enough to be heard only by his fellow cupboard companions. "Aye, you can count on us!"

"I'll just nudge the doors open a fraction first," said Meston, summoning up his courage. "I used to hide in here years ago on bath night, so I know the dangers of being cornered, then venturing out and admitting defeat."

As he peered out, he watched Thelma get up from her seat to go and turn off the light switch. The resulting gloom in the cupboard caused Ted to whimper and clumsily grab hold of Norman's head. He in turn called for calm, although in a rather muffled manner.

Thelma and Monica, meanwhile, appeared slightly sinister as the contours of their faces danced and glowed by the light of the thirty odd little candles. Joe, now unable to see the shelf on which he was sitting, and still wearing his rucksack, had lost confidence in his now untenable perch, and thus succumbed to gravity, sliding off and pushing Norman forwards against Meston. By now, the ladies at the kitchen table had given up their vigil, and had begun singing *Happy Birthday* - albeit in a rather dirge-like manner - and completely unaware of their apparently absent guest of honour's imminent return as part of a human avalanche. Greg could now feel himself being propelled outwards by the gathering force behind him, but he had the presence of mind to grab hold of a large bag of pinhead oatmeal that he felt by his feet, so as to cushion himself when he fell out. He assumed that the cupboard doors were always kept ajar for situations such as this.

Just as Thelma and Monica reached the final '*Happy Birthday to You*!', Norman urged his men to 'roll with it', and so the six cupboardsmen spilled out en masse on to the sofa, rolling and bouncing off, whilst happily avoiding any mishaps or injuries to each other. Greg was well-protected by his oatmeal from being struck by Ted's foldable chair that had come adrift, but the bag then burst open just as Joe's tea tray flew over his head and slid on to the table, stopping just short of the illuminated cake. Meston immediately stood up from the melée of men on the floor, and with perfect timing went and blew out the candles in front of the two ladies' horrified faces.

"Goodness!" said Thelma.

"Sorry to have kept you both waiting," said Meston as he leaned across the table and kissed a spellbound Monica whilst the front of his jacket dangled over the smoking candles. "We got a bit side-tracked."

Greg took it upon himself to shed some light upon the proceedings. He thus fumbled for a switch on the wall and smiled reassuringly at the two stunned ladies, although their faces were still in the shadows as he'd merely switched on the outside security light.

"Surprise!" called Tom as he stumbled over Norman's rucksack to present Thelma with the tin of fruit. She also was honoured with a kiss, this being on her forehead. "They don't know it yet, but I've finished at the bank!" he enthused. "I'm going to work with these guys making music!"

Neither mother nor daughter spoke, but instead gazed uncomprehendingly at the sudden influx of visitors. Norman felt that Thelma was staring at him in particular, and so he too approached her, stepping carefully over Joe, still prostrate on the floor. He hesitated, but presumed that he was expected to greet her in a similar manner to Meston and Tom. He stooped and kissed her hair, then stood upright and blew sharply through his lips as though expelling an excess tress.

"Hello madam," he said before solemnly summoning Ted and Joe to repeat the ritual. "One for all and all for one. Ted, you're next."

Meston, meanwhile, had left the room, but Greg wondered whether he should try another switch and illuminate the room better, or allow the more romantic ambient external lamp to continue providing just enough light. However, mother and daughter, in perfect synchronicity, rose from their chairs and moved towards a cutlery drawer. Thelma picked up a knife and walked back to the table, whilst Monica hurried out to bring back Meston. Greg gulped and thought that perhaps the atmosphere might not be so romantic after all. He quickly enjoined Norman and his two comrades, now recovered from their encounter with Thelma's head, to repeat the chorus, but they'd forgotten the tune. Thelma stared at them, then dug the knife into the cake. "I see there's eight of us. Just as well. I couldn't divide it into any odd numbers."

"You'd better all sit down," said Monica, pleasantly, as she returned holding Meston's hand and pointing to the various chairs placed around the kitchen. "What a shock, though! Mam and I both thought Mesty was outside cleaning his carburettor!"

She smiled at him, but he avoided eye contact and proceeded to whistle '*Happy Birthday*' - in the Ionian mode.

"Anyway, however did you all get in that cupboard without us seeing you?" asked Monica. "And you all look so tired!"

Greg glanced round at the others to see if anyone wished to explain, but their eyes were all focused upon him, and so he assumed the role of spokesman. "Well, we have something rather unusual to tell you," he began tentatively, but Thelma was now holding her head in her hands. He hoped that Joe hadn't been too rough when he'd dutifully bestowed his comradely kiss. "Er, we've all been to a sort of investiture - to do with musical composition," he continued.

"Told you they were up to something, didn't I, Monica?" said Thelma, quietly. "None of them have stopped singing or whistling all day. They're all exhausted, poor things."

"Mesty must have been showing them where to hide in case they were hounded by talent spotters," said

218

Monica as she took the knife slowly from her mother, before setting about dividing the cake.

Greg realised that duplicates of himself and the others must have been present at the farmhouse that day, but he trusted that the dimension that controls the auditory arts had now recalled them. This was just as well as the complexities of dividing the cake into fourteen segments would have been quite an inconvenience for the two ladies. Tom, meanwhile, was surveying the Great Cupboard and deftly arranging a few misaligned jars of mustard, although he seemed more intent on producing pleasing notes by clinking them together. "Cool!" he said at regular intervals.

Norman, Joe, and Ted were standing rather awkwardly near the sofa as though awaiting instructions, but Greg had no idea about what they should do; either now or in the morning, when presumably he was meant to lead them all to some field and hopefully locate the tree that would deliver the sounds they had always desired. Right now he would defer to the ladies for instructions, and partake in some of the cake when Monica was ready to allocate it.

"I just realised," said Tom suddenly, turning to face the three old soldiers. "Whatsaname will still be waiting for me at Mother's house. I should have got hold of her on my Blackberry, but I think I left it on that Tamara's desk in the pyramid! What am I like!"

Ted seemed to find this confession slightly unnerving, and his hands tightened into nervous fists.

"It's a communication tool," assured Norman, quietly. "The young people use them to send messages in code."

Greg thought he heard the sound of an outer door

219

being closed, and the unmistakeable barking of Dawn. He presumed that she'd just returned from a walk, but who had returned with her? Tom also seemed to be distracted by the sound and absent-mindedly handed a jar of Dijon mustard to Joe before gesturing to Greg that perhaps they should investigate.

"We're just going outside for a minute!" called Greg to the two ladies carefully slicing the cake.

Both men hurried along the hallway. Greg assumed that Tom was also concerned that a clone might still be at large. They could see a large human form bending over to wipe Dawn's feet, but the hall light hadn't yet achieved full brightness.

"Hello!" said Greg, welcomingly, at least reassured that the crouching figure meticulously attending to the dog's feet was neither Meston nor any of their temporary clones.

Dawn wagged her tail and struggled to go and meet the two men, but then it became apparent who her minder actually was.

"Oh, it's that strange man from the bus with just two weeks left!" said Nurse Newnes, as she stood up straight and turned to face them, unsmiling. "And your friend must be one of those hippies from the tent. I've just kindly taken Thelma's dog for a walk because Meston *apparently* had *more important things to do*!"

Meston was at that moment walking purposefully into the hall to welcome Dawn, and yet nervous as to who could possibly be her guardian.

"Oh, wondered where you'd got to," said Nurse Newnes with obvious tedium as she let go of Dawn's lead and allowed her to go bounding up to Meston, almost knocking him over. "Anyway, good work for collecting me this afternoon, but you won't need to take me back tonight."

"Sorry, I...." but the dog's effusive and yet contented barking was drowning out any more of Meston's apologies or attempts to explain his absence.

Nurse wasn't really into bounding anywhere herself, but she'd now barged into the kitchen and was standing in front of the table, studying the demarcated cake with a sense of mistrust. Meston and Greg had remained in the hall to discuss possible avoidance strategies in case any of their temporary substitutes were still around.

"Who's that then?" asked Tom, watching the nurse through the doorway as she commandeered one of the kitchen chairs. "Some gatecrasher?"

"She's a friend of Thelma's," said Meston. "Apparently my other self must have invited her here as a guest. Sorry."

"But there's all us lot to be your guests, and it looks like I'll be needing somewhere to crash tonight!" said Tom.

Greg felt that everything would automatically slot into place, and so he calmly knelt down to stroke Dawn's head, rather than contribute to any discussion. "Shall we go and eat some cake first?" he said. "It looks like the first course has already gone!"

They duly walked in, overtaken by Dawn whose boisterous attention to a drinking bowl was distracting Nurse Newnes from her warnings to her hostesses about the dangers of icing exacerbating cholesterol levels. The dog then hurried round the table to gaze at the three older men sitting silently on the sofa, but Greg noticed that Norman and Ted appeared quite alarmed at being scrutinised so intently. Nurse wondered what

221

had engaged the dog's attention and so she turned round, seeing the sedentary trio for the first time.

"Well I never! You kept quiet about these three, Mrs. Throstlethwaite!" she said, mildly shocked. It was now her turn to stare at them, as Monica had opened the back door to let Dawn out to "finish off in the garden", but whereas Norman and Ted were both wary of the large visitor, Joe happily made eye contact with her and took on the role of spokesman.

"We roar and we're raw!" he proclaimed, smiling broadly.

Nurse Newnes turned to Thelma as she concentrated on slicing the cake. "Did the Kremlin send them here?" she asked, her voice lowered by one decibel as a gesture towards being discreet.

"They're our campers," explained Monica. "Apparently they have a marching song!"

"Really? What's that in aid of, then?" she challenged. "I don't see any point in all this singing nonsense. You can't turn the radio on these days without hearing some tuneless rubbish going thump thump thump, or some dreary orchestra going plink plink plink."

Greg thought her comments completely fatuous, but he wondered whether her radio might need retuning. Then he noticed Ted's hands go into super-clench mode. Was he preparing to finely-tune her dial?

"Why don't they just play music that people like?" she continued. "They could just delete all that other stuff!"

Ted's whole body had now become rigid and his breathing was deep and deliberate. Greg thought he could even hear the thump thump thump of Ted's heart,

222

and the plink plink plink of the buttons of his jacket as they yielded to the little man's apparent stress.

"Who's first for a slice?" asked Thelma as she finally held a small plate bearing cake to whosoever wished to approach the table.

It was Ted who first responded to the call, but his bearing was mechanical, and he stationed himself right behind where Nurse was sitting, grabbing the back of her high-backed dining chair. Greg assumed that he was about to reach across the table for his segment, but when Nurse suggested that concerts should be banned because of the audience's tendency to cough, and that listening to hospital radio interfered with patients receiving their medication, Ted appeared to have become rooted to the spot. Thelma raised the plate and made the sing-song sound that Greg had sometimes witnessed when older ladies proffered cake - something like 'here you are' but in cuckoo tones - and yet Ted remained motionless, except for his hands going into an overdrive of dynamic tension. Was it a seizure, wondered Greg, or was it the manifestation of SuperTed, defender of the cause of musical expression? Unaware of the pent-up energy behind her, Nurse Newnes suddenly found her seat being given rocking chair status as she was pivoted forwards against the table. She screamed, then blurted out: "Have you gone mad?"

Thelma gasped and put down the cake. "Now, now," she said, but invoking the present moment had no effect, as Ted then pulled the chair backwards to the same degree of tilt.

"What on earth are you doing?" screamed the hapless nurse.

"This!" replied Ted, in a voice devoid of any quavers, but replete with power.

Thelma and Monica conferred briefly, whilst Norman and Joe also formed a huddle. Meston appeared apologetic, while Tom muttered something to Greg about wishing he could take a picture. "This could go viral!"

"I'm sure it's just high spirits, Nurse Newnes," said Thelma, smiling sympathetically at her pendulum-like guest. "It is a sort of birthday party, after all. Shall I pour you a nice cup of tea? It's Darjeeling - just for today!"

Nurse's lips were tightly shut, but her eyes were wide open with an expression of rage as she rocked to and fro.

"Perhaps later, then," said Thelma before proceeding to pour tea into a cup which Meston was holding nervously.

Greg thought it best not to intervene in the hostage crisis, but he nevertheless went and stood close to the chair briefly until he was satisfied that the seat was still firmly attached to the legs. "I just wanted to make sure the connecting pegs weren't working loose," he explained to Ted, but the latter now had a resolute expression that transcended any possible concern about wood fatigue.

Norman and Joe seemed to have come to some sort of agreement, but rather than ask Ted to cease his chair-thrust calisthenics, they began to accompany each rhythmic thud of the chair legs by stamping their own feet on the floor, louder even than Nurse's protestations. "We will rock you," they chanted, emphasising and repeating each "rock you" with an

224

even louder thump.

Dawn barked in time too, but on the offbeat.

"What do you think we ought to do?" said Thelma, concerned, but Monica and Meston were swaying to the beat, too.

Greg glanced at Norman and Joe as though to ascertain whether their comrade often performed such stunts, but they were too engrossed in stamping their feet and spurring him on. Tom had also joined in the chorus, and so Greg thought that it would do no harm if he were to add to the vocals, but without the percussive footwork.

"There's no room in art for your brand of musical fascism," roared Ted to his captive, suddenly. "Have you ever listened to Korngold, Cream, or Klezmer?"

"Have *we* done that, Mesty?" asked Monica, but Meston was too entranced to respond.

"A slice for you, Greg?" said Thelma, in tones that implied that everything was perfectly normal. She waited for him to approach, before pulling him down towards her as though to impart something private to him. The recipe, perhaps?

"What's got into him, do you know?" she asked as Ted continued to berate the nurse with names of composers, folk traditions, and genres. "He'd hardly say boo to a goose before, now he's become all pushy and his friends are tap-dancing. Did they *find* their inner men?"

"Well, er, something *did* happen today," said Greg. "Actually, we've....we've all been selected to become....well...."

Thelma maintained her grip around Greg's neck, whilst staring intently at his lips as though prompting the words to flow. "To become well?" she suggested.

"Er....to become conduits, you might say," said Greg, wondering if he should gently extricate his head now from her motherly grip. "Composers, but ones who can download, so to speak, by being receptive to a....to a tree! It's a great privilege!"

She looked uncomprehending, and yet cautiously pleased for him. "Did *you* know anything about all this, Monica?" she asked. "He says they're all going to receive a great privilege tree so as to become composers!"

"I know!" said Monica, regarding her husband with admiration. "Mesty's just told me. It sounds like fun!"

"Sorry, I think it's a Horse Chestnut," Meston interjected. "We'll probably need to take packed lunches tomo...."

"Stop this nonsense at once!" screamed Nurse Newnes, but Ted merely persisted with his catalogue of musical history.

Greg wondered what the nurse might do to Ted were he eventually to stop. Order him to bed in a mixed ward with a plateful of diuretic pills? Administer a vigorous blanket bath with horsehair fibres? Perhaps for his own safety he was now doomed to continue rocking her indefinitely, or would he at some point convince her of the importance not to suppress the aural arts, which apparently - they'd been told - all emanate from H?

Greg was released from Thelma's arms, and wondered whether he should join in with Meston and Monica's rhythmic clapping as they swayed in time to Norman and Joe's foot stamping and chanting. However, Tom had approached him, looking slightly concerned.

"Have you got room for me in that caravan for tonight?" he asked. "I've kipped on the sofa here before, but I don't fancy any of those replicas of ourselves you were talking about tumbling out all over me from the cupboard in the middle of the night."

Greg put aside his reservations about the caravan tipping up, but he nevertheless tried to reassure Tom that normal laws of unilateral existence should be in operation once more, now that the clones had returned to their right time and space.

Thelma then grabbed Tom to pull him down for a private consultation. "There's a pair of your Uncle Bill's old pyjamas under the other bed - Paisley," she advised him.

He tried to nod, then pulled himself free and looked at Greg as though in need of further advice. "Do you snore?" he asked.

"I believe I do," admitted Greg.

"You could have had the spare bedroom, Tom," said Monica, speaking in the same rhythm with which she clapped. "but Dawn sleeps in there and she's a *terrible* snorer."

"Perhaps Dawn could sleep on the other bed in the caravan, and Tom could have the bedroom," suggested Greg. "I'm a heavy sleeper."

"This is definitely the last party I'll be going to," called out Nurse as she lurched forward yet again. "This is how Stalin began his reign of terror! No offence, Mrs. Throstlethwaite."

"That's all water under the bridge," said Thelma, giving her hapless guest an icy stare.

"Troubled waters, calm seas, stormy weather, old

227

man rivers; they've all been transmuted into art by notes on a stave," declared Ted as he lectured his intransigent passenger. "Even you with your NVQ might one day become a song on everyone's lips."

"Help!" shouted Nurse, but the rocking continued.

Greg could see there was a dialectical deadlock between her and her instructor. He wondered if he could step in and broker a deal between them but Tom wanted another word with him first.

"Is that all right with you, then? You don't mind the dog sleeping with you?"

Nurse looked warily at the two men and screamed again, but louder this time. "I'm being pushed into some kind of vice ring!"

"That's fine with me if it helps you get a good night's sleep," said Greg to Tom. "We've got work to do tomorrow!"

He smiled reassuringly at Nurse, but she failed to look reassured.

"Oh, I've got something for you, Mesty," said Monica as she ceased clapping and picked up a cylindrical-shaped parcel from under the table. "Happy Birthday!"

"Yes, and from me too," said Nurse, pleasantly, then, remembering her predicament: "Help!"

Meston thanked her and carefully unwrapped his present, apologising for each accidental tear of the giftwrap whilst Norman and Ted provided the accompaniment of rhythmic foot-stomping as his wife clapped and grinned.

"If that stuff's alcoholic you're allowed four units maximum a day," stated Nurse, followed by another appeal for freedom.

"Ever listened to Mongolian overtone chanting?" asked Ted of his captive chair-woman. "They deploy circular breathing and can sing two notes simultaneously. Can *you* do that?"

"Can *we* do that, Mesty?" asked Monica, but her husband shook his head.

Nurse was now either too shocked to scream, even on one note, or saw no point in it - none of her protests had been taken seriously. Greg thought the duel between her and Ted represented the recitative in Beethoven's fourth piano concerto in which the gentle piano - dominated by the strident orchestra - eventually attains oneness with its oppressor by melodic mollification. However, in this case, the timorous Ted - stirred to overwhelm his ignorant detractor - used argument and a dining chair.

"It's a bottle!" said Meston, surprised as he began to draw his gift from its crêpe paper sleeve. "It's lovely!"

He held the bottle proudly in his hands, its bright yellow contents drawing admiring gasps from Tom and Thelma, currently in conclave about whether Uncle Bill's pyjamas had street cred.

"Don't worry, the Paisley design's a bit more blue than that, and not quite as dominated by egg," she assured Tom.

"I'll put this next to my bottle of coconut liqueur," said Meston. "It's like liquid sunshine!"

"Ever heard of Monty Sunshine?" asked Ted of his detainee. "Played a clarinet. Do you even know what a clarinet is?"

"You are my sunshine, my only sunshine," sang Thelma, quite unselfconsciously as she gracefully waved the cake knife in front of her in lieu of a baton.

229

Greg knew the words of the song, and, having earlier that day been 'handed the baton' for downloading new music from the ether, he felt moved to accompany her in a recital of some of the old. He was delighted that she'd correctly sung the two syllables of the word 'only' with a semitone interval - which he felt conveyed perfectly the poignancy of the phrase, and the rhythm accorded well with the on-going decision to 'Rock You.' Nurse now appeared to be closing her eyes as though she might have succumbed to being rocked to sleep, but as the others joined in the rendition of the song, the combination of foot-stamping, singing, chanting, and clapping had increased the volume of sound within the kitchen quite considerably. Nevertheless, Greg's sensitive ears had detected a disquieting squeak coming from Nurse's chair. There was now a distinct possibility of its incessant contortions causing wood failure, precipitating its involuntary occupant noisily on to the floor. Meanwhile, Ted still showed no signs of tiring, and he was currently advising her on east European folk traditions, focusing on the Hungarian Cimbalom.

"A keyboard *far* wider than *your* imagination!" he told her, with a sneer in his voice.

Had Nurse mentioned to Meston when she arrived that she didn't need a lift home? Was she too intending to stay the night at the house, or was she going to be collected later by persons as yet unknown? Greg shared his concerns about her with Meston, who offered to find a can of lubricating oil for the squeaking chair, but as he stood finishing his slice of cake, whilst presumably pondering on how to apply the oil, a sharp knock at the front door interrupted his inertia.

"That must be her lift now!" said Meston. "I'd better let them in. Excuse me, everyone."

Greg had often heard people announce who was at the door even before verifying the fact. However, visitors, or even collectors, rarely arrived the moment they were first anticipated. Whoever it was that had arrived, there was no discernible small talk, but their entry in to the house was accompanied by some rather clumsy knocking and scraping sounds in the hallway. Was the nurse about to be removed with the aid of specialist equipment?

"Sorry, can you put them on the table?" said Meston as a young man carrying six heavy carrier bags entered the room. "We'd forgotten all about you!"

The man wore a jacket with a supermarket logo and seemed startled at witnessing Thelma's waving knife; Nurse's charges to and from the table; the chanting and foot-stamping from the men on the sofa behind him; and being serenaded with: '*You'll never know, dear, how much I love you*', accompanied by clapping. He made an attempt at a polite smile as he dodged the knife from one side of the table and Nurse's head on the other, and carefully placed the bags in the centre. He then appeared to be making a retreat, but Tom interceded.

"You can wait while we check it's all there," he said firmly. "You'll need us to sign for it, so we need to know what we've got!"

"Can I see the dog food?" asked Monica. "Dawn can't eat anything that's come from a dented tin. She's a bit fussy!"

"No problem," said the man as he duly decanted the bags whilst Tom carefully arranged the cylindrical items methodically on an adjacent work surface and ticked off items on the invoice.

"Sorry, we're having a party!" said Meston by way of explanation, but the man merely nodded weakly as he stood waiting.

Greg thought that the visitor deserved some sort of inclusion into the gathering. "What sort of music are you into?" he asked as the man emptied the final bag into the safety zone on the table between Thelma's sharp knife and Nurse's blunt head.

"Well, I usually listen to Dazza's Hits on Radio Buzz FM. He's a laugh!" said the young man, now slightly less tense.

Nurse's chair stopped abruptly as the room fell silent. Their working guest was then subjected to stares from all those present.

"Oh dear, oh dear," said Joe, whilst Norman shook his head.

"I think you'd better leave," said Tom as he glared contemptuously at the man.

"What's wrong, Tom," said Thelma, gently. "didn't he bring the semolina?"

"He didn't bring his brain, Auntie Thelma," said Tom. "Go on, pal, get back to your flippant radio DJ who makes all your choices for you."

Greg regretted having asked the question, but at least it had subdued Ted, if not completely the nurse.

"Wait a minute. I'm coming with you," said Nurse as she rose swiftly from her chair which promptly fell backwards on the floor.

"Sorry, I'm not allowed to take passengers in the van," said the now rather frightened man as he quickly exited the tense kitchen.

232

"I am *not* a passenger," said Nurse, proudly pulling herself to her full height. "I am a trained nurse. I am an SRN!"

She hurried out of the room in hot pursuit of the delivery man, but paused briefly at the door. "I'll be glad to get out of this madhouse. It's like being interrogated by the Bolsheviks. No offence, Mrs. Throstlethwaite."

"To be honest, Nurse Newnes," said Thelma, glaring at the departing visitor. "Mrs. Krupskaya and I were merely exchanging recipes. That's *all* it was." She then turned towards Greg and expounded. "Mrs. K. was awarded the Order of Lenin for her borshch."

"Well, it's probably comforting to eat a hot dish after a cold war," said Greg, hoping that peace would now reign in the kitchen.

"I'm feeling a bit tired," said Ted, now using his familiar rather feeble voice. "Have you got room on there....", but the loud slamming of the front door startled him as he quickly squeezed into a place of safety on the sofa between Norman and Joe.

"My arms are aching too," he added. "It must be due to falling out of the cupboard. I'd *never* do that at home."

His companions merely nodded knowingly, but said nothing about his recent role as the strife and scold of the party.

"It's getting rather late," said Norman, looking at his watch.

"It certainly is, it certainly is!" said Joe. "I wonder where it's got to!"

"I think I'll give those pyjamas a miss," said Tom, addressing Greg sheepishly. "Perhaps Dawn might

233

want to wear them!"

"Perhaps," said Greg, noncommittally, but then he observed a puzzled look on Thelma's face. "On second thought - no. I'm sure Paisley wouldn't suit her!" he assured her. It occurred to him that Tom had mellowed since his recent brusque dismissal of the musically passive delivery man, as had Ted after his even harsher treatment of the opinionated nurse. Both men had exhibited defensive stances on behalf of musical appreciation, but was this tendency applicable to everyone who had attended the hectic course in the Pyramid? Might he himself at some point become enraged at hearing a false note or an ignorant belief being aired? He observed the gentleness with which Meston and Monica sorted out the groceries and proffered the more traditional items to Thelma for her approval. He watched Tom who in turn was now overseeing their handling of unsalted butter, as though it were a consignment of gold bullion. Meanwhile Dawn was relaxing contentedly in front of the men on the sofa whilst Joe seemed to be singing some canine lullaby in her ear. Norman was patting her head delicately with his fingertips, but Ted viewed her warily as though afraid she might gaze at him and appeal for the sliver of cake which he had somehow obtained from the table during his assertive period. So far, any discussion of the day's events had remained private, but had Meston been able to prepare his wife yet for a rundown of their recent initiation, or even of their impromptu odysseys, taking in Hungary, The Hebrides and Cairo? And did she passionately embrace the diversity of music with neither arrogance nor ignorance?

234

"Sorry," said Meston suddenly whilst handing Tom a small tin of pineapple chunks to stack. "There's something you ought to know, Monica."

"Oh, they've not sent rings, Mesty, have they?" she enquired, only slightly concerned.

"No, but something wonderful happened today," he said tentatively. "Sorry, it's hard to know where to start."

"Start what?" said Monica, staring first at Meston, then at her mother.

"He wants to go and live with his new friends in a tent," whispered Thelma. "It's probably just a phase."

Monica looked at Greg for reassurance. He smiled back - reassuringly. "He wants to do great things!" she declared.

Tom had now organised the three older men to form a human chain in order to pass items to them to place in the Great Cupboard. They seemed to relish this activity and had begun to chant as they performed the task. *"Custard powder with the rice, put the herbs next to the spice. Marmalade goes to the back, make room for the multipack."*

Meston had begun an attempt at explaining to Monica how music hath charms to overcome the normal conventions of time and space, but she merely shook her head in synch with her mother and smiled at him.

Greg knew that he had a duty of care to his fellow musical messengers but should he intercede with the full story? He positioned himself near to them and idly tapped his fingers on a drum of baking powder as though to convey a sense of musical satisfaction. Meston picked up on this and invited him as back-up in

235

his presentation to Monica. "Shall the three of us go outside and chat in private?" he suggested.

"Do you want me to come too, Monica?" asked Thelma, but Greg shook his head on Monica's behalf.

Thus they stepped outside, whereupon Monica began to gaze at the night sky as though its vastness would assist in comprehension. Greg was the last out and, having closed the kitchen door quietly, he stood near to them, wondering whether he should produce the manuscript book, or perhaps offer her the tub of apricot yogurt as a souvenir from the Great Pyramid of Cheops. Silence prevailed, punctuated only by the old soldiers in the kitchen chanting about the distribution of sponge fingers.

"Sorry, but you know I've always wanted to find the key, as well as the bars, and clefs, and things?" said Meston, before looking up at Orion's Belt. "Oh, and the notes, of course!"

Monica studied him seriously, then followed his gaze into outer space. "I don't think astronauts have time for music, Mesty. They're too busy floating in a tin can and reading altimeters."

He glanced at her impassively and said nothing, and so Greg pulled the book from his pocket and brandished it. "I think that sometimes we're bestowed with a gift that's so powerful that even space and time are distorted to allow us to receive it!"

"It was only a bottle of Advocaat," said Monica. "Mesty can make space for it in the cellar in no time!"

"Sorry, I don't think you understand. We've actually been *specially selected* to receive keys and notes etc!" enthused Meston. "We learnt about it today during an unexpected adventure, although you probably thought we were here all the time."

"Specially selected?" She looked at him warily, then at Greg, as though seeking clarification. "It's not one of those time-share things, is it?" she asked, pitiably.

Greg was about to intercede, but he noticed Meston's face assume a look of barely suppressed rage. Then he saw that Thelma was standing at the back door window, quizzically peering out. He felt moved to act as diplomat and so he opened the door slightly to advise her that they needed a quiet space.

"*Fabric softener - litre size, individual cherry pies,*" chanted the old soldiers from within.

"We're rather busy at the moment....looking for black holes!" Greg advised her. "We may be some time!"

"No, Monica, it's nothing to do with any scams," seethed Meston. "This is about the power of music to percolate and permeate!"

Thelma looked as though she was about to step outside to intercede in any fomenting family friction, or possibly scan the heavens for any gaps, but Greg gently pushed against the door, smiling politely at her as she shuffled backwards into the kitchen.

"It's good to have a hobby, Mesty," said Monica, "as long as it doesn't involve committing yourself to any cons."

Meston then committed himself to utilising an adjacent garden incinerator as a percussion instrument, beating the steel lid with his hands, his eyes wide and focused on his dubious wife. "Seventeen beats to the bar!" he shouted. "Can you feel the energy?"

Greg quietly suggested to her that she say 'yes', but

237

instead, she began to accompany the tempestuous tympani by dextrous foot movements like a whirling dervish. Thelma appeared at the door again, this time accompanied by Tom, but they sensed that this was a private performance and so refrained from intruding. Greg thought this might be an appropriate moment for him to withdraw - Meston's drumming was becoming increasingly frenetic, and Monica's now rapid rotation emulated that of a pulsar. He walked over to the kitchen door, just as Meston began to launch into a detailed chronology of his long, long wait for the muse, and asked Thelma if Dawn was ready to retire yet.

"If you're sure you don't mind," she said as she handed over the dog. She glanced across at her son-in-law, then at Greg. "It's probably all those liqueurs he collects - gone to his head. He's a lovely boy, though. He sings arias in the bath, too!"

"I'm sure he's a dedicated quantum of the opera!" said Greg as he took hold of the short lead attached to Dawn's collar. "Anyway, we'll be getting to bed. We've all got a busy day tomorrow!"

He pulled the door closed, then waved goodbye to her through the window.

"How many different tunes can be created out of just twelve notes?" Meston challenged his rotary wife. "And where does all the inspiration come from? Soon I'll tell you where!"

Greg left them to disseminate the quest for the tree of musical knowledge, and proceeded to escort Dawn to the caravan. Once inside, he put her to bed in the opposite bunk to his own, and partook of a cheese and chutney sandwich that had been kindly left for him on the small table. After settling down in his own bed, courtesy of some mysterious captain, he heard the three senior men return to their tent, softly humming 'The Galloping Major' in three part harmony. Dawn joined in at this point, although in a pseudo-soprano register.

CHAPTER 14

Greg was awoken by the sound of heavy rain beating on the caravan roof. He pondered on the resemblance between rain pouring on a roof and the rapturous applause of a large audience, but the drips tortuously running down the window when he pulled aside the thin curtain suggested that this performance hadn't been well-received. The prospect of leading his little party across wet fields to a vigil with an unknown tree to await providential notation now held little appeal. He watched Dawn's thin head stir in the bed opposite, but her eyes indicated that she had no wish to venture out either. He knew the old soldiers would also be reluctant to go far today, but he felt a responsibility to motivate his team, and make an attempt to infuse the surrounding area with freshly-caught music. He looked out again and gazed disappointedly at the puddles in the grass.

Ted left the tent and was standing dejectedly in front of a micro-morass of mud as though contemplating how he might make it across to the security of the path to the house, but Norman had now joined him in a lugubrious appraisal of whether conditions were safe for them to venture anywhere today. He put his arm round the little man's shoulder in comradely stoicism, then felt the top of his beret, presumably to gauge its water-repellent qualities. Joe had also now emerged from the tent and seemed to be delighted at the prospect of a new day. He joined his companions and merrily attempted to blow raindrops off Norman's headgear.

Greg took his cue from Joe, and decided to perceive the dismal day as a fun-filled challenge, and began to emerge from bed. Dawn also now saw the pervading gloom in a positive light, barked with excitement, and leapt out of hers. Ted glanced nervously at the noisy and slightly wobbly caravan and scuttled back to the refuge of the tent. Dawn, meanwhile, stood at the door and gave a series of sniffs, then exhaled - a classic canine request for freedom. Greg opened it for her, whereupon she looked up at him in an 'aren't you coming too?' expression.

"Soon!" he advised her, and so she bounded off through the damp grass, several puddles, then on to the path towards the house. Greg remained in the open doorway to assess more accurately the day, then dressed quickly before departing the caravan himself. He loped towards the path, but paused to tap gently on the canvas of the tent as though to ask: 'Aren't you coming too?', aware that a more verbal invitation might alarm at least one of its occupants, but the sound of rain hitting the canvas was louder than his delicate knocks. He thought about coughing, but his throat was in perfect order. Reveille, perhaps? Too officious. As he stood getting wet, inert with patience, the flap opened, revealing a startled Norman on his hands and knees looking up at him. "Oh! Would you like to come in?" he asked. "We're debating what to do."

Greg greeted him, then knelt down on the groundsheet and shuffled in to their cramped domain. He found a space and sat on one of the foldable chairs between Joe and a picnic hamper. Ted sat opposite them on a camp bed and nervously handed him a jam jar containing tea.

"We never bring cups with us," explained Norman. "The handles are vulnerable features, but you can always rely on a jam jar for strength and safety, plus you can make a quick assessment of what it contains by checking for any suspicious sediment! Isn't that right, men?" He glanced at his comrades as though to seek their approval of his words of wisdom. Joe raised his jam jar and grinned at Greg, wishing him "Good health, good health!", but Ted used his to mask his face as he silently sipped his tea.

"Greg, we've been talking amongst ourselves," said Norman, thoughtfully.

"That's all right. You didn't disturb me!" said Greg.

"No, I mean about this adventure - waiting for music to cascade from a special tree. There's a hawthorn growing outside one of your caravan windows. Couldn't we all sit in there in the dry and maintain surveillance of that one instead? Obviously, we won't discover anything on a grand scale."

He appeared to be half-smiling as he made his petition, but Greg winced at the thought of six people all sitting at one end of the rather fragile-looking vehicle and peering out of a steamed-up window until the whole thing tipped up. He also noticed the reference to a hawthorn. Had his former temporary clone resumed his true arboreal identity?

"Well, just a thought," said Norman, seeing concern in Greg's eyes.

"It's such a terrible day," added Ted. "The doctor told me I don't want to get water on the knee, and I hate getting moist feet."

Norman nodded. "He gets through copious numbers of towels."

242

"But we have to go!" said Greg, surprising himself with the passion in his voice. "I'm sure the rain will clear up soon. It's our destiny to find this tree and fulfil the Harbingers' plans for us. Such enlightened tutors too. They really taught us well!"

"They're merely tortoiseshell?" said Joe. "Could be hard, like Norman's corns."

Norman nodded again. "I get through copious numbers of plasters."

"But we've been waiting all our lives to compose," pleaded Greg. "Now at last we've got the chance. That moment of creation when man is raised to the genius of art! And in our case - a truly altruistic co-operative effort!"

The three old soldiers shook their heads. Greg almost shook his fist. He briefly considered various road movies for inspiration. Surely, Dorothy hadn't had to cope with this degree of indifference from her disparate friends when going off to see the lizard? Perhaps he could gain some confidence from another musical odyssey - the family who walked up Mount Everest with an ex-nun who enjoyed raindrops on kittens might be suitable role models, although his knowledge of the cinema was rather patchy.

"Who knows how long this expedition is going to take?" asked Norman. "I was hoping to rationalise my sock drawer when I got home. I found a potato in one of my bed-socks last week."

"I once found a thermal vest in my cardigan drawer," said Ted. "I must have put it in there by accident. I can be a bit accident-prone when I'm tired."

Greg felt himself losing control - yet in a positive way. He knew that his eyes must be blazing now with

Beethovenian rage. If he had the great man's celebrated ear trumpet, he'd blast the three reluctant adventurers out of the tent with a sustained note of H - if he could only produce such a sound. Instead, he gazed at each of his hosts in turn, willing them to make the move. The effect was that they quickly finished drinking their tea, placed their jam jars neatly under their camp beds, and then fastened their jackets as though ready to depart. Standing was difficult within the confines of the tent's low and sloping headroom, but before they had a chance to emerge from their refuge Meston and Tom pushed their way in.

"Sorry, I did knock on a flower pot, but I don't think you heard us," said Meston. "Are you ready to come and have breakfast before we all set off?"

"I've opened a tin of grapefruit," said Tom. "The shelf life is phenomenal, but it must be consumed within three working days once opened, so let's get moving! Oh, our leader's in here too. Hi!"

Greg nodded. "We're just going!" he said, but Meston seemed concerned at the men's living conditions.

"Sorry, I didn't realise it was so small in here. Cosy, though."

He was almost knocked off his feet as Dawn came bounding in, barking excitedly, keen to greet the huddled occupants. Meston's attempts to usher her out were in vain as she shook herself in what little space was left, spraying second-hand rain which resulted in Ted sustaining moist feet. The little man looked at Greg for guidance but Greg was pre-occupied, having been pinned up against the rear of the tent whilst his feet were now pinned down by Dawn's haunches. The crush was almost as intense as the group's arrival the previous evening in the Great Cupboard. However, Greg felt conscious of a united will to leave the tent - and yet there was a sense of inertia too - as though here within the enclosed space was a place of security and peace, enhanced by the drama of the downpour without. A plaintive gust of wind whistling in further enhanced the comparison, but soon Greg's feet were yielding to the effects of pins and needles as Dawn remained contentedly suppressing them. His neck, meanwhile, was pressed against a suspended wind-up lantern, and the hooked top of Joe's knobbly stick was somehow exerting pressure on his thoracic vertebrae.

"Shall we all go and have breakfast, then?" he suggested pleasantly. "There might be eggs!" He thought that the possibility of eggs being available might provide an added spur, and Meston was now nodding, as though eggs definitely *would* be on the menu.

Tom opened the flap and ushered everyone out. They emerged with heads down, and mostly they stayed down in deference to the rain. There was no chanting from the senior men this time; they were already receptive to whatever music might be on its way for harvesting. Greg and Norman formed the rear of the quickly-moving procession towards the kitchen door.

"We'll get a clue soon as to where this tree is, I suppose?" said Norman.

"I'm sure it'll all make sense," said Greg, crossing his fingers, but quietly confident. "Like the way you instinctively knew what items needed taking upstairs when you were young."

"Yes, but I never brought anything *down*," said

Norman. "Anyway, I do seem to have a sixth sense for some things. I can usually tell when my wheelie bin has been emptied, even before I open the lid to check!"

"Do you find you resonate with the collection of recyclable items too?" asked Greg as they leapt in tandem over a patch of saturated and horizontal grass.

"Well the sounds of bottles and jars being tipped into the collection van is quite pleasing. It brightens up those alternate Tuesdays," said Norman. "I usually try and remove the labels when I wash them out, so I suppose that improves the tinkling effect! I've never told anyone that before!"

Greg smiled. He felt confident now that the pursuit of pleasing polyphony was paramount to the party.

Tom and Meston had just carefully swung little Ted over the final puddle, and were now almost at the back door. Monica welcomed Dawn back from her sleepover with a towel for her wet feet, and smiled as the men entered and congregated in the warm kitchen.

"Mesty told me all about your plans last night," she announced excitedly. "I couldn't take it all in at first, especially that man playing a triangle at your tables, but then I'm not musically gifted."

"Wipe your feet," said Norman as Ted hovered on the doormat. "They're moist."

"Mother once thought I should train as a ballerina in the Bolshoi," continued Monica. "But then Mesty came along and swept me off my feet!"

"Yes, sorry about that," said Meston as he proceeded to sit on the floor and remove his shoes.

Places were taken at the table and a general murmur of excitement seemed to be developing amongst all present - both about imminent food and the prospect of a trek to a benevolent tree. Greg remained pensive and hoped that a sign would present itself. He discreetly sought pointers amongst the tableware, and even perused the names on various packets and jars placed on the table for clues. He hoped he wouldn't have to formulate a route based on merely numerical factors - converting calories to yards, or even grams to metres.

"Can't beat an omelette in the morning!" said Joe as he sat facing him at the table. "Although I've certainly tried!"

"Best to use a whisk," said Greg, as he studied the tablecloth for any arcane letters in its border pattern.

"Life's full of risks!" said Joe, breezily. "Best not to tempt providence, though. Oh no. You might come unstuck!"

Greg noticed that the label on a jar of cowslip honey was coming unstuck. Had Norman been trying to steam it off in order to present uncluttered cullet to the council collection van, or was the address of the beehive significant to their quest?

"Anyone lost a comb?" asked Tom as he picked up a small black item off the floor.

"Yes, I have!" claimed Ted, whilst Greg felt as though he'd just found a connection.

"Could I have a look at that?" asked Greg. "I've always been interested in....fine teeth!"

Ted handed it to him, warily. He examined it for its manufacturer's embossed trademark, but the legend 'Ted's comb' was all he could make out.

Norman had been rummaging covertly in his day sack and eventually extracted a sandwich bag containing two slices of bread which he placed discreetly on his side plate. "It's ryebread," he confided in Greg. "Apparently I'm wheat intolerant."

Greg handed the less than helpful comb back to Ted with an almost imperceptible nod of thanks, before turning to Norman. "Let me know as soon as you start to experience the onset of anaphylactic shock if we pass too close to any wheat fields," he advised quietly, but Ted looked puzzled by this remark and studied his comb nervously.

"You mean this could retain static and be responsible for creating those crop circles?" said Ted.

"Well, no, I really meant Norman," said Greg, but apparently the proximity of any farinaceous crop in its raw state was of little concern to Norman's health.

"If this doesn't work out for me, I suppose I could apply to become a road manager for a band," said Tom, also confiding in Greg. "Or should I opt for being a *band* manager for the *road*? I'd only need to adjust my CV slightly, and I'm sure I could soon get used to supervising a band on the road!"

"Surprised to be banned from the road? Oh dear, oh dear," said Joe. "You'll have to walk then!"

Tom stared at him, but then emulated Joe's unique way of misinterpretation. "No problem. I'm ready to go when you are!"

Now it was Joe's turn to appear puzzled, which he assuaged by pouring himself a cup of tea from the large teapot as though to stake his claim on the imminent breakfast. Meston and Monica were jointly addressing a grill pan in the manner of two trainee cooks about to perform some unspecified task upon it, but then they turned and watched the door to the hall as footsteps were heard descending the stairs.

"Ma's coming!" said Monica, with a hint of relief.

248

"She'll sort us all out. She used to be a dinner lady!"

Thelma stood framed in the doorway, smiling warmly at the crowd in the kitchen, until she was heralded by the boisterous Dawn with enthusiastic barking and jumping.

"Hello! Where's my precious one been?" she asked the dog as she stood cuddling and patting her neck, concluding with the formality of shaking her paw.

Greg answered on the dog's behalf, but the reply: "In the caravan!" had little effect and the question was repeated several times. Joe left his seat opposite Greg and came and sat next to him as though he too wished to confide in him. Was he about to supply Greg with a clue about the way to the tree? Would it be in the form of a riddle? Hitherto, Joe had mostly made casual observations based on inaccurately heard statements, but his manner right now was much more serious. He leaned slowly towards Greg whilst Thelma gave Meston and Monica instructions regarding multiple servings, during which Tom in turn interjected to instruct his aunt to wash her hands thoroughly in hot soapy water before 'prepping'.

"Your precious one's been in that musty caravan all night!" Tom reminded her. "Possibly adorned in those dodgy Paisley pyjamas!"

Greg noticed a creak from Joe's chair as he leaned towards him. He thought the note was familiar.

"When I was young, Reverend Gatherglow asked me one day if I'd like to sing in the church choir," began Joe, "but I wanted something deeper, oh, *so much* deeper!"

"You wanted your voice to break first?" asked Greg, as another creak emanated from the chair.

"I didn't want anything to break, but the human voice didn't interest me. I spent most of the sermon transfixed by huge pipes. Such power! Like terrifying grey torpedoes, and yet ably controlled by little Miss Sweeting, the local National Savings collector and organist."

"Sorry, do you two want scrambled?" called Meston.

"Yes please!" replied Greg, before turning to Joe to elicit his request, but Joe had no concern for the menu. "Er, we're both scrambled!" he added, hoping that Joe would be amenable to such a category.

"I was transfixed by the largest pipe," continued Joe. "Its aperture was big enough for you to post a parcel, as though our very souls could be wrapped up in hymn-sheets and sent to St. Peter, care of the Celestial City - courtesy of Miss Sweeting!"

"Here's your hot milk!" said Monica as she presented Greg with a large steaming jug. "Ma's boiled it just the way you like it!"

Greg thanked her and helped himself to wheat flakes, offering a similar packet and most of the milk to Joe, but his companion was too intent on eulogising about the organ pipes to be distracted by food. He leaned towards Greg again, his chair now having developed a slight cracking sound.

"The beautiful lyrical chords she produced!" he continued. "And the shocking vibrating discords too! It was as though her fingers could create earthquakes - the keyboard must have had its own special faultline!"

"She must have achieved mastery over the tectonic sol-fa!" said Greg, hoping that such a comment didn't sound frivolous.

"One of the stained glass windows rattled so violently during '*Hail The Conquering Hero*' I thought the figure of St. Thomas might fall and land headlong on to our pew!" continued Joe. "I was only thirteen."

"I doubt there was any real damage, though?" said Greg, but then he recalled hearing of a village somewhere nearby called Deeping St. Thomas. Was that to be their venue? Was it thirteen miles away? Little Ted would never survive the journey.

"No breakages," assured Joe. "But the power! I once got out of my seat during an accessional hymn, pushed past a man on his knees, and walked up to Reverend Gatherglow as he stood at the altar watching me with a puzzled expression. Choirboys stared at me too, giggling, but I hadn't come to apply for a singing job. Oh no."

"You wanted to claim sanctuary?" said Greg.

Joe moved in towards Greg once more, but this time the chair emitted a loud snap. Whatever had been the reason for Joe's confrontation with the minister would now have to be put on hold, as Joe's seat split into several slivers of sharp wood as it collapsed in a heap under him. He crumpled on top of it, a distant expression on his face.

"Man down! Man down!" called Norman in alarm.

"Goodness!" said Thelma as she heard the sound of crashing wood. She spun round from her position as senior cook at the stove and saw Greg looking concerned at the floor next to his chair. "Has there been an accident?"

"It's that weird nurse from last night!" shouted Tom. "She's trashed the chair and one of the campers needs first aid. Look!"

Joe was as disinterested in his present state as he had been with the offer of hot milk and wheat flakes. "I told him," he continued. "I want to play the organ. Can someone give me a lesson?"

Tom had by now dragooned Meston and Norman into assisting Joe's ascent, but each of them was reluctant to exacerbate any injuries by moving him. Ted hovered next to his fallen comrade like a referee about to count to ten over a routed wrestler, but Greg merely listened as Joe continued with his story.

"He told me I'd probably be of more use playing the fool instead, and that he'd already got a deputy for whenever Miss Sweeting was unavailable to exercise her skills at the keyboard."

Thelma and Monica were now standing by the table, listening attentively to Joe's confessions whilst jointly stirring a bowl of eggs with a brisk whisk.

"What a shame," said Thelma. "Your father used to play the fool, Monica, but that was probably down to those pink tablets. With him it was a Miss *Keating*, though; she had a Remington. He told me he used to help her with her exercises in the typing pool after work. He even used to change her ribbons for her too! I think people took advantage of his easy-going nature."

"Don't move him!" said Tom as he noticed Ted attempting to loosen the polo neck on Joe's thick pullover. He might have broken something. Feet contain metal tassels or something, and they can wear out."

"Don't talk to me about feet," said Norman.

"Sorry, only trying to put in some useful input," said Tom, slightly hurt.

"He's just broken the chair," said Greg. "His coccyx might be bruised, though."

"Oh dear. Shall I try and get Nurse Newnes to him?" asked Thelma, but Monica squeezed her arm slightly as though to say no.

"Oh well, as long as he's all right. I've got some Coxes for you men to take with you when you go out," she continued. "They're probably slightly bruised themselves!"

"So she liked wearing ribbons, this Miss Keating, then?" enquired Tom, as he half-seated himself on the table.

"Not now, young man," said Norman. "I think we need a strategy for raising him, although we must respect his human rights."

"You'll never guess what I did next!" continued Joe, oblivious to all the attention being paid to what he might *do* next - here and now.

Greg shook his head, whilst Thelma looked knowingly at Monica.

"I ran up to the organ loft, pursued by the churchwarden, Mr. Plankforth," said Joe, animated. "Revolution was in the air!"

Ted was carefully eating a bowl of frosted flakes to feed his inner wolf, but he was almost at the stage when spoon and bowl tend to produce an impatient clatter. "I'm nearly ready for my cooked breakfast, please," he asked nervously of the two ladies at the table, "But can I not have any tomatoes if they're tinned? The taste can be a bit strong."

"Oh, can you make sure his plate isn't too hot?" asked Norman, smiling. "He burns easily."

"Sorry, yes, we'd better be getting on," said Meston

as he guided the two ladies back to the job in hand. "Anyway, the tomatoes are straight from the garden. They're tin-free!"

"What happened next?" asked Greg as his offer of a slice of toast to Joe was declined.

"All Hell broke loose, and in a church too!"

"Goodness!" said Thelma as she tipped a plate of mushrooms into the hot frying pan. "Sounds like our wedding!"

Greg wondered what might have produced sizzling sounds at Thelma's ceremony. Or did she mean that an infernal row had developed? Had Miss Keating attempted to stop the service by clamouring at a stained glass window with a loaded Remington?

"Miss Sweeting fainted as I burst in to her organ loft," continued Joe. I seized the moment and took over with a rendering of the 'Crossroads' TV theme tune!"

"Well, that didn't happen at our service," said Thelma. "Our problem was that Miss Keating went slightly mad and tried to set fire to the register while we were signing it. Bill said it was nerves, then she started screaming. Marvellous acoustics, but I think she was jealous of my bouquet. She kept pulling the heads off my Peace roses and glaring at me."

"These things happen," said Greg, although he felt sure that with recent legislation church registers were now fireproof. He looked down at the crumpled heap of wood next to him on the floor. Did it constitute a fire hazard for the man resting on top of it? Norman and Tom were trying to make Joe slightly more comfortable by inserting fire-retardant cushions under him.

254

"We should try and make the patient comfortable," said Norman. "Although we don't want to make him soft."

Dawn was of the same opinion as she'd now taken up a position of sitting on Joe's feet. Greg hoped this wouldn't lead to a compression fracture.

"So how did your premiere performance go?" asked Greg, prompting Joe to continue his story.

"I was forcibly removed by the sexton before I'd even finished the tune," said Joe. "The suspense for the congregation must have been terrible, but my hands were tied. Tied with Miss Sweeting's Motoravia double knitting wool, to be honest. Four ply!"

"I think Miss Keating must have been keen on knitting," said Thelma. "Apparently Bill used to provide her with four ply, she told me. Anyway, it wasn't nice of that sexton to subject you to bondage, Joe. Especially in a church."

"What's a sexton?" asked Tom as he tried arranging Dawn's feet in order to make her more comfortable too.

"I think he's a church official who supervises the digging of graves," said Greg.

"Wow! They certainly took unauthorised organ playing seriously, then," said Tom.

"My parents tried to pretend nothing was happening," continued Joe. "They sat there in their pew reading their 'Hymns Ancient and Modern'. They didn't like fuss. Anyway, it turned out all right in the end. After Miss Sweeting came to, she suggested I be given the job of pumping the bellows for her!" He exhaled contentedly as though to indicate that he had finished relating his memoirs. He placed his hands on the edge of the table and nodded contentedly.

Greg clasped his hands and looked at the window for signs of an improvement in the weather, but it was steamed up due to the boiling and scrambling of eggs, and lack of breath control from those awaiting them. He sat wondering whether he might have picked up any more clues as to their destination from the revelations of both Joe and Thelma. Was Motoravia - wherever that might be - significant? Was the quest for H indeed still on?

"Breakfast's ready, everyone!" called Monica. "Joe, would you like me to bring you a small tray?"

"That's all right, thank you dear," said Norman. "He's brought his own. He made it years ago in metalwork at school. We all made one, although Ted's has a more substantial guard rail."

"Yard of ale, you say, Norman?" exclaimed Joe. "That'll go down nicely after a good walk!"

Greg thought this a positive sign. Joe had obviously found his calling by having been invited to operate the organ pump in his youth, and now, in his later years, he was set on braving the rain and going on the quest to help pluck more music from the air. He gently pushed the sleeping dog from off his feet, then stood up briskly - showing no signs of injury - only to kneel down again at the table, his knees resting on the cushion. Did he imagine himself to be still in the church and that the plates of hot food being placed on the table by the two ladies were the sacraments?

"You'll need a new chair!" said Monica as she served him a large 'traditional English breakfast', but he only had a chance to say "thank you" before Norman interjected. "He'll be fine; please don't worry. He's got his own chair clipped on the back of his rucksack, but it'll be character-building to eat in a penitential manner for now."

Monica and Thelma must have decided to build their own characters too as they also proceeded to eat without the comfort of chairs. They stood together at the Formica worktop near the stove, and ate eggs on toast, whilst the six men sat - or in Joe's case - *knelt* at the table and tucked in to theirs. Dawn had spread herself out on the sofa, and was catching up on some sleep, her deep breathing complementing both the light clatter of cutlery on plates, and the windblown rain lashing against the window.

All conversation in the cosy kitchen had ceased, and Greg felt a great sense of peace as he feasted on his scrambled eggs, augmented with juicy tomatoes and hash browns. His sense of taste was now sharpened, and his hearing had also intensified. A sudden relaxing contraction of metal inside the grill merely harmonised with the other gentle ambient sounds. He felt as though, somehow, his ambition to find the source of H was already realised, amidst the quiet contentment that he believed they all shared at this moment. But then his reverie yielded to discursive thought once more. Was H to be found in *Hash*? And wasn't hash the common name for the symbol identical with a musical sharp, and found on telephone keypads? The keypad of H? Should he eat it or listen to it?

"Sorry," said Meston, quietly as though aware he was interrupting a contemplative atmosphere. "I think it might be clearing up. Should we be making a move soon, do you think?"

Greg looked once more at the window, but this time there was a hint of sunshine, and the rain was no longer lashing, but caressing the pane. All eyes were now on the window, but it was Tom who went and opened the back door to assess whether it was indeed better weather there too. There was no draught, and the final fling of rain was diminishing by the second as though a tap were being turned off. He pulled a flower off the clematis that grasped the wall outside and placed it in Thelma's hair, as though he were a dove returning to Noah's Ark with evidence of dry land. "I'll organise the crisps and flapjacks, then!" he announced, happily.

"Christmas backpacks?" said Joe, as he put down his knife and fork on an empty plate. "Can I order one now?"

Tom stared at him in bafflement for a few seconds, before walking over to the Great Cupboard and carefully standing on the sofa next to Dawn. She sat up and watched as he pulled open the double doors with a sense of occasion and surveyed its depths. The others watched Greg as he went over to the single back door, opening it with a sense of humility and surveyed the weather. The air was fresh and fragrant, permeated with the heady aroma of greens growing in the vegetable plot. He wondered whether to go and pick a floret of broccoli to place in Monica's hair as a gesture of goodwill, but decided that such acts of chivalry were Meston's prerogative, and that his priority now was to advise 'his' party that the adventure should begin in half an hour.

However, as he turned towards them to make his appeal, he noticed them all waving enthusiastically, and yet he'd hardly even set foot outside the door. Surely he'd not been subject to another leap in time; those recent temporal and spatial voyages of discovery undertaken by the group had merely been a convoluted means of getting them to experience the power of music to transport the listener, and to meet the Harbingers of H. Their last aberration of the space / time continuum had terminated in the Great Cupboard. He naturally assumed that the waving indicated a growing sense of loyalty towards him, but then he realised that they seemed to be staring beyond him, and that Norman especially was waving avidly. Greg turned round again and followed their gaze just as two men were walking past. What were they doing outside, and didn't the younger of the two men resemble the late Buddy Holly? He wasn't all that familiar with the singer's art, but it was the man's thick-framed glasses that brought him to mind. He waved too - out of politeness - and then observed the man's companion. He too wore thick-framed glasses, but his rather anxious expression definitely looked familiar. Then Norman cheered, prompting Greg to make an improbable deduction. Buddy Holly and Dmitri Shostakovich had come to empty Meston and Monica's wheelie bin. He went back to the door and peered out, half amazed, half apprehensive of them suspecting he was checking up on their method of waste collection, but there was no sign of either of them. He wondered what to tell the others but Meston was now standing at his side.

"Sorry, but this path outside the back door is actually part of the public footpath to the woods," he advised quietly. "It's quite rare to see anyone going past, but that's probably why the imagination can play tricks." He winked, and went to ask Tom what flavour crisps he'd found.

259

"Sardine and sprout with reduced fat," he said casually as he threw a large multipack on to the table.

"*Who's* out there?" asked Thelma, currently preoccupied with scraping some burnt toast over a pedal bin.

"Just some walkers, Ma," replied Monica.

"Hmm, your father liked walking," said Thelma. "Miss Keating once gave him a compass inscribed with a lovely cross on the back. He used to go to bed with it clutched tightly in his hand. He had a tendency to stray."

"He had a tent to see her safe?" said Joe. "Very discreet, very discreet."

"Shall we get going in about ten minutes?" said Greg. "We might even catch up with….those two men. They might even know the way!"

CHAPTER 15

Greg thought it highly likely that the two celebrated, if unfortunately deceased, musicians had come specially to escort the six unknown composers-to-be to their correct location. If so, they were probably now eagerly awaiting them somewhere in the vicinity to assume the role of spirited guides. After all, other dead composers had kindly given up their time to accompany or advise Meston and himself. This gave him renewed assurance, but then he noticed that Thelma's toast-scraping action had almost ceased, as though she'd somehow lost some of hers. Monica clutched her mother's arm, perhaps to comfort her, or possibly to reactivate her wrist action. Might there still be regrets that Bill had taken his cherished compass with him when he'd escaped from the theatre in Mablethorpe, care of the magician's assistant?

"Well, he's made his bed now," said Monica, coolly. "So it's up to him to lie in it."

Thelma looked at her, warmly, then at Greg, with a sense of admiration. "I'm sure he has, Monica, and it's a captain's bed too! One day we can ask for a blue plaque to be fixed to it to commemorate our talented guest!"

"I meant my Dad, actually," said Monica.

"You shouldn't worry about him," said Thelma, before blowing gently on the toast to disperse the last of its black film. "Dawn has been a wonderful substitute - an excellent role model for you, and an inspiration to Meston!"

Greg was still sitting at the table, finishing his cup of tea and trying to disregard the adulation and the suggestion that his bed deserved a plaque, although another blanket would be useful. Dawn had jumped off the sofa and was now nuzzling him as though asking him for another walk, but he doubted that she had the will to be part of a musical co-operative. The others were all engaged in packing, either in the tent or in the house, and as he'd already got everything he needed with him he thought it might be best to stand near the back door looking keen to depart, and yet patient. "The last time I went in the woods I met a German Shepherd called Spike!" he said, not knowing what else to say to the two ladies as they regarded him benevolently.

"Ahh, it's always good to meet our European cousins," said Thelma. "You might see him again. It's amazing who you can meet if you put your mind to it!"

Norman and his retinue had arrived outside the back door, each with a foldable chair, and replete with tray. Meston and Tom then emerged from the hall carrying a slightly disintegrated Ordnance Survey map and tape measure.

"Follow the Chief Harbinger!" said Norman, rallying his troops behind Greg as he stood on the step checking his pockets.

"Swallow the cheap Bollinger!" said Joe as he took a swig from his plastic bottle. "Cheers!"

Thelma and Monica saw them all off at the door with coordinated waving, and so at last the search was underway. Greg pondered on the dynamics of who should pair up with whom when walking in a group, but as Tom was right behind him and Meston was still embracing Monica as though his imminent adventure would be fraught with danger, it was Tom who began to walk abreast with Greg as they headed for the woods. The three older men were leaning against the incinerator waterproofing each other's boots from an aerosol spray can.

"Try to avoid inhaling the fumes," warned Norman. "This stuff is *twice* as toxic as vinaigrette dressing."

"Those two guys we saw with the black frames - did you recognise them?" asked Tom. "I mean in a weird historical way?"

"Yes, I think they've been sent here to support us," said Greg. "The younger man was a singer who died tragically and the older one was a composer who, some say, *lived* tragically."

"That's tough. I'll try and cheer them up with some office jokes," said Tom as he proceeded to tread a fine line around a series of muddy puddles.

Greg hoped that Tom's office had been kept clean, and that they could then all listen attentively to whatever knowledge the musicians could provide. "Shostakovich had to tread a fine line between his art and toeing party doctrine," he said, sadly.

"You probably sussed he was cheating, I suppose?" said Tom.

"You mean plagiarising?" said Greg, shocked that the great man might have been borrowing tunes from his comrades.

"Is that what they called it then?" said Tom. "I know Auntie Thelma used to play second fiddle for years."

"Really!" said Greg, amazed at this additional revelation. He had no idea that she'd ever performed in a Soviet orchestra, although she'd obviously developed a liking for borshch at some point. "Does she still play?"

"Well, she plays innocent, but I think she suspects what he was up to."

Greg hoped that Tom might have been confused and that there had been no compromise of collective copyright.

"I still can't get my head round us getting to meet all these dead musicians," said Tom. "Anyway, I suppose the internet must play a big part in breaking down barriers. I've even got a ringtone that's supposed to have come from Mozart! Sad to think that after writing those cool tunes in Australia thousands of years ago he had to supplement his income producing jingles for mobile phones. That guy was ahead of his time."

Greg humoured him with an acquiescent nod and considered whether Mozart's penury might have been reduced if he'd invested any royalties in a deposit account at Tom's bank. He then heard the approach of synchronized wheezing and the syncopated squelching of frustrated footsteps. He turned round to see the three old soldiers trying to catch up by means of delicate pirouette movements around the larger puddles. Was it only yesterday morning that he'd seen the same little procession on the same path, and then avoided them by sitting behind a large oak tree where he encountered an animated dog and his irritated master?

Meston had now joined the little band of brothers, and so the inevitable pairing took place. Probably from an innate sense of duty to support Ted as he trudged dolefully through the mud, the straggler proceeded to walk alongside the little man, apologising for the state of the track. Norman was teaching Joe to search for rocks to use as stepping stones when the going got tough. "It's a trick I picked up on the Isle of Wight," he added.

"Trust you to pick up a souvenir!" said Joe, laughing. "Trust you had a good time there too!"

"It's being cut off from the mainland that's made those islanders so self-sufficient," said Norman. "You should have seen the methodical way they presented their galvanised iron dustbins on collection day!"

By now Greg and Tom had reached drier ground where the canopy of trees had kept the path free from becoming saturated.

"Are you sure this is the way we're meant to go?" asked Tom. "We've got a duty of care to the others not to lead them up the creak!"

A cow in a neighbouring field mooed loudly. Greg translated it as a bovine affirmative. "I'm sure this is right," he said, confidently. He thought he could identify the oak tree in the distance where he'd sat throwing a broken ball before being transported to a conjurer's cabinet. He half expected to see the man and his dog still sitting there, but instead two men wearing black-framed glasses stood idly kicking pebbles as though expecting something to happen.

Greg was now certain that they must be Dmitri and Buddy and that their purpose was to conduct Greg and his party to an even more important tree: their access point for downloading H. However, the scene in front of him reminded him of a play he once saw in which two Irishmen wait for ages for a character who never appears. Was that an omen? Would the manuscript book still in his pocket prevent their meeting and whisk him, and his friends too, to yet another location? He decided to override the book's instantaneous satnav feature, and removed his jacket, discreetly allowing the book to fall out into a gorse bush. "Look everyone!" he called out. "Our guides are waiting for us!"

Dmitri cast a nervous glance at the approaching deputation but Greg waved at the two men reassuringly and urged his friends to do the same, although this might have appeared rather militaristic as six hands shot up in unison.

"I bet those two were big in their day," said Tom as he strode purposefully towards the slightly anxious-looking pair. "They probably hung out with Mendelssohn too, sailing round the Med. on luxury yachts. If only they'd had charter planes in those days!"

Greg suddenly pretended to have discovered a rare bird's nest. "Well, well!" he said in an exaggerated manner in order to reduce the impact of Tom's last statement. "You don't see many....er eagles' eggs round here!" He then whispered loudly in Tom's ear. "Don't mention flying!"

"All right!" said Tom, sensing a slight reprimand. "I'll try not to offend the eggs."

Greg could hardly clarify his advice now as they were almost upon the awaiting duo. He wondered about the protocol of who should introduce whom, and whether Dmitri Shostakovich was fluent in English, although he was fairly certain that Buddy Holly was. Meston and the others were right behind, and so Greg, probably due to nervousness, extended his hand cordially before he'd even reached those of the guides.

Dmitri looked at the approaching hand with apprehension, whilst Buddy smiled, bemusedly. Greg weighed up the options. Should he introduce himself first, or should he present Tom and then the others? Or would it be more fitting to let their two 'hosts' initiate the greetings? Ultimately, the exchange of names wasn't all that relevant when the pursuit of music was their single goal. Besides, this was a mission to which the late composers had already been summoned to assist.

"Hi, I'm Tom!" said Tom as he grabbed one hand each of the two great men. "I've come with these guys to look for a tree. Fancy some crisps?"

"Crisps?" said Dmitri, suspiciously, as Tom then proceeded to take off his rucksack and unzip its upper section.

"We've brought apples too!" said Greg, acceding to the more informal style of making contact. "I think they're Coxes."

Norman, Ted and Joe were already erecting their foldable chairs by the tree, nodding and making polite grunts and smiles to the two bemused men in lieu of anything more vocal whilst each regained his breath.

"Hi, I'm Buddy!" said the younger man, stepping forward to assist Norman in opening out his chair.

"Can you spare a dime?" asked Joe, sufficiently oxygenated and grinning broadly at the man.

"Sure," he replied, as he caught a packet of sardine and sprout crisps thrown to him by Tom. "They told me you'd been having a depression over here too."

"You could say that," said Tom. "I worked in a bank, but I'm glad to have got out in time before it crashed!"

Greg gulped and called Meston over as a means of distraction.

"Sorry, I'm Meston!" He leaned awkwardly over Norman's chair to shake Buddy's hand.

"No kidding!" said Buddy. "Here, this is my friend from Moss Cow. I can't really pronounce his name!"

Dmitri's attention had been caught by Ted's hapless attempts to insert a bent straw into his tiny carton of apple juice. He appeared to have recognised a twin soul in the little man's persona, and so he walked over to him and kindly punched a hole in the top of the carton with a toothpick. "They denounced you too, did they?" said Dmitri, as he proceeded to hold the straw in place for the surprised Ted to quench his thirst. "What did they accuse you of - formalism?"

Ted's eyes betrayed a look of anxiety as he hurriedly sipped his juice whilst presumably wondering if his friends had complained about him greeting the composers with too much reverence. Conscious of this, Greg tried to create a relaxed mood by sitting on the ground and ignoring the wet nettles, but now his own eyes betrayed a look of unease as he realised he was sitting in precisely the spot where he was when the angry man and his friendly dog had discovered him. Nevertheless, he patted a clump of sprawling roots next to him as a gesture to all those standing; inviting them to sit down for a few minutes, but they chose to remain upright, clutching their sealed packets of crisps as though awaiting permission to open them.

"No, no-one's complained about me being formal, I don't think," said Ted. "Norman encourages us to be polite, but always with a hint of *lion*."

Dmitri stared at him for a while, then nodded his head, almost as despondently as the manner in which Ted had spoken. "With me it was that Lady Macbeth of the Mtsensk District that got me into trouble. How about you?"

"Me? I don't know anyone in....where?" said Ted, looking towards Norman for assistance.

Norman was engaged in chatting to Buddy about map-reading, advising him that he often read the Landranger series cover to cover. Greg was eager to help Ted out of his current conversational crisis, but he was even keener to hear more about Dmitri's tribulations at the hands of the authorities. He stood up and whispered in Ted's ear. "It's the name of his opera, based on the Scottish play."

"Oh yes, I wrote an opera too," said Ted, avoiding eye contact. "I called it.... Mrs. Le Frith of....The Lake District."

Dmitri stared at him again briefly, whilst Greg wondered where to look before sitting down once more. He thought it might look desperate if he were to pat the roots again, but Buddy had now observed the vacancy in the impromptu seating area and courteously asked Greg if he could sit there.

"Feel free!" said Greg. "This land is your land - as someone once sang!"

"Thanks. I've been looking at some of it on your friend's map. Lots of green, but I used to think that Blue Grass was where it's at," confided Buddy as he clasped his hands around his knees and vacantly rested his eyes on a passing squirrel. "I like your wildlife, but since I joined the Brotherhood of Musical Mentors I've been getting hooked on the singing of Minke whales. Gee, those creatures have sure got soul!"

Greg acknowledged this revelation with a nod whilst formulating an intelligent reply, but the odd snatches of recollection from Dmitri's former career were what really held his attention.

"They panned my fourth symphony," continued Dmitri, shaking slightly with tension. "My advice to you would be to skip your fourth and go straight on to the fifth."

Ted looked at him with awe. "I'll pan it right away!"

"May the fourth be without you!" called Joe.

Greg was now in that classic conundrum of hearing various conversations simultaneously and being unable to decide which was the most interesting. Buddy was now recalling some woman called Peggy Sue who had apparently jilted him, but had he actually just declared an interest in the choral music of Minkes, and announced that he was a member of some brotherhood of mentors?

"Apparently we're the Harbingers of H," said Greg, slightly embarrassed at how grand he sounded. "Are you part of the same organisation?"

"Well, I guess I am," said Buddy, repositioning himself on to a slightly drier clump of tree root. "I think you've already met some of our other mentors. Someone called Haydn sends you his good wishes!"

Greg felt his pulse quicken, although hopefully not too fast for the usually sedate Father of the Symphony. "Wow, I *did* meet him, although I was fragmented at the time, and he might have been an extended version himself. Jimi Hendrix was with him. We ate goulash!"

"You don't say!" said Buddy. "Those two are fully-booked for the next two years now!"

Greg leaned back against the bark of the tree and closed his eyes for a moment whilst trying to take it all in. When he opened them again Meston and Tom were standing in front of him.

"Sorry, I thought perhaps we could get going," said Meston. "I'm a bit keyed-up!"

"He's keyed-up with H!" said Tom. "I think I will be soon. There's an awesome-looking tree in the distance and it seems to be pulsating with rainbows!"

CHAPTER 16

"How are your knees today, Little Tedders?" asked Norman as the party duly moved off along the track. "You don't seem to be genuflecting as much, I've noticed."

"I'm bearing up, thank you," replied Ted, his improved condition having no bearing on his usual doleful delivery. "How are your feet? Those surgical stockings must be a boon."

"Hmm, I think I've been cutting corners with my toenails," said Norman, regretfully. "I foolishly trimmed them with my curved scissors designated for finger nails, or - unofficially - for levering reluctant drawing pins. Now my nails are convex, which some podiatrists claim can escalate to them in-growing. I rang a men's helpline, but they don't advise on medical matters that far down."

"What about propping them up on a pillow?" suggested Ted.

"What about stopping and hugging a willow?" asked Joe, glancing quizzically at Norman. "Well, why not! Comrades in arms, comrades in arms!"

Dmitri kicked a small stone and muttered something privately in Russian.

Greg kicked a fir cone and uttered something publicly in Latin. "Salix Officianalis - the common willow," he said, thoughtfully. "What if we were all willows, or elders, or even....hawthorns?"

"Come again?" said Buddy. "I've met a few elders, but they usually go round in twos."

272

"We've all recently undergone various changes of time and location," explained Greg. "There were several versions of me, and I'm still wondering if I'm actually the same Greg as before, or perhaps I'm just *a* Greg."

"In my language we have no concept of 'the' or 'a'," said Dmitri, sagely. "It has helped Slavic people avoid problems of identity crises!"

Tom shook his head, and smiled, then whispered something to Buddy about them all probably having had "flights of the imagination".

"I wonder how far it is now!" said Greg, eager to counteract the effects of the sensitive *f* word on the young man.

"Sorry, is it me, or can anyone else hear humming?" asked Meston.

"There are eight of us," said Dmitri. "We have formed an octave. Soon we will merge with H! H for humming!"

There was by now a general, and yet understated, excitement within the group about the musical revelations to come. Greg especially found himself radiating goodwill towards his fellow man whenever he was anticipating some mutually appreciated musical experience. He recalled once listening in awe to an orchestra tuning up and hoping they'd play an encore, hearing the notes not as a grating practice run of stage-struck instruments, but as an enticing introduction to *The Wasps Overture* that was to follow. Since that performance he'd felt a much greater affinity towards both musicians and winged insects. He turned to Dmitri and addressed him deferentially. "Mr. Shostakovich, I think your *Gadfly Suite* is sublime!

273

Oh, and you speak English extremely well!" He trusted that he hadn't sounded too patronising. "And *your* English is excellent too, of course, Mr. Holly!" he added, before wondering whether this might indeed have sounded crass.

"Gee, thanks!" said Buddy. "So's yours!"

"We have already crossed barriers of time and place with no difficulty," said Dmitri, seriously. "It was therefore inevitable that any language barrier would also be breached just as easily in quest of musical enlightenment. Perhaps we are all gadflies!"

"I guess we're all on the same plane of existence today," added Buddy.

Tom coughed loudly and pointed out a solitary bluebell so as to deflect attention from Buddy's *faux pas* with the *p* word.

Buddy's attention was on a young holly tree, which he proudly pointed out. "And that's probably a more recent version of me!"

By now it seemed that everyone was checking out each tree they passed, and yet they knew it was the glow in the distance that was the reason for their pilgrimage - the tree of H with its constituent cascade of chromatic creativity.

"Sorry, I think I need to stop at this ash for a moment," said Meston, waving them all on. "I'll catch you up in a minute!" He stood diffidently with his back to the sizeable tree, smiling self-consciously as they all passed by, and called Greg's name softly. He repeated it slightly more loudly until Greg turned round, averting his eyes, but facing Meston, rather thrown.

"Just face the trunk and imagine you're at home," advised Greg. "I'll wait for you by the clump of wild

274

garlic if you're nervous!"

"There's something resting on that side branch," said Meston, pointing upwards. "It looks like that manuscript book I gave you!"

"Sorry," said Greg, regretting having jettisoned it in a gorse bush, but now fearful of its ability to stalk them. "I think I might have emptied my jacket pockets a bit too zealously."

Meston stared at him uncomprehendingly for a few seconds, before gazing back up at the branch. "A bird must have planted it there, then. The book must have been destined to accompany us!"

Greg nodded and wondered what sort of bird could have carried a book in its beak, but then he conceded that it must have been placed there by H. "It was probably a heron," he suggested as Meston tried jumping up and down in order to retrieve it.

"Sorry, can you possibly help me out?" asked Meston. "Apparently it's possible to clench one's hands and form a step for someone else to stand on to reach things, although I've never tried it before."

Greg had never got involved in such acrobatics either, but he stepped forward and formed a stirrup, as did Meston. Greg wondered which of them was going to volunteer to bear the weight of the other, and who would attempt the balancing act whilst grasping a book that had hitherto been a travel guide in its most literal sense.

"I used to milk cows," said Meston, after a long pause. "Manually sometimes. Perhaps *my* fingers would be more agile for this type of weight-lifting?"

Greg wondered if Meston's dairy had incorporated a gym, and whether the rewards for those donating milk

275

had been the availability of exercise machines for maintaining agile hooves. He thought the support of a cow's foot might be more reassuring than Meston's palms. "What is your maximum load?" he asked.

"Er, I think I can probably run to however much you weigh," said Meston. "We all passed the medical in the pyramid!"

"I'll remove my jacket. That should help," said Greg, recalling that it was his jacket that had brought about the present situation in the first place.

Meston stood rigidly with his back against the tree, his eyes closed and his hands clasped, as though he were at a service of remembrance. Greg hung his jacket from a rather spindly branch that waved gracefully as it received the weight, and stared at the motionless man standing before him. The juxtaposition of the gently rocking jacket and Meston's static pose was now affecting his sense of decorum but he overcame his urge to giggle and remembered his responsibilities as Chief Harbinger. Should he take a run at him and leap nimbly into his clasped hands? Or should he walk up to him with more dignity, carefully raising his foot and placing it gently in the awaiting hands whilst avoiding depositing too much mud from his size 9 shoe? And where would his other foot go once the first one was in place - on Meston's shoulder? He began to wish he'd watched more escape films for tips on such matters. How would he cope when they finally reached the Tree of H?

"Ready when you are," said Meston, confidently. "My hands can probably take any shoe up to size 12."

Greg had decided on the more restrained approach, although he was still trying to quell an urge to laugh.

276

He marched up to Meston's awaiting handclasp and raised his left leg, gently allowing his foot to slot into its mounting. His friend almost buckled under the weight, but it was Greg who felt precarious as he tried balancing whilst raising his other foot to try and gain a purchase on a tiny niche carved in the bark. "At least the rain's held off!" said Greg, slightly high-pitched.

"Yes!" said Meston, in an equally strained voice.

"Is the men's free?" called Norman, hurrying back towards the scene. "I've brought Ted, he needs the....oh."

"We're a bit tied up at the moment," called Greg, carefully turning round to see Ted anxiously running on the spot and Norman's lips quivering.

"So I see," said Norman. "Tedders, you go and find another location. Remember, when you've found one, look left, then right, then down."

"We're keen to retrieve a book," explained Greg. "We....accidentally dropped it!"

"Sorry!" said Meston in an even higher voice as he leant his head to one side of Greg's leg to smile stoically at Norman.

Norman stared back for a few moments, the tremor on his lips having spread to his chin. "If you want something to read, I've got some magazines with me about refuse collection - and there are several illustrated easy-to-follow recipes on the back pages."

"Thank you, but the book's up here on this branch," said Greg as he nervously extended his hand to try and grasp it. "We think it was deposited there by a passing heron."

"Heron!" squeaked Meston, his face red with the exertion of hoisting the foot further skywards.

"Oh, I see what you mean!" said Norman, looking up, the tone of authority back in his voice. "Joe could have dislodged your book with his stick, but Tom's teaching him how to spot forged banknotes. What *you* need is a fisherman's keep-net."

Greg hadn't anticipated any arboreal angling but as he made a leap of faith to grab hold of the book, a sudden breeze dislodged it, causing it to descend gracefully to the ground as though it were no heavier than one of Norman's rubbish magazines. Greg decided to follow suit and jump, eager to be back on the ground too, but in the absence of a fisherman's net to receive him he landed equally gracefully on a mulch of last autumn's leaves.

"Thank goodness you landed before reaching terminal velocity!" said Norman. "Excellent librarianship, too!"

"That's the man we need to thank!" said Greg, pointing to Meston, now recovering on a prostrate log upholstered with moss.

"Sorry, but can one of you grab the book before it disappears again?" said Meston.

Just then another slight breeze caused the now-empty branch to rub against a neighbouring maple. This produced a plangent cadence similar to the tones of a double bass.

"It's the final bars of Schubert's String Quintet!" exclaimed Greg. "Even the tempo is correct!"

It was Norman who had undertaken to rescue the manuscript book, but he had heard the sounds differently. "Actually, I think it's a signature tune I used to hear years ago at 10pm on some foreign radio station on short wave played on a glockenspiel. It was

278

the highlight of my bedtime!"

"Sorry, wasn't it a TV ad for firelighters played on a trombone?" suggested Meston. "I can almost smell the paraffin!"

Norman ignored him and stood leafing through the book, turning the pages randomly, then handed it to Greg. "A veritable mine of information, this!" he said, grinning broadly. "The index has details of every musical work that's been composed - as well as those works yet to come!"

Greg had seen no such index before, and Meston was looking surprised at this revelation also. Was music subject to the same laws as the Periodic Table of elements? Could new compositions be predicted? If so, that would mean that there was only a finite amount of new works to write, or discover. Deep down, however, Greg knew that there was an infinity of music still to come, and the format of the index seemed to concur with this theory, as each time he tried to peruse the final page, another one appeared. He regretted having been so cavalier as to try and lose the book, but at the time it seemed to have fulfilled its purpose and he was still slightly dubious about its powers. He handed it to Meston, its original owner, and wondered what he might find within its seemingly limitless pages.

"There's a whole chapter on the speech patterns of the citizens of Belfast!" said Meston, pleasantly surprised and at once engrossed. "Apparently the rising fourths were powerful enough to find their way across the sea to Liverpool, but mutated to a faster tempo there due to the influence of the currents in the Mersey!"

Greg had had close encounters with the fourth kind when he'd stayed on the Northumbrian coast - where answers were often voiced as questions. This was puzzling at first, but he thought his confusion might be due to foggy conditions on the Tyne. However, when visiting Colchester once, he'd noticed that the locals tended to transform questions into statements: rising octaves would occur when asking directions, then descend gently by a semitone. He attributed this practice to the influence of the curlews soaring above the River Colne, then, without asking directions, descending gently at Brightlingsea. The two trees made contact again, this time producing an extract from Dvorak's New World Symphony, or was it folk music from Peru? Whatever it was, there was a rapturous harmonic accompaniment coming from the direction in which they were headed. It was time to move on.

"Sorry to sound self-centred but I just had a quick look in the index," whispered Meston as he warily gave the book back to Greg. "My symphony isn't listed, but it seems I'm going to write a trombone concerto! The premiere's in Portsmouth next year!"

"I look forward to hearing it!" said Greg as he shook hands with him to congratulate him on his unusual opus.

However, even though Meston's hand was flecked with mud, the book appeared to be immaculate. Greg then thought it best to put it carefully away in his pocket before his own curiosity - he didn't really do pride - made him wish to look up his own name. Norman, meanwhile, was oblivious to any biographical references being discussed as he was currently absorbed in examining the track.

"You can learn a lot about your fellow man by observing the impressions their feet make," he declared, proudly. "Footprints are the windows of the sole. I think they went *that* way!" He duly pointed the way that the rest of the group had gone - not that there was any mystery about their route - but it afforded Norman the opportunity to act as leader, heroically leading his replacement platoon into the promised land - a land flowing with H!

They moved on with a lightness in their step, as though drawn onwards by the power of the tree in the distance. It was only the shimmering that they could see, but the exquisite sound of pure notes, augmented by the voices of the rest of their party just a few hundred paces ahead seemed to guide them effortlessly along the stony track. The three men moved in silence; even the squelching of their boots in the residual mud was now nothing more than a whisper. Greg felt that Norman and Meston had at last surrendered the mundane for the profound, but then Norman sighed and shook his head. "You've probably noticed that Joe is inclined to get hold of the wrong end of the stick at times, even though he carved it himself from the branch of a sycamore."

"He seems to be astute," said Greg, thoughtfully. "Perhaps he sees things from an unusual angle."

"Well, yes, there is a kink in the middle," said Norman. "I've noticed him trying to straighten it out. Of course, Ted won't risk handling sticks in case his fingers get stabbed by splinters, but he is a bit of a wild sort. He said he felt the claws of a clay pigeon scratch his head once as it tried to snatch his woollen hat!"

"I don't think clay pigeons are native to these parts," Greg assured him. "His hat should be safe here and his hands seem to be firmly clenched much of the time."

281

"Not *all* the time. You might be surprised to learn that he plays air guitar!" said Norman. "He's quite accomplished at the chords!"

"I wanted an air guitar when I was young," said Meston. "I never got one, but my dad let me have a go with his airgun once. I shot an empty cocoa tin, but, sorry to say, I dented the label."

"Well, just think - you might well soon be plucking keys from the air and finding the component keys that emanate from H!" said Greg, enthusiastically. "A power shower of cascading creativity!"

"With all the music that's already been written, do you really think the source is limitless?" asked Meston.

"I know it's incomprehensible to the human mind how a new tune can be created when before we heard it, its existence could never be imagined," said Greg. "But then suddenly it's there, part of a constant stream of audible beauty! And like Planck's Constant - this phenomenon has been given the name H too!"

The voices from the others who had gone ahead suddenly became silent. Now only the mellifluous fusion of humming, singing, and orchestration could be heard as Greg, Meston and Norman wended their way along the path. They too had become silent, until they found themselves alongside the rest of the party who were standing motionless on a ridge facing the scintillating tree. Were they having a brief rest before making the final putsch, or were they overwhelmed by the vision and the sounds before them?

Greg scrambled up the grassy slope to stand shoulder to shoulder with them, then saw their dilemma. Between them and their goal lay a deep watercourse about thirty feet wide or more, stretching in either direction as far as the eye could see. Joe stood prodding the ground with his pole as though considering vaulting across, whilst next to him Dmitri was nervously checking his pocket watch. "I'm sure it's running backwards!" he said, holding it to his ear as though to make sure it wasn't going 'tock tick.'

Ted was in the process of sitting down carefully on an inflatable mat, propping himself up on his hands to prevent himself falling off.

Tom turned and faced Greg. "We can't swim across. I've heard that crayfish are active in some parts of the country," he said, despondently. "We're stumped! What we need is for some rich farmer to loan us a bridge."

Buddy gazed ahead. "That is one swell Christmas Tree!" he said of the tall, ultra-symmetrical tree with pulsating colours, chords, and rhythmically fluttering leaves. "I wonder if Santa's brought us any stepping stones to help us cross the river and open our....oh. I guess we'd need to *get* there first to pick them up."

"Actually, we tend not to believe in Santa Claus in this country after the age of twenty seven," said Norman. "Anyway, I understand that items have to be requested in advance."

"Sorry," said Meston, now peering down into the water below them. "I'd no idea that this ditch ever existed."

Greg nodded slightly as though to assure everyone that whatever their predicament; it would somehow be resolved. "We might as well eat our snacks now while we wait for...."

"While we wait for what?" asked Tom, irritated. "Wading boots? Does anyone know how deep that water is?"

"Low salt crisps, anyone?" asked Greg, pulling a large bag from within his rucksack. "Apparently it's as well to reduce our daily intake of sodium!"

"Take to the podium?" said Joe. "Well, we've all got our batons. Now we just want to get the music and we're all set!"

CHAPTER 17

Greg was delighted at the positive vibes that only Joe could bring to this impasse. It was at that moment that he looked upstream and noticed a barge heading towards them.

"Better late than never!" said Dmitri as he waved his hands grandly at the approaching craft. "It's the Valkyrie sisters!"

"The *what* sisters?" asked Tom, querulously.

"I think that's our lift," said Greg, assuming that the crossing was to be on a pre-booked ferry operated by some Fenland franchisees of a Wagnerian epic. "I don't think you'll be seasick this time!"

"Can someone give me a lift up?" asked Ted as he struggled to rise from his cushion. "I'd have used my folding chair instead, only I thought I saw a ladybird crawling menacingly on one of the armrests."

"Don't worry about ladybirds, Tedders," said Norman as he tried to help him up. "Some of those insects are actually male, like we are! The red and black polka dot costume has the same status as a flak jacket!"

"I think polka dots would hurt my eyes," said Ted as he stood up. "Anyway, can someone help me slither safely down the bank? My knees have turned to jelly!"

"Really! We call it Jello in the States!" said Buddy as he gave him a helping hand to get down the bank. "My mom used to make it in a glass mould shaped like a rabbit!"

Ted looked at him nervously, then slipped on the

wet grass and slid elegantly down towards the water, until his progress was halted when his foot became anchored in a rabbit hole. Buddy dashed to his rescue, and gently extricated the trapped foot. "Maybe I shouldn't have mentioned the glass mould. Of course, we ate blueberry pie too. That's probably good for gammy knees."

Meanwhile, the barge was steadily advancing, but so too was the sound of agitation from within. Greg suspected there was some dispute on board, evidenced by shouting and the sight of assorted clothes being yanked from a washing line slung between a chimney and the guard rail. Was there a problem with soot on the whites, or might they be re-enacting a scene from an opera? A young lady dressed in a kimono stood on deck holding a megaphone to her mouth as the craft slowly drew alongside them.

"Nice dress!" called Tom. "Any chance of you ladies taking eight of us to the other side?"

The lady glanced at him disdainfully, then shouted indistinctly through the loud hailer. "We represent characters from opera, ballet, and various ballads. We exist purely within our specific roles and we oppose the proliferation of replacement choruses, choreography, and arias. I should warn you that we are armed with secateurs and retractable saws."

"Hear, hear!" said another of her comrades, currently engaged in tearing a shirt into shreds. "Listen to Sister Butterfly and help protect our roles from unfair competition. Stop tree downloads!"

"Here, here!" cried a chorus of distressed voices from within. "We've been hijacked!"

Greg realised that the piracy issue was based on a

286

false premise of musical substitution. He raised his hands as though to quell the insurrection, but the two ladies took this as their cue to inhale, ready to be conducted in singing their standard repertoire.

"Let me assure you we're not trying to flood the world with a tidal wave of replacement themes!" he called out, whilst Sister Butterfly and a matronly Valkyrie held their breaths as though awaiting the maestro's direction. "Our task is to expedite the bringing forth of fresh music, to be enhanced by composers and arrangers, so that every person can find something accessible with which to resonate!"

"Sorry for interrupting," said Meston, "but I'll tell you what gets my vote. Abide With Me."

"Come fly with me?" queried Joe. "Or we could *all* go by boat. I'm sure it's safe!"

Buddy suddenly went pale, then looked up at the sky as though recalling an incident, but then gazed at the charismatic tree and took on a serene expression. A man dressed as Nebuchadnezzar appeared from below on the craft and stared suspiciously at Greg and the opposing line-up of artistic expressionists, all eager to feed the world with an unlimited supply of what he, Nebuchadnezzar, probably believed to be counterfeit notes of excess melody. He then turned and stared at the pulsating tree, before settling his ominous gaze on jovial Joe's stick. "I see you've helped yourself to a bit of it already!" he called out scathingly. "I'm glad it's not got a tree preservation order because we've got tools and equipment on board to reduce that oversized humming squirrels' nest to sawdust!"

A face then appeared at one of the windows on the craft, prompting Dmitri to whisper furtively to Greg. "I think they're holding George Gershwin captive. He wrote a rhapsody in blue instead of a proper key. They won't like that."

Greg nodded seriously, and realised that the operatic ladies were at least still compliant with the custom of awaiting the command of a conducting baton. Should he produce it and quell the mutineers into providing safe conduct on to the boat for the eight Harbingers? During the impasse, Greg noticed that Tom was very gradually moving down the bank towards the prow of the vessel. Gershwin waved to him encouragingly, and was now accompanied at the window by Marc Bolan, waving excitedly at a white swan gazing benignly from its nest, just a few feet away from the craft's potential liberator.

"I want to see if there's another way in," whispered Tom to Buddy and Dmitri, before subtly mouthing his intentions to the others. "There must be a lifeboat somewhere with a ladder. The Navy's bound to be hot on health and safety!"

"That young man's going to get moist feet," said Norman, from the corner of his mouth. "Such courage."

"I had no idea there'd be this sort of opposition to our mission," said Dmitri, his words directed at Greg whilst shaking his head. "Liberace assured me that nothing would go wrong with our transport arrangements. He's been so keen to make amends after murdering Rachmaninov."

"I had no idea," said Greg, shocked. "Where did this happen?"

"On his Blüthner Grand. Destroyed him with ostentatious flights of fancy in four octaves," said

Dmitri, before glancing at Buddy and suddenly appearing uncomfortable.

Greg thought it regrettable that safety issues concerning showy interpretation had been so lax in the 1950s. He'd once heard of a loud pedal becoming stuck during a recital of a Beethoven sonata after the pianist had pumped up the volume from nought to ninety decibels in only six seconds. Meanwhile, the tone on deck had diminished to little more than quiet murmuring between its operatic pirates, whereas the tree had now become distinctly more vibrant; radiating hues of ultra-crimson and the greenest of gold, plus chords and cadences that obeyed only the highest laws of harmonics. Even the pirates had now grudgingly turned round to observe it as though anxious of what it might do next. Greg decided to wait until they turned round once more before engaging them in more argument. They were obviously unsure as to what strategy to use to defuse the tree's power. He sidled inconspicuously to his right to deflect any undue attention towards Tom who was now moving in a crouching manner towards what he presumably hoped might be some sort of fire escape. His training at the bank had probably included such tactics in case of hostages being held in the strong room during panic over a weak pound. However, wading inconspicuously in the weed-strewn waters around a boat in distress might prove much more hazardous. Should Norman and his little band of military mates be gently nudged to seize control by uttering their warbled war cry?

Another mutineer had now stepped out on deck bearing a cut-throat razor and a jar of shaving foam.

"We could bring that thing down with fire power!"

he said in a Spanish accent. "It worked at Cadiz, although I'm a Seville man!"

"We come in peace," called Greg, hoping his words wouldn't be construed as too other-worldly. "Your roles are safe. We merely want access to the source of limitless raw music to refine it for mankind!"

The barber stared at him, then at his companions all lined up in a pose that comprised of confrontation towards the singers of discord on the boat, and veneration towards the bringer of concord on the opposite bank.

"Why don't you use your folding chair, Tedders?" asked Norman, suddenly aware of his companion's inability to get comfortable on his unwieldy sitmat. "Surely the ladybird has moved on by now?"

"I think one of the bolts is loose," said Ted, tremulously. "I'm afraid it might go at any time, like my knees."

"Always check your kit," said Norman, sharply. "The French Foreign Legion would have withdrawn your Camembert rations for a month for such a lapse. Now try and sit still on your mat and focus on the tree. It's within our grasp now! "

"Sir! Yes! Norman!" whispered Ted, saluting vaguely before his unstable sitmat capsized on to a cluster of buttercups.

"You know they're not real, don't you?" said Dmitri, nervously, having sidled up to Greg.

"You mean the buttercups?" said Greg. "Or do you mean that Ted's knees are prosthetic?"

"Neither. I mean that the pirates are aesthetic!" said Dmitri, averting his eyes from the usurpers of the boat. "They are merely the products of musical genius who have lost the plot. See those two women standing in front of the helm? Leonora and Rosamunde - the fearful manifestations of two 19th century overtures who have assumed the identities of wronged works of art!"

"I see," said Greg, thoughtfully, amazed at this explanation, but very relieved by it. "So how have some misguided operatic characters, as well as some orchestral scores, been able to overpower the ghosts of their collective creators?"

"They're just desperate to be heard," said Dmitri. "They all believe that musical appreciation is subject to whims, but they want it to be regulated! Strict curbs on crossover and fusion, referees' whistles synchronised and tuned at halftime, licences for church bells."

"Just as well you guys got us on side!" said Buddy. "The music sure ain't dead yet, even if we can no longer write it!"

Dmitri nodded. "I met William Tell yesterday. Wonderful man, and his bowing technique is amazing, but he too had let this idea of identity go to his head; his son's head was somewhat cluttered with fears too, as well as fruit. I told him they had nothing to worry about and that we are all made up of the same eternal twelve notes. He saw the light, heard the sound, and once more merged into cosmic concord!"

"Comic encore?" said Joe. "Let's ask them for something from The Pirates of Penzance, then!", before proceeding to clap vigorously.

Greg took his cue from the solitary clapper, more out of etiquette and convention than of appreciation of the bizarre characters on board the vessel. Norman and Greg joined in, although with serious expressions, whilst Dmitri nodded diplomatically and glanced either side of him nervously. The captors ceased their malevolent gaze upon the tree, and swiftly turned round to glare bemusedly at the line of applauding spectators. What they didn't realise was that the applause was actually for Tom's emergence on the starboard side. Greg assumed that the words which appeared to be on Tom's lips were: "So, what do I do now?" to which he responded by taking immediate action. He pulled out the baton from his jacket pocket, held it aloft and proceeded to make the down stroke that would create the necessary distraction for Tom to attempt to rescue the hostages. A cacophony of arias, overtures, and musical mayhem thus ensued, augmented by apparent social disharmony amongst the egotistical artistes. However, the manoeuvre didn't quite have the desired result as Tom was seized by a standby Valkyrie and pushed down below, although his breach of security was of little consequence to the desperate entities vying with each other for musical dominance.

"They've kidnapped him!" said Ted, anxiously. "They might try and extract information from him until he sings!"

"We must stay calm!" said Norman, his lips twitching violently. "And remember, *they're* the ones with most to lose. If you extract DNA from kidnappers, then what you're left with is….kippers!"

"Kippers! There's a thing," said Joe. "Don't worry, I'll extract the little bones for you, Ted!"

"They won't survive this din for much longer," said Dmitri, quietly as the conflicting rhythms and keys assailed their ears. "Look at the expression on the face of Leonora Number Two!"

292

Greg was well aware that Beethoven had written several Leonora overtures, but he didn't know whether the great man had envisaged any rivalry developing between them. However, they in turn had been superseded by the Fidelio overture, although in the opera it was one of the Leonoras who liberated their husband from captivity. Greg saw a parallel between their multiple existence, and the various extra Gregs that had co-existed recently. Perhaps it was his turn to make overtures at attempting liberation himself? Suddenly, The Tree, which had been providing a subtle kind of background harmonics, and which was currently eclipsed by the disharmony on board, seemed to pause before bursting forth with a fanfare akin to a hundred trumpets in majestic accord. The aggrieved players on the boat suddenly froze as though pausing to draw breath for a chorus of reconciliation, but instead they remained silent and apparently stunned. Greg knew that it was now the time for him to affect the rescue. "That's you, you're on!" he said to himself as he steeled himself to climb on board. The force of the fanfare, however, had knocked Ted to the ground, or more accurately, on to his sitmat. He then slithered down the bank towards the prow of the boat on his unintentional sledge, hitting it with his moist feet and causing the boat to turn in the water as though on course to face The Tree.

Meston had come to Greg's aid and was once more offering him the inept support of his clasped hands to provide a step up - this time on to the vessel. However, aware that the boat was now gently swinging away from the riverbank, both men rushed the task and collapsed into a heap in front of a rather vacant Barber of Seville.

"Sorry about that," whispered Meston. "Our little friend with the balaclava seems to have regained his superhuman strength and has slightly launched the boat."

"He's a powerful little man," said Greg, whilst glancing up at the motley collection of characters on board whom by contrast appeared to have lost all strength and were standing motionless and impassive. "He told me he does weight training with bottles of bleach augmented with lemon!"

Norman and Joe had raced down to the water's edge to rescue their little friend, leaving Dmitri and Buddy to stare in wonder at the combined spectacle of an assortment of musical manifestation standing frozen on deck; two potential liberators chatting in a heap in front of them; and the recreational soldiers placing Ted in his foldable chair as they plied him with a jam jar of hot tea.

"The British might seem rather hesitant about bursting into song," said Dmitri. "but they certainly know how to have fun in a crisis - and they love their tea!"

"I guess they don't have much space for singing in such a small country," said Buddy. "In the States we have more land, but as for tea, we lost quite a few cups of it at some crazy party in Boston."

"Sadly we lost some of *our* land. We foolishly exported the whole of Alaska to…." said Dmitri, giving his friend pause for thought. "But happily, our indigenous people in Siberia have no reservations about bursting into song - especially with an accompaniment of vodka!"

294

"Hmm, I guess *our* reservations have been a little different in that respect," said Buddy.

Greg and Meston weren't too sure about their next step, other than to try and get up without causing too much provocation to the suspended musical creations in front of them. "Should one of us try and turn that big wheel do you think?" asked Meston. "Sorry, I'm not really sure about driving boats. Thelma and Monica usually help out when I drive on wet surfaces."

Greg looked at the staring faces, as though to elicit their consent in steering the boat. Perhaps one of them could blink, or even give some clue as to where the handbrake was located. He was intent on rescuing their hostages but their captors seemed to be fading from view. Had he become slightly concussed from his tumble on to the boat, or had their discord been resolved, so as to diminish from both auditory and visual range as The Tree conquered them with its power?

"As long as the stern stays close to the bank, it looks as though we're just moving round to face our destination," said Greg. "I think the opposition might be waning, though!"

Meston stood directly in front of Leonora Number Three and asked: "if it would be all right now to enter the downstairs?" There was no reply, and apart from the victorious trumpets, the only other sound was that of Norman and Joe wheezing and creaking as they ran towards the stern, carrying Ted in his latter day Sedan chair. Within seconds, the entire assembly of pirates had dissolved into sub-notational particles which then seemed to disappear into Greg's pocket, and quietly entered the manuscript book.

"Would you all like to come this way?" suggested Greg, but aware that such an invitation might have sounded rather genteel. "It's quite safe to get on board now. The entities have abandoned ship!" he added, slightly more boldly. He extended a hand to help the three old soldiers climb on deck, although Ted was hoisted up still in his chair. Dmitri and Buddy waited their turn, casting lingering looks towards the woods behind them before they too boarded, prior to the voyage to the other side of the river.

Meston, meanwhile, was offering everyone crisps. "For sustenance," he said. "Sorry, I've only got plain."

Greg wondered about the protocols of rescuing imprisoned composers. He knocked gently on a nicely finished oak door and awaited permission to enter, but Norman and Joe had decided to use Ted's chair as a battering ram, in which the rather bemused Ted remained seated, draining the last of the tepid tea from his jam jar. *"Storm the hatch and set them free, we don't stand on ceremony,"* they chanted. The brassy fanfare of liberation from The Tree had now softened to a more graceful accompaniment befitting the gentle blows of Ted's tarnished steel chair on the more attractively stained oak door, while those below deck could be heard conferring on orchestration. "I'm putting in a C sharp on the word 'hatch', Mr. Sibelius," said one. "Just a semi-quaver."

"We're from Grimsby, we can roar, we'll fight for peace, you write the score," replied Norman's troop, their voices also quavering.

The gentle pounding on the door had had little effect on gaining an entry, but suddenly it opened to reveal Tom standing there.

"Hi, come in," he said casually. "Come and meet the team!"

"Do any of them require medical attention?" asked Norman as he peered inside before entering. "I have cotton wool."

Tom raised his eyebrows and shook his head slightly. "It's a bit late for that. They're all....you know....they came *back* to help us!"

"Overtime, you mean?" asked Meston before tripping over the step. "Sorry, we got held up by a missing manuscript book!"

"They're from the other side," advised Dmitri. "Like myself and young Buddy!"

Greg noticed Meston take a glance across the river, presumably to alert those on board to any more composers who might wish to join the team, but his view was dominated by the pulsating light show from the Tree that awaited them all.

"From the other...?" said Meston, confused. "Sorry, did everyone wade across?"

"He means from beyond the stave," said Greg in suitably hushed tones.

"Oh, sorry," said Meston. "Yes, it's really good that they've been able to appear to us. I've only ever seen a spectral cow before! She'd had a bad case of TB."

"Horrible complaint," called out a young man from the vicinity of the galley stove. "I'm Fredric. Who's for tea with lemon?"

The Tree responded by bursting into what sounded to Greg like Chopin's Revolutionary March, although he realised that what he could hear was the prototype for many familiar tunes and great works. He then pondered on the fact that whereas in physics light moved quite fast and was ascribed the letter C, music moved at varying speeds and had been designated the letter H. Might tea, therefore, often sipped slowly, be the source of universal taste - T - the catalyst for appreciating musical scores under good lighting?

"Excuse me, but who's the captain of this thing?" asked Tom, concerned with the practicalities of the voyage they had yet to make.

Ted had remained just outside the door, still seated in his chair, whilst Joe attempted to adorn his little friend with a lifebelt. Greg quickly considered volunteering for the captaincy of the boat for the short crossing to the opposite bank, but instead he decided to give precedence to Chopin's offer of refreshments, having already acquired a taste for the great man's preludes. "Yes, please! Can I give you a hand?"

"A big hand for the people who work down below!" called Joe. "No sugar in mine, thanks."

Tom appeared to be frustrated that his call for leadership was sidelined in favour of a tea break, and so he assumed the role of second in command, and proceeded to harangue a Mr. Dankworth on the importance of efficient record-keeping. "I didn't push too many investment products. I didn't need the hassle but my ledger was the talk of the district! I drew little saxophones in the margins, and it all balanced!"

"I used to play the saxophone! I'm Johnny," said his friend. "Didn't you have the use of a computer where you worked?"

"Yes, but head office wouldn't let me have a monitor until I achieved monthly targets. Stupid, really. I just sat there moving the mouse around, but I had nothing to look at. I'm Tom, by the way. At least, the ledger was cool."

"Yes, we met in a dentist's waiting room in Milton Keynes! You were about to be scaled and polished!"

Tom shook his head, as though to deny any involvement with health care so far south, but Greg, currently adopting a sort of presidential stance as he wondered which one of the available composers he should confer with, politely interjected.

"You were probably cloned like the rest of us at the time," he suggested. "Apparently one version of me was involved with a pigeon on top of The Old Bailey!"

This time Tom nodded, conceding that this was a rendezvous between those who had lived to create, and those with links to either dentistry or avian law. Greg then spotted his hero, the amiable Franz Schubert, sitting opposite and currently engaged in an animated conversation about ball point pens with Marc Bolan and King Henry VIII.

"If I'd been able to buy these in Vienna I might have completed all those works that I had to abandon due to a scarcity of Prussian Blue!" said Franz as he borrowed Marc's to write an accompaniment for the minimalist theme emanating from The Tree.

"I too erred," admitted Henry. "If I'd brought forth occasional albums of songs praising the delights of my other sleeves, I might have been far better occupied and less inclined to tyranny."

"I really took off with Tyrannosaurus Rex," said Marc. "but then I settled on plain T. Rex. The sleeves on our LPs looked great!"

"You intrigue me sir!" said Henry. "Pray, where was this land over which you were conferred the title Rex?"

"The UK, I suppose," said Marc, nonchalantly.

"I know not of such a domain, and who were the LPs?" asked Henry. "Did *they* bestow you with the T?"

"Here we are, gentlemen," said Chopin, placing cups before them. "Tea for two, and I've brought coffee for you, Franz."

Greg considered asking Franz for his autograph, but wasn't he forgetting his important role as Chief Harbinger, committed to the very essence of what made each composer great? Tom and Johnny were gazing out of the window at The Tree and humming, whilst Norman had deployed his foldable chair next to Scott Joplin who was giving him a brief lesson on the structure of Ragtime by tapping vigorously on the chair's legs, causing its occupant to choke slightly on his cherry flapjack. Greg felt rather detached from all the ensuing conversations, and yet he craved involvement in the mystery of composition to which they all aspired. He then noticed that The Tree had quietened down, and that this was reflected within the boat. The hum of conversation had become pianissimo, and all attention was directed upon a door at the far end, flanked by Johann Sebastian Bach and John Cage.

"This is what we've all been waiting for!" said Dmitri, quietly in Greg's ear.

The Tree was not only on pause, but out of sight. The boat's slow starboard progress had finally brought it at right angles to the riverbank, such that from the windows at either side Greg now had a commanding prospect up and down river. However, even though he was slightly apprehensive at the prospect of other craft being obstructed by the boat's broadside position while he and his companions awaited developments, he didn't

300

feel like volunteering as harbourmaster with duties to channel boats. But he did feel more enthusiastic now about taking command as Harbinger with duties to channel notes. The scene within was as peaceable as the river; even Richard Wagner and Max Bruch were chatting convivially over their cups of tea.

"Two lumps in mine," said Richard as Max contemplated the sugar bowl in front of them.

"I'd get that attended to," said Max, earnestly. "I'm sure my doctor would fit you in for a consultation. He hails from Patagonia so he's seen it all."

"Thanks," said Richard, puzzled. "I don't need a physician but isn't that where the natives worship a sugar loaf mountain?"

"No, you're probably thinking of Brazil - in a naïve sort of way!" said Max.

"Ah, the land of nuts and coffee!" said Richard. "And wonderfully rainy forests too!

"Quite so," said Max. "And natives who are so cut off from civilisation that they only need to count up to three!"

"Himmel! I should have based my Ring Cycle there instead and written only *three* operas," snapped Richard.

"Or you could have based it in Israel," said Max. "We'd have encouraged you to write only two, then there'd be fewer performances for us to cancel!"

Joe was helping Ted to negotiate the step. "One step for a small man, one leap for a kind giant!"

"Would you like to sit here?" asked Jim Morrison, offering them a place by the stove."

"No thanks; we've brought our own chairs," said Joe. "My friend's got poorly knees so he doesn't stand on ceremony. He loves being out of doors, though!"

"I'd forgotten he was ever in the band," said Jim. "Wild times."

All attention was now focussed on the door at the far end, although after a minute of expectation it remained closed.

Greg was reminded of those intervals he had spent in cinemas when the light was too dim to read the programme and yet bright enough to identify all those who had come alone. He wanted to glance at the manuscript book in his pocket but the light was poor, and yet strong enough to reveal him as the only person not engaged in pianissimo level conversation.

"I wish you well, young man, in getting hold of this ultimate key!" said a voice in his ear. "Hi, Gershwin's the name!"

Greg turned and faced the looming figure beside him, slightly embarrassed at not having recognised the man, although it would hardly be appropriate for musical spirit guides to wear name tags. Greg introduced himself, and then asked Gershwin salient questions about his compositional methods, and especially why he'd written a rhapsody in blue.

"Everything was in short supply in those days," he replied, as he placed his empty coffee cup on Chopin's wooden tray, thanking him for the addition of sprinkled chocolate. "Couldn't always get the right key, so I took a risk and borrowed the colour blue from those jazz musicians!"

"Well it worked!" said Greg, maintaining an eye on the still closed door. "Although poor Stockhausen had to resort to using neither key nor colour."

"Brave man," said Gershwin. "He didn't know

302

where he was going, but he still went."

"Excuse me," said Norman, whispering in Greg's ear, whilst gripping his own metal tray. "When shall we be going? My men are getting restless."

"I think we're expecting a guest speaker," said Greg. "I'm sure we'll be off soon, though. The prow's almost touching the opposite bank even while we...."

A thunderous organ chord comprising the instrument's entire lowest octave reverberated throughout the interior of the boat, causing Norman's lips and Chopin's cups to tremble in awe and amplitude. A display of scintillating colours provided the visuals, as The Tree, still out of sight, burst into life once more and illuminated the windows. The door also burst into life, swinging open with such force that its guardian, J. S. Bach, was flung from his chair into the arms of Luigi Boccherini, whom Greg recognised from the statuette on Tamara Trotman's desk in the Great Pyramid. Peering through the doorway, however, revealed nothing, but the mighty chord continued as though it were the fanfare for an equally mighty writer of great music.

A small figure then became apparent, stationary and indistinct in the comparative gloom. Greg suspected that it was the lack of applause that deterred him from making an entrance. He thought about taking the lead by initiating a 'big hand', but on the other hand, should he procrastinate a bit longer in case the fervent fanfare turned into a dramatic drum roll? Whilst hesitating, he noticed Meston running towards the door.

"Sorry, sorry!" he called out as he hurried to meet the motionless visitor. "Have to help....it's er...."

"Someone ordered a pizza?" asked Joe, helpfully.

Greg glanced at some of the faces around him for clues, but they looked neither hungry nor curious, and so he shook his head. Meston now appeared to be attending to the mystery figure in some way. Was it a neighbour complaining about the noise? The fanfare gradually attained pianissimo level but was superseded by the sound of a squeaky wheel, as the figure, now borne on a large crimson cushion atop a rather narrow tea trolley, progressed sedately through the doorway propelled by a somewhat proud Meston together with a slightly subdued Sibelius. There was still no applause - which might have affected the dignity of the occasion - but a gentle flourish of glittering glissandos heralded the entrance of what was none other than Sir Lammington Lyons, late Chief Harbinger of H.

Gasps and appreciative murmurs from the assembled company greeted him as he rode between them, in turn nodding and waving effetely. Chopin then ran up to him with a glass of blended water served on an inverted saucepan lid, before reversing reverently as Sir L. thanked him and took a tiny sip of his frugal refreshment. As he nodded benignly in all directions he noticed Greg and gave him a special wave before trembling with laughter. "Scuffed my veneer!" he said in a high octave, recalling Greg's comment in the Great Pyramid. As this was the first utterance of the great man to the assembled company it was seized upon and repeated by almost everyone, although querulously as though no-one had any idea what it meant.

Sibelius certainly looked baffled and slightly put out as Wagner collected various empty cups and saucers and placed them on the lower shelf of the now stationary tea trolley whilst Sir Lammington delicately shook more eager hands of those who wished to touch him.

"You and I could have collaborated on a mighty Teutonic-cum-Nordic epic," whispered Wagner into Sibelius' ear. "Ninety hours of Norns and Trolls!"

"Norns and Trolls?" asked Gershwin as he gently placed his own cup behind Sir Lammington's dangling legs. "Didn't that premiere on Broadway in 1950?"

"Every note is everywhere and every when," said Sir Lammington, softly, raising his hand as though indicating he was ready to move on. "Even your incinerated eighth symphony has been recycled and renewed, Mr. Sibelius."

The great Finn looked shocked but nodded gracefully, before gesturing to Meston by means of eyebrows and a quick nod that it was time to begin the second movement. Thus in perfect synchrony they propelled the old gentleman to a position near the sink where Chopin carefully removed the dirty crockery from between the former's dangling feet, whilst he slowly began to raise his hands, and thus bring forth a chord of unsurpassable beauty from The Tree.

After a while this sublime chord faded, and yet the light show had intensified, gracing the windows on both sides of the boat with the appearance of stained glass whilst a more modest opalescent light shone upon Sir Lammington's face. He smiled serenely at Greg before closing his eyes in a state of reverie and - apart from the soothing sounds of Chopin gently washing the cups and saucers - a silence of deep intensity had taken hold. The prelude from the sink continued, culminating with a coda of bubbles popping within the three old soldiers' jam jars, after which the great man opened his eyes and nodded graciously to his rapt audience.

"Let us welcome Gregory, the new Chief Harbinger, and his five comrades in composition," he said softly. "May they carry the batons of harmony, tempo, and melody to all those who yearn for it!"

The composers in the audience burst into a fit of gentle applause, each tapping the fervent fingertips of one hand on the passive palm of the same hand. Here was the answer to the philosophical riddle of what would be the sound of one hand clapping, thought Greg, but now there was the question of how to respond to the acclaim. Might it be appropriate to stand up and extend his arm to his five friends, a gesture employed by conductors keen to show off their soloists when facing rapturous dual-handed applause after a concerto? There was no need on this occasion as his comrades in composition were already getting to their feet, and waving wildly. Greg stood and waved in an all-encompassing rotating motion, but Sir L. then kindly gestured to them all to be seated, and for the single hand-clapping to cease.

"Well, here we are!" he began, rocking slightly with the magnitude of his declaration. "Thank you all for coming here today, as well as calling at various other places *en route*, not to mention time zones!"

"Don't mention it!" shouted Joe. "Last year we went to Skegness so we were ready for anything this year!"

"Shhh!" said Norman. "Don't show off."

"I'd like to apologise to everyone for the recent hostage crisis on board," continued Sir L. "Some of our creations can be very wary of what they see as competition. I once had to rule in favour of a squeaky

306

shoe after a complaint from a WW2 marching song."

"I suppose you'll have to do some ruling yourself now and again," whispered Meston into Greg's ear. "I can help with that if you like. It's probably important to prevent the notes escaping from the manuscript by having neatly defined bars! Oh, sorry, Sir L.!"

The great man looked at Meston and nodded as though to confirm he had taken on board his comments. "I hope that no-one here has been too inconvenienced by those episodes of sharing yourselves with parallel universes," he said, directing his words at the six new Harbingers, but then he was heckled by a latecomer at the back.

"Excuse me, can you hurry up?" shouted Benjamin Britten, anxiously. "I just spotted two people fishing. They might become curious if we stay here too long. They're on the bank *opposite* the Tree, but they look like the sort who wade."

"It's probably Bizet's Pearl Fishers," said Wagner, dismissively. "I can imagine them wading but they wouldn't be able to carry on like that in the Rhein!"

"Shall I go and ask them if they've got permits?" asked Tom. "If they have I can tell them the fish are hibernating or something."

"If you don't mind," said Sir L. "Although we won't be much longer. You'd better take…." but Tom was already halfway out of the door, followed attentively by Britten.

Ted sustained a paper cut on his index finger from a sachet of granulated sugar and was receiving care and cotton wool from Norman and Schubert. Sir L. realised that his presentation was not holding everyone's attention, and so he raised his voice an octave.

"But sometimes the available space on a stave isn't enough for our purposes. We need to add extra lines to accommodate the notes, and add repeats to allow us to play them again. Space and time - our dedicated servants!"

"Shall I try and get the tannin stains off the cups now?" asked Chopin, making a subtle wave to attract the attention of Sir L. "I had a go at polishing the cutlery while we were held by the choir invidious."

"It doesn't really matter," said Sir L. patiently. "The china will undoubtedly vanish into the ether once we've finished chatting here."

"Hear that?" said Joe, excitedly. "China's going to shout at the Spanish, and Ibiza wants a Finnish captain here!"

"That proves the power of nationalistic tone poems," said Sibelius, proudly. "I'm sure Finlandia is at this very moment guarding us from further invasions. Rumour has it that The Pirates of Penzance were massing upriver this morning, but that my 'Swan of Tuonela' hissed at them and they disappeared."

"It's rather like Eurovision, isn't it?" said Greg, conspiratorially to Dmitri, but the latter was looking at his watch and shaking his head.

"As for those of us who have already penned their individual finales, as we like to put it, and then taken their places in the Celestial Concert Hall, they have suspended copyright restrictions and sent copies of themselves to assist our esteemed team of Harbingers find their way here today," said Sir L. his voice now flat-lining to a pitch similar to that of a priest in high church mode. "I'd now like to thank the following." He produced a long strip of paper from his pocket, took a sip of water, and began reading out names in alphabetical order. His delivery was portentous but dull, and included a pause after each name to let it sink in.

Only Joe sat enthralled. Greg was wondering how long the list of acknowledgements would be, and whether he could discreetly dip into his manuscript book in order to monitor the forecast compositions that would issue from The Tree. A few feet away Marc Bolan was teaching Buddy Holly how to play noughts and crosses, a game he'd never heard of before. He was convinced that the diagram was actually a fret for designating chords to be played on a guitar, and which he vocalised with a "Yippy Aye..." before stopping ashen-faced and glancing nervously at the sky. George Gershwin was asking Henry VIII if he'd ever been to Paris, but the monarch declared that he had a much greater interest in Calais. Chopin, still busy at the sink, had dropped a cup which smashed on the edge of the stove, whilst Dmitri was gesturing awkwardly to Sir L. in an attempt to indicate the time on his watch. Greg was reminded of the last day of term at his school when teaching was suspended and adventure comics were read conspicuously on desk tops to prevent rioting. Right now, this group of altruistically determined and yet mildly deceased composers probably didn't pose any major threat to decorum, as they would already be sedated by listening to the recitation of a seemingly endless list of names. "Dina Appeldoorn....Cyprian Bazylik....Christian Ludwig Boxberg...."

Greg discreetly removed the book from his jacket pocket and turned to the last page. This was classroom reading at its best; containing neither missions to Mars, nor androids with cars, but a serious chronicle that constantly updated itself automatically with each new entry revealing the name of some new work, its composer, projected date of publication, and opus number. His eyes were transfixed, scanning numerous entries, whilst his mind dwelt on the idea that at this very moment the creative sap in The Tree was onstream and that it required collecting *now*!

Meanwhile, the great man droned on in a monotone, relieved occasionally by a chord from The Tree as if it were an exclamation mark to emphasise a particular composer's merit, although most of them were completely unknown to Greg, and were merely being intoned due to having been instrumental to this odyssey. "Arnold Brunckhorst.... Felix Benda.... Dietrich Buxtehude." At least he'd heard of, and listened to Buxtehude, but he'd also heard of Norman Nacton, sitting yawning with Ted, and whose opus one had yet to be inspired and energised by The Tree. At some point it would appear in the list in front of him, as would his own, but such anticipation was currently being overwhelmed by tedium. He would have to make some excuse and abandon ship. Perhaps when Sir L. reached the letter C would he make a move and attempt to reach out for 'H'.

J. S. Bach, meanwhile, was assisting Chopin in brushing up the broken china. "Don't worry, young master," he said as he held a small plastic dustpan in position. "Only the cup is broken, the handle survived! Your fingers probably need strengthening. Have you considered writing for the organ instead of that pianoforte?"

Handel had indeed survived another nine years after

310

Bach's death, recalled Greg. Was there symbolism at work here? The Tree then produced a powerful cymbal clash and Greg knew that it was calling him. He put the book back in his pocket quickly, and stood up slowly. He was about to assert his authority as the new Chief Harbinger.

"Er, would you mind if I go and see if Tom's all right?" he asked, hesitantly. "And Mr. Britten as well, of course." Having asked permission so humbly, he tried to impose his will somewhat more forcibly by walking purposefully towards the hatch, but The Tree suddenly emitted a melodic refrain in waltz time, prompting him to begin sashaying towards the exit instead. He turned his head towards Sir L. to convey a mood of determination tempered with deference, only to find that his fellow Harbingers had also succumbed to dancing, and appeared willing to follow him anywhere. The former Chief cast a benevolent gaze upon his departing successors and waved them off gently, pausing briefly after honouring the name of Cornelius Cardew on the interminable roll of sponsors and supporters.

Greg opened the hatch and breathing in the fresh Fenland air he peered upriver, his eyes focussing on a narrowboat in the near distance. Two familiar figures were crouching on the riverbank alongside it, blatantly pressing their faces against its windows.

"Wow, illegal fishing!" said Buddy, having told Sir L. that he too wished to go for a short walk.

Norman nodded in agreement, and having helped Ted down from the boat on to the grassy towpath, they all set off on a secondary adventure to act as river bailiffs. Greg thought that Britten's concerns were that the crew might be curious about The Tree, not that *they* warranted investigation from the Harbingers. However, a short stroll on the rather dull grass might get them all in the mood for crossing to the greener grass on the other side of the river. Besides, Greg's manner of acting as leader was to let someone else act as conductor - just as in any orchestra. Norman was the conductor, but Greg was in charge of the strings.

"Sorry, isn't that the support vessel for this one?" asked Meston. "It looks quite law-abiding, so perhaps the rumour was unfounded. They could be lightly poaching crayfish, of course, but let's hope there's not been another coup by disaffected opera parts like we had on our boat!"

"That's actually a houseboat!" announced Norman confidently as he surveyed the scene. "Observe the washing line attached to that sycamore tree. Right under the gingham tablecloth there's a black wheelie bin - 120 litre capacity, but incompatible with hot ashes."

"In that case we'd better recall Tom and Benjamin before they alarm the occupants," said Greg. "Tom can be highly strung at times, but some of Britten's pizzicato passages can soar even higher!"

"Britain's pixies score even higher!" shouted Joe, pleased to have something useful to add. "Shall I go and rescue the two men?"

"Yes, Joe, you go, but don't shout," said Norman. "And put your gloves on. I spy nettles."

Joe loped off cheerfully along the tow-path whilst a loose lace on one of Ted's boots had necessitated remedial intervention from Norman. "When we get home I'll teach you some basic knots!" said Norman, quietly. "Either that or we can go down the Velcro road. Something for you to consider, anyway."

"Is that the way Dorothy went?" asked Ted. "I saw a film about her life when I was a youth in Louth. She sang about a rainbow and walked along a road built of brick. I still have nightmares about it."

Greg's first film had featured a path through a forest - rather than a road consisting merely of hardcore. Seven diminutive mineworkers marched along it on their daily commute as they sang lustily about a hoe, whilst their young housekeeper remained at home singing softly to linnets and fending off travelling crones who offered complementary apples garnished with poison.

"Would anyone like a Cox's Orange Pippin?" asked Norman as he reached into his rucksack and produced a slightly dented apple which he then held aloft to show off its best side.

"Pippin?" questioned Greg, momentarily concerned that one of the group might have been merged with a humble hero in another epic film he'd seen: some mission about conveying a precious ring. "Not at the moment, thank you," he replied. "Although I'm sure it's not been tainted!"

Norman looked at him quizzically for a second, his lips trembling slightly, before proceeding to peel the apple for a salivating Ted.

"We've checked out the other boat," called Tom as he came running back towards them. "No potential threats."

Benjamin took a slower pace, but he sounded less than relieved. "I once wrote an opera about a disturbed soul called Peter Grimes. Goodness knows what he'd

313

have done if our paths had crossed again. I'm beginning to regret scoring all those F sharps now."

"You regret storing all those dead sharks?" asked Joe. "Well, we can all make mistakes in our youth. I taught myself to play the kettle drum but I really wanted to learn the saxophone."

"Peer pressure, you see," said Norman, quietly into Benjamin's ear. "Our peers can exert such power over us musically."

"You don't need to remind me," said Benjamin. "Peter's F sharps were the talk of Aldeburgh. That's why I felt I had to score them."

"We should be getting back to the...." said Greg, before turning round to see that the boat that they'd recently left was now shimmering colourfully and humming gently in harmony with The Tree on the other side of the river. It also appeared to be fading from view. "Er....I think we need to hurry!"

"Tell me, is it true that you call your rivers 'broads' in this part of England?" asked Buddy as they began to walk briskly back to the now less solid boat.

"Well, that's the name given to some of the waterways in Norfolk," replied Greg. "But in these parts you're more likely to find them referred to as dykes."

Buddy stared at him for a moment, then shook his head. "I really can't figure this country out, but it's been fun to visit, and those old soldier guys are great. I'm sure you'll all be OK distributing that H."

"Thanks, we'll find out soon," replied Greg, dealing with the last remark first. "The three 'reserves' have hidden depths - their plan was to get away for a few days to get in touch with their masculine side.

Anyway, thanks for bringing us here safely. When do you have to go back to...."

"Gee, right now!" said Buddy, quickening his pace and pointing at the boat, now only a matter of yards away. "We're almost there, and yet it's fading from view!"

Greg also noticed the fade-out, and that Buddy had begun to move in a kind of gliding motion. He attributed the gliding to his interests in aviation and the fading to an imminent finale. He looked round to make sure his comrades were keeping pace, but they were not only right behind, they appeared to be leaping in cinematic slow motion. Even Ted had become imbued with an aura of strength and bounding agility, whilst Benjamin had opted for the gliding gait.

"This way!" said Greg as he stood to one side to allow everyone to leap or glide aboard the now visibly-challenged vessel. The theme from The Tree had become a tremolando which perfectly captured the mood of urgency and ethereality, but there was confusion in the air also as the men awaited Greg's orders as to whether they were to re-enter the hatch or move swiftly along the deck to assemble at the prow.

"We'd better ensure that Buddy and Benjamin are safely inside," said Greg. "Then we must thank everyone, briefly, before positioning ourselves on deck, ready to take up the challenge!"

Thus they entered the conclave of composers, most of whom were chatting animatedly amongst themselves about either polyphony or middle eights, whilst others drummed their fingers in common time. Meanwhile the Chief Harbinger continued wearily recounting names of other dead composers deemed worthy of acknowledgment, if not royalties. As he reached Manuel de Falla, Wagner voiced his objection to the reciting of middle names on the grounds that it wasted precious time. Greg tried tactfully to interrupt by waving, but Tom beat him to it - by shouting.

"Hi, we're back! Do you know your boat's getting blurry, chief?" he announced. "You might want to abandon it, but we're going to leap to the other side. Thanks for the teas and the info. Keep in touch!"

"Yes, thanks for the refreshments!" said Norman. "Oh, and Ted says the teaspoons were nicely contoured - he's got sensitive thumbs!"

Meston then shook hands warmly with the Chief, although the old gentleman's hand was so sensitive that it almost disintegrated. "Sorry." said Meston as he gently withdrew his hand and smiled sincerely so as to dispel any panic about blurriness.

Greg ushered his men towards the far door and thought a farewell hug might be appropriate, but the Chief began convulsing with laughter as Greg stood before him wondering whether he should place his head to the left or right of the head of the great man.

"Don't scuff my veneer!" giggled Sir Lammington, lowering his head and yielding to a fit of mirth. Greg thought that he was about to be head-butted, but he didn't flinch and merely construed any physical contact to be the transmission of potential genius. He gently nudged the vigorously nodding head with his own, at which point the room erupted with a rousing cheer sung to a sequence of ecstatic chords emanating from The Tree. Buddy and Dmitri then glided up to him, smiling benevolently, and escorted him to the deck where Greg's fellow Harbingers now stood waiting to make

316

the final leap to the opposite bank.

"We'll always have Leningrad," said Dmitri wistfully, as he waited for them to take off.

"This could be the start of a beautiful harvest!" said Greg as he looked up admiringly at The Tree and then at the water that separated them. "One, two, three...."

CHAPTER 18

In a supreme act of co-ordination the six men leapt gracefully across the water from the prow of the boat and landed in perfect concord on the soft grass opposite. The Tree provided their accompaniment in the form of an augmented sixth that transcended any instrumentation.

"We did it our way!" called Joe proudly as he helped Ted up. "Like Franck's Sonata!"

"Well...er...." said Greg, before gesturing to everyone to turn round and bow to the crew of composers on the boat. However, as they proceeded to face their benefactors there was little left to observe other than a hazy spectacle of hands waving in soft focus, and a compressed chorus of ethereal cheers. The men stood respectfully and some sighed regretfully, but within seconds the last vestiges of their mentors' existence had completely faded. All that remained was a slight impression in the water where the craft had rested, together with the dregs from an industrial size teapot.

"Surely, that was all some sort of re-enactment, right?" said Tom, standing next to a thistle and looking confused. "Like war-games, except without the wars. Anyway, I vote we should just get on with chilling out under this special tree and see what happens. Like Buddha, or was it Newton? One of those explorer fellas."

"Well...er...." said Greg for the second time. "Shall we all make our way to the trunk and perhaps encircle it holding hands?" He'd meant this to be an invitation rather than a petition but Tom looked at him as though considering whether to call for a *show* of hands, rather than a *clasping* of hands.

"Tree hugging, you mean?" said Tom. "Yeah, if we must. *Then* we can....whatever it is we've come here to do."

"Receive the gift of unpublished music, I think it is," said Norman, hesitantly. "I'm sure it'll all make sense."

"Sorry, can I just measure the girth?" said Meston as he proceeded to run past them with a tape measure trailing from his eager hands.

"Treasure the earth? That's the way to live!" said Joe.

"I'll give you a hand," said Greg. "You and I go back a long way when it comes to engaging with trees. Probably about half a mile away when we retrieved the manuscript book from that branch of the ash tree."

Although they were undoubtedly walking over The Tree's root system, there was still no sense of the huge significance of the creative energies into which they would soon be tapping. Should they approach it with extreme reverence, or would it be appropriate to pat the bark affectionately, or even examine it for excrescences of sap so as to avoid getting resin on their clothes during the big hug? The play of light from the branches had become somewhat subdued, as had the sounds, although this could be merely a coda, marking time until a climactic theme heralded The Tree going on-stream.

"If you'd like to hold one end of the tape in place I'll walk round it with the other end," said Greg as they stood just inches from the trunk. "Hopefully we'll meet

319

up again back here."

"Sorry, will you be surveying in a clockwise direction?" asked Meston. "Just so I know which side to expect you!"

"Why not," said Greg. "Always as well to trust the wisdom of clocks. I should appear again on your right, but can I ask if you have any particular reason for measuring it?"

"Sorry, I just want to make sure there's room for us all," explained Meston. "Monica gave me a 5 metre tape this morning but it's actually my birthday present from the no-nonsense Nurse Newnes. She thinks I'm underweight, so I must check my waist and inside leg daily."

"She didn't give you any scales, did she?" asked Greg.

"Sorry, I had enough of them when I was learning the piano," said Meston. "My teacher wanted to introduce me to some triads but I avoided getting mixed up with those too." He looked at Greg as though seeking the nod to take the momentous step, and seeing no objection, duly proceeded to make contact with the trunk by pressing one end of the tape firmly on the bark. He shuddered slightly as a number of birds took off from the upper branches with urgent squeaks as though announcing an imminent change of occupancy.

It was Greg who was alerted to a much deeper sound - a pulsating rumble from way below middle C. He nevertheless delicately began to wind the tape around the circumference of the vibrating trunk. But now the response was an allegro arpeggio that broke through two sound barriers - first from subsonic to audible, then from audible to supersonic, until he found

320

himself experiencing the higher frequencies in a state of tactile waves as the top of his head underwent a massage in multiple keys. Meston appeared to be entranced too, and not only were his outstretched arms firmly pressed against the bark, but his head was pressed lovingly against it, as though playing a Stradivarius in raptures of auditory delight.

Greg turned round to beckon the others and also to convey to them his own sense of joy, but Norman was still in outdoorsman mode as he stood demonstrating to his loyal comrades, as well as a bemused Tom, the art of telling the time by observing shadows cast by a fixed post.

"The gnomon, we call it," he said with authority.

"Norman by name, Norman by nature!" said Joe.

Solar time, however, had effectively stopped as the sun was currently eclipsed by clouds. Instead, the superior source of light was the renewed display cascading from the branches and dripping from the leaves.

Norman looked up with a sense of wonder. "And young people say they're bored!" he said.

"Are we nearly there yet?" called Ted, as he stood leaning against the gnomon for support.

"Yes, let's go for it!" said Tom as he grabbed hold of his arm and pulled him the last few yards towards their journey's end.

Greg grabbed hold of Ted's hand, whilst Joe connected with the little man's other hand. Tom grasped Greg's free wrist, as though determined to see the task through without their chief escaping, and Norman duly joined them and placed his fingertips delicately on Tom's sleeve.

"Sorry, I got side-tracked by a squirrel watching me," said Meston, instinctively clasping Norman's hand as though forming another stirrup. "I began measuring in centimetres, but then I seem to have changed to decimetres. I think it was about fifteen from where I started."

"Give me strength," said Tom.

Greg wondered if it was important that the six of them should fully encompass the trunk, but Meston's vague surveying suggested that there was a large gap yet to be populated. Tom's frustrated appeal for strength might need to be taken up by all of them.

"Shall we all try and stretch as wide as we can?" called Greg with his face even more firmly pressed against the tree.

"I don't want any ants crawling on my face," said Ted. "They go for sweet things and I've just been sucking an extra mild mint."

"Come on, let's expand," said Tom. "We've come this far, so we might as well do whatever it takes to get this concert started. One, two, three, pushhhhhh!"

It was as though their combined effort at stretching in order that Greg's hand might mesh with Meston's was having the desired effect. He could definitely feel a circuit being made, even before he detected Meston's index finger touching his own.

"Oh, sorry," said Meston. "I mean....oh, good, we've made it!"

This minor success was confirmed by a loud roar as though a vast quantity of sap was now coursing up from the roots within the trunk at great speed.

"I think that what we did just then is known as a Heimlich manoeuvre," said Norman, his voice rich with tones of satisfaction. "Our multilateral squeezing has meant that any moment now the tree will eject from its....er, throat.....the...."

"The key of H?" said Greg, hardly able to accept what might be happening.

"Sorry, I think that squirrel might be staring at me again," said Meston. "Perhaps I should stare back."

Only Greg and Tom, standing either side of him, could hear what he was saying as the thunderous roar of sap filled the air.

"Probably best to avoid too much eye contact," suggested Greg. "They can be rather hypnotic, like Ravel."

"It probably wants to ask you out," said Tom. "Tell it you're busy this evening washing your Lambretta - works for me. Hey, I think we're moving!"

The tree began to vibrate violently as a virtual stampede of squirrels, along with assorted birds, descended and gathered around the hapless tree-huggers. Joe was heard to laugh with a hearty: "Well, well!" whilst Ted was just about heard whimpering with a mournful "Help, help!"

Norman told his two charges to remain composed, and to remember their training with the instructive Tarzan films. "Soon we might learn the correct notes to allow us to yodel!" he added. "We might even have the beasts of the jungle at our command too!"

Greg felt rather self-conscious, which prompted him to explain to the woodpecker currently perched on his left arm the purpose of the group's presence. "We er...we've come to collect something. Not eggs, just some notes. Sorry to disturb you."

This must have been a password, as the assembled

wildlife immediately began depositing small colourful objects as though bestowing gifts. Beakfuls of what appeared to be plastic lozenges were scattered amongst the men's feet. A flotilla of herons also joined in the operation - their contributions being even more generous. The bark of the tree appeared to be bathed in sunlight, which each member of the group commented upon favourably, although this was odd as the sun didn't normally illuminate 360 degrees of a vertical object in the late afternoon.

"Of course, the object placement might be a means of marking their territory," said Norman egregiously. "Don't flinch, I'm sure when they've finished we'll receive the knowledge we came to collect."

Reinforcements of other native species of birds, augmented by squirrels - both grey and red - continued the dainty bombardment until the men were up to their knees in small plastic items. Norman's lips were on the verge of quivering, whilst Meston's feet were being alternately raised and lowered in a morass of green and yellow as though he were treading grapes - both red and white.

"Sorry, Monica said that Nurse Newnes thinks I shouldn't stand still too long in case I develop varicose veins, and not being able to see my feet is a symptom of flab, apparently," said Meston.

"We've only been standing here a few minutes," said Greg, comfortingly. "Anyway, I don't suppose it'll get much deeper. It's probably some de-cluttering process, as when Sibelius dispensed with that entire symphony."

"I've never actually seen birds downsizing before," said Norman, with a sense of wonder. "Although I did once witness a jay jettison a fish-head into my Uncle

324

Ed's new wheelie bin whilst I was disposing of a matchstick."

"We've *all* been there," said Tom with a hint of exaggeration.

"I resolved to follow the bird's example and go and catch my own fish after that incident," said Norman. "I considered a job as a trainee trawlerman, but they didn't have any sou'westers in my size and there was no heating on deck, and so I took a job as a typesetter for an angling magazine instead."

"Funny how things work out," said Meston. "I knew I wanted to write a symphony, but then I developed an empathy for Friesian cows, which in turn led to me becoming a security guard in an umbrella museum. Now here we are, knee-deep in little plastic....sorry, whatever they are!"

"They're memory sticks," said Tom, confidently. "Millions of them."

This statement elicited a rousing chorus from the birds, presumably of approval, who then hovered for a few moments before flying off in formation as though their work was done. The squirrels made eye contact with Greg before scampering away as one, and the tree responded with a single sustained note of such purity and mystery that the men listened enraptured. Greg knew what this all meant, and he could see in the faces of the others, or at least in those standing next to him, that they knew too. They nodded, and slowly released their clasp of each other's hands. Joe and Ted emerged from behind their side of the tree, trampling carefully through the pile of plastic, and exchanged expressions of having found wisdom with all those present.

"That's H that we're listening to," said Greg after a

while. "Progenitor of all other notes. I think we're meant to open these little gifts from the birds, or take them to someone who...." He remembered the manuscript book still in his pocket, and trusted that its automatic updating hadn't made it too thick to be extracted. He hoped he'd find the answer within as to what to do with what Tom had identified as memory sticks, although he wasn't sure what the memories had retained. The book came out easily, and he instinctively searched the first page for some advice. "Make music, not war!" it said in bold letters. "Let the pen drive out the sword!"

He read the words out loud and observed Norman nodding portentously. Tom was nodding too, but more passively.

"Pen drives, that's another name for memory sticks," said Tom as he looked down at the sea of plastic. "Seems like we've got what we came for! There's music at our feet!"

"Sorry, ought we to take it somewhere to get it analysed?" asked Meston.

"It's hardly moondust," said Tom. "We probably need to get this lot to a registered composer with a powerful computer."

"I think we just need to trust that the right course of action will present itself," said Greg. "If only we had something to put all these sticks into while we wait."

"This is one of those occasions when a wheelie bin would be useful - one designated for plastic, of course," said Norman.

Tom seemed to disagree with this idea, and reacted by banging his head repeatedly on the tree trunk in an allegretto rhythm.

"I hope he's not annoyed," said Ted quietly. "Should I offer him a peppermint cream, Norman?"

"No, I think he's just a bit tired," whispered Norman. "He probably doesn't share your resilience!"

"Doesn't care for Brazilians?" queried Joe. "My Sunday School used to give us Brazil nuts at Christmas, but I didn't care for them. I was more the monkey nut type."

Norman, Ted, and Meston then conferred on the merits of macadamia and the advantages of almonds, whilst Tom groaned.

"Monkey?....type?...." muttered Greg, thoughtfully. "Monkeys....typing....er....I've had an idea."

Five pairs of eyes gazed at him expectantly. He had become their oracle and had responsibilities. He discreetly touched the book in his pocket for security, then considered reading aloud the treatise on plagal cadences as though delivering great wisdom but his innate humility prompted him to try and explain his idea.

"Well, apparently there's an old legend about six monkeys being allocated a typewriter each and asked to type randomly." He paused, and observed bemused but mostly loyal expressions of trust. "The theory goes that given enough time they should eventually type out all the works of Shakespeare."

"Sorry, but I don't think they'd understand his use of English," said Meston. "I doubt if we'd even find a stray monk in these parts, anyway."

"I feel like I've ended up in a version of Miss Summers' Ice Cream", said Tom, with exasperation. "Can't we get a move on and drop some of these sticks off at the nearest local composer's if he's still open?"

"Well, what I was thinking," continued Greg, directing his attention to the ever optimistic Joe, "was to feed all these sticks into a few computers and just let them process the raw H and convert it into music via the random fingering of the person at the keyboard. There shouldn't be any need for primates."

There was no reaction to this proposal - even Joe was speechless - although the Tree was keen on the idea, or at least the sudden appearance of a wheelbarrow, together with another sublime chord from on high, indicated that it was.

Norman took it upon himself to be the first to start loading the barrow, and soon, in silent reverie, the rest of the group eagerly assisted in the task. Greg trusted that the barrow would instinctively know where to take its precious cargo and that there would be adequate room within for the sea of plastic that would soon supply those whose ears thirsted for the sounds it contained.

The barrow was a sizeable one and it took some time to fill, but with six pairs of hands employed in the task it was eventually full. Norman then levelled out the load of plastic to form a satisfying flat surface.

"That'll reduce wind resistance when we proceed!" he said with a sense of pride. "It should also lower the centre of gravity."

Greg had often noticed people leaning languidly on supermarket trolleys as they pushed them along the aisles. Now he realised that this was to improve speed and stability rather than losing the will to shop. "Well, I think we can set off now!" he said.

A blackbird flew out of The Tree and on to a nearby bramble as though to indicate the direction they should take. With tacit agreement, the men jointly grabbed hold of the shafts of the barrow and with little effort moved it along the path towards the bush, at which point the bird flew towards the next one along the route to await them there, singing encouragingly.

"Thank goodness we didn't have to climb that tree after all," said Ted. "Even climbing up on to my grandpa's knee used to make me dizzy, but he was quite tall. He used to recite Edward Lear to me while I sat on his left one, but the right knee was out of bounds after being hit by a hailstone in Hornsea."

"Afflictions of the knees are hereditary in his family, you see," said Norman to everyone, but in hushed tones. "Mid-leg crises, they call them now."

Greg sympathised. "I once bruised my knee on a kitchen table in Whitley Bay, although I couldn't vouch for my own grandpa's misadventures, except for his tendency for unregulated whistling."

Onwards they went, following a meandering path through the woods in the late afternoon sun with just a blackbird as guide.

They crossed a stream via a wooden bridge just wide enough for the barrow, and yet when Greg glanced back after crossing it he thought the stream appeared to have widened slightly. He also observed a carelessly discarded crisp wrapper floating past. The brand looked familiar - who had ignored the country code of waste disposal? He said nothing, but noticed the blackbird nodding at him knowingly. They had re-crossed the river, and, thought Greg, Norman must never know about the litter infringement.

After a while the men burst into song, although the accompanying blackbird still had the edge on sonority.

"Fight our way past ferns and dock, we've got plastic sticks in stock.

Guarding music is our job, fending off Hobgoblin's mob."

Such singing had a tendency to produce a jogging motion in the men's gait, but then a bout of coughing would ensue, on this occasion resulting in the bird issuing a distress call until the barrow was once again allowed to trundle in peace.

A large Victorian residence loomed up in the distance and the barrow seemed to be steering itself towards it on auto-pilot, although the shafts still retained a modicum of human contact. Norman, walking in front of it, had taken up the role of escort.

"Do you think it would be appropriate for six men with a wheelbarrow to seek advice from the owners of that house as to where the nearest composers live?" suggested Greg. "Bearing in mind it's the middle of a Sunday after...?"

"Sorry but I think I know this place!" said Meston excitedly. "If it's where I think it is, we've almost come full circle!"

"Wow! So they're neighbours!" said Tom. "Are you on good terms? Do they know any local bands?"

"It used to be the manor house but, sorry, I don't know who lives there now," said Meston. "All I know is, if I stand on top of our henhouse I can just about see their weather vane. It's a wrought iron rabbit."

"Forget the rabbit. I suggest we call there," said Tom. "Just as long as that loopy nurse isn't giving their chairs a hard time."

Although the prospect of visiting the first house they'd seen nearly all day had the effect of quickening everyone's pace, Greg noticed that Ted was lagging behind. He offered him a supporting hand, but Ted's own hands were covered in blisters from having handled so many memory sticks.

"I should have worn my gloves but they get a bit uncomfortable after a while," said Ted. "They're made of rabbit."

Tom muttered something incoherent, and Norman invited him to assist with the escorting.

"Try and keep clear of the wheel," advised Norman. "The tyre's caked in muddy leaves."

Joe led the next refrain, with further collective jogging:

"Cross-ply tyre caked in mud, quavers coursing through our blood.

Surround the house, watch out for Nurse, Ted's got blisters fit to burst."

By now they were fast approaching the main gates which were wide open, but even more inviting was a large brass sign fixed to one of the brick gate posts. It, however, stopped them in their tracks. Greg read the words aloud with due reverence.

"The Jack Macadam Academy of Music." He paused for the gasps to subside. "I think this might be our destination!"

The bird flew off whilst the six men stood still pondering and gazing across a gravel forecourt towards the entrance. Two modest cars were parked near an outbuilding, and a bicycle was leaning against a wall. The main door was open, and it was obvious that there would be people about.

"So," said Greg, looking kindly at Meston. "Who wants to go and find the person in charge?"

A side door opened and a young lady emerged with a bag of rubbish which she carefully placed in a nearby wheelie bin.

"I think I'll go and ask that lady over there," said Norman, obviously impressed. "She's bound to know!"

Tom was also keen to ask her what she knew, but as he ran across the car park, overtaking Norman, Ted cried out in pain. Norman pointed to him as though to say: 'you sort him out,' and Tom duly complied, rendering his own brand of altruism.

"Alright. On the barrow," he shouted as he manhandled the little man on to the cart, resulting in further cries of pain as he sat on the load of rather uncomfortable plastic gadgetry.

"I think I've got a stone in my shoe," complained Ted, whilst Joe loosened his collar and prayed for his sole.

"If you'd been an oyster you could have turned that stone into a diamond," said Tom, obviously put out.

"Sorry, but I think you'll find that oysters turn grit into *pearls,*" said Meston.

"Whatever", said Tom as he arranged the hapless man's feet so that they dangled freely over the barrow.

"Good afternoon, can I help you people?" called a man in a bright red suit who suddenly appeared, framed in the main doorway. "I'm afraid you're too late for the recital! Oh dear, is the gentleman hurt?"

The delegation made its way to the steps whilst Norman continued chatting to the lady as they enjoyed quality time at the bin. Greg braced himself to give an account of their mission to the sympathetic man, together with a request for access to six computers, and a resume of Ted's battle-scarred anatomy. He decided instead to produce the book as a means of introduction and as he held it aloft and wondered how to begin, the young lady excused herself from Norman and came over to share her own understanding of the deputation to the man, as he stood bestowing upon the car park an expression of benign welcome.

"Her name's Consuelo, she's a student," said Norman as he rejoined his party. "From Andalucia. She says they can probably offer us the use of their facilities for half an hour! Buena!"

Greg mouthed his thanks to her and advised the group to await the man's own invitation. This was presumably the man in charge of the academy, thought Greg, and his red suit presumably ensured that he could easily be located.

"Bring your barrow up the disabled slope," called the man. "I'm Harold Eaglescliffe. I can get a first-aider to your friend, but I've just been advised that you travel the countryside finding musical inspiration in birds' nests. Well *done*, everyone!"

This was received by a burst of applause - from within the building. A group of students was watching from one of the ground floor windows and they were obviously keen to endorse Harold's welcome: it seemed a very democratic set-up. The men immediately began to propel the barrow up the slope, but it took little effort, and was soon through the main door and careering along a lengthy corridor, following the man in red as Ted assumed the role of fearful charioteer. Greg ran ahead so as to catch up with Harold to try and give a fuller explanation and soon he was providing him with a garbled account of the mission which the Harbingers of H hoped to fulfil.

They entered a room containing desks surmounted with computers, each of which had a pair of headphones attached. There was also a large whiteboard displaying a series of dominant chords which the desks faced submissively. A grand piano stood cowering behind the whiteboard, and any grandiosity it retained was further offset by a suit of grey overalls slumped across its keys.

"Ah, those will be Mr. Bubwith's," said Harold, noticing Greg's look of curiosity. "He had to change rather urgently this afternoon to double up as our coffee and canape waiter. By the way, does your friend in the barrow require any oxygen?"

"He's fine, thanks," said Greg. "He usually extracts enough of it from the air to keep going. We gave him a lift because his knees are under-performing, and one of his feet was suffering from true grit!"

"What a remarkable man," said Harold as he switched on the computers. "And so thoughtful of him to carry his own tea tray around with him on his back."

"He's definitely one of the old school," said Greg. "His classroom had no computers, but lots of monitors, so I was told."

Ted duly entered the room upon his conveyance, steered lightly by his retinue, where they paused to survey the educational facilities until Harold invited them to take their seats.

"I understand you all wish to try out some themes you found in the woods today," said Harold. "Be our guests. I trust you all know how to operate the Gibbons Music Writing Program?"

"Sorry, did he say gibbons?" whispered Meston, anxiously peering at a large metal cupboard.

334

"I think the program might have been inspired by Orlando," replied Greg, reassuringly. "Simians tend not to work Sundays."

"We're new to all this, but we've got a few ideas we want to try out," said Tom, pointing to the material in the barrow. "We'll leave everything exactly as we found it, or perhaps even better!"

"Fine. I'll leave you to it, if you wouldn't mind all signing this form first and adding your home addresses. I'll ask Mr. Bubwith if he's got any more canapes."

"Raw cannabis?" exclaimed Joe. "Miss Sweeting used to grow that in the organ loft, but I got my highs from the fugues!"

"They're actually small snacks," advised Norman, discreetly, whilst Harold placed the form on Meston's desk. "It's not really warrior-food, but dainty rations can help to build us up into lean, mean, song-writing machines!"

The form was passed around, whilst Harold went off in quest of Mr. Bubwith. A group of students then arrived and congregated in the doorway, intrigued by whatever was about to take place within the room. They said nothing audible but peered in at the visitors and their mysterious wheelbarrow and whispered amongst themselves. Greg took it upon himself to get up from his seat and gather handfuls of memory sticks from the barrow which he placed on each desk. He helpfully pointed out the ports on the computers where they could be inserted, and assured Ted that he was not at risk from electrocution.

"Then we can just type randomly!" announced Greg self-consciously, aware of the bemused but supportive audience hovering in the doorway.

335

The words 'Welcome to Gibbons!' appeared on each screen, although how they should proceed was uncertain. Random typing, however, would probably mitigate against any helpful advice or instructions that the program might wish to offer. Greg was conscious of being required to give a lead, and so he extracted and extended his baton and held it high, mentally counting to three, before making a dramatic downsweep. He promptly sat, and immediately began typing gibberish with the others following suit. Nothing appeared on the screens, nor did any sound issue from any of the headphones, but after about a minute of concerted typing - incorporating the crescendo keys F1 to F12 and the esoteric keys on the right - a printer situated beyond the piano began to activate, spontaneously producing manuscripts. The students gasped in unison and then watched open-mouthed, which was handy as after a few seconds they began to sing. The impromptu choir looked at each other puzzled and yet were delighted at their contribution - even if whatever they were singing was completely new to them. The lyrics consisted entirely of the tonic sol-fa, and after a few bars they were harmonising and producing complex polyphony. Sheets of manuscript paper continued to be dispensed by the printer, as the men carried on typing whatever keys their fingers chose.

Harold returned with a small tray of microscopic snacks and genteel coffee cups. Initially he appeared surprised to encounter the singers at the door, but as he entered the room and observed the printer churning out sheet music and a typing pool for whom keyboards held no syntactical structure, his hands promptly released their grip of the refreshments tray.

Greg recalled being told in the Great Pyramid that the power of music exceeded that of gravity, and thus in this room where music was being created the falling tray's contents were launched horizontally and followed a perfect trajectory to land on each man's desk, unspilt and intact.

After Harold had composed himself sufficiently he went to examine what his guests had composed by perusing the printouts. He sifted through a few and then slumped in a chair where he studied the notation. There was elaborate orchestration, and some of the themes were already slightly familiar due to the students' own choral interpretation. He appeared to be both delighted and incredulous, and after a minute's reflection he suddenly jumped up and went to examine the screens. Occasionally the words: 'Then the next bit goes....' would appear on a blue background, which was the prompt for the insertion of another stick.

"And all this was inspired by birds' nests?" asked Harold as he observed Tom typing haphazardly with his right hand whilst his left was busy feeding himself cocktail onions.

"The birds were actually pro-active - cool or what!" replied Tom. "By the way, cheers for the nibbles but that bubbles guy really goes in for twee."

"Indeed. We had to cater for five civic dignitaries today - they had to leave room for their next banquet," said Harold as he grabbed hold of further supplies of plastic from the barrow and placed them on each desk. "But you're all so proficient. I can only type with two fingers myself and yet your fingers are as deft as Paganini's! It's as though you've bypassed the program and that the music is actually....writing itself!"

337

Reinforcements took over at the door whilst the first contingent of students allowed themselves an interval. Two of them attended to the printer and fed it a fresh batch of A4 paper just as another printer started up and went on stream.

"We're just conduits," explained Greg, modestly. "We've been charged with the task of letting new music flow through us. Apparently the receiver in Egypt where we had our induction could no longer cope, and the late Chief wanted us to find a special tree that would tap into the source. It's been quite hectic!"

"Astonishing," said Harold. "I've always been intrigued by how the mind can conceive a new musical theme. Our students rely heavily on algorithms but I've always felt that we just need to let it pour in - as though from a garden sprinkler!"

"Er, well, that was how he put it," said Greg. "I....*we* have a mandate to inundate the wolds and beyond with refined H!"

"Incredible," said Harold as the replacement choir selected their soloists and Conseulo seated herself at the piano.

"Let me declutter the keyboard for you, dear," said Norman as he rushed to her aid, but the presence of Mr. Bubwith's overalls on the keys created no undue muffling effect as her fingers produced a glissando worthy of Rubinstein.

"Hey, Meston!" said Tom, suddenly full of warmth towards his in-law. "Do you think we could play randomly on your piano when we get back and see what happens? We could get Monica and Auntie Thelma to do the vocals. They weren't too bad on that birthday song!"

338

"A choral symphony, perhaps!" replied Meston. "I won't be sorry to get that opus one off my chest at last. It already sounds like we've had a great jam session!"

"I think my hands are feeling better now," said Ted. "All this typing must have massaged them. It's like the relief when I've applied moisturiser after being caught in the cross-wind from my fan heater."

"Don't forget, Little Tedders, I've got some cold cream in my bag if you need any", said Norman. "Cold for the bold."

Greg too was feeling the powerful effects of composition by committee. His nostrils were being caressed by the aromas of freshly boiled tar - or was it raspberry summer pudding? His keyboard also provided pleasant sensations in his fingers evocative of immersing them in a packet of soap flakes - or was it finch feathers? Visually, however, he was now aware of the entire room being bathed in a dense haze of every hue of the rainbow - or was it no less than the vast spectrum of the Orion Nebula? He sampled a bruised vol au vent, at which point his entire sensory palette was complete as instead of bruised vol, his taste buds detected the ultimate Rich Tea biscuit - or was it nectar itself?

"I believe my varicose veins might be downsizing to a subcutaneous format!" announced Norman as he bent down to replace a memory stick. "I can't remember when they last felt this good. It must be the economy size servings of caffeine."

Greg wondered if his manuscript book might also be downsizing, or was it expanding as the music it had forecast continued to spill from the printers? He felt in his pocket but the book seemed to be unaltered and had no doubt completely surrendered both its capacity to arrange impromptu transport and its tendency to update itself. He also wondered whether there was any need for the anarchic typing to continue, or if the flow of music worked on a similar principle to that of siphoning water by suction and induction. Was it worth the risk of abandoning his post and hoping the process would carry on, and could he advise the others to give their hands a rest also? What breaks did the legendary monkeys take?

An answer then appeared on a green background on each of the screens - 'Intro complete'. Greg took this to be confirmation that the frenzied fingering could cease, and so he got up and advised his five fellow harbingers accordingly. Typing came to a halt; only Consuelo continued playing the keys, the discarded overalls now forming a cosy rug for her knees. Tom tried unsuccessfully to catch her eye by waving to her with his right hand whilst with his left he ate a feta fritter. However, her eyes were serenely closed as she played on harmoniously, ably accompanied by the choir at the door. Even the plangent chugging of the printers contributed to the overall aural delight.

"She's playing and they're singing entirely from memory!" said Harold incredulously as he delivered more sticks to the men who now resembled members of an orchestra during a 'free period'. "And the whole atmosphere has changed, the room is full of rainbows!"

"Music is so powerful in its pure state that it affects *all* the senses," said Greg. "It might be best if we leave soon and just let you continue - as long as you take frequent breaks devoid of any stimulus. You could contemplate the properties of a rice cake!"

340

Ted was taking the opportunity to suck an additional peppermint but the contortions of his tongue had alerted Harold.

"Are you quite sure you're all right now, my friend?" he asked, concerned. We have lint in our first aid box if that would help."

"I'm fine, thank you," replied Ted, stoically. "We only set off to find our inner men, but then we had to go on tour and climb hundreds of steps, then we met lots of composers from the other side after falling out of a cupboard!"

"I'll get Mr. Bubwith," said Harold reassuringly. "He can give you a hot bath. He's got tea tree oil."

"Thank you, but he's a bit wary of water," said Norman. "He uses a flannel but of course it's still in the tent. Anyway, we'll probably be going soon so could you say goodbye to Consuelo for me? I can see she's totally absorbed in our repertoire!"

"Of course, and you've certainly brought us a vast amount of material," said Harold. "I'm most grateful to all of you, and the students will gain experience by adding the finishing touches before releasing it into the world but your source omitted all the clefs! What is music without those elegant treble clefs! By the way, who owns the copyright - it's not an ornithological issue, is it?"

"I think you'd better take this," said Greg, offering him the book. "That will give you all the information you'll need. We must be getting back now but you're welcome to retain the barrow in case you're guided to collect some more yourselves - it has a cross-ply tyre. Anyway, I'm sure we'll meet again or make contact somehow!"

"Sorry to butt in, but I have to go home and feed a hen," said Meston. "Anyway, we're almost neighbours - I only live the other side of the copse!"

"You've never lied to the cops?" queried Joe. "Hear that, Ted? I'm sure his milk quotas were always above board, too!"

Ted seemed embarrassed and quickly assembled his belongings. "Yes, we had better get going before it rains."

Tom was leaning awkwardly on the grand piano, gazing into Consuelo's unreciprocating eyes as she played a pianissimo passage. "It's really cool the way you play those quavers!" he whispered, but then he noticed that the glare he was getting from Norman was rather cool too.

Greg made a tentative move towards the exit, prompting the choir to move aside into their respective vocal ranges and allow the team to depart. Then, after a protracted farewell between the visitors and Harold, plus numerous nods and smiles to the choristers, the Harbingers emerged from the birthplace of many opuses, and into the long corridor.

"So, what happens now?" asked Tom. "I thought we might have done a deal over the memory sticks, or try and wow the public on sell-out tours. I could be a roadie helping Connie shift her piano!"

"What you've done has been invaluable!" said Harold as he accompanied them towards the main door. "Your gift to music, the academy *and* to all those who will hear the end product of your nature ramble. You will surely be rewarded."

"I pulled the plug on three tenners some guy presented at the bank once," said Tom, who was clearly put out. "They were duds! I never got any reward for *that*, though."

"You pulled the plug on three tenors? Had you been giving them a bath?" asked Harold. "Extraordinary. Did you offer tea tree oil to your....buds?"

"What?" asked Tom.

"I'm sure we will be guided by the power of H to receive whatever our rewards should be", said Greg, reassuringly. "We've achieved our mission, now we just need to find our way back to the farmhouse. Meston thinks it's close by!"

"Sorry, I know where it is, but I think we'll need to climb a stile", said Meston.

"Don't worry," said Norman. "I'm sure we can take a stile in our stride. The art is to ensure we don't slip on a damp foothold which is why I always carry a handy size packet of rock salt for greater traction. It was mined in Cheshire!"

"Mr. Bubwith might have a spare bag of salt if you'd like back-up," said Harold, pausing outside a door. "Shall I ask him? I think he's in the refectory tuning a tambourine."

"I think we'll be fine now," said Greg. "Thank you for helping us with our task. We were told that the world was in urgent need of a fresh injection of music of all styles. Apparently all of this proceeds from the proto-key of H, before it's stepped down into its constituent keys."

"Ah, we don't really cover music theory here," said Harold as he opened the door wide for his guests to depart. "We just give the students a grounding in elementary harmony and the life and times of the late Delphin Strungk, then hope they've got it. We're rather

343

short of funding."

"I'll be short of funding myself soon," said Tom. "Anyway, nice meeting you. Mission accomplished and all that!"

"Yes, we'll get to work on refining the wonderful canon of music you brought us," said Harold as he shook hands with all his guests on the porch. "Thank you all again, and do keep in touch!"

"Sorry, shouldn't he have given us a receipt?" asked Meston, quietly.

"I don't think he needed to," said Greg, turning round and waving to Harold on the steps and the students at the window. "We were meant to come here, and so whatever happens is as a result of the power of music. Let's get back to the house - there could be some residual birthday cake waiting for us!"

"Sorry, I think Monica will have recycled it by now," said Meston. "We can probably rustle up a Welsh rabbit!"

Harold was waving farewell with both hands to his musical benefactors as they crossed the forecourt. The students stood facing them at the window, singing the latest release from the wheelbarrow. Mr. Bubwith remained inconspicuous, but the happy Harbingers marched proudly towards the gate, turning to wave at frequent intervals.

"Which way now?" asked Tom. "We came from the right, so it's got to be left, right?"

"Left, right, left, right!" called Joe as he stood marching on the spot.

"Yes, thank you Joe," said Norman, "but remember you'll need to break step when we reach the stile."

"Sorry - yes, it's left," said Meston as the members

of the group glanced towards the academy for the last time. "Have you still got that manuscript book, Greg?"

"I have," said Greg, checking it was in his pocket. "I suppose you'd not realised before you gave it to me that it incorporated a complementary travel feature?"

"Sorry, it belonged to my Great Uncle Hermes - there's a small 'H' on the front cover," replied Meston as they began walking along another woody track. "He was prone to playing a muted trumpet in temperance halls all over the greater Scunthorpe area so I suppose his wanderlust must have permeated the paper. I was partly named after him!"

The track was broadening out, and giving way to a path across a field of turnips. The chimneys of the farmhouse were now visible, with the henhouse roof peeping above the hedge. The only slight obstacle now was the anticipated stile, but the mood amongst the six Harbingers - if such a title still applied after the completion of their odyssey - was one of vigour and joy. The trio of tea trays jostled loudly against the tubular chairs as the older men strode purposefully across the field as though leading the others to victory. The rhythm was in perfect synchronicity and was the prelude to the entire group breaking into spontaneous song at unabashed volume.

"Turnips inches from our toes, we don't care - just scare the crows.

Back to base is where we're bound, we've been freeing great new sounds."

"Sorry, it's not a stile after all," said Meston as they approached a five-barred gate. "But it's got a galvanised iron sliding bolt - that should make a great sound too!"

Greg was instantly impressed at the appearance of the gate and halted, prompting the others to look at what it represented.

"It has the five lines of a stave!" he said, his voice betraying a sense of supreme satisfaction. "Music is indeed everywhere!"

There was no verbal response to this statement, merely a communal nod and an appreciation of the call of a distant cuckoo.

"Well, well!" said Greg. "G and C - it's singing a descending fifth!"

"Indeed," said Joe. "A perfect fifth to end the day and the key of C to open the gate!"

"After you, little Tedders!" said Norman, kindly. "We can do some drumming when we return to the tent!"

THE END

www.ingramcontent.com/pod-product-compliance
Lightning Source LLC
Chambersburg PA
CBHW021253050726
47498CB00003BB/824